Ravenmocker

Ravenmocker

Paul R. Hargett

Writer's Showcase
San Jose New York Lincoln Shanghai

Ravenmocker

Writer's Showcase
an imprint of iUniverse, Inc.

For information address:
iUniverse, Inc.
5220 S. 16th St., Suite 200
Lincoln, NE 68512
www.iuniverse.com

This is a work of fiction. All events, locations, themes, persons, characters
and plot are completely fictional. Any resemblance to places or person,
living or deceased, are of the invention of the writer.

ISBN: 0-595-20451-1

Printed in the United States of America

For the Cherokee, the "Real People";
Never forget the mountains.

For my sons,
Zachary Paul Hargett and
Morgan Reid Hargett;
I will be with you always.

Thanks to:
Papaw and Mamaw (Paul and Bea Petty), my family one and all, Dwan for the patience and the most precious of gifts; my sons, Sylvia Waters for continuing to believe, George Fischer, my Si-hing Brian Edwards, Glennis West, Jeannie and Angie Wiggins, Cary and Les Robinson, Warner Montgomery, Rusty and Shebra Auten, Eddie Noles, Marilyn Hoyle, my MSC family and friends worldwide and to Gina, for too many reasons to count

Special thanks to:
The Museum of the Cherokee Indian,
Cherokee, North Carolina

BOOK ONE
"LEGACY"

"Well, it seems to be a good book. Strange that the white people are not better, after having had it so long."

> Yonaguska, prominent Cherokee Chief and
> adopted father of Col.W.H. Thomas,
> after hearing translation of the book
> of Matthew
> Spring 1839
> Soco Creek, Cherokee, N.C.

"The only good Indians I ever saw were dead."

> General Philip Sheridan to
> Lieutenant Charles Nordstrom
> December, 1868
> Fort Cobb, Kansas

PROLOGUE

The sickly sweet smell of old death lingered despite the rush of warm summer air washing through the rusty pick-up. The nasty stench clung to his clothes and his mind like an angry snapping turtle, refusing to let go no matter how hard he tried to think of other things. It was all he could do not to turn the truck around and go back. He even pulled off on a side road once before changing his mind and continuing towards home. Jason knew, felt it deep down; he had done something wrong, but he wasn't sure what it was or who the hell to tell.

The high mountain air filled the cab, its roar fading the sounds of the radio to a bare whisper. He opened every window, even the little triangle shaped ones in the front, but the wind brought little comfort. The odors of shaded earth, high altitude and mighty pines were full of life, yet even they failed to mask the ugly smell of death he so recently unearthed. The memory of what he had done, at what he had found, hung on just as strong, haunting him. It was an accident, sure, but he was still guilty. Even though he wasn't quite certain what he was guilty of or how much damage he had caused. No matter what he tried, the whole thing nagged at him like his ex-wife. Something was strangely wrong with his "discovery" and he wished the hell he could figure out what.

Jason Hodges began his morning like every other morning of late, operating his bulldozer, clearing a job site for a new condo construction near Murphy, North Carolina. He began from the hot asphalt road and just started dozing his way into and over the thick mountain forest. You could do this with the really big machines; pulling the levers and pushing the gears as the big tracks and the mighty blade responded to his touch like a knowing lover. He respected the earth and the world around him, a respect he had learned from his grandfather, Zachary Hodges, a full-blooded Cherokee Indian. Jason was proud of his heritage and remembered what he was taught and often marveled at a world which found him destroying the very thing he cared for the most, the mountain land his people had called home for thousands of years.

The thing was; he loved being outside, loved working with his hands, and loved the feeling of shaping and moving the earth like a sculptor with clay. Jason did his job well and respected nature as best he could. That's why, when he first struck the large obstacle near the stream and a great portion of it just fell away, he knew something was wrong. It didn't feel right. There was nothing he could put his finger on at first, and yet, his uneasy feelings grew for a time as he sat on his machine deciding what to do, the huge engine idling patiently beneath him. He finally gave a sigh of impatience and shut down the big diesel to take a look. Jason figured he best investigate as there was no use breaking a tread on some unseen obstruction. He had done this once before and it cost him a week's profit and a week waiting for parts.

The awful smell hit him before he got to the front of the huge dozer. It was like the time he and his father found the cave and a bear, which never awakened from its long winter nap. It was late spring by then and it had been slowly rotting for weeks. Small animals and flies had already been at the corpse and he had gone outside and been embarrassingly sick. The odor reminded him faintly of that, but there was something else about it he couldn't quite place, something familiar, like a partial memory or a lost dream.

As he drew nearer, the smell grew stronger until finally he had to pull an old bandanna from his pocket and wrap it around his nose and mouth. It didn't help much but, combined with his growing amazement at what he found, he was able to ignore it for a time.

He struck the large pile of what he thought was dirt and rock and dislodged a large, oval-shaped stone forming some sort of a seal for what appeared a large cave. The fading sun allowed just enough light to suggest a large open area inside the freestanding rock structure. Carved into the cold stone were markings he remotely recognized. They resembled some of the characters of the old Cherokee, the language before Sequoia.

Jason visited the museum on the Cherokee Reservation several times in his life and the shape and style suggested something he saw there. He had no idea what they meant and suspected there may not be many people alive who did.

Jason was taught that his forefathers had built primarily with log and thatch. What he was looking at was nothing like that, but he was still sure it was connected to the Cherokee. It was once their land before being stolen by the whites and the carvings proved as much.

Jason moved closer and peered inside. The opening was still not big enough for him to enter; he was just able to put his head in and peer about. The walls were moist and damp with fungus. Water trailed down the sides and he could hear the faint dripping of water into a puddle somewhere within the blackness. It reminded him of a leaky bathroom faucet he could never get around to fixing. The water may have fed into the cave by way of a nearby mountain stream, but it was hard to say for sure. Further back in the darkness, he heard a soft, rubbery scrapping and gathered, whatever else it might be, it had become home for a large number of bats. He considered, for a moment that the bat smell might be the odor he recognized, but quickly ruled it out. The overpowering stench was very strong, unknown and yet somehow vaguely familiar. It wasn't the bats, of this he was sure, it was something else, something which caused his stomach to knot and his skin to crawl.

As darkness continued to grow around him and his men headed for their trucks and home, he walked around the structure, perplexed. A few of the men called their good-byes and Jason waved back absently. The cave, for lack of a better word, was maybe sixty feet across, thirty feet wide and appeared to be solid rock. Over the years, undergrowth and even a few small trees covered it, hiding it for untold decades, maybe centuries. He had no idea what he found but he knew he wasn't about to bulldoze it until someone who knew about such things could have a look. He knew a fellow down at the reservation museum and Jason finally decided to leave things as they were for the night. If he gave his friend a call when he got home, they could maybe explore inside first thing in the morning. There would be more daylight then, and hopefully fewer odors, he thought to himself as he removed the cloth from his mouth and nose.

Something about the idea of entering the enclosure at night didn't appeal to him. Actually, he felt sort of funny about the whole thing. From the time he first caught the smell, his senses screamed at him to pay attention. It was a feeling he rarely sensed. Something his father claimed was a gift from his ancestors. Whatever the reason, he felt something about the cave. It seemed to seep "wrongness" with the smell; a feeling so thick he could almost see it like morning fog across the forest floor. He had a little itch right at the top of his spine. As he walked towards his truck, he kept looking over his shoulder expecting to see someone. Jason tried unsuccessfully to laugh at himself as he started his truck and headed towards home. He just couldn't seem to find anything funny at the time.

The smell kept coming back to him. His mind kept replaying what he saw, the cave, the carving on the stone. His memory teased and probed at it like a sore tooth despite his best efforts otherwise. He couldn't erase the tattooed smell or ignore the mystery of what he found on the mountain. The night wind carried a suggestion of coming rain. He could just make it out over the vile stench clinging to his clothes. He spoke out loud, "Good, maybe the rain will wash the damn stink away."

Several hours, a hot bath and several beers later, he reclined in front of his television and watched a rerun of some sitcom with the sound down, not caring what was on but enjoying the single person's idea of company. Jason's grandfather built the little cabin he lived in with nothing but a carpenter's adze, a sharp ax and his bible. Almost a century later, it was home for Jason.

The big man tried to eat but found he had little appetite and decided to drink instead. A light breeze from the thick mountain forest blew through the rusty screen door of the cabin like the dull drone of a far away plane. His mind barely registered the growing sound of the windswept trees and the approaching rainstorm. It was too busy exploring the imagined interior of the old cave he found, wondering what treasures they might find inside the next day. He missed his friend at the museum but left a message for a return call.

It all continued to nag at him, gnawing into the back of his mind, nipping and tugging at his memory but not hard enough he could put a name to it yet but it felt, well, bad somehow. He had to tell someone, anyone, what he had found, of that he was certain. He felt like a little boy, with a secret he couldn't wait to relate.

Jason laughed at his rhyme and retrieved another cold beer from the fridge before settling back into his worn recliner. He glanced through the open screen door for a moment, absently scratching the stubble on his chin and watching the growing force of the wind whipping the tops of the big oaks near the cabin into a frenzied dance. It was going to be one hell of a summer storm.

One sitcom became two, then three as he finished his beer, then another. Time passed slowly as the storm gathered force. Sleep tugged gently at his pant leg as his father used to say.

Sometime later, he jerked awake and glanced around, startled from a troubled, light sleep. The television lit the room with ever changing

patterns of light and color as David Letterman joked soundlessly with
Paul Schaffer. Nothing seemed amiss. He looked through the door and
watched the rain that had begun to fall as he slept. It was not a hard rain
as yet, but huge, wet drops splattered loudly onto the tin roof overhead
and lulled him back towards sleep with its peaceful, steady rhythm.

The smell woke him the second time. He thought for just a moment,
in that fleeting instant between waking and slumber, that he was dreaming of the cave. The odor was mixed with the musty scent of mountain
rain, but beneath, hidden like a rat in a basement, lingered touches of
something else. The same evil stench he had exhumed. It reminded him
of a wet animal and rotting meat too long in the sun. He tried to push
the dream away and reach for another, more pleasant one; but it was not
to be.

He came full awake just as the old screen door was thrown inward
with enough force to bang it off the opposite wall. Jason's mind,
numbed by sleep and the beer, tried to decide what to do in the seconds
that followed. His eyes made for his gun over the mantle piece, but
when he met the gaze of the figure filling the shattered doorway, all
rational thought left him in one mad rush.

Everything happened so fast, his mind was left to trail slowly behind
in horror and disgust. The smell of rotting death washed over him in a
great wave of revulsion, gagging him as he tried miserably to rise from
his chair and face his attacker.

Jason was a big man, well over two hundred pounds and seldom felt
overwhelmed by anyone, but his body was effortlessly lifted and tossed
off the far wall of the cabin like a child's doll. When he hit, Jason felt
something pop in his back. His mind briefly registered a white hot flash
of pain just before he slumped to the floor like a sack of wet mud. A
mighty hand tightened vice-like around his throat and he was pulled
from the floor and shoved roughly against the wall.

He flayed his arms uselessly; sending old black and white photos of
his family crashing to the floor at his feet which dangled without

touching, just above the cabin floor. Jason didn't notice. All he saw was the terror that held him. Ancient, dark eyes pinned him to the wall like stakes to a vampire's heart. Jason tried unsuccessfully to search for pity in the hate filled marble orbs, tried to plead, but his words were caught by the strong claw which held his throat with a power like nothing he had ever felt or imagined.

Jason felt an explosion of pain, which he never would have thought possible. His chest and mind screamed in agony and torment, followed almost immediately by the soothing numbness of shock and an approaching veil of darkness. But before that final veil settled over him, before his pain ended forever, he was treated to one last glimpse of true horror. Through his great anguish, his mind understood what was happening in the fleeting seconds remaining. His last glimpse of life as he drifted towards death, robbed him for eternity of all sanity and hope. His own beating heart was raised to the mouth of his attacker and devoured. The killer managed a wicked, bloody smile, which said so much more than mere words ever could. The demented eyes held so much anger and hate it seemed to flow in tangible waves. Jason tried valiantly to draw one last breath with which to scream, but managed only a final, weak sigh of dying.

After that, there was only the deep, eternal darkness of death. And by then, it was most welcome.

CHAPTER ONE

I was running when the demons finally caught up with me. I had been running as far and as fast as possible for a very long time. In the end, it didn't matter. Our past is as much a part of us as breathing and dying, and forsaking it changes nothing. I should have known better. Maybe Charleston wasn't far enough from the North Carolina Mountains to guarantee my sanity and safety. Who knows? Now, I believe the demons of my family's past would have chased me to another world to draw me back if necessary, and basically did. I never really would have gotten away, but, for a time, I thought I had. I was wrong.

It was a day like any other; at least it began like that. I walked into the bar as I had a thousand times before. Nothing was different, yet everything was about to be. Myskyns Tavern had been a meeting place and watering hole for my friends, business associates and myself for as many years as I could remember. I didn't really drink that much but was comfortable there. I'm not really sure why and don't really care.

Anyway, Charleston wouldn't have been Charleston without Myskyns. The bar was in the old section, just off Bay Street near the Customs House, moving there a few years before from its original location in the heart of the market. A narrow cobblestone road passed in front of the ancient brick building and a bright green awning marked the entrance. It was said that all the cobblestone streets of Charleston were constructed from European and English stone, transported in the holds of trading ships as ballast, hundreds of years earlier. They were pretty to look at, but pure torture to drive over and I've been told hell on earth for high heels.

Not so many years past, I used to drive from Boone to Charleston during occasional breaks from my academic pursuit at Appalachian State University. Myskyns had always been the "place to be" when in Charleston, with a reputation for always having the best musicians around. It wasn't unusual to walk in and find a big name band cramped on the little stage with the pictures of the old jazz musicians on the back wall. A friend of mine owned the bar and I often used it as office, meeting place and a source of an occasional adult beverage after a hard day of work. I felt among friends there, in an environment I knew well. There wasn't much about my life at the time that I was comfortable with, so I didn't question it too much—didn't want to look a gift horse in the mouth.

This day, near the end of August, was like all summer days in Charleston; hot, and so humid people looked as if they had just stepped from the shower if they were outside for too long. The sky was the normal beautiful color of blue that the Greater Charleston Chamber of Commerce managed to arrange on a regular basis to satisfy the constant flow of tourists and visitors to the "Holy City". On my short walk to Myskyns, I passed the normal crowds moving through the market in waves. There were old men ambling wearing straw hats, a camera in one hand, a local map in the other, accompanied by their wives who strolled through the old market intent on purchasing the "buy of a lifetime". College of Charleston kids peddled their bikes around the masses of tourists passing through the market. Citadel cadets walked the streets in-step and in pairs, clothed in military uniforms of white and gray. There were businessmen on family vacation, seemingly hundreds of small children, and the inevitable flock of young couples traveling on honeymoon. The street vendors in the lower end of the market pushed their wares in the sing song voices of the surrounding islands; Kiawah,

Wadmalaw, James Island, the accents differing ever so slightly. The clop of diaper clad horses mixed with the voices of uniformed tour guides as rented carriages passed the rainbow colored houses facing Fort Sumter in the city's harbor. This was the low country of South Carolina, home of shrimp boats, tourism and trade. A city where every meal could be served with shrimp and rice and every building had a history all it's own. These were the sights the locals of Charleston claimed as their own and took about as much notice of them as they did the changing of the tides.

This was all part of the mystique that was Charleston, center of southern tradition and dignity and the true heart of the old south. Little had changed since the days when Scarlet and Rhett supposedly walked the flagstone sidewalks. Time seemed to move differently in the "Holy City," so named due to the large number of Churches found within the town limits. These were many of the reasons I had come to love the city. As a "mountain boy" born and raised, I had never cared for life in any city, but Charleston was an exception to a lot of different rules including a few of mine. By choice and by deed, I was exiled from my mountain home and I chose Charleston as both residence and "place of recovery"

My trip to Myskyns this particular afternoon was for a rather different reason than usual and even I wasn't real sure at the time what it was. The night before, I had returned home to the sound of a ringing phone and I tried to hurry upstairs racing against the answering machine. As usual, it beat me and I had to start yelling for the caller to hold on while I cut the recording of my own voice from the background. While I was doing that, my grocery bag fell open and canned goods fell all over the kitchen floor.

"Hello!" I barked into the phone.

"Morgan?" The male voice on the line was familiar.

"Yeah?" I managed to take some of the frustration from my voice while fighting to retrieve cans and hang onto the phone at the same time.

"How's it going Cuz?" The hick mountain accent was unmistakable.

"Great!" The short mystery cleared itself up. Steven was my first cousin on my mother's side. I hadn't seen him in over a year and it seemed much longer, but that quickly passed. "What's up Steven? How's life in the mountains big guy?" He was my closest living relative if I didn't count my brother and seldom did.

"About the same as…well…except…for a few things here lately, everything's bout the same as always I reckon. How long has it been since you been up this way anyhow dweeb? Year? Two?" We gave each other hell whenever we talked, joking and needling each other in most every conversation. It was sort of a tradition. Outsiders would never think we actually cared for one another. It felt good in a familiar sort of way to hear the taunting tone in his voice and yet, it brought back painful memories that I had been struggling so long, and so hard, to forget. For a moment, I experienced major guilt for not having called him.

"It's not been that long, smartass, just a few months. Fortunately, I didn't get down to see you. I was sight seeing with a friend of mine, a female friend, and didn't want her to see your hideous features, us being related and all—I didn't want her to think ugly was a family trait." I wasn't about to be out done by him and decided to get my "shots" in early. "You know, we sort of rode around and watched the leaves change colors, took a short trip on the bikes, stayed at the cabin for a few days, that sort of thing." I tried to sound just a little more serious. "Really though, I meant to call…" and I did, "…but we were fast in fast out." I paused for a second, stacking food in the pantry to buy time. If he was going to ask about the trouble I had been in or where I had been since, he would have done so then. I gave him a chance to work it in and felt strangely relieved when he didn't.

I moved the conversation quickly past the silence. "You still got your old Harley?"

Steven chuckled, "Yep. Matter of fact I'm looking at it from the phone booth even as we speak." We both knew what I had been thinking and what he hadn't said. I was thankful and silent for a moment before I finally realized why I hadn't quite picked up on Steven's voice right away. There was something different about it, something faintly tense and foreign. Steven, like me, was one-half Cherokee Indian and prided himself on his uncanny ability to remain calm in the face of anything. Even a slight edge in his voice was an unfamiliar sound for Steven. Something was going on he wouldn't, or couldn't, tell me about. We had been apart a long time, but not so long that I would not have noticed.

"That's great. Where are you anyway?" I asked, trying to sound casual.

"I'm in the mountains, up-near Maggie Valley. I was kind a' sort a' on my way down to see you, if you're gonna' be around. Then maybe down to your good-for-nothing brother's place."

I knew then, something was most certainly wrong. Steven and I had seldom been apart growing up. We were pretty close and did most everything as a duo. We hung out together at family reunions from early childhood, partied through our teenage years, hunted, courted women and fought each other, and everyone else who got in our way. True mountain rednecks to a degree. We had sort of drifted apart over the last few years, but that had been my fault. You might say, I had a few personal problems that kept me away. Even though we lived only a few hundred miles apart, I hadn't made any serious efforts to see him since my release. I had my reasons. Even so, Steven remained closer to me than just about anyone I knew. We shared a hell of a lot more than ties of blood. Over the years we explored together, drank together, and learned about life together. He was more of a brother to me than my real brother, Jordan, had ever been.

Still, Steven was different from me in a million ways. He never left his mountain home unless he had to and clung stubbornly to the old ways. He remained proud of his Cherokee heritage and tried to be a true

Indian warrior in every aspect, but, to his great sorrow, he was born three hundred years too late. He was forced to accept a stallion of steel rather than a painted war pony and that seemed unfair to him. My cousin Steven was a misplaced soul in a wrong century and that fact haunted him his entire life. He rarely left his home in the mountains, feeling closer there to the past and his true destiny. More than that, he stayed because of his love for the high mountains and his general dislike of "non-mountain" people. That I understood completely because I pretty much felt the same way. We may have been different, but we were of the same blood and heritage, and that link was centuries old and stronger than most.

A call from out of nowhere was totally unexpected and very unlike Steven. It was more than welcome, but the vague edge of his voice during the phone call didn't register right. Combining the unscheduled visit and his unusual desire to see Jordan, I knew something had to be wrong. My younger brother and Steven had never been close, quite the contrary, they hated each other. That, of course, was not unusual in Jordan's case. He was never the most popular kid on the block so to speak. If Steven wanted to see Jordan it had to be one hell of a reason...one I couldn't wait to hear.

"Well come on down Steven. I'd like to see you." I commented on his announced visit with some hesitation. "It's been too damn long, but...is anything wrong, Stevey? You okay?" I knew the use of the nickname would get some response out of him. He hated it. Over the years, I used it to aggravate him as much as possible, but not up to the point of him bashing my head in, of course.

"Watch your mouth smart ass. Just because I ain't seen you in awhile, don't think I've gotten scared of you or nothin'. Up to now you've just been lucky is all." The sound of his familiar dead pan humor was a relief of sorts.

"Sure. That's your opinion anyway." I taunted him with a slight chuckle.

There was a moment of silence over the phone line before he continued, "Morgan, everything is okay really, but I got something I need to
talk about. I think I need your help with a little problem I got…we got."

"We got?" I let the question hang in the air.

"Don't ask questions—just do this one thing for me Morgan."

"Sure…" I hesitated, "…yeah, sure, whatever. I don't like this mystery
shit though."

"I know. I'll explain it all later, Cuz." There was something else in his
voice that was unusual, and I finally came to recognize it as concern.

"Alright. What you got in mind?"

"Is there somewhere we can meet, bout four maybe?"

"No problem, how about Myskyns? I know you remember where
that is."

"Yeah, I remember." He snorted, then after a moment's silence,
"Morgan…they'll be an FBI agent with me."

"What?" I couldn't keep the irritation from my voice. "I've seen you
hang out with some strange people Cuz, but that's weird even for you."
I took the milk from the useless bag and put it in the fridge having finished stowing all the canned goods by then, "What's up Steven? What
are you getting me into man?"

"Look, it's nothing really. This guy was coming anyway Morgan. He
planned to talk to you and I told him I thought it might be easier if I
was there. He thought it was a good idea and didn't seem to mind a
whole lot, so I'm tagging along. Look, it's not a big deal Cuz. He has
some stuff to talk to you about same as me…that's all. I'll tell you all
about it tomorrow after he's gone, but don't say anything about this in
front of him. Just answer his questions and I'll fill in the gaps later. You
gotta' trust me on this Morgan. I know this sounds strange as hell and
you're probably gonna' think I'm crazy, but just try to hear me out first.
It's very important to me…to all of us."

Steven prided himself on never asking anyone for anything, yet he
was always there for his family or close friends. He considered himself

totally independent. He needed no one and because of that, he owed no one and liked it that way, just another of many ways in which we were a great deal alike. If he asked for something, it had to be important to him, and near impossible to tell him no.

"You've said that twice now. Who is this "all of us" Steven?" I asked, not happy with the situation or the way the conversation was going. Years in the military taught me to be wary of blind meetings. "I don't like walking into a scene I can't rehearse for, you know me better than that Steven." I looked out the window at the white caps in the bay. The early evening moon left shadow and light patterns on my arms as I waited for Steven to answer and so much time passed I thought for a second he may have hung up.

"You're the all of us Morgan, you, me, Jordan and a bunch more. We're all part of this. Just let me explain tomorrow, alright?" The line grew silent yet again as he waited for my answer.

"Fine, I don't like it, but I'll be there." I answered reluctantly.

"Good, see you tomorrow at four." He responded equally as short. Neither one of us had ever developed an appreciation for talking on the phone and eliminated all needless words whenever possible.

"Keep it between the lines Steven"

"You know it, man." he said as he hung up.

So, as I opened the door to the bar, I was more than curious to hear his explanation for such radical behavior. I immediately noticed him sitting with a rather uncomfortable looking gentleman at a table near the front of the tavern. A long mahogany bar stretched all along the right side of the room, supposedly the longest continuous bar in the South. A shiny brass rail snaked along beneath a number of leather covered stools down it's length. The walls were rough brick and the ceiling exposed oak beams. The lighting was sparse, but adequate, and it gave the place sort of a homey, comfortable feeling.

Steven rose as I walked towards their table well away from the bar. My cousin hadn't changed. His long black hair was pulled back in a familiar ponytail, faded blue jeans, scuffed up cowboy boots he seemed to live in, topped off with what seemed an endless supply of black Harley-Davidson t-shirts. He smiled as he wrapped his big arms around me in his traditional bear hug greeting. I felt as if my ribs were going to be crushed as my feet left the floor. This was no easy task, as by normal standards I am not a little person. I measure out about six feet three, give or take, and weigh in around 200 pounds, depending on how seriously I'm working out at the time. Steven, on the other hand, was different. Steven was,…well, he was huge. He outweighed me by more than seventy pounds and was a full four inches taller. I remember basketball and football coaches in high school always wanting him to go out for their teams but he had no time for sports. With a family to feed and a father who drank too much, all his extra time was spent with a trowel in one hand and a stone in the other. Steven's father and his father before had been stone masons and he carried on the tradition. He worked hard and played hard. Cold beer and bar brawls were no strangers to Steven. The former was evident in the slight paunch he carried over his Harley belt buckle and the latter in the many scars marking his face and hands. The paunch did nothing to take away from the years of hard muscle evident on his body, or the hard look constantly in his eye. I had seen very few men able to stand in his way once he decided otherwise.

"You can let me go now, Steven." I uttered harshly through clenched teeth. "It's good to see you've not lost your charm. Your mind still as muscle-bound?" It was a running joke between us. Steven's uneducated rough exterior masked a surprising intelligence no one would expect from his appearance. He had finished high school, never went to college, read more than most, and had common sense. It was enough for him. He constantly exploited others expectations to his advantage when they showed a tendency to judge a book by its cover. I quickly surmised such was going to be the case during this meeting. He evidently did not trust his traveling companion, or was intent on playing the dumb country hick for some reason or another. I was becoming more and more curious at his actions.

"How's it going Cuz?" he chided in a heavy, exaggerated mountain accent. He gave me a quick wink only I could see. "It's good to see ya' man." His broad back masked the real concern I saw in his eyes and the truth to his remarks.

"No problems, just lots of work and never enough money. It's good to see you too." And it really was. "Who's your drinking partner here?" I nodded towards the man with him.

"Morgan Roberts, meet Agent Fred Smith of the FBI. Mr. Smith, my cousin, Morgan."

I extended my hand to little man at the table. Agent Smith was about five eight or nine, if he stood on his tiptoes, and probably weighed one hundred and thirty-five pounds soaking wet. He was dressed neatly in a very stylish dark blue pinstripe suit; a crisp white starched collar and one of the new flower print ties that seemed to be gaining popularity. His collar was marked with moisture, evidence of the high humidity and heat of summer in Charleston. His handshake was limp, as if he wanted to draw it back and wipe it on his handkerchief. He didn't meet my eyes as he introduced himself. Instead, his eyes contacted a point just over my shoulder as we spoke and he pasted a fake used car salesman smile on his face. I amused myself sometimes by judging people by the way they handled their eyes. Eye contact, or lack of it, said a great deal about a person's psyche and Agent Smith wasn't acquiring very high marks from the git go, to use an age-old mountain expression.

"How do you do Mr. Roberts?" His accent was Yankee, maybe upper New England.

"It's very nice of you to agree to see me on such short notice. Would you like to sit down?" Agent Smith peered over his glasses (preppy Polo frames, of course) and asked, "May your Uncle Sam buy you a drink?" He asked, gesturing toward the empty chair on his right.

"If you don't mind Fred", I saw him wince as I used his first name, "I'll buy my own until I hear what this is all about." I didn't like the situation and wanted to set the tone early. "I'm here so easily because my cousin asked me to be. It's not my habit to visit with government employees without having a damned good reason first. It usually means trouble for me of some kind, and I've had more than my share of that." I gave him my best icy stare, "Now, what can I do for you?" As we sat down around the small table, I caught Kent, the bartender's eye, behind the bar and he motioned to Steven's broad back with a questioning look.

"Beer, Steven?"

"Now, have you ever known me to turn down a free brew Cuz?" His feigned backwoods accent was so comical it I was all I could do to contain a smile.

"Fred?" I inquired and saw Smith's obvious displeasure with the familiarity. For some perverse reason, I was pleased by his negative reaction to the informality.

"I suppose I'll have another club soda, thank you." His response was condescending, obviously impatient with my request and attitude.

"Of course, what else?" I commented and gave a slight nod to the bartender. "Now, Fred, what the hell is this all about anyway?" My tone did little to mask my frustration and I didn't really care by then.

"Well, there's no reason to be hostile Mr. Roberts. If I'm not mistaken you've spent some time as a government employee yourself. Let's see," he made a little pyramid with his fingers and began to speak in a slow monotone as if reading from a file; "Morgan Roberts, age thirty-two, current residence Charleston, South Carolina, owner of a small but very successful motorcycle dealership featuring a particular German import. Served a total of eight years as a captain with the Special Forces primarily stationed at Fort Bragg in Fayetteville, North Carolina. A specialist in tactics, field reconnaissance, hand to hand combat and other things of that sort." He commented with obvious disdain. "Graduated both officer training school and Appalachian State University, in Boone, N.C. with top honors. Degrees in Economics and Philosophy of all things, honorable discharge from the Army, just under two years ago under rather vague circumstances, for reasons I don't yet know, but could find out if I deemed it necessary I'm sure." He finished his narrative with smug satisfaction, seemingly "paying me back" for my obvious disrespect for his position.

I shook my head and smiled. His type was always the same. "Well you're definitely full of information Fred, but that stuff is old news and you still haven't come any closer to telling me what we're doing here." I placed my palms on the table. "Now look, I have plenty of better things to be doing with my time. Even though this meeting has been extremely pleasant and informative. I believe my cousin and I will be going now. You have a nice evening Fred." As I finished, Steven took the hint from my sarcastic tone, and we both rose as if to leave.

The little man moved quickly. "Now wait just a minute, you can't leave like this I came all the way here to talk with you on a matter of some importance."

I turned back to him and stepped close, within a foot of his face. "The hell I can't Fred. I do not, repeat, do not, need some pompous Washington asshole dictating policy to me. I haven't seen any kind of warrant and you haven't read me my rights, so I assume you are not arresting me. I have an attorney you are more than welcome to speak with and his office is only a couple of blocks away." I smiled at him; "You want his card?"

I punched lightly on his chest with my finger just to see how much he would take. "You obviously came here for something, Fred. Just spit it out! I don't have time for you to pull your bureaucratic bullshit. I'm not impressed with your organization and even less with you. I can already tell there is no danger of you and I developing a deep love affair, Fred. I just want to know what you want. It's that simple. So, unless you're willing to have a two-way conversation, we're out of here. Bye again Fred." I had my own reasons for disliking "government men", as my people used to call them, and he seemed to be cut from the same cloth as most others. We turned again to the door and didn't get five feet.

"Mr. Roberts, wait please, I'm sorry. I didn't mean to offend you. Can we please try this all over again?" I knew by his forced, semi-friendly tone, it hurt him to ask. My strategy of invading his space seemed to have worked. At least he wasn't as smug and sure of himself anymore. I don't know why I felt a need to push him. I just did.

"You don't sound too sincere to me Fred." I turned to my cousin, speaking loud enough for the FBI man to hear, "What do you think, Cuz? You got time for another beer with Mr. U.S. Government here?"

"Well, I do got a pretty busy schedule you know, but I reckon he did come a hell of a long way to see you. I think it's only fair he should buy the next round though."

"Good point, I like the way you think Cuz. We need to get those tax dollars back whenever we can I guess, and we might never get another chance if we don't take this one." I turned back to the agent, "Okay Fred, here's the deal; we'll try this again, but only if you'll order something besides club soda, I never have trusted someone who wouldn't drink with me. It makes me nervous and I hate being nervous." I smiled genuinely, having way too much fun at his expense.

He hesitated. "Alright. Thank you." He indicated our chairs. "Please sit down gentlemen." He waited for us before returning slowly to his own seat.

Kent, who had been watching my little performance from behind the bar, took the opportunity to bring over the drinks and deposited Steven's beer, my Absolute rocks, and Fred's club soda. Kent had been the bartender in Myskyns for as long as I had been coming to the bar. Nothing I said or did surprised him anymore. I caught his eye and nodded towards the agent.

"Can I get you something else sir?" Kent asked.

"Sure." He seemed to think about it for a moment. "I'll have a glass of white wine please," glancing at me as if for approval while Kent retreated back to the bar.

I replied with a slight nod, "Well, we're on the right track anyway. Now…" I took a long swallow from the frosty drink, "tell the truth Fred, is that your real name, Fred Smith?"

He glanced down slightly and away before replying, again not making eye contact," Yes, it is on both counts. There are actually real Smiths around." His exasperation with me was just barely hidden.

Steven, who had been surprisingly silent through the whole performance and was evidently growing tired of it, took the opportunity to interrupt, "If you two have finished your little dance here, I would be right pleased if we could get down to business. I haven't got all night, you know." He tilted his chair back and looked directly at me as he spoke, "Morg, I'll tell you how I got together with this here guy, just to get things started and all. He came up to the mountains looking for some of our family and asking a lot of crazy questions. He said he was going to come down here to see you. I said I might be persuaded to meet him down here as you had sort of a reputation as being antisocial when it came to strangers, especially when they work for the big Uncle." He turned to Smith; "Can't figger why anyone would say that. You?" Steven had a sadistic grin on his face as he asked and I could tell he too was taking pleasure in needling the guy.

Agent Smith said nothing, just looked uncomfortably at his newly arrived glass of wine as Steven continued, "Anyway, I thought you might find what he had to say sort of interestin'. I tagged along. And that brings us up to here and now." As he finished speaking, he turned back to Agent Smith and nodded signaling the end of his brief narrative, which, for him was a lecture. He folded his hands behind his head and closed his eyes, seeming to lose all interest in the conversation. At least that was the image he was trying to project. I knew whatever was said he would miss nothing. I couldn't help but wonder at the silly game he was playing and why.

"It's a rather strange situation," the FBI agent began, "several weeks ago, in early June, a man was brutally murdered in the mountains of North Carolina. The man was Jason Hodges, no relation to you, other than the fact that you all have a large percentage of Indian blood. I understand you're half Cherokee, Mr. Roberts, and I already know your cousin here…" he nodded towards Steven, "…is as well. It just so happens, the deceased also had a high percentage of Indian blood…excuse me…" he gave us a forced, perhaps sympathetic smile, "…Native American. This Hodges was not an actual relation of yours though, and that point really caused us some problems initially." He paused and shook his head as if it was a personal failure of some kind on his part. "Anyway, there have been a surprising number of murders committed by the same person, or persons, unknown. The murders have taken place in various cities in Arizona, Alabama and most recently Georgia. We've had the computer checking any and all connections and it would appear all the victims are within the same family tree, or tribe." He met my gaze. "Yours. We have reason to believe you, yourselves, may be in some danger."

As he spoke his air of superiority began to resurface, "So you see, that is why I'm here Mr. Roberts. I came to see if you might have information that could possibly help our investigation and put an end to these killings."

"I don't." And I truly didn't have a clue as to what he was talking about.

"Well, that is yet to be seen isn't it?" A touch more of his previous smugness returned. "I need to ask you a few questions before we'll be sure won't we?"

I ignored his snide comment, "Excuse me, but what makes you think the same person is committing these murders?" My curiosity kicked in about then and I was determined to find what in the hell he was getting to, and why.

"The murders have a number of definitely related points in common. The only thing I'm able to say at this time is that they share the same…how can I say this…brutal characteristics?" For a brief instant, his face paled and took on a blank look as if remembering something unpleasant, then he quickly washed the look away and replaced it with his properly authoritative mask.

"Fred, I thought we had gotten beyond all this bureaucratic nonsense. How do you know these things aren't a plant to throw you off?"

"Well Mr. Roberts, I know by your military background you may be familiar with such matters but this is not the same thing. We're the professionals here not you." His tone suggested how much he enjoyed bringing that to my attention. "I've been investigating bizarre murders for almost ten years. I've seen the worst. The serial killers, the really sick ones, and I can tell you I've never seen anything to match this. Someone, only one is my theory, is really insane. Really, really sick." He faked sadness, "Honestly, I can't say anymore under direct orders from my superiors. We're making it a top priority to keep this from being blown apart by the press." The little man shook his head with obvious distaste, working hard at the pity angle, "God how I hate the media!" He gave a little wink as if taking us both into his confidence.

He was a good actor I had to give him that, a little too comical for my taste but good nevertheless.

"We don't need them in on this. They're already beginning to notice a pattern and we can't afford to help them in any way. Wide scale panic will not help anyone, especially potential victims. Surely you gentlemen can understand that?" He tired to sound sympathetic and concerned and fell just short of pulling it off. "You two could easily be targets yourselves."

"Okay, I'll buy that much, but since it involves only personal theory as you put it, what makes you think it's only one person and not

a group?" I rattled the ice in my then empty glass and forced myself
to be patient.

"Honestly? I can't imagine anyone committing such…such atrocities
to another human being. To believe that someone could do
things…things like that, to another human just to cover their tracks is
just too hard for me to believe. I feel it has to be just one very demented
person, someone with unbelievable strength and ferociousness and an
inhuman disregard for life." His face took on a rather sickly pallor, as he
seemed to recall something that didn't fit his normal concept of what a
killer should be. "Anyway, to continue along my train of thought, so far
there have been no murders within your immediate family but I'm
sorry to say some of your second and third cousins have been among
the victims."

The agent went on to list a number of relatives, the majority just
vague memories and people I had been told I was related to, but a few of
the victims were more familiar, including a great uncle and a cousin I
knew quite well. There were a total of fourteen dead scattered across the
South and the Western United States. All apparently by the same killer,
or killers, if Smith was wrong.

The Agent continued, "The victims seem to be primarily men. To
date, the only female victims have been grouped by male victims as if
they were…" He seemed to search for just the right word, "…irrelevant.
Plus, they weren't…disfigured in the same fashion. We think the men
are the primary targets…" he paused, "…we have several reasons for
believing this." Something about his demeanor made me certain he
wasn't going to tell us what they might be. "We've made every effort to
ask the families to remain as quiet as possible about this, and considering the particular…unpleasantness of the murders, they have been very
cooperative." He paused long enough to finish off his white wine. I
noticed he kept his pinky finger raised politely as he delicately lifted the
glass to his lips, and I wondered briefly what such a man could possibly
know about catching a killer.

"The computer printed a list of all additional family members within your specific tribal tree and we dispatched agents to contact everyone on the list. I was assigned your names and subsequently, here I am. My partner is still interviewing in the mountains." He smiled smugly and opened his hands as if he just explained the meaning of life itself, "Do you have any idea of anyone who might have a reason for doing this to your family members? Can you think of anyone who might have a motive? Anyone who might have any ideas?" He adjusted his wire-framed glasses with his index finger and glanced expectantly at me for an answer.

"Definitely not, at least on such a widespread scale. I mean we all make enemies but I can't relate all these people to any one individual or incident." I glanced to my cousin, "What about you Steven?" Steven, we both knew, had enemies running every backroad in the mountains, but none of them killers, at least not the kind Agent Smith described.

I saw Steven's face darken ever so slightly before he forced the expression away and replaced it with his best look of hick innocence. If I hadn't known him very well, I never would have caught it and I felt sure Agent Smith missed it, but it was there nevertheless. Something was turning around in his head for sure.

"Nope, can't think of anybody. I already told him that." He gestured towards Smith and used the same "down home" accent he had adopted for the meeting. He knew something he wasn't saying and didn't intend to discuss it with Smith present. It was all I could do to contain my curiosity. I struggled to exercise the patience that was supposedly a birth right of my people.

"Have you gentlemen heard of any of this before?" Smith inquired, peering over the top of his glasses, which seemed unable to stay on the bridge of his nose, and which he kept adjusting with his middle finger.

I glanced at Steven before answering for both of us. "No, this is most definitely a first."

Agent Smith slid his empty glass aside. "The last murder, as far as we know, was committed two days ago in Gainesville, Georgia. The pattern is getting closer gentlemen. Anyone could be the next victim, even one of you." He pointed at me and smiled for dramatic effect, seeming to take particular delight in bringing this to our attention. Smith then waved his hand in the air with an air of dismissal, "Look, I've got a list of things to do a mile long and never enough time. I would appreciate it very much if you would take my card and call me with any information you might remember, or might hear. Don't forget, you two could very well be on the killer's list yourselves." He looked at us seriously before continuing, "If you find anything or need our help, don't hesitate to call. We're operating out of a temporary regional base in Charlotte, North Carolina."

"I think I can manage that." I took the offered card, "I don't know about you Steven, but I sure feel much better with Smith here protecting us. Our tax dollars at work for us at last!" I raised my glass in mock toast, perhaps knowing I was pushing too far, but not really caring by then, "Thanks, Fred."

"Don't mention it. We'll let you know if anything pertinent occurs." he said, seemingly ignoring the sarcasm in my remark. "By the same token, this works both ways. If you two hear anything, it's your duty to report it to me, understand?"

I shook my head and smirked. "You know Fred, we were doing so well up to this point. I have finished with the days of doing my "duty" for little shits like you. We'll be glad to help if we can, but not because you insist on it. I don't give a damn who you think you are. Do we understand each other?" The more he talked, the more he irritated me. I struggled to keep my growing anger at bay, my hands clenching and my voice rising. I felt like a bully but couldn't stop myself it seemed. My inability to control my emotion brought familiar frustration with myself and served yet again to make the situation worse than it should have been.

Smith looked at Steven who sort of shrugged his shoulders and gave him a sympathetic look as if to ask, What could he do? "Fine, fine, whatever." His feathers ruffled at such an unaccustomed attack on his precious authority. "I really appreciate your time and consideration in this matter. I'll contact you with anything further if necessary." His snobby attitude resurfaced, as he seemed satisfied we weren't going to be of any help to his investigation. "One last question, Mr. Roberts," his voice loaded with sarcasm, "Why did you leave the service anyway if I might ask?"

I just stared at him. I didn't say a word. The asshole undoubtedly knew my past the entire time. I should have realized if he had access to my file, he would have known everything. The anger began to reach for me then in earnest. I felt it's first true touch and I struggled within myself to keep it in check. I wanted to strike the man. All my months of "psychological" healing seemed for naught.

He looked from my face to that of my cousin and could find no trace of emotion in either.

I met Steven's eyes and read genuine concern, but he didn't do or say anything. When I returned my gaze to Smith, I don't think he liked what he saw and looked away nervously and quickly. "Well, I'll be going now. You two don't forget to call if you think of anything else. I'll be in touch." His smile infuriated me even more. It was all I could do not to tear it from his face.

"You do that." I attempted to keep my emotion to myself, but it was a struggle. I had worked hard to keep my demon, my anger in check— had to, had fooled myself into believing I was making progress—and the FBI jerk had brought it all back to the surface with one smartass comment. Some progress.

He extended his hand in my direction as he pushed back his chair. I casually looked over his shoulder towards the bar for several moments, ignoring his existence. His hand stood in air between us like a refused offering. He finally snorted with frustration, admitted defeat, and snatched his hand briskly back to his side.

Agent Smith mumbled something I couldn't hear, spun on his expensive Italian loafers, and stormed towards the door. Two local college girls were just coming through the entrance. They parted to allow him passage as he blew past them in a huff. The two girls turned to frown at him. His head never wavered as he rushed through the wood and glass doors and out into the hot sunlight. I was glad to see him go.

"Nice guy." I said.

"What an asshole!" Steven said with a forced laugh. "I thought he'd never leave."

Without further hesitation, I turned to him, my ill concealed anger just beneath the surface, "Okay, I've had enough of this crap! What's going on Steven? I want to know and I want to know now! I hate this soap-opera, cloak and dagger bullshit and you know it."

"Fine, but I definitely need a real drink for this. Can I get you one while I'm at the bar?" His huge frame towered above me as he rose from the ladder-back chair and smiled a silly grin I had seen a million times before.

"I think you better make it a double." I took a deep breath and tried to be patient with him.

"You don't know the half of it yet!" He called back over his shoulder.

I watched as two men slid unobtrusively out of his way to allow him room at the bar. They weren't obvious about it; they did it in a way that allowed them to be cool, but they moved over just the same. The male ego is such a strange animal.

As I watched him talk and joke with Kent, I wondered what could possibly be bothering the normally quiet giant. I recalled a night just before my college graduation in Boone when Steven came up to celebrate with me. He brought a few of his friends I had come to know over the years, some fairly interesting individuals in their own right, and the five of us went out for a beer or twelve. Ultimately, his group of friends began to discuss who had the most nerve and backed up their claims with various stories of glory and gore. Before the night was over, we ended up near a clearing on top of the Blue Ridge. A bet resulted in a game which consisted of one of the group taking a 45 automatic and shooting a target drawn on a tree twenty-five yards away. The only catch was the "test" person stood directly under the target, the outer edge touching the top of his head. If he flinched, he lost. Steven won.

As I watched, after trying in vain to stop the foolishness, one of his buddies, Bill Mason, a typically terrible shot, emptied an entire clip, rapid-fire into the target inches above Steven's head. My cousin continued to smoke his cigarette as if he were home watching his television set. He never even blinked. His friends called him a crazy son-of-bitch and paid him their money.

Nothing ever shook Steven, but something had and I was growing extremely tired of waiting to find out what.

CHAPTER TWO

Steven walked back from the bar carrying a drink in each hand and dropped heavily into the chair beside me. I heard it creak distinctly under the strain of his massive weight.

"Nice looking young lady back shooting pool, eh?" he asked, still feigning the thick backwoods accent.

"Okay, Steven." I replied, ignoring his remark. "No more bullshit, okay?"

The pretense left his voice. His down home talk was still intact but not nearly as pronounced. His vocabulary improved a little and phrasing changed completely to his normal manner. "Listen Morg, you and I go back a long ways, I need to know something right off the bat—you ever remember me telling you a lie? Ever?"

I didn't even have to think, I knew his nature better than my own "No, never." One thing he had never been guilty of was dishonesty. He may have broken a number of commandments, but that particular one he honored. Honesty was a true virtue of the Cherokee and he would do nothing to dishonor his heritage. Steven lived that heritage like no one else I knew.

"Morgan, I want you to listen to me. I want you to hear me out. I know this is going to sound totally crazy to you—hell, it sounds totally crazy to me—but I gotta' believe it…at least a little." He took a big drink from his glass and looked uncomfortably towards the back of the bar. "I know…I mean I think I know, who or…what is doing the killing."

"Good! I thought it was something like that. Why didn't you tell Maxwell Smart before he left? They need to catch this asshole and quick. I know he was a dweeb, but…"

"It's not like that Morgan, it's not that easy. If I told them, they would never believe me. Never! You just don't know."

"Well then why don't you tell me Steven?" It came out more sarcastic than I meant, but my aggravation with the situation still clouded my thoughts.

He drained the remainder of his bourbon in one long swallow, then signaled Kent for another. "Morgan, I know you don't give too much thought to your Cherokee up-bringing." He turned to face me, "I mean you and I used to spend a lot of time in the woods just like our grandfathers did, but that's not the kind of stuff I'm talking about. You're part of today's society, man, not like me. I could never give it up and come down the mountain; I'd never make it. You know some of the tribe's history and problems; I'm not saying that. I'm just saying you've only been to the reservation what? five…six times in your life? And that just for a family get together or something." Unfortunately, what Steven said was true. I had grown impatient with all the tribal nonsense long ago.

Kent brought our drinks and perhaps sensing the intensity of the conversation, he left without saying a word. The mark of a great bartender, knowing when to speak and when not.

"You know, I still try to maintain a lot of the old ways when I can. I've been trying real hard. It's all gone by the wayside over the years, but a few of us try to remember and respect."

He waved his hands as he talked and I could tell he was nervous. That was most unusual for him. "What I'm saying is; I've stayed a lot closer to this stuff than you have. It's real important to me, for reasons even I don't get…but it's real important Morgan and not just to me. You know, I'm still trying to live all those stupid old stories we used to hear from our folks, you remember? I'll never have the head for it I guess, cause I'm only a half breed maybe, but I try my best to keep the faith." He stopped long enough to light a cigarette; his dusty red skin brightly illuminated for an instant before he continued. "You know what I'm saying here, Morgan?"

"Steven, the percentage of your blood mix hasn't got a damn thing to do with it and you know it. Your soul is, and always has been, positively pure Cherokee through and through. You're more Indian than just about anyone I know, but what the hell has all this got to do with anything?"

"You're not going to believe me Morgan."

"How can you say that man? I haven't even heard you yet. How can I not believe you? At least tell me what's going on and let me make my own decisions. You know who you're talking to here…it's me for God's sake! Just spit it out and quit playing around."

"All right, just right out then—these people are being killed because of something in our past—a curse."

"A curse?" I couldn't hide the slight smile. I tried not to, but the absurdity of it and the look on his face was more than I could take after all the dramatic build up.

"Morgan! Damn it! I knew you were going to look at me just like that!" He shook his head with a disgusted look and blew smoke in my direction. "Shit man, I knew it! Look, I don't know the whole deal I just know what I know, okay?"

"Go on." I said, trying to be more patient, something I had always had to work at. Being patient would never be listed among my virtues despite my heritage.

"Well to make things worse Morg, it sort of involves…well it involves Kathy." He looked uncomfortably away from me. "Well not really Kathy, it involves her grandfather, Rising Wolf."

I carefully ignored the reference to Kathy, "You mean that old guy is still alive and well? How old can he be anyway?" I asked, changing the subject rather smoothly I thought, but fooling no one but myself.

Ben "Rising Wolf" Parker was the epitome of the ancient shaman from the Cherokee tribes of yesteryear. His wrinkled face resembled the old Indian on the television commercials a few years back, the one who thought about ecology and cried as he paddled his canoe through the polluted waters of a stream.

Steven smiled. "Old, definitely old, but he still remembers more about the tribe and the traditional ways than anyone else. He's the one who sent me to find you." He pointed his cigarette at me, "You know, your grandfather and him were pretty tight, both being the "last of the great shaman" and all that. I know your grandfather died early on, but he's the reason I'm here."

"Okay, I'm still listening." The reference to my grandfather evoked an automatic sense of respect. He brought that out in everyone who knew him and he still held that power even in death.

"Well the first murder, this guy Jason Hodges, was clearing a building sight for some new building project in the mountains near Murphy…I don't know…some ski resort shit or something. Rising Wolf tried to get the developers to build somewhere else but they didn't want any part of that. He claimed the ground was a sacred place, a bad place and that they shouldn't go digging it up. He told them something bad would happen if they did, and sure enough it did." He shook his head and pulled on his ponytail, a habit he had developed over the years, "The place was on the southern side of the Hiawassee River near an old creek the Indians called Peachtree. Members of the tribe had watched over the land around the area "unofficially" but they legally had no rights to it. The land was taken from them along with everything else before the Trail of Tears. Anyway, the tribe members that managed to hide out from the troops and not get killed or forced off their land—they watched over that piece of ground real close."

He paused long enough to ask, "Still with me Cuz?"

"So far." I replied, taking a long sip of the cool, clear liquid in my glass. The bar had filled with people as we talked. It was a good mix; people in suits, and shorts, and jeans. They all stopped by for a quick drink and a little relaxation, all sharing a common goal. Bars were a great equalizer.

"Over the years they were able to talk whoever owned the property into letting that certain little piece alone. Well, last year the owner died and his sons sold the property to some company for development, and that's where all the trouble started."

He paused, taking a long drink from his almost empty glass, and looked at me over the rim. I knew he was trying to judge my reaction so I purposely kept my face blank. He took a draw from his cigarette and slowly exhaled before continuing.

"Rising Wolf, and a group from the reservation, asked the company not to develop that parcel. Of course the company, like most companies, was run by little assholes that didn't give a shit about anything but money. They basically told the council they had no legal rights, and to take a long walk off a short pier. Rising Wolf tried everything he knew, but it didn't work. Construction started anyway and he was told to stay the hell off the property or else." He looked past me as he spoke and I knew, without turning, he was following the actions of the girl in the poolroom.

"The old man says the land was cleared, and in the process something bad was released, something real bad." He stuffed out his cigarette in the ashtray; the butt nearly lost among the rapidly growing pile and immediately lit another. "Ben says they were white people here before us…I mean albino people, people that lived in little caves and hated the sunlight. One of these people, a witch it turns out, stayed around after her kind was all gone. The villagers put up with the woman over the years because her magic was great and they thought she was a "Sacred One" because of her skin color. They were afraid of her but they paid her with gifts to work her magic, to bring luck to the hunt, or rain for the crops. Ben says the whole thing has to do with her. He is not sure of all the details. That is about all he can remember of the story."

I listened as he talked and found myself marveling at the change in my giant of a cousin since I saw him last. He spoke about the past events as if he firmly believed them, not as if they were myth. His unfamiliar tone suggested a respect I had never seen in him before. He had changed—but then so had I.

"Anyway after whatever happened, happened," he continued, "they put this bitch in this cave. Then the white man came and all our troubles started. The people who knew exactly what went down, and why, were either killed, run off, or died over the years. Rising Wolf says the only reason he knew the story was because your grandfather told him and the other council members about it years ago. Your grandfather had this book of formulas..." his hands formed the shape of a book, "...legends and stuff he was given by his teacher. The story was recorded in it. This book was old—real old. Shamen had been keeping it through the years, writing things down as a way to keep the history alive." His voice changed, becoming strangely sad for Steven, "You know, over the years, it's been real hard to find people to listen to the old stories. There are no real shamen anymore except maybe for Rising Wolf and a few others. Turns out these guys have been writing this stuff down since the 1800's. Even then they couldn't find students like they once could." He shook his head in disgust at the painful history of his people.

I interrupted, "You know, all this is interesting, but you think we might could...I don't know...get to a moral of this story sometime soon?" I tried to lighten the mood with a smile.

"Look, you wanted an explanation, I'm giving you one. Just shut up and pay attention, smart guy."

Kent arrived with two new drinks, "I hate to interrupt two gentlemen in such intense conversation, but here are those matches you asked for Steven. Can I get you guys anything else?"

"Yeah…" replied Steven without cracking a smile, "…the little blonde in the back will do just fine…straight up, no ice."

Kent shook his head and smiled, "I knew I missed seeing you around here for some reason." He laughed all the way back to the bar.

"Okay, where was I?" He absently sipped his drink and slipped the matchbook into his T-shirt pocket. "Oh yeah…when your grandfather figured he wasn't going to have anyone to pass things on to, he worked harder on the book. Rising Wolf says he took it real serious. He added all the myths and legends he could to it and even asked others, people like Rising Wolf to help. No one did that till then. See the medicine men have always been real secret about their craft you know? They didn't want anyone to know what they knew unless it was somebody they were teachin.'" He rubbed his eyes and leaned back in his chair. "Turns out in the end, they might have kept those secrets too well."

I knew it was a sore spot with him. He had always had a real problem with what happened to the Cherokee in the name of "white civilization"; an entire world sacrificed for little or no reason but greed. A world quickly forgotten and casually shoved aside in the name of supposed progress.

"Your grandfather was given this book by his teacher and Rising Wolf saw it, even read it and gave him a few formulas of his own that Screaming Eagle didn't have. He doesn't know what happened to it after your grandfather died. He says it was a leather book, maybe five inches thick." His big fingers illustrated his words as he talked. It was mostly written in old Cherokee and in that book he figures to find out about the killings and this "Ravenmocker." That's what he says; this white witch, this killer is a "Ravenmocker", a demon from the past. He thinks the book will tell how she came to be there, why, and hopefully how to send her ass to the hell she deserves." He leaned his muscular arms on the table and swirled his drink in little circles in the liquid that formed beneath. "And there you have it." He didn't look up as he said it.

"What do you mean, "and there you have it"…what the hell does that mean? You're telling me you actually believe this old ghost story?" I asked in genuine amazement.

"Well, I'm not saying I don't believe it, or I do believe it. I'm just saying the old man believes it. It's like the old folks used to say, "I know not how the truth may be, I tell the tale as it was told to me." He asked me for a favor, so here I am. Plus, Kathy sort of egged me into it and you know what a bitch she can be." He smiled at me knowingly.

"Yes, that I more than understand." I replied, my mind flooding with memories I didn't want or need to recall, "What's the favor anyway?"

"He wanted me to come find you and get the book so he can figure out how to stop this shit."

"But I don't have the book, Steven."

"Shit, I was afraid of that." He shook his head and drained the remainder of his drink. "Then I'm supposed to find Jordan and get it from him, and I hate that shit let me tell you. The old man seemed sure that, even though your father had no use for that kind of stuff, he would still have enough respect to keep the book, maybe even give it to one of you. Rising Wolf felt sure either you, or Jordan, must have it somewhere. I was, of course, hoping it was you so I wouldn't have to see that asshole brother of yours."

I ignored his last remark, "Before we continue with this conversation I want you to know one thing. I do not, repeat, do not, believe any of this bullshit. You were right on that part anyway. I do not believe in ghosts, monsters or the bogey man, for that matter. I will, however, continue this pointless conversation in an effort to humor you. Now, that said, I'll tell you I very seriously doubt Jordan has any such book. You know my old man and I weren't the closest father and son in the world, but I'm sure even he would have enough sense not to leave something like that to Jordan." I hesitated, "But then if you remember, the way he died didn't really allow him to do much in the way of planning if you know what I mean. Of course, when you get right down to it, he probably just didn't give a shit. You never know he might have burned the damn thing just to get back at my grandfather. He was capable of anything there at the last."

I paused as I felt my heart beat just a little faster and my palms turned sweaty. Thoughts of my father did that to me. I moved my hands off the table so Steven wouldn't see them shake. Sometimes it seemed to me, my father's ghost was never going to leave me in peace.

"We can check with Jordan, but I don't think he's got this book, I really don't. If he doesn't have it, then I have a good idea where we can find it." I was thinking of all the boxes I had packed in a rented storage building in the mountains. The last thing I wanted to do was sort through their contents. I didn't think I was quite ready for that yet.

"I'm sure glad you said "we" paleface!"

"Well, I understand why you felt you needed to explain this in person." I shifted uncomfortably in my chair, "We're going to have to do that with Jordan too and you can't go alone." I smiled and shook my head, "Hell, if you show up on Jordan's doorstep he's more likely to shoot you than talk to you. Keep in mind, if I do go, it's because I care about Rising Wolf and respect his wishes. I may not know as much about the old ways as you, but I do know that if I don't show my respect for the old shaman, my grandfather will roll over in his grave." I moved to rise, "Now, all that said, let's go get another drink and go back and shoot some pool or something. I need to think and I'm tired of sitting in one place looking at your ugly face."

We stopped by the bar, picked up a couple of drinks, and walked to a vacant pool table in the back. The recorded music wasn't near as loud, and it was far less crowded back by the tables. In the time we had been in the bar, the crowd had grown and filled most of the available tables. It was a popular place. The young blonde girl and her boyfriend happened to be at the table right next to us. I watched as Steven surveyed the situation with an approving eye, his gaze lingering on her

short, leather skirt and long tanned legs. He noticed me watching him
and grinned.

"Are you ever going to change?" I asked with a smile.

"Let's hope not, I'm too set in my ways and sudden changes to the
system ain't good for you, right?" I watched as he chalked his cue, a look
of serious concentration on his face, "Who's gonna' break?"

"Well, since we know you're going to beat the crap out of me, I'll
break first. It may be the only chance I get to see you rack if I don't."

"Okay Cuz. Do you want me to spot you a few balls or something…you know, just to make it more even? I don't want to embarrass
you or anything."

"Just shut up and rack the damn balls you dumb Indian."

As he racked, the balls seemed to disappear in his huge, callused
hands. The sometimes-friendly giant looked up as he worked and
asked, "So, you can take off from the shop for a few days?"

"Sure, the place pretty much runs itself." I rolled a cue over the green
felt of the table as I talked, checking the stick, "I've been taking more
and more time off lately anyway, riding and trying to get myself back in
shape, spending some time at the beach, you know. I'm just trying to
enjoy life for a change. I've been trying to sort things out in my head." I
twisted the cue tip in the powder blue square of chalk and lowered my
voice almost unconsciously; "its just taking longer than I thought is all."

He politely ignored my last comment. "You don't look out of shape
to me. Check out this spare tire I'm carrying around." He cradled his
stomach with his hands like a pregnant lady and I couldn't help but
laugh. "Too many beers and not enough work, I reckon." He removed
the wooden rack from the carefully arranged triangle of multi-colored
balls.

As I lined up the cue I asked casually as I could manage, "Kathy does-
n't believe all this mess, does she?" The cue ball struck the triangle with
a loud crack and the bright balls scattered over the table. A solid ball
dropped in the left corner pocket.

"I wondered when you would get around to a question like that." He smirked and continued, "I think she feels about it sort of like I do; she doesn't necessarily believe it, but Rising Wolf is her grandfather, you know. She's afraid he's about to leave this old world and she'll do anything to make him happy. He told her this stuff way before the first murder ever happened, that's probably why she's so concerned. Hell, I don't know! Who the hell knows what Kathy thinks but Kathy? She's as crazy as you are." His smile slipped a bit when he realized what he said and he added, "I'm sorry."

I brushed it aside with a smile, "No problem."

"Well, Kathy thought I better come get you because if I didn't, Rising Wolf was gonna' come himself."

I turned to get my drink from the shelf near the table. "Yeah, she had a point there. He's even more stubborn than she is, if that's at all possible." I replied absently, briefly lost to personal reflections. Long black hair, deep brown eyes and emotions I thought forgotten crept unwelcome into my head.

Steven quickly moved on, "Anyway, once this guy got slaughtered—that's the word for it—she paid a little more attention to the old man. Later, when we heard about the other murders through the tribe grapevine, she decided I better find you quick. After Mr. F.B.I showed up, I figured I'd just come down when he did so you'd get the whole story at one time, you know? Nice shot there bud, you been practicing eh?"

"Not really. That was just pure luck." As if to prove the point, I missed the next shot. Pool was never my game and was obviously never going to be. I leaned on my stick and watched as Steven walked to the end of the table. As he lined up his shot, I knew further conversation would be pointless until he finished his run. He was one of those pool players who took his game seriously and refused to talk while he worked the table. He thought it was perfectly fine to talk while you were shooting, but you damn well better be quiet while he held the stick. He even extinguished his ever-present cigarette before he picked up his cue.

I noticed the guy at the next table move back to allow him to shoot even though there was plenty of room between them. Steven had that effect on people to say the least. His broad back and long arms seem to make even the regulation-sized pool table seem like a child's toy. I patiently finished my drink and listened absently to the jazz beat of the music flowing from the CD player as I watched my cousin casually run the table. As he shot, I ran through all the information I had heard the last few hours.

It was a strange situation with no immediate solution on the horizon and tons of problems I didn't need at the moment. It seemed the only thing I could do, was ride with Steven down to see Jordan and try to find the crazy old book. If my brother didn't have it, then I figured it was probably packed with my father's stuff in storage.

The thought of going through "his" things sort of made me squeamish. I felt the familiar tightening in my stomach...the same feeling I had growing up when he walked into a room...never knowing when, or if, he was going to explode. The subconscious twinge was something I thought I could control...something I thought I had managed to leave behind. I was beginning to realize that legacy of fear still lingered. It might not ever go away. Just when I was sure I chased every damn memory of him from the dark folds of my mind, an errant thought would bring that familiar touch of fear back, just for an instant...then it was gone just as fast. I knew the son-of-a-bitch was dead but I still couldn't forget, no matter how hard I tried.

After some reflection, I thought the motorcycle ride with Steven might even be good for me. I was due a little time to myself, and a week or so of riding with Steven didn't seem like such a bad thing. It would seem like old times again. In addition, I thought it might be finally time to talk about what had happened to me since I left the mountains and Steven was the best listener I knew. Maybe by the time we finished all the running around, Agent Smith, or one of the other secret agents, would catch the creep who was killing my family and I wouldn't have to face Rising Wolf with my skepticism. The old man was not one to listen very well to "white man's logic." He preferred his own unique outlook on the world. The only thing he had ever liked about today's society was television. Crazy as it seemed, he loved to watch television. Certain favorite programs he watched religiously. He claimed they were a vast source of knowledge but I think he just enjoyed it myself. Getting him to admit it was an entirely different problem.

Remembering Ben "Rising Wolf" brought an involuntary smile. Just the way he "came about" his name said a great deal about the man. Actually, about both he and my grandfather, John "Screaming Eagle" Roberts. When they were young, it was not popular to be Cherokee, not for a century or so anyway. Parents named their children "white" as an attempt to save them from potential discrimination and hatred. That was their hope and intent anyway. When the two Cherokee friends came of age, they "renamed" themselves, as was traditional, but with the most "typical injun" names they could devise. They stubbornly claimed those names as their own, then defiantly wore them with pride and determination. Through the years, even their own tribal members favored the atypical Cherokee names. What were originally monograms of youthful defiance, became badges of lifelong heritage and honor.

Ben "Rising Wolf" Walker definitely had a way about him. I knew if he decided; Steven, Kathy, or anyone else for that matter was going to do something for him, you could bet it was going to happen. Ben was not the kind of man someone said no to, whether they agreed with him or not. He could rationalize anything if he thought about it long enough, and to top it off he could make anyone believe it about as easy.

So, basically like it or not, ready or not, I was going on a trip to southern Florida. I was going on a trip, I particularly didn't care to take, to see a brother I didn't particularly care for, to find something that might or might not exist. After all that was done, I was supposed to take this book to a potentially senile old man to combat something I didn't really believe existed in the first place.

Life sure played some weird tricks sometimes.

CHAPTER THREE

After several games of pool, (all lost by me), and numerous adult beverages, we left Myskyns Tavern and walked out into the hot, muggy Charleston evening. We debated our sobriety for a time and decided the best bet would be to walk the few short blocks to the dealership. The shop was down on the bay near what once served as docks for banana boats from South America.

I bought the building almost two years prior and converted the bottom to offices and a showroom. I maintained a small parts supply, bought and sold a few bikes, and had one hell of a mechanic when we opened. The building had a total of four floors and the third floor was converted into living quarters for myself, thus reducing the need for a house payment in addition to all the other bills. After eighteen months, we had three mechanics and one of the largest motorcycle showrooms in the South. No one was more amazed than I. The saying "right place at the right time" did indeed seem to have at least some basis in fact. I guess I was surprised most, as life had been sort of stingy with luck when it came to me. It was sort of growing harder and harder for me to accept such "good things" in life without looking around for a hidden price tag or "the other foot to drop".

We turned left on the cobblestone pathway and followed it one block up to Bay Street. The lights of the Customs House showed brightly in the distance as we headed in that direction. The sound of a late night jazz band drifted through the open doors of a neon-marked bar across the street and I heard a woman's distinct laughter amidst the familiar tinkle of glasses and the echoes of conversation. As we passed, the sounds dimmed and faded. We walked slowly, admiring the many facets of the old city, and just thinking. When walking in Charleston there seemed to be an unwritten rule; one never went anywhere in a hurry; one sort of ambled, especially at night.

The evening air felt good after the long hours in the bar and the intensity of our conversation. Neither of us said anything for a few blocks, both lost in private thoughts. The silence was not an uncomfortable one; we had spent too much time together for that. The spell was broken when several young guys walked towards us, then split up and passed on each side of the sidewalk. They wore khakis, white button down oxfords and deck shoes, undoubtedly Mt. Pleasant boys from across the river. The standard "uniform" was easy to spot for the locals. It was rumored that Mt. Pleasant had a city ordinance requiring all males over the age of four to wear a duck logo somewhere on their clothing. I found that easy to believe and wouldn't have been surprised if they set up checkpoints on their side of the Cooper River Bridge insuring residents complied. We caught the young men's voices as they whispered comments among themselves. As they got further away, we heard their half-suppressed laughter.

"You are an ugly son-of-a-gun, you know." I commented to my dark-skinned cousin with a smirk.

"How do you know they were talking about me?" he asked with mock sincerity.

"Well, I've lived here a few years now, visited more than that, and don't recall seeing many giant Indian motorcycle thugs every day. You've got to admit you don't look like your normal run of the mill tourist. You look like you're on your way to rob the nearest liquor store."

"Maybe so, but who the hell cares? How long do you think those guys would last back home on the mountain?"

"Not too long." I laughed as we turned the corner, continuing our short walk towards the water.

"So let me ask you something Morg, why are you living here in the first place? Don't you, like, miss the mountains anymore? All this city livin' gittin' to ya'?" He shuffled along with an easy stride that looked slow and clumsy but was neither. I found myself walking a little faster than normal just to match his wide strides.

"You know I love the mountains, Steven". And the strange thing was; perhaps no one understood that more than he. "It's not that. I'm just not comfortable there right now." I hesitated before I said; "You know why as much as anyone. Plus, I really do like this city. It sort of has a calming effect on me for some reason or another. I've lived all over, and this is about as good as it gets off the mountain." We passed another loud bar and stopped just long enough to look in the window. It was a country music club and the dance floor was filled with line dancers, their well-practiced movements in perfect sync.

We walked on down the slate sidewalk and I continued to ramble, feeling myself comfortable with conversation for the first time in a long time. It felt good to be with him again, just talking as we have always done. For a time, it didn't matter why we were together, or why we had not been, just that we were. "I think I've moved every year or two for as long as I can recall. Hell, the old man didn't stop moving from shack to shack until after I left home that last time. You know how it was. It was time for me to settle in one place for a while and it sort of worked out this was the place."

I stopped moving and he walked a step ahead before noticing and turning back to me with a quizzical look.

"I just had to have some time to sort things out Steven, you know? I needed to be away from everything and be by myself for awhile." My voice was calm and relaxed, contrary to what I really felt.

He met my gaze and sort of smiled and said: "Yeah, I can understand that I reckon." He waited on me to start walking again and, as I did, he fell back into step beside me. We crossed at the corner after allowing a carload of tourists to pass, and then he continued, "Well, if this was the time to settle down, why not come up to the mountains? It might be fun to see your ugly face every now and then and that is our home. I could help you "work things out" as you call it."

"You know why Steven." I replied rather dryly.

"I know some of the reasons, or I think I do." He grinned broadly; "I for sure know one female reason in particular. What is it with you guys anyway? She acts the same dumbass way you do. Why don't you guys grow up already?"

"Just let it go Cuz." As we talked and walked, we passed a busy restaurant overflowing with semi-intoxicated patrons. They clustered in a group awaiting their tables and laughed and talked loudly in the otherwise quiet Charleston evening.

He waited until we were well past before continuing. "Fine, and you think I'm close mouthed about things. Talk about the pot calling the kettle black." As we cut down the short block towards the water, the cycle shop came into view and he exclaimed, "Damn! What the hell is this? You've got to be kidding me. You never told me this place was so damn big." His face took on a comedic look of wild-eyed amazement and he asked in his most deep country accent, "You think you got enough room here Morg?" I couldn't help but laugh. It felt good yet somehow foreign and unfamiliar.

We walked towards the building the bank and I owned on the bay. I guess over the last year or two, I had been blinded to the size of the place. It was fairly impressive, but it still needed lots of superficial repairs. It was at least structurally sound and that was a vast improvement over when I purchased it. The four-story brick building was built over a hundred years before and looked it, in my mind anyway. Strangely that was one of the things I liked most about it. It had a little more age and a lot more character than the majority of the newer build-ings in the area. The yard was totally fenced for security purposes and the complete enclosure was a half-acre, maybe a little more. The only reason I was able to afford such a place was the area was not exactly the best Charleston had to offer. In addition, the old building was in a seri-ous state of disrepair and neglect when I purchased it from a bank, which had to foreclose on the previous owner. It was indeed a case of "right place, right time", I guess.

I led us to the gate and disarmed the security system underneath the big BMW DEALERSHIP sign, which brightly lit our path. Big summer moths butted against the lighted plastic. I absently flipped the switch, dousing the bright white light. I turned to Steven. "Walk through the gate and be perfectly still, don't move until I tell you."

"What the hell are you talking abou…?" and he stopped dead when he realized Dog was standing quietly about thirty feet away in the shadow of the building. I knew he was not afraid of any animal on earth, but he was most certainly respectfully cautious when necessary. With Dog it was necessary. Dog was about four years old; a cross between a black German Shepherd and a hybrid wolf, and bred for intelligence. I found her through a friend who knew a breeder near Spencer Mountain, North Carolina. She was undoubtedly the best dog I had ever owned and smarter than most people I knew. She seemed able to put up with me pretty well too and that earned points in her favor.

"Come here Dog." I said evenly. Dog was her name. I liked it even if no one else did, and few did. Hell, I thought if John Wayne could call his animal that, so could I. She moved noiselessly to my side and awaited further direction.

"It's alright girl. He's just another dumb Indian. He's ugly as sin but he's okay. Hold your hand out Steven and let's see if she remembers you."

As he lifted his hand he said, "I can't believe it. When I saw her last she was just a little pup, you had just gotten her that weekend. Christ, how the hell much does she weigh?"

She reached her nose out tentatively towards his hand with a short silent sniff, seemed to nod her approval and immediately moved to my left side, waiting patiently for me to resume walking. She was as familiar to me as my shadow.

As I closed the gate behind us, I answered, "She weighs nearly a hundred I guess. She probably looks lighter because she is just so damn dense, not a whole helluva lot of fat on her."

"Yeah, I can see that. She turned out to be a good dog huh? I always thought she would be."

"Unbelievable. She's just unreal sometimes." I often caught myself thinking of her as more human than canine and frequently I found myself sounding like a father proud of a child rather than an animal. It's strange what you latch onto when you're alone in the world for the most part and I spoke more to her than any one else during the previous year that was a certainty. "She thinks she's human and I haven't had the heart to tell her anything different. I generally have more intelligent conversations with her than most humans I know." I smiled. "I'm sure that will more than likely be true tonight for instance."

"Smartass."

We entered through the showroom, and I couldn't resist showing him around. The bottom floor had been completely renovated to allow the biggest motorcycle display floor in three states. Mirrors on one wall increased the perception of size. Still, we currently had about thirty bikes on the floor with plenty of room to spare. A section had been converted into individual offices, a meeting room, lounge, and small kitchen all with the original rough brick walls. Restrooms and the shop area were through a center door to the back.

As the lights gave life to the room, Steven whistled through his teeth. He didn't say anything else; he just began walking silently around the room spending time with each bike as he passed. The current inventory, much larger than I would have liked, featured several of the new BMW machines, the sporty RS, the touring RT and even a few off-road bikes with an amazing 1000 cc of power. The models were all displayed in almost any color my customers might like, each with a custom, hand-painted finish signed under the tank by the "artist". In addition, in one corner were several late model bikes I had taken in trade. I didn't like to do this, but I made some exceptions depending on the quality of the motorcycle. A half-dozen Harley-Davidson Sportsters, Customs, three of the tour models in various stages of dress, and a few Goldwings completed the inventory. Steven, of course, gravitated to the Harleys and sat on each one, touching and tinkering.

"God, how I love rich people." Steven said after his circuit of the showroom.

"Yeah, right. I'm surviving thanks, but the bank still has the biggest chunk of this place. I'll owe them for the rest of my life and half of what's after that. It will be a damn long time before this is mine, thank you. Come on upstairs and I'll make us a night cap." I moved to extinguish the lights and we climbed the stairs to the third floor, bypassing the second, which was used for storage and additional office space as needed. Dog moved along as we did, not needing an invitation, a queen in her castle.

The third floor was my own private domain. I hit the light switch and illuminated the living area. The wall facing the harbor was mostly glass and off to the left was the Cooper River Bridge. I looked out over the bay as Steven wandered around the place. Across the harbor, in Mt. Pleasant, I could see the lights aboard the battleship docked there to lure the tourists. The brackish water of the bay appeared rather calm and still. I could just make out the white crests of the small swells in the faint moonlight. Wet marsh grass bent slowly in the light summer breeze, providing a home for sand crabs, clams and the tiny marsh birds that ate them.

"Now, this looks a little more homey anyway." He walked over, dropped into the old beat up recliner, which I had for years and refused to get rid of, and lit another in what seemed an endless supply of cigarettes.

"I guess you could say the money hasn't reached this floor yet, but it's home." The room itself was covered with original oak hardwood floors, open and airy. I sweated long hours over a sander to get them that way. Ancient beams were positioned throughout the room supporting the exposed rafters of the ceiling and floor above. Sparse furnishings and lots of open space completed the floor plan. This level still sported bare brick walls and was occasionally touched with a few prints I had carefully accumulated during years past, some there for reasons only I understood. I didn't have much of an eye for art; I just knew what I liked, to borrow a well-worn expression. Charleston was filled with many exceptional local artists and I liked a few of them. The rooms, kitchen, two bedrooms with separate baths, and the large living area all had an unfinished look. The funny thing was, they probably always would. I have always been a firm believer in function over fashion as anyone could tell. Other people's opinions meant very little to me when it came to their judgements influencing my life. The place served my purposes very well and I could care less if anyone approved of my interior decorating skills, or lack of them.

"What's on the top floor?" Steven reclined in the chair and stretched his long frame like a big cat.

"Right now it's an area I turned into a training room, you know; a few weight machines, heavy bag, speed bag and some other training equipment. That's about it really. It doesn't even have heating and cooling as yet."

I went to the small bar in the corner as I spoke and mixed us a drink, walked over handed Steven his, and slumped heavily onto the couch opposite him. The big black dog made a small circle before finally settling at my feet, once again positioning herself between us. She liked my cousin just fine, but she trusted only her master, and she never forgot her job as she saw it, protecting me. I sort of liked that in a dog.

"Steven, tell me for real man; you honestly believe any of this stuff about this witch, or whatever you call her?" I had pushed the question aside as long as I could.

After a moment's hesitation, he responded, now more serious; "All I know is; I don't know. It doesn't sound real I admit, but hell, there are a lot of things in this world that don't sound real to start with and they sort of grow on you later. The old man definitely believes it's real. Morg, he might be old and gray but he's still sharp as a razor." He started to open a fresh pack of cigarettes as he talked, "The Cherokee people and their myths go back longer than the white man has been around. They were doing just fine before the white man came to "civilize" em, if they needed it or not. Some things just can't be explained by science and you know it, man. Some things just are, and they don't need to be explained to be real. Hell Bubba, you say that same thing all the time yourself. Somebody pretty damned real is killing a lot of our people and I want to know why. If you or I are on the hit list, I want to be ready that's all. I won't take this shit lying around and waiting for a late night visit from God knows who, or what. It don't matter what I believe."

"It just seems so far fetched to me, but I guess we can ride down and see Jordan tomorrow." I still didn't believe I was agreeing to go. "At least we'll get to enjoy the ride. If we leave early, we should be there late afternoon or early evening. I'm sure Jordan is going to think we have totally lost our minds. He has no respect at all for his heritage or his elders anyway, as you already know."

Steven replied, "Who gives a shit what that asshole thinks? That little dweeb needs his ass kicked and if you hadn't stopped me I would have done it a long time ago. If he wasn't your brother I would never let him run his mouth the way he does and he knows it too!" He stopped and looked around, his unlit cigarette dangling from the corner of his mouth, "Got any ashtrays?"

"Yeah." I made no move to get up.

"Well?"

"They're over in the drawer in the bar. Get it yourself if you want one. If you insist on smoking while in my house, I'm not going to help you do it."

"Thanks. Thanks for the friggin' hospitality Morgan. You're too nice to me." He reluctantly managed to get out of the recliner.

When he returned I asked, "You want to ride one of the bikes downstairs tomorrow? I've got a nice demo RT just like mine that will be a hell of a lot more comfortable than that old hog you're riding. Better yet, why don't you just trade that thing to me? I'll make you an offer you can't refuse."

"Nah, you know what they say; "Harley born and Harley bred." I know it's old, but that bike has seen me through too many miles to let her go now. She's sorta' like a wife and I ain't ready for divorce, you know what I mean? It's like that old piece-of-shit rust bucket I saw parked around back. How long have you had that old truck? At least fifteen years I know of. So you've got no room to talk."

"You're right, I wouldn't take anything for that old truck. In four-wheel drive low it will still pull a house down. I don't even drive it anymore, its just kind of comforting to know it's there." Steven knew better than most, why I kept the truck. It was one of the few things my father had ever given me, that is, if you didn't count the black eyes, busted ribs and the bruises. After a time, I lost count of those anyway. Of course, I had to work all of one summer just to have the blown engine rebuilt, but I was reluctant to let it go just the same. I didn't completely understand why myself.

We finished our drinks and talked over some of the details of the short trip down to Florida and generally what we had been doing since we last saw each other. We both kept carefully away of anything too specific. I returned to the bar several times to freshen the drinks as the night wore on. Much later, I showed him to the spare room and to the toiletries and supplies. As I turned to leave, I stopped and leaned on the door frame, "How is she anyway, Steven?" I tried to look as casual as I could manage but he was having none of it.

"Well, it sure took you friggin' long enough to ask didn't it? And don't think I didn't see it coming either big guy. I may not have seen you in awhile but I still know you pretty damned well." He shrugged; "She's doing fine though; beautiful and feisty as a wild mare and mean as a copperhead. You and her are both just too damned stubborn for your own good."

"Maybe so." I turned away with nothing else to say but, "Goodnight Steven."

"See you in the morning, cousin." He seemed to know just when to stop asking further questions. It was a strong quality, which I wished others possessed.

I went into my bedroom and performed all the well-worn rituals we all became intimately familiar with. As I brushed my teeth, I looked at myself in the mirror and asked my reflection what I was getting myself into this time. As expected, I didn't know the answer, or at least didn't offer one. I ran my hands through my close cropped hair, a style I had grown accustomed to during my years in the Army, and noticed my eyes were a little bloodshot around the brown. I decided sleep, hopefully, would help everything become clearer. As I slid into the big king-size bed, thoughts of the evening danced around my head long into the night. When sleep finally came it was fitful at best. I tossed and turned for hours, unable to get comfortable.

Around five-thirty I gave up the effort, slipped into an old pair of sweat pants and a T-shirt and went into the kitchen for a glass of orange juice. As always, Dog paced along behind me, sleeping when I slept, waking as I did, and walking when I walked. The deck I had built outside the living room was covered with a slight sheen from the evening dew, so I turned a cushion on the lounge chair to hide the wet side and propped my feet on the wooden rail. The light, morning wind felt cool on my damp feet. The semi-wonder dog drifted down to the deck by my side and turned so she could watch for the hidden marsh birds stalking their prey in the puff mud. The cold orange juice was fresh and pulpy, just as I liked it and I sat the empty glass on the table by my side and watched in the faint light as droplets of moisture formed together before trailing down the sides. For a time I just counted the drops and thought.

The cool musty, odor of the marsh grass drifted up and I inhaled deeply, filling my lungs to capacity and then slowly exhaling. The fresh saltwater smell of the harbor combined with the pungent scent of the marsh confirming the essence of old Charleston, a true city by the bay. I heard the stirrings of early morning city noises in the distance, loud garbage trucks, street sweeping machines and the other sounds rarely heard. The night work force was usually asleep when we were awake and vice versa; nameless ships passing in the early morning light, some retiring, others just beginning.

I could make out car headlights crossing the big Cooper River Bridge, their owners lost to their own unique, early-morning thoughts and dreams. The humidity was so high I could taste moisture in the salty air and in the distance, I heard the vintage clock in the Church Street steeple signal the bottom of the hour with a solitary gong. The lonely sound of that single heavy note seemed to hang in the morning air for an eternity, drifting out over the harbor and finally fading in the distance. Off towards the open water of the ocean, I could just make out the faint tendrils of light as the sun reached her long arms from somewhere around the earth to pull slowly over the horizon. Not anything definite yet, just the first, brief insight into the coming day, as yet unspoiled by people and events.

I had the strange feeling something was about to upset the balance I was finally beginning to achieve in my life…something that could take away all I had worked so hard to accomplish. Premonition was something I didn't have a great deal of faith in, but had to give some credence to. Things were about to change for me once again. I knew because I had felt the same way before and always with the same certainty in my heart. The familiar feeling usually turned out to be right on the money. My grandfather once told me it was part of "my gift". I didn't know if it was hearing all the Cherokee "curse" crap or actually hearing Kathy's name spoken aloud, but something stirred the feeling. I hoped I was wrong. Things were just beginning to look up in my life and I damn sure didn't want to give up any of the emotional ground I had fought so hard to gain. It had been a hard struggle for me the last couple of years, a solitary battle for sanity, which I chose to fight alone. It was a lonely decision sometimes, but I found it worked out better that way. At least, that's what I kept telling myself.

As the morning sun slowly lit the surrounding landscape and city skyline, I remembered a night when I was very young and I was visiting my grandfather for one of the last times I was to see him alive. I was spending a few weeks with him over the summer before I returned to Jr. High School. We walked over the mountain to visit one of his friends. His seventy-five plus years prohibited hiking anywhere in a hurry, so he always had plenty of time to point out things about the woods, stories of our family, the Cherokee and their tales and myths. As he talked and walked, pride rang in his voice and his eyes became young again as he remembered running as a boy through the very forest we were exploring.

It saddened me to think back to those times, because I had come to realize that he must have known, even then, I would never feel the same as he about our family's past. He would never be able to pass on the legacy of our past or his hopes for the future. My father, of course, was not one capable of carrying on anything but a good drunk. His life was a total mockery of everything my grandfather stood for and believed in. Me, I was already completely apart from the old ways, and I would never be the one to fulfill his dreams for him. I was his last hope, his last chance…perhaps his greatest disappointment, and I was too young and full of myself to grasp it at the time.

I understood that the book, the one Steven was looking for, was perhaps my grandfather's only legacy and there hadn't even been anyone left for him to entrust it to. It had to be frustrating; devoting his entire life to maintaining and keeping alive knowledge he revered as sacred, only to find in the end no one really cared about it anymore. It wasn't until then, that early Charleston morning that I realized how much I had let him down. At the time I had no idea because I had never understood. I loved my "Papaw", my grandfather, more than any man I have ever known, yet, I failed him greatly. When my grandfather passed away, my love for my heritage passed with him. I gave myself up totally to the current lifestyles of the time and tossed my family's past aside like an old sock.

I would never be able to repair the damage in my wake, but I could do what Papaw would have wished; I could help Ben "Rising Wolf". If I didn't believe enough in the old Indian's tale, I could believe enough in my grandfather to do what was right. I owed him that much. I could never hope to repay his memory but I could damn well try. I might not ever get another chance to redeem myself, and it would give me something to do—something to focus on—and that was something, which had been missing from my life for some time.

I walked into the house to wake Steven. A new day had begun.

Chapter Four

After some preliminary arrangements, we planned to get on the road around ten. I had to wait for my shop manager to come in and run over several things to be taken care of while I was away. My RT had to be prepped and my motorcycle bags packed, the ritual, which always proceeded any trip involving overnight travel. Preparing all my "stuff" for departure was nearly a ceremonial occurrence, almost as important as the ride itself, or so it seemed to me. I guess I was sort of "anal" about it, but it had worked out to my benefit too many times to count. It was always a challenge to pack everything I could possibly need in a limited space and still not clutter my luggage. The mandatory items were things like; tools, spare sparkplugs flashlight, the appropriate maps, clothes, rain gear, and anything else that might be needed.

Steven, of course, thought it was all so needless. "Just throw some shit in your tankbag and let's get the hell down the road okay? It looks like it might rain and I don't want another bath." He was sitting in a chair beside my bed drinking coffee and complaining.

"Just hold your damn horses alright? You sound like an old woman. In Charleston it always looks like rain, and you could always use a bath. We can't leave until I get someone in here to run this place anyway. Besides, I may need this stuff, you never know. We've had this same conversation before, if I remember right."

"Yeah! Every time we ride anywhere together! You have this thing of getting all your shit together and taking forever to do it. I just don't understand why you have to go through this stupid ritual every damn time."

"It's just become a habit over the years, and I seem to recall a time or two when you were glad I pack heavy." I pointed my finger at him, "Remember that time near Knoxville when you had the flat in the middle of the night? You would have walked a long way without my handy can of fix-a-flat. Don't criticize what you use, my unappreciative and foolish cousin."

"Fine, you got me alright?" He held his hands apart in surrender; "I give up. But, can we leave today you think? If we ain't, I'm going back to bed, I need my beauty sleep you know."

"Well, you're right about that part anyway. You sure you don't want to ride one of the demos downstairs? You need anything for your saddlebags?" I wrapped a flashlight in a thick plastic rain suit and shoved it deep in the bag that would form my back support as I rode.

"No, I'll stick with my ol' Harley and I've got all I need thanks. Anyway, if I don't, you've got everything else to hear you tell it. I've got two changes of clothes, clean underwear in case there's an accident, and my forty-five. What the hell else do I need?"

"I don't know. Toothpaste, perhaps? I was going to say something to you about your breath, but since you brought it up…"

"Yeah, yeah, funny. Real funny."

As we walked downstairs, I spoke to Dog who had been glued to my side all morning long. She seemed to have a sense when I might be going away for awhile. "And what is your problem? Can you give me a little space here, huh?"

She cocked her head with a quizzical look, as if to better understand.

"Why don't you go and eat the breakfast I was kind enough to set out for you? Go on, beat it Dog."

She turned and trotted up the back stairway. About that time, my sales manager walked in and did a double take as he saw Steven.

"Good morning, Morg. What's happening?" He asked in his normal, disgustingly cheerful voice.

"Not much Mike. Meet my cousin, Steven Waters. Steven, Mike Thomas."

They shook hands and Mike looked up at the tall Indian, "Damn if they don't come big in your family Morg. I think I'd dearly love to meet some of the females from your clan."

I laughed, "You'd love to meet any female and you know it. Steven, Mike here knows more about motorcycles than I do, but he has one great downfall; an addiction to anything female."

"And what's wrong with that?" Steven asked seriously.

Mike laughed and replied, "All right! My kind of guy! There are worse things in life to be addicted to that's for sure." As he glanced out the window, he continued, "Now here's a reason for any man to become an addict for the female form."

We turned to follow his gaze out the big show window as Marilyn got out of her car and walked towards the building. I guess you could say Marilyn Bates was the office manager. She was a CPA and basically ran all administrative functions. She kept up with the shop, a few other business interests I maintained and basically kept me straight, which was a full time job. As Mike suggested, she was indeed something to look at. He had been trying for years and could never even get to first base with her. She and I had a brief "friendship" when we first met and quickly determined we would be better off as just that: friends.

Marilyn was very tall herself, taller than most women. She was about 5'11" with long blond hair and a complexion that seemed forever tanned. Her figure was known to stop traffic on King Street on some summer afternoons when she shopped downtown in a short skirt, and that made the situation with Mike that much worse. With his reputation as a "ladies man", he took it as a personal insult that she wouldn't give him the time of day. Like the good salesman he was, he never gave up. I had to admire him for that.

"Good morning gorgeous!" He began with a huge smile on his face.

"Drop dead Mike." She replied without missing a step, "What's up, Morg? Who the hell is this good looking giant you've got with you? Decided to hire a body guard and didn't tell me?"

"I don't know what the hell you're talking about with that good looking stuff…" I pretended to look around in confusion, "…but this big guy here is my cousin, Steven Waters."

Before I could get any further, Steven stepped up between us and took her hand. "Please ignore my little cousin here, he never did know how to act around beautiful women."

For just a moment, I honestly thought I saw Marilyn blush. Recovering quickly, she said, "Well, I'm just charmed, pardon the pun. I'm Marilyn Bates and I unfortunately work for your "little" cousin." She looked over his shoulder at me with a humorous glint in her eye at her use of his words. "So I'll leave all the comments about his nature to you, even though you do seem to have him pegged pretty well."

Their hands seemed to take an unusually long time to separate. I noticed a look on Marilyn's face as she stared up into Steven's that I hadn't seen before. Of course, it could have been that she wasn't used to looking up at anyone, male or female.

"Alright, if you guys can get over this mutual admiration bullshit, I have some things to discuss with Mike about a short leave I'm going to take with Stevey here. Marilyn, could you maybe show this big Indian around the kitchen? I think if he gets another cup of coffee his attitude about life might change."

"Attitude? What attitude? I think life is a wonderful thing, and getting better all the time," he retorted, his gaze never leaving Marilyn's face. "Take all the time you need. Who needs to hurry? You can never be too sure about travel arrangements." He gave me a sly look only I could see. "And don't you think you better check your tank bag again before we leave? You know I keep telling you how important double checking your stuff is and you just don't listen! And don't call me Stevey, it's Steven, even sir to you, but not Stevey." He turned back to Marilyn, "I keep telling him over and over again, but he…" He continued talking non-stop as he took her by the arm and headed off toward the kitchen in the rear of the building.

I shook my head and smiled as they walked away, then turned to discuss my departure with Mike.

Before I could begin, he interjected, "Did you get a load of that? What the hell has he got that I don't? I've never seen her act like that before." He shook his head in exasperation. "Man, damn!"

"Maybe it's the height, Mike. Have you ever considered elevator shoes?" When he didn't laugh at my joke, I continued, "Anyway, I'm going to be riding for a few days, and here's what I need…"

Less than an hour later we had the two motorcycles stopped in front of a gas station just off Savannah Highway. Steven topped off his tank and handed the pump handle to me, as I straddled my bike and used my key to unlock the gas cap.

"That Marilyn is sure some piece of work. I understand why you hired her," he said with a mischievous wink.

"Oh hell no you don't! That woman is as smart as she is beautiful and you're just too stupid to know it. You wouldn't know smart if it bit you on the ass." As I began to fill my tank I added, "She did seem to take sort of a liking to you though, why I'll never understand." As I swung my leg over the seat, I asked, "Need anything from inside?"

"No. I've got everything I need."

I walked into the gas station and paid the attendant, a college-looking kid of about twenty.

"Nice looking bikes."

"Thanks."

"You fellas heading far, are you?"

"I sure hope not." I absently replied as I walked out the door, then found myself whispering to myself; "I sure as hell hope not". The little bell over the door chimed as I exited into the growing heat of the morning.

We started out following Highway 17 towards Savannah and stayed off the interstate. Riding the interstate was not something we liked to do, and since we had a need for speed, I-95 towards Daytona Beach was going to be mandatory as it was. The route we chose gave us scenery to look at and time to think before we had to ride the last leg of the journey on the overcrowded highway into Florida. Our shadows chased behind us, speeding through the wet marshlands of the South Carolina countryside, the land of early morning duck hunting and the watermelon patch. The occasional roadside ponds we passed sported small Jon-boats with fishermen aboard. Frequently, we passed cars parked along the highway with their occupants visible on the shady bank of a nearby marsh pond, rods bobbing gently above the water, beer coolers by their side. The sun rose higher, hot and in an extremely bad mood. It beat down on us mercilessly as we continued our journey south. We purposely held the speed down, as the road was notorious for speed traps. They were planned to snag the unwary trucker moving ocean containers between the piers of Savannah and Charleston and, unfortunately, a lot of other people got caught in the web.

I hadn't seen my brother since my mother's funeral, nor had I spoken to him on the phone. We never talked on the phone. As a matter of fact we rarely talked at all anymore. I had almost given up trying to talk to him and it seemed to work out better that way for us both. We may have been close when we were young, but that had long since passed.

Jordan lived just outside of Daytona Beach in a large house near the water. He had finally "made it big", after years of using every person he came in contact with. Jordan was one of those men who went through life finding one hair-brained scheme after another to get rich quick. Each idea seemed crazier than the last, definitely the deal of a lifetime for someone. Unfortunately, it was usually only a good deal for Jordan and rarely anyone else. Over the years he managed to alienate every family member and friend he knew, the latter were few in number and generally even less before he finished. He could find a way to talk anyone out of their money to finance his latest enterprise and didn't care about the consequences of his actions. Jordan had one person in life he cared about, Jordan. Everyone else was just a tool as far as he was concerned, put here to serve his needs and fuel his dreams. When we were young, he was a shitty little kid and he grew into a shitty young man. Of course, the way we were raised and the father we shared went a long way towards shaping his abrasive personality. Over the miles of our southbound trek, I attempted to form a way in my mind of telling him the crazy story and getting some fix on what his response might be. If he did have the book, there wouldn't be a problem getting it…that is, if it benefited him in some way.

It seemed I was the only hope for understanding Jordan was ever going to have on this planet and, even my patience was wearing paper-thin. I had my own problems to deal with of late and it was only due to the brother thing that I even made the effort. Steven was right; Jordan was as asshole of the supreme order, but he was still my brother. Too many times I took the heat or the physical blow ear marked for Jordan and just accepted them as my due. Too often I stepped between my father and my younger brother to accept the brunt of his drunken rage, but after awhile I didn't care about that so much. By then, I had already come to hate my father. But it seemed Jordan came to expect it from me over time and provoked the old man just to see me take a beating. Nice guy my brother. Maybe that was part of the reason he was so screwed up. Hell, who knows? I never claimed to be a psychiatrist.

This "Ravenmocker" story was, unfortunately, just the type of thing he liked to chastise. He didn't care about his cultural heritage or our family history. I knew he would never understand what would possess us to go to such effort to appease a dying old man. Of course, I didn't really understand myself, yet I found myself buzzing down the highway with a half crazy Indian riding by my side. Another problem I had to consider would be the interaction between Steven and Jordan. To say the least, there was no love lost between them. Steven once had a young girlfriend who fell prey early to Jordan's sinister charm and was hurt deeply in the process. Steven was not the kind of man to forget something like that. The only thing that kept Jordan from being the physical recipient of his wrath was my request for amnesty. In retrospect, I should have let him beat his ass. As it was, Jordan left town on his most recent get-rich-quick endeavor and time smoothed over the wounds. It generally does. Anytime they were together since the air was volatile and tense. Jordan seemed to have a sick desire to taunt and prod, like one would a caged lion at the zoo. I was charged with keeping the lion at bay, just like always, and in his own perverse way; Jordan had confidence in my ability to do it. One day I was afraid I wouldn't be able to stop my crazy cousin and even though, in a way I wanted to see it, I hoped this wasn't the day.

If we kept to schedule we would reach Jordan's house in seven hours give or take a little. Our moderate pace allowed us some time to enjoy the ride and to stop periodically for food and drink, especially drink…the hot sun took it's toll on the best of men. It's hard to remain on the back of any motorcycle for several hours without a break. Eventually all feeling in your rear evaporated so to speak. It was a long, hot ride for crazy reasons but I was enjoying it just the same. The land flowed by and the wind pushed us along our way through the morning and into the afternoon.

We stopped near Jacksonville for a late lunch at a deli type bar, and over a submarine sandwich Steven commented; "You've been sort of quiet about Kathy and I know it's not something you want to talk about, but…"

"You're right, I don't want to talk about it." I bit into my sandwich.

"Fine, fine, but you know you're gonna' have to see her. We can't deal with this without going up to the mountains. You know we gotta' go up man."

"Well, I'll cross that bridge when I get to it. Now, let's change the subject." I foolishly held out my bag of chips and his big hand disappeared inside and left only a crumpled chip or two and a few crumbs. "How are your parents? You haven't mentioned them, what's up?" I took a long swallow of the cold soft drink, crumpled my empty bag of chips and reached for his.

He snatched the bag away and put it out of my reach. "They're doing fine. Hell, the old man's as mean as ever and mom is always the same. She calls him a cranky old Indian and he calls her an uppity old white woman. It's the only true love I know of. They never say one kind word to each other, it's truly beautiful to behold."

"Your dad got over the heart attack then?"

"Pretty much." He shrugged his big shoulders, "It's slowed him down a bit, did a fair amount of damage to his left side, and he had to give up drinking and smoking entirely, and to him that was the worst part. All in all, it may have been a good thing. It has definitely changed his attitude."

"You still living at the house?" I managed to ask between the final bites of my sandwich.

"All my stuff is still there if that's what you're asking, I'm just not around very often. Something always seems to come up, if you know what I mean."

"Yeah, I know. I've seen some of the "things" before. Still playing the field are you?"

"You know it! I'm getting older so I have to get my licks in while I can, pardon the expression." He finished his sub and attacked his bag of chips without offering me any.

"Thinking of adding Marilyn to your list?"

"Well, the thought did cross my mind. When this thing is over I might need to come visit you more often, see what happens—maybe buy the lady a drink or something."

"Be careful of this one cousin. She's not your run of the mill mountain girl; she grew up wearing shoes. You're might bite off a little more than you can chew with her, big guy. She's not exactly a one night stand type." I pointed my finger at him, "Trust me on this, Cuz."

"Do I detect a little attitude here? Nothing going on between you two is there?" He raised one eyebrow comically.

"No, nothing is going on between us. She's just a good friend and I don't want to see you get any wrong ideas about her, that's all."

"I gotcha'. You worry too much, always have." He rose to empty his tray in a nearby receptacle. "Anyway, 'nuf said. Let's ride. I'd rather ride in this heat than listen to you bitch."

"Who's bitchin'? I was just curious that's all."

We paid the bill and stepped out from the air-conditioned comfort into the sweltering heat of the Florida afternoon.

"Jesus, but it's hot as hell down here! What am I doing out of the mountains? I bet it's twenty degrees cooler there."

"You're doing a good deed, remember? You conned me into coming along. I'm not sure I understand why either one of us is here really." I swung my leg over the saddle and put the key in the switch.

I was surprised when Steven looked at me seriously. "I know this all sounds like something from a horror comic book, but what if it's true Morgan? You know yourself we can't explain everything that goes on around us. The old ones have their own explanations and sometimes they make a hell of a lot more sense than others I have read in any school book, you know?"

"I know all that, but a curse? A witch? Get real Steven, you know better than that." I removed my sunglasses and rubbed my eyes.

"Stranger things have happened. I don't know myself. Right now we're just humoring an old man and trying to make a pretty lady happy."

"And you've always been good at that last part right?" I kidded him as I put my helmet back on followed by my glasses and gloves.

"Yep...good enough that they'd throw rocks at you sport," and he laughed, kicking the big Harley to life and prohibiting any rebuttal I might have made.

The remaining leg of our journey was uneventful but extremely long, and hot. I felt the heat of the bright Florida sun beating down on my arms and was thankful for the gift of my Indian heritage which made my skin nearly immune to it's effects. The riding helped me relax and unwind as it usually did. If nothing else, it felt good to be out on the highway again. It also felt good to be with Steven. I had forgotten I missed him I guess, and hadn't realized how much because I had been so caught up in dealing with my personal problems.

I had never been to my brother's house. The pictures he sent, his way of bragging about his "final hard earned success" as he called it, were hanging around in my memory somewhere. His address and directions he included with his last postcard, placed his home just north of Daytona Beach in a rather well to do Florida suburb. It was the kind of neighborhood that major "money cities" all seemed to have in common; semi-secluded location, lots the size of small towns with one ostentatious dwelling, complete with an Olympic-sized pool and separate guest quarters.

We turned from the nearly deserted, oak-lined street, into the massive entrance gate which marked Twelve Oak Lane. The house was barely visible in the distance through the palm trees and the pampas grass. I was not sure seeing my brother was such a good thing for me. I never wrote him about the "unpleasantness" I had gone through over the last few years. He would have been no help anyway and I really hadn't wanted him to know what happened. I was embarrassed and I didn't want to try to explain to him what I had done because he never would have understood. He couldn't understand because he was incapable of comprehending anything but his own greed and desires.

I briefly wondered again what I was doing and why. Jordan was definitely not going to get behind such a crazy story and all hell was probably about to break loose between he and my traveling companion. I almost wished my brother would not be in the large white mansion we rode towards. The day could turn hotter in more ways than one, and very quickly.

I took a deep breath and rode ahead.

CHAPTER FIVE

The long driveway wound through a grove of trees towards a massive, white house just past a well-manicured lawn. The trees lining the drive echoed the sound of the motorcycles back to us, the tranquility of the summer afternoon violated by our passing. Two doors of the four-car garage were open and empty, their previous contents parked in front of the large ostentatious dwelling. A new, bright red Corvette and a two-year old black Mercedes sat in startling contrast to the stark white background of the house. The dwelling was constructed entirely of white brick and marble, with a clay-colored Spanish tile roof. The grounds were lush, green and well cared for. The bright Florida sun lit the sparkling, white, house like a concert spotlight. It was very impressive—everything Jordan had always said he would have one day.

We coasted beside the automobiles and cut power to the engines. An almost forgotten quietness greeted me as I scratched my head after removing my helmet. I breathed deeply and could just make out traces of salt water in the air. The ocean couldn't have been far away. I thought I heard a gull off in the distance. My brother had to be spending a small fortune just to keep the place up—I knew he would never do such honest work. To hear him tell it, he was beyond manual labor, always was, and probably always would be.

"Jeeesuus!" Steven whistled through his teeth. "Who the hell did the little shit steal this from?"

"Give it a rest already, you know this isn't going to be easy as it is. I don't want to have to play referee between the two of you the whole time we're here. Why don't you at least try to refrain from being your normal charming self long enough for us to get what we came for, okay? You can control your emotions cousin, I've seen you do it." He shook his head in disgust. "Stay cool and let me do all the talking." When he started to interrupt, I held my hand up. "I mean it Steven. Don't make things any worse than they already are. We've got enough problems without adding to them."

"That sounds like one plan I guess."

"Well, if you have another one I'm prepared to listen." I swung my leg over the seat and stretched my tired back by reaching for the sky, then slowly bending towards my toes.

He smiled, "Sure, you ring the door bell and when the little shit comes out, I politely beat the crap out of him until he comes across with what we want." He raised his eyebrows comically. "Now, that's a much better plan, if you ask me."

I couldn't help but laugh, "You stupid shit."

"Thanks. I try real hard."

"You know, sometimes you definitely give new meaning to the word idiot." I took off my sunglasses. "Now look…no kidding, you got me into this, and if you want me to help you with this crazy plan of yours, you've got to promise to keep your mouth shut and follow my lead. We definitely do not, I repeat, do not need your macho bullshit making an already bad situation worse. Get it?"

"Yeah, I got it." He reluctantly agreed.

"Good."

"Let's just get this over with okay?"

"And as peacefully as possible?"

"Sure. Fine. I've got it already. I'll try to behave Massa' Morgan."

"You do that."

Large, double doors were viciously guarded by two huge grimacing lions. They reached fifteen feet or more with their pedestals, stark white against bright blue sky. The doorbell chimes sounded some tired tune I couldn't quite place, as we waited patiently on the steps. I placed the palm of my hand against one of the mammoth lions and felt the smooth marble; felt the heat it radiated from the hot sun of the late afternoon. Steven leaned one arm on the other lion and tried to look bored with the whole situation.

The door opened, revealing a remarkably attractive young woman with hair so blonde it had to be real. For a moment I was stunned. Her hair reached down her back, almost to her waist, and the print sundress she wore concealed a body like something from a man's magazine. The bright green eyes took both of us in quickly, lingering for a second or two longer on the huge Indian leaning on her lion. It was then that I realized just what an impression we made, dressed in motorcycle gear and looking like trouble waiting to happen. Her eyes changed slightly, taking on a worried look.

As I regained my composure, I glanced at Steven and motioned for him to remove his glasses. I attempted to put her at ease. "Lori? I'm sorry to bother you, but I'm Morgan, Jordan's brother. We didn't mean to startle you." I smiled my most reassuring smile and attempted to look as respectable as I could. Steven also tried a smile, but it was probably more unnerving than reassuring coming from a man of his size and appearance.

After a moment or two, her beautiful eyes cleared. A look of worry changed to what appeared genuine pleasure. "Morgan! This is just great! I have wanted to meet you for such a long time. Please, please come in." Her voice was as magnificent as she was, light and cheerful and pleasant.

She moved aside, allowing us to enter and we stepped into a beautiful foyer filled with tropical plants, lots of open space and very little furniture. The floor was thick, marble slab polished to a mirror shine and bright sunlight flowed into the room through a number of tastefully positioned skylights. It was cool and comfortable inside as Lori closed the large door in our wake. It was a vast and welcome change from the heat we had ridden through most of the day.

Lori continued politely, "Jordan talks about you all the time. He'll be so excited you're here."

I wasn't so sure of that myself. "I hope so." I let my expression show something other than what I really felt. "I'm sure we must look pretty rough by now. We've been riding in this heat all day." I turned to Steven. "This is my cousin, Steven Waters. Steven this is Lori Roberts, Jordan's wife."

She extended her hand to Steven and smiled; radiance, charm, and Southern hospitality all displayed in her manner. He sort of stammered as he took her tiny hand in his huge paw and I thought for just a second he was perplexed about what to do or say. "It's a pleasure to meet you ma'am."

I smiled inwardly at how truly embarrassed he seemed, clearly uncomfortable; as if he would rather be anywhere else but where he was. Despite his normal brash outward appearance, he was still just an old mountain boy at heart, and he was totally out of his element. Lori exhibited all the signatures of old money and good breeding and the giant Indian was a like a pauper in a palace here; a wild timber wolf cub among a litter of French poodles.

"And you," she replied, "My, but you're a tall one aren't you?"

"Well, some people think so anyway. You've got a great place here, Lori." Steven may have been a mountain redneck, but he could still be charming when dealing with members of the opposite sex. He somehow managed to say just the right thing. I could tell by the light in her eyes and the pleasant smile, which lit her features nicely.

"Why, thank you so much. I'm sort of proud of it actually. We've only been here about a year, so I haven't gotten the place quite to my liking yet, but it's definitely getting there." She paused with a shy smile; "I've been doing the decorating myself." Her voice reflected obvious pride. "I guess you guys didn't come down just to see me and my new house though, did you?"

"Well of course we did!" I replied without hesitation, "But while we're here I thought we might visit with my little brother for a spell. Is he around?"

"He should be home any moment. He and some friends went to play golf over at the club. They should drop him back home anytime now." Her refined features and porcelain skin accented her classic beauty. Her speech echoed polish and education and I caught myself wondering how such a woman could be married to my brother. Maybe I was in the wrong house and had the wrong Lori. She continued speaking with a never fading smile, "Why don't we step into the den and I'll be glad to fix you gentlemen some refreshments. How does that sound to you? Something cold and wet for such a hot summer day?"

"That sounds wonderful." I replied readily and Steven politely echoed the sentiment.

"Great! Just follow me and we'll get you fixed up!"

She turned and walked down a long hallway and I glanced briefly at Steven as we followed. He looked quickly at her retreating figure in the tight summer dress and winked at me. I quickly shook my head in his direction and gave him a smirk, even though I had caught myself looking in the same place just moments before, probably thinking the same thoughts. Whatever else Jordan had, or had not accomplished, he had definitely found a prize in her. Lori appeared to be a beautiful and surprisingly pleasant young woman and I couldn't imagine what she saw in Jordan. I suppose love really was blind.

We followed her down the long hallway as she made brief stops in the different rooms we passed along our way. She showed us each and indicated recent renovations she was particularly pleased with. As she described the rooms and the additions, her voice became more alive and as light and cheerful as the bright white motif that seemed prevalent throughout her home. She had done a fine job and had every reason to be proud of her accomplishments.

At the rear of the first floor, we found a large open den with a glass wall and double patio doors. An adjoining cabana, as large as most homes, sat beside a sparkling pool and was visible through the glass. Resin patio furniture rested in abundance poolside, white tables and matching umbrellas. The whole house was sparkling clean and it seemed about as livable as a museum. It had a great deal of decorative and not a lot of functional.

"Why don't you gentlemen make yourselves comfortable? You can sit anywhere you like. What can I get for you?" She asked, as she walked towards a large glass bar.

"You don't by any chance have a cold beer?" I asked.

"Of course. Light or regular?"

"Leaded will be fine thanks."

Steven added, "You can make that two, if you've gottem."

"Coming right up." and she floated over to a small refrigerator behind the bar.

Steven whispered quickly, "Where the hell do we make ourselves comfortable in here?" He gestured apprehensively at the spotless couch and matching white recliners.

I smiled at his discomfort, "Lori, do you think it would be okay if we stepped out by the pool? The shade underneath that umbrella looks very appealing."

"Sure thing. That'll be just fine. You two go ahead and make your-selves at home. I'll bring your drinks out in just a second."

I slid open the glass door and Steven followed me to the patio table and sat uncomfortably in the chair beside me. His large frame filled it completely, the top of his head almost touching the open umbrella.

"Now that is one classy lady," he said.

"Yeah, you're right. She is definitely not what I expected. I'm not sure what I did expect, but she is not it."

"No kidding! One thing I don't get is how Jordan got this one on the hook and into the boat. He must have sold her some more bill of goods." I knew he was remembering what Jordan had once done to his friend.

We heard the polished slide of the glass door and Lori appeared. Steven rose quickly and smoothly to his feet, moving from his chair quite gracefully for a man of such size. Before I could react, Steven rushed ahead to help Lori with the drink tray.

"Why, thank you. I'm not used to such chivalry. I don't know if my little southern heart can take it." She placed her hand demurely over her chest as she feigned an exaggerated, southern accent like Scarlet in Gone with the Wind. The difference was she sounded a great deal more natural doing it. She laughed pleasantly at her little joke and followed Steven as he sat the tray on the table. Her laughter was soft and musical and real and I could smell her light perfume, which hinted of roses and musk. She sat beside me and removed two icy beer mugs for each of us. Lori had whipped up some kind of fruity concoction for herself and she sipped delicately from its frosty contents.

"So what brings you boys so far south? Came down to see the pretty Florida girls I bet?" She asked with a mischievous smile, which could have lit half of downtown Charleston on a Saturday night.

I replied with the first thought that came to mind, "Well if we did, we could leave satisfied anytime now. I don't think we're going to see any better than what we've found here." And I meant it. I paused as she laughed politely at the compliment. "Actually, we came down for a short visit and to maybe discuss a little business with Jordan. It was an added benefit getting to meet you and believe me, I'm sorry it took so long. I'm really sorry I didn't get down for the wedding," changing the subject rather smoothly I thought. If she noticed anything, she was enough of a lady to take the hint and didn't pursue the subject further.

"Well, I totally understand. I know how busy you must be. Jordan has told me what a successful businessman you are. The way he talks you must own half of Charleston by now."

I thought to myself, Jordan must have been trying to impress someone for him to say something like that. He was so full of shit it was amazing he didn't have the odor sometimes. "Well, that's just like Jordan to brag that way, but in all modesty, I'm just a small business owner. I'm self-employed and in debt like most of the free world. I'm afraid there's nothing very glamorous about it and I definitely don't appear to be doing anywhere near as well as Jordan by the looks of things around here." I indicated our surroundings, trying to change the direction of our conversation and move it away from me.

"Well, Jordan never discusses business with me, but he does seem to be doing rather well. He's moving in some rather exclusive circles and he knows all the right people, I guess." I noticed as she crossed her magnificent legs beneath the glass tabletop and had to force myself to pull my eyes away.

"Great! It's good to see a successful marriage for a change. I'm glad Jordan found someone to make him happy after all these years."

She seemed to hesitate slightly before she replied, and a look drifted behind her eyes that I couldn't quite identify. For the first time her radiant smile slipped a notch or two. "Well…yes he…we're very happy."

Quickly regaining her composure, she continued, "I tell you, I think I may have married the wrong brother, Jordan never mentioned you were such a charmer." Being the perfect hostess, she politely turned to Steven to bring him into the conversation. "Let's see, if you two are cousins, then that means you and Jordan are cousins as well, right? You know Jordan doesn't speak much about his family, but I'm sure he never described you. I feel certain I would have remembered. I mean he never mentioned anything about a huge, good-looking cousin that I recall."

Steven looked somewhat uncomfortable as he replied, "Well, I'm sure he just doesn't think about me much. I pretty much hung out with Morgan here when we were young, being slightly older and all."

I thought to myself that he handled his response really well and made a mental note to congratulate him later on his diplomacy. Before any of us could respond, the patio door slammed open with a loud bang.

"Who in the hell parked those piece of shit motorcycles in front of my friggin' house?" My younger brother walked out to the pool area. I caught the slight grimace on Lori's face from the corner of my eye just as she heard his voice. It was fleeting but I caught it just the same.

Jordan and I shared a few of the same physical qualities, but most notably the facial features. We both had the same dark brown eyes, high cheekbones, and nearly jet-black hair. His hair was cut in a preppy, stylish fashion and mine was cropped much closer, more functional than fashionable. He was about four inches shorter, and over the last year or two seemed prone to do what the majority of men do as they approached the big milestone of thirty years; he developed a slight bulge around the middle. I guess too many beers and not enough exercise brought about that result in the best of men. His relative attractiveness and his gift of persuasion made him a success with women over the years, but there was nothing attractive about his attitude and it seemed this day would prove no different.

"I want to know and I want to know now! Who is respons…" He finally realized he had company and caught my eye. "Well, well, well…look what the wind blew in! If it isn't my big brother." He spoke with obvious sarcasm, then without pausing; he addressed Steven in a rude and hateful manner, "What the hell are you doing in my house? I guess my brother's taste in traveling companions hasn't changed much has it? You need something here or are you just along for a free ride like always?"

I held my breath and waited for the fireworks.

CHAPTER SIX

Surprisingly enough the fireworks never came, at least not then anyway.

"Jordan!" Lori's surprised tone suggested how unprepared she was for his viscious verbal assault on Steven.

My big cousin stiffened slightly before meeting my eyes, but other than that, made no comment. I could sense the fire barely suppressed beneath the calm facade of his features. How he kept his composure, when I knew he wanted to tear Jordan into little pieces, was something I'll never figure out. For all my talk, I don't know if I could have handled the insults as well as he did. I knew the next few minutes were going to be the hardest.

Unfortunately, another, a totally innocent victim, was sacrificed to gain an uneasy peace.

Jordan spoke to Lori, his tone venomous, "You stay out of this! No one spoke to you did they?" He jerked his head in the direction of the patio doors, "Now go in the house and get me a beer." When she didn't respond right away he yelled at her. "Well…what the hell are you waiting on? Go!" He turned his back to her, facing me with a silly grin on his face, "And another of whatever Morgan is having." He didn't mention Steven at all. Even I wanted to punch him then. It was all too familiar and unsettling.

Lori, her eyes averted as if to hide tears, went into the house without speaking. It was obvious to everyone that the last thing Jordan needed was another beer. Well, like father, like son, they always say, whoever the hell "they" are.

"And might I say it's nice to see you too, little brother. Your attitude seems as chipper as ever. Have a bad day on the links did we?" I kept my voice level and flat. I made direct eye contact with him and he quickly turned away.

I would like to think that Jordan, even though always the consummate asshole still managed to maintain at least some respect when dealing with me over the years. Maybe he remembered how often I had pulled his worthless hide off the firing line in the past, or maybe it was the memories of the times he had pushed me to the point where I had to physically adjust his attitude. Either way, I could tell by the sudden change in his voice such thoughts were not far from his mind.

His attitude did seemingly alter for the better as he settled into a chair, "Of course I'm glad to see you! I'm just surprised that's all. Why didn't you call? I would have had some friends over and we could have had a little party. I tell you, Lori has some girl friends that you wouldn't believe. I gotta' say, I've been a little tempted myself, if you know what I mean." He gave me a lecherous wink and I found myself wondering, and not for the first time, how we could possibly be of the same blood.

Lori returned with the beer, sat two bottles on the table, handed Jordan his, and quietly returned to her chair. She made no comment. Her cheerfulness had seemingly evaporated though she kept a hollow smile for our benefit. Her eyes were red around the edges and I noticed her hands shook as she folded them in her lap. I noticed she clenched them together so hard her knuckles were white.

"Thanks honey." He commented dryly without even looking at her. "So tell me, what brings you down to my neck of the woods anyway? You decided to come down and see for yourself your little brother could actually make it on his own?"

Steven had yet to say a word. He just sat and stared at the pool. I decided the situation might just work out after all. As long as they continued to ignore each other, we might survive the night.

"Well, we rode down for a short visit to see how you were and maybe discuss a little family business. Lori was kind enough to show us around. I have to say it looks like you're doing very well for yourself Jordan. I'm happy for you." I surprised myself when I realized I was telling the truth. He was my brother after all and if I couldn't be proud of him, who would?

"Why thanks Morgan." He beamed so much at my comment it made me feel a little awkward. "Yep, we're doing all right Lori and I." He turned on a fake smile I had seen on every used car salesman and attorney I had ever met. "You see, real estate down here is the thing. You get to meet the right people at the right time, know when to get in and when to get out, and you can make a million. I'm going to do just that this year!"

I smiled to myself at the number of metaphors he used, sounding like an over used sit-com character. He reminded me of Herb Tarleck, of WKRP fame, except he didn't have white patent leather shoes, a matching belt and a sports jacket like the seat covers on a 65 Ford Fairlane.

I knew all I had to do was ask about whatever he was currently into and he would talk for hours. Jordan would always take time to tell you about his favorite subject…Jordan. True to form, he continued to chronicle his exploits in the financial world of Florida. I nodded as he spoke but I wasn't really listening.

I watched over his shoulder as the sun began to set. As it faded into the western sky, tropical colors painted themselves on the distant horizon and the day slipped into soft pastel focus. As Jordan's voice droned on, I made the appropriate comments to keep him talking while my mind raced ahead, trying to find a way to present our "situation". I knew that if he felt the desire to make fun of Steven for his part in our little endeavor, then problems were going to develop and fast no matter how well Steven had done up to that point. There was just so much he could take and I wasn't going to kid myself thinking otherwise. I had to find a way to turn the conversation in the direction I wanted and away from Steven.

Lori made a trip back to the house to restock our beer supply but basically hadn't said a word since Jordan first arrived. It was amazing to me she would put up with such treatment, but then again, I guess love made people do and accept things they normally wouldn't.

Jordan described his most recent, moneymaking exploit into the world of Florida finance. "...Then we bought this parcel of land from this old couple see, for less than a quarter of a mill and sold it one month later for almost three times that! Of course, it helps having the right kind of friends down at the courthouse to let you know what parcels are slated for development next. You know those old geezers were really pissed when they found out what was happening. I guess they just had no clue how big business really works, right?" His selfish sneer gave me cold chills but it also gave me an idea.

I glanced quickly at Steven to catch his eye. "You know, funny you should bring that up, I have something sorta' strange to ask you. No big deal or anything but we might could make a little money, so to speak. It's probably not much to you, but I was talking to a friend of ours up in the mountains. I know you probably don't remember Katie Moore over on the reservation, but she was telling me the other day she knew this wealthy collector of Cherokee artifacts. This guy is looking for an old book of some kind, some Indian legend or medicine man junk, stuff like that, you know?"

"Yeah, yeah, go on." Jordan's interest definitely tweaked when I mentioned money in any form or amount.

"Well, it seems some of those old guys up at the reservation told her they remembered our grandfather having a book like that." I shrugged, "Anyway, she called to see if I could find it in dad's things or to see if maybe you had it. I told her I had never seen anything like she described, but maybe you had. Have you? She says it might be worth a good bit of money."

From the corner of my eye I noticed Steven lean slightly forward in his chair, paying real attention for the first time.

"No, I don't know anything about any old book…" Jordan hesitated for a moment and I could sense the wheels turning in that greedy little brain of his, "…no, not that I know of, but that doesn't mean it's not in dad's stuff, you know."

Steven slumped back in his chair and thankfully lost interest in any further conversation involving my brother. I hoped anyway.

After he had a few moments to think more about it, Jordan continued, "Now look Morgan," his tone got serious and the fake smile was gone, "…you got to realize if that book is worth anything I get my share, right? I mean we're brothers right? You should pay me my share just like you did on the cabins. If it's his, we should split the money just like everything else." He held his hands apart and looked at me with red rimmed eyes, "That's only fair, right?"

I put on a fake smile of my own, "Right Jordan, I wouldn't have it any other way. I definitely believe you should get what's coming to you." Inwardly, I was disappointed at my brother's obviously insatiable greed. It was always hard to admit the faults of those you love, even if they were complete assholes.

If he noticed my sarcastic comment he made no reference as he continued, "Hey! Enough about that!" He clapped his hands together. "You know it's getting pretty late and I'm hungry as hell, how about some dinner? You're going to stay over, aren't you?" He was still addressing all conversation to me and didn't appear conscious of Steven. I liked it that way and mentally knocked on wood. "We'll talk more about this junk later, okay?"

"Well sure, it's been a long ride down and I'm sure we could use some nourishment. Right Stevey?"

Steven moved for the first time in at least half an hour and re-crossed his legs before he replied, "Yeah that sounds real good. Thanks." For once he didn't even comment on my unwelcome use of the nickname. That worried me.

Jordan made a face as Steven spoke but he looked to me. "Yeah, well...okay. Hey Lori! Why don't you be a doll and whip us up something and we'll eat out here by the pool. I'll run in and change out of these golf duds and we'll have some real drinks. You need to use the head or anything?"

"Yeah, that would be nice. How about you Steven?"

"Yep, those last fifty miles or so were pretty rough." He was attempting to be civilized and doing a damn good job I thought.

Jordan indicated the cabana and spoke to Steven as I held my breath. "Well, that cabana is open. It's all yours. There's two beds and a bath, use whatever you need; everything is in there. You should be comfortable in there for the night." His voice was only remotely civil and filled with contempt. He spoke to Lori with a tone not much better, "Honey, why don't you make up one of the guest rooms upstairs for Morgan."

Lori responded with a puzzled look, "But Jordan, why can't they both stay in the house? There's plenty of..."

"Just do as I say Lori!" He snapped at her in a commanding voice, an inherited trait that I easily recognized from our youth.

I quickly interjected, "No, that's alright. You did say there were two beds in the cabana? We'll both stay out here. It'll be easier on us all I'm sure. We don't want to intrude." I glanced out of the corner of my eye and tried to gauge Steven's reaction to the obvious insult, but could read nothing on his passive face. I again felt the urge to belt my brother myself. I knew Steven was making a supreme effort to control his temper and he was doing much better than I would have.

"Well suit yourself! There's a frickin' Holiday Inn down the road for all I care!" His voice rose in anger, slurred by the alcohol.

"Jordan!" Lori began.

"Shut the hell up!" I think he would have struck her had we not been there. He struggled to bring his emotions under control and I was amazed at how much he reminded me of our father. I had seen this same scene a million times before. The sins of the father being relived by the son, and the bad thing was I felt as if I were looking in a mirror that only time and events kept from being me.

Jordan continued, this time a little less angry, "Alright, whatever. I'll see you in a few minutes then. Well come on Lori, let's get cooking!" He slapped her loudly on her rounded rear end and laughed maniacally as he walked into the house, his rudeness forgotten only by him.

Steven looked at me and shook his head. I didn't say anything.

Lori lingered behind to speak to Steven, "I'm really sorry about Jordan. Sometimes when he's had a little too much to drink he gets, well, somewhat overbearing." Her voice was soft and pleading. "Please try and forgive him okay? I don't understand why he's acting this way to you and I'm very sorry. I'll go fix us some dinner. Anything special you guys want? We have practically everything." She tried valiantly to smile, to restore some civilization to a totally uncivilized situation. She was surely one hell of a woman.

Steven answered for us both, "I'm sure whatever you want to fix will be just fine."

"Well, okay…I'll make you something nice." This time her smile was warm again and real as she pointed a delicate finger in the direction of the guest quarters and some of the light returned to her voice. "There are plenty of towels, soap, or whatever, in the bungalow. Please help yourself. I'm sure Jordan will be right down. Just yell if you need anything." She hesitated as if she wanted to say something more, then slowly turned and walked into the house with a quick wave over her shoulder.

"That asshole is still one of the biggest pricks God ever put on this planet, and one day I am going to squash him like the pissant that he is!" Steven stood and stomped around the swimming pool, a lit cigarette trailing smoke in his wake, "I hope you are happy that I sat there and took all that bullshit from that…that…"

"I know! I know! You're right but what the hell can I say? He is my brother. I know how bad the kid is, but some of it could be my fault. You know, with dad like he was I should have taken more time with him, maybe did the big brother thing a little better. Hell, I don't know anymore." I knew my voice betrayed the frustration I felt as I found myself again at a point in life where I tried to defend by brother's juvenile actions.

"Done more for him?" His voice rose, "Done more for him?" He moved to tower over me, "Have you completely lost your mind? I've personally seen you haul his ass out of more jams and stand behind more of his hair-brained schemes, which you knew were a crock of shit to begin with, and another thing…"

"Okay, okay! I get the point! Now let's not forget what the hell we're doing here in the first place. We're not here to debate the loveable points of my brother's personality. Let's go into the house and clean up before he comes back down. Let's just leave the bags on the bikes for now, we'll get them later. We'll eat, sleep, and then go home. All right"

"Fine." He said, even though he was obviously not happy with the situation and had more to say on the matter.

"Fine."

We walked into the small guest house, cabana, or whatever term was popular, just as the sun took it's final dive of the day and passed on it's journey around the world. It seemed as soon as the sun dropped, the loud night sounds became audible. The ever-present cricket symphony, the croak of the bullfrogs from the nearby marsh, the night wind moving through the palm trees, all seemed to click into instant volume like the power switch on the TV remote control. In truth the sounds had really been there all along, just gradually increasing with the darkness. Night always seemed to bring a heightening of the senses.

A short while later, we returned poolside, physically, if not mentally, refreshed. Steven settled back into one of the chairs, slid an ashtray over and lit a cigarette. He had calmed down considerably to his more normal demeanor. He tossed his matchbook and cigarette pack onto the table beside the ashtray and moved another chair over to use as a footrest. As I slowly paced in front of the pool, he watched me for some time before he finally spoke.

"That was pure beauty the way you suckered him in about the book. That almost made the whole conversation worth it, you know. He sure is a greedy little shit." He made an oval of his mouth and blew perfect symmetrical smoke rings and smiled, "Yes sir, you sure got him with that line, it's no wonder you're making a killing selling bikes. Hell, with natural bullshit ability like that, I bet you could sell a bike to a ninety year old grandmother."

"Yeah, right. I feel really great about it." I didn't want to discuss it any more with him and I knew he was just baiting me as a way to return to our earlier conversation.

"Look, no matter what you think, it's not your fault he's like that. I mean, what are you going to do, eh? I've tried to get you to beat the shit out of the little twerp too many times, and do you listen? Hell no! All I get is bullshit about "poor little Jordan" or "he's just misunderstood", "he's had a tough life…" Bullshit! That's crap and you know it! You lived the same life and turned out half-way alright anyway."

"Thanks. Thanks a lot." I felt my temper start to rise a notch or two, "Let's give it a rest, okay Steven?"

"No problem." But he continued on without missing a beat, "And you know what else? He is going to be an asshole no matter what you do. Some people are just born like that, and he's one of 'em, the end, period, dot!" He pointed his cigarette at me. "Get off your own back already and show some of those brains everybody is always telling me you got. Let's tell the little dweeb "adios" and get the hell up to the mountains where we belong. We don't need anymore shit from him and if I have to stay around that asshole much longer all bets are gonna' be off. You know what I mean?"

I stopped pacing and came to sit beside him in one of the plastic chairs. When he started to speak again, I held up my hand for silence and he gave a sigh of frustration but at least remained quiet. I stared silently towards the house without responding. The large, great-room lights were on, as were those in the kitchen, and a room upstairs showed light through heavy curtains. Night sounds again rose to consciousness, filling my senses with the sounds of darkness in the far south. The smells, so familiar, reached me and I took deep measured breaths, trying to clear my mind as I slowed my body and my breathing. The emotional roller coaster I had been on for the last twenty-four hours was not something I was prepared for and I truly needed to settle myself down. I was tired and I was nervous. As I sat there, I caught the briefest hint of something tainted. It reminded me of the smell of some small animal, which maybe came close to the house to die. It was faint and sickly-sweet like something several days past dead. Then the soft Florida breeze blew the odor away from my senses as quickly as it came. I broke my train of thought and turned to my cousin.

"I suppose you're right about one thing at least, we do need to get out of here"

"No shit I'm right. Who the hell are you talking to?" He snorted and leaned back in his chair, his face partially hidden behind a cloud of cigarette smoke. "I say we eat and leave."

After a few minutes, I decided I wanted to try to explain myself a little better, and I reluctantly re-opened the topic from before. I felt I owed him an explanation. "With Jordan I've tried everything I know to help, and I still come up empty. Nothing seems to work, but I feel I've got to keep trying, or I've failed in some way." I shook my head and laughed, "There you go, I guess I'm not really chivalrous at all. I don't defend him for him; I'm doing it to help me. I guess it's really selfish and I should just say the hell with it and give up. Take my word for it, that's what a shrink would say anyway." As a matter of fact, I had been told that, nearly verbatim by one of the "miraculous" mind-healers in person.

"Well excuse me Sigmoid Fraud! Did you figure that out on your own or did you read it on the back of a cereal box? Give me a break! You know what your problem is Cuz? You try to analyze everything to death. If you would spend more time livin' and less time…"

At that moment a sound drowned out his words; a sound I will never forget and will never be able to describe. It was way beyond words—it defied words. Attempting would be like trying to depict a sunrise to a man blind from birth; it could only be experienced, not expressed. A horrible female scream came from the open, second floor window of the house. A scream so intense it was only remotely recognizable as human, filled to overflowing with terror…and worse. It was not a bottled scream from some television or movie track, but a cry of anguish and physical pain that could never be duplicated. The terrible cry continued for what seemed an eternity and was suddenly cut short in a violent and abrupt manner.

Steven and I responded as one, both running as fast as we could for the rear door. Seconds later, as we ran we heard another sound, somehow much worse than the first. It wasn't a scream or a cry as before; it was something else…something I had never heard…something so horrid it defied description. It seemed no human throat could have given voice to such a thing. The hair stood on my arms and I had to force myself to continue moving towards the house. I noticed that the…the wail…for lack of a better word, had a similar effect on Steven as his stride slowed for an instance to match my own. When I glimpsed his features, his expression was grim and focused. Something in the weird cry was wrong. It was primitive and primal, off key in a bad sort of way. Yet it also held a vague hint of something familiar that I couldn't identify.

Then, as quick as it came, the sound faded and died.

CHAPTER SEVEN

As the strange sound died away, Steven and I resumed in earnest our flight towards the house. As we ran through the kitchen, I noticed a pot of something boiling over on the stove, obviously left in haste. I moved quickly through the den with Steven barely one step behind. The screams had ceased, but all manner of noise came from the second floor as we rushed towards the stairs. It sounded as if furniture was being overturned above our heads and I could hear the voice of my brother as he yelled and cursed in obvious rage or fear. As we started up the stairs, a terrible odor greeted us, similar to that I encountered earlier only much, much worse and it got stronger as we got closer.

Steven passed me going up the stairs, taking them three at a time, and ran towards the closed door at the end of the hall. All the sounds emanated from behind the bedroom door, which he tried unsuccessfully to open. He looked quickly to me, gestured with his head, and moved to one side. I brought my right foot forward and kicked hard just above the knob, and the door flew open, banging violently against the wall. Steven was through the opening before I could react and I noticed he had drawn his gun from its normal resting-place near the small of his back. I had never known him to be with out it and for once I was glad.

The horrible smell washed over us, enveloped us in a cloud of overpowering stench that made me feel sick to my stomach, and it got worse as I entered the room. At one time, the room had undoubtedly carried the same white motif as the rest of the house, but that had been grotesquely altered. No matter how long I lived I knew that bedroom scene would never leave me. It was as if a crazy painter didn't like the decorating and decided to splatter buckets of bright red paint about the room. It covered the floors, the curtains and the furniture. It trailed down the walls like icicles melting in the spring and pooled together on the bleached hardwood floor in little puddles that seemed to join together as we watched. Only it wasn't paint. It was blood. Lots of it—more than I had ever seen, outside of a cheap horror flick anyway.

For a brief time all we could do was stare. The only remaining light was an overturned lamp, knocked from a dresser by the door. It cast a weird glow from its new resting-place on the floor. The glass shade had shattered and the bare bulb illuminated the room and it's contents with a harsh light. The smell of the blood was greatly overpowered by the vile stench, but it was still there, faintly familiar in a disgusting sort of way.

The impersonal brightness of the bare lamplight revealed the remains of her body, draped across the lower portion of the king size bed. What was once a beautiful woman was instead a heap of mutilated flesh and ripped apart clothing. The remnants of the print dress and the huge amount of blood in the room suggested the absolute brutality with which she had been killed. It was obvious she could not conceivably have been alive. Her body had been ripped up the front from groin to chin and the size of the wound was so large it was hard to imagine what could possibly have caused such extensive damage. The bare bulb reflected in her dead green eyes, an empty, stony stare, which seemed to settle upon me. My stomach knotted with emotion. Her expression still seemed to hold the surprise and terror she must have felt as she died. The room was so quiet I could hear our harsh breathing and a steady drip of blood as it filled a puddle by Lori's head. From outside came another sound—one I didn't, couldn't possibly, recognize.

It was similar to the rumbling purr of a cat though there was nothing soft about it and it moved me in an entirely different way. The sound was louder, and stronger, and much more powerful than any cat, no matter how large. It seemed to permeate my whole body and sink right into the bone. I felt fear, yet something greater than fear. Strange as it may seem, especially considering the life I had lived, there was very little which actually scared me. Hell, I had almost convinced myself, over the years, I had nothing to loose. But something…something about the noise scared me…it touched me in a strange, primal way that made me want to run in the opposite direction as far and as fast as I could. Then, I wanted to go towards it just as quickly. Something drew me towards the sound, called to me, made me want to come closer, both magnetic and repulsive at the same time. Unfortunately, I knew the only thing to do was move closer.

I nodded to Steven and inclined my head towards the deck and he shrugged his shoulders and moved ahead. The sound continued, primitive and strange, yet possessing a remotely familiar tone, something just past the fringe of recognition or understanding.

The glass doors to the balcony had ruptured outward, leaving a thousand shards of glass glinting in the faint light through the billowing curtains. The eerie sound came from the darkness beyond. I nudged Steven and motioned for a flanking movement. He crossed to the opposite side of the patio doors, his gun in a classic combat stance covering the opening as he moved. He cast a hurried side to side glance as he crossed the open doorway and when he reached the other side, he shook his head, indicating he had seen nothing. I motioned for cover as he held the only weapon, and just before he stepped through the broken glass onto the wooden deck, I rolled through the door and to his right. Steven quickly fanned the gun from side to side and then stopped, pointing the powerful handgun towards a far corner of the deck.

The deck ran almost half the length of the entire upstairs. In one corner, about twenty-five feet away, my brother lay on his back in an exposed, awkward position. I knew it was Jordan because I could just make out his loud golf pants in the faint light. They had been pulled carelessly around his ankles. One shoe lay off to the side and his legs appeared ghastly white in the semi-darkness. Stranger still, I couldn't see anything above his knees. A deep, dark shadow covered his upper body, hiding it from view—hiding his face so I couldn't tell if he was alive or dead. From this living shadow came the eerie sound we had heard, and whoever the figure was, he never moved one inch to acknowledge our presence. Also, it was obvious we had found the origin of the horrible smell. It was even stronger so close to the killer and I could almost visualize the stench, like morning fog rolling across a lake.

The killer was big, really big, bigger than Steven even was, but it was hard to tell as some thick, dark cloak seemed to shroud his entire body. We both saw the evidence of great strength inside the butcher shop that had once been a bedroom. I started to move further to the left in hopes of seeing the weapon. No one could inflict the kind of damage to a human being I had seen without using a weapon. Over the years of my military training, I had seen scores of serious fighters, the best in the world, and even they could not hurt someone that badly without a weapon of some kind.

Steven barked a command, "Alright you son-of-a-bitch, you move one damn inch and I'll blow your damn head off. You move your hands where I can see them! Now!" the gun was trained on his target; his finger rested lightly on the trigger, relaxed and ready. "Now!"

The dark apparition didn't move, but the strange sound stopped. The foul smell hit us in waves, sick and putrid as we waited for the next move.

"Alright, let's try this one more time. Move now!" He fired a warning shot over the head of the killer, not wanting to hit my brother. The single retort filled the silence between us and yet, at least for a brief instant,

I thought I heard a muffled sound from the killer, perhaps a single gruff word, but I couldn't be sure and couldn't make it out if it was.

The next few seconds passed so quickly, with movement so fast, I didn't have time to respond. As I watched helplessly, the killer grasped my brother's head. I quickly moved forward, breaking my momentary daze, and as I moved, I regrettably saw all too clearly what occurred next. It happened so fast, I had no chance to get to my brother or his attacker. Two large hands appeared from under the folds of the killer's cloak, grabbed Jordan's neck and swiftly and easily snapped it like a Thanksgiving wishbone. I caught a brief glimpse of what appeared to be metal on the ends of each finger just as the madman left my brothers body with the speed of a spitting cobra and I realized too late he was coming for me.

I could see very little of the murderer's features in the dark. As the massive body closed on me, light was blotted by his bulk and he seemed to spread the huge coat or cloak in his wake. It appeared strangely opaque, further blocking out the already dim available light. I had no time to register anything else, because the speed of my attacker was like nothing I had ever seen. The movement off of my brother and across the deck to me was accomplished so swiftly I barely had time to think, and no time at all to react. The fetid odor was too nauseating to describe. It hit me like a fist in the face. A feeling of dread filled my mind as I shifted into a more defensive stance, bracing myself for the onslaught of the charging form. It was all I could do in the little time I had.

The large caliber slugs from Steven's gun tore methodically into the killer's body. Each powerful slug jerked the body back like a puppet on a string. Steven placed the shots close together, textbook perfect. He did it by the book and emptied the clip in a matter of seconds scoring a hit each time. The smell of spent gunpowder and cordite momentarily masked the rancid odor. My attacker hesitated, unbelievably still upright, and emitted yet another unexpected sound. This time it was a high-pitched squeal of pain…and yet something else. It was harsh and unsettling, and seemed somehow…feminine. A swirl of long, light-colored hair was briefly exposed, intertwined in the layers of the large, dark cloak.

Steven rapidly ejected the empty clip, still with one round in the chamber. He slammed another into the weapon with the muzzle never leaving the retreating figure. The shrill cry changed from one of anguish to one of anger, and again the killer came towards me, almost as fast as before. He had taken an entire clip from a 45-caliber weapon and had not fallen! The whole thing was like something from a nightmare or bad late night television, only it was real and it was coming for me again, and this time even more angry than before.

I caught a brief glimpse of the hand attacking me. It was attached to a large, light colored arm. In that split second, it appeared as if razor-sharp cutting blades of some sort were attached to the end of each finger like the movie demon Freddie Kreuger. That was all I could see. I jumped to my right as fast as I could but not before a sharp, piercing pain exploded across my left leg. At the same time, the explosive sounds of the large handgun erupted just above my ears as Steven's bullets again blasted my attacker.

The force of each bullet shoved the killer back, closer and closer to the edge of the deck. Steven placed the last four slugs close together in the center of his target and the last one toppled the murderer up and over the short railing. The huge figure screamed as it fell; a high-pitched cry of anguish and pain that was abruptly cut short. It seemed I could hear my heart beating in the quiet that followed. My breath sounded like a runaway freight train beyond control.

After a moment, Steven broke the silence between us and said, in an uncharacteristic show of emotion, "That was one hard assed son-of-a-bitch! I was beginning to think that was Superman or something. Nothing can be that hard to kill! Nothing!" As he talked, he did not allow his feelings to override his common sense. He loaded his third and final clip into the gun and still kept it leveled on the deck where the killer went over. "Must have been on crack or angel dust or something! Damn, but that had me worried there for a minute!" It may have been the most agitated I had ever seen the quiet giant.

"You're telling me." I couldn't hide the amazement from my voice either; "Did you get the size of that guy? He was at least as big as you are. Jesus...." Then I remembered my brother, and turned with apprehension towards the corner where he lay, absolutely motionless.

I checked Jordan's neck for a pulse. There was no heartbeat. I glanced at his face, still locked in a grimace of total and absolute terror. The eyes stared sightlessly into mine, as if trying to communicate something with that last frozen look of fear. My brother was dead and I allowed it to happen right in front of me. It brought a painful memory abruptly to mind; how my mother must have felt when she watched my father die. It was a thought I had refused to acknowledge for well over two years but I was face to face with it again. It seemed I would never be able to hide from myself no matter how I tried.

"Morgan, damn man!" Steven's voice was lowered to an awestruck whisper, " Look at the rest of him."

I stood and looked at the lifeless body of my younger brother. The sight of him lying there, helpless and hurt, filled me with surprise and disgust, somehow making the already bizarre spectacle even harder to understand. Above the waist there was no sign of struggle other than large rips of his preppie pink golf shirt and a splattering of blood which may not have been his own. If he had been in the bedroom when Lori met her tragic demise, he could have been literally drenched with her blood. Below the waist, the crazy mystery got more difficult to understand. His pants and underwear had been torn from his body and pulled down to his ankles. Long, deep scratch marks trailed down his legs and blood seeped from the shallow furrows. His genitals were exposed and covered with a thick, mucus-like substance.

I looked at Steven and gestured towards the wall switch, "Hit that light".

The weird, yellow glow of the outdoor bug light badly illuminated a disturbing sight. It appeared that, well, his body had been left in an obvious state of arousal. The slimy stuff gleamed on his manhood, yet erect in a grotesque parody of sexual excitement. Death had not even altered its intensity.

"This is completely crazy!" Steven turned to me, perplexed. "He's been...he's been raped Morgan! What the hell is going on? That...that was a female Morg! Rising Wolf was right! I thought so when I heard her scream, but damn, what a big bitch! Jesus! I told you Rising Wolf knew what he was talking about."

"Alright already. Check up big guy." I held up my hand to slow him down, "We don't know for sure it was a woman Steven. That wouldn't make a whole hell of a lot of sense if you think about it now would it? We'll go down and check the body in just a minute, hold on a second okay?"

I knelt down to get a better look at something in the weak, yellow glow, moving to allow the light to better reach the body. I pulled Jordan's shirt collar to one side, exposing a previously obscured wound. It had been partially hidden by his shirt and inflicted just above the heart. Some substance other than blood seeped from the wound, which appeared a bite mark of some kind. It seemed unusual for one wound to have been inflicted, considering the damage done to Lori, yet I could not see another.

I glanced to the face of my younger brother, so much like my own. The sightless eyes mirrored mine almost exactly. I gently closed the eyelids a final time. A brief feeling of hurt touched me, tightening my chest like it was a vise, making it difficult to swallow. A quick, fuzzy memory entered my mind; a small four year old boy with skinned knees, wearing cutoff overalls, yelling from the past for me to slow down because he couldn't keep up. "Don't leave me Morg, please!" The tiny voice cried. The skinny little legs pumped as fast as they could go, trying to cover ground without falling, as always seemed to happen. I turned my face away.

"Come on! Let's go down and get a look at that body. I want to see what kind of a person could do this kind of damage. This whole thing is getting too crazy for me. This is just totally and completely illogical!" I felt control leaving my voice and changed the subject hoping Steven wouldn't notice. "We're not going to have much time, so we better move fast." The wound on my thigh throbbed with pain and leaked blood in a trickle, but didn't appear life threatening. I would have to deal with it later, but for the moment, it could wait. Adrenaline makes a strong anesthetic sometimes.

We moved through the ruined white bedroom without glancing again at Lori's remains, we rushed down the stairs and back through the kitchen. I absently reached for the knob on the stove and turned it off. Smoke had started to rise and the smell of scorched food was heavy in the air and even that was a welcome change. As we emerged at the rear of the house, we came to an abrupt halt at the edge of the area beneath the deck.

There was no body.

The body of the killer seemed to have vanished into thin air. It wasn't underneath the deck where it logically should have been and to make it worse, directly under the deck was the swimming pool. It was crystal clear—no body—no blood. It rippled with empty, serene tranquility, reflecting the shimmering starlight as if nothing had happened at all.

"What the hell?" Steven looked around. "Where's the body Morgan? I hit that asshole at least ten times in the damn chest! Nothing could have lived through that." He stopped and turned to me, arriving at a conclusion I had already reached. "Morgan, there was no splash!" He fanned the area around the pool with his gun. "That body had to land in this damned pool and there should have been a splash! I don't like this shit Morgan. I don't like this shit at all. Let's get the hell out of here."

"You know for once, I think you're right. I don't want to stick around and explain this to some officer of the law when I have no idea myself as to what the hell is going on."

As if to illustrate the need for flight, the distant sound of a police siren filled the newly quiet Florida night air, still some distance away, but closing fast.

"Let's get out of here, Steven." As I turned, the painful wound in my leg reminded me it needed attention. "Let me borrow your bandanna Cuz." As he handed it to me, he returned his gun to the ready and glanced methodically side to side as we moved towards the front of the house. I stopped long enough to tie the cloth tightly around the top of the wound and the flow of blood began to slow immediately as I applied pressure.

Steven made it to the bikes before me and was already kicking his big machine to life when I got there. He had not removed his helmet from the back bar of the bike and I didn't take time for the luxury either.

"You all right?" he asked.

"Yeah fine, the bleeding is about stopped." I turned the key in the switch, and hit the start button as I kicked up the stand. "Let's get out on the highway, and put as many miles from this place as possible. Don't stop for any police."

"Don't worry!" Steven yelled over his shoulder as he roared away, "...you just try to keep up!"

We raced away into the muggy night air; exiting quickly via the same drive we had entered so casually just hours before. It is always amazing how so many things can change in such a brief period. The neighborhood receded in the rear view as we sped onto the interstate and twisted the throttles to put as much distance as possible between us and the bizarre murder scene. We buzzed around cars as fast as we safely could. The automobiles were only brief blurs of color and light as we whizzed past. The wind blew through my hair and made my eyes sting. My mind raced as fast as we did, refusing to accept the horrors I had witnessed.

The speed of our flight felt good as the adrenaline flow returned closer to normal levels.

The two of us sped northward through warm night wind. The miles parted and flowed beneath our wheels like the prow of a speedboat through the ocean; time and distance disappeared in our wake. It required concentration to control the machines at such speed, perhaps fortunately so, for I had little time to reflect on the events left behind…or the brutal death of my brother and his new bride.

After we covered sixty or more miles, I pulled up beside Steven and signaled for a stop. We rushed up the next exit ramp, well away from the city, and turned toward the bright flashing lights of a service station. It seemed best to pull into the dark area beside the station and away from curious eyes. There was an ancient picnic table near the restrooms beneath an old light, which had been knocked out and never replaced. The place seemed deserted, but as we killed the bikes the sound of a television reached us from inside the small store, the words distant and unreadable.

I unsnapped my tank bag and searched for the first aid kit and my leather, riding chaps. I got off the machine and limped towards the picnic table. "Well, I guess this is one time this stuff came in handy, huh?" Purposefully trying to mask my anger and confusion at what had happened.

Steven smiled briefly and walked over to where I was removing the now bloody bandanna. "How's it feel?"

Before I could stop myself, and in a hateful tone that seemed to come from nowhere, I said, "Oh, it feels just wonderful! How do you think it feels? Idiot." I immediately regretted the remark and the tone, but couldn't take either back.

"Sorry…excuse me for asking." He moved away from the table and back towards his bike. I could tell he was disturbed by the speed at which my emotion had changed. Hell, sometimes when the anger came, it was often so fast, and so vicious, I couldn't sense it coming myself. It was almost as if it didn't come from inside me at all, but from outside myself completely. I couldn't control the switch no matter how hard I tried. I didn't mean for it to be that way, but then again, that was one of my problems.

"No." I shook my head slowly; "I'm the one who's sorry Steven. I didn't mean to be an asshole." I was embarrassed by the uncommon outburst of emotion and knew I was losing control faster than I thought.

He forced a smile, "That's okay—I know it's hard not to be what you are." His timing was perfect. Humor was always his answer for anger.

I tried a smile myself; "It's not really that bad, I don't think. Whatever he used cut me deep but clean, I think the bleeding has already stopped. Another day and I won't even know it's there." I looked at him seriously, "I'm really sorry Steven, I'm still a little hyped I guess."

"No shit! Me too." He re-joined me on the old picnic bench.

I cut the fabric from around the wound and poured peroxide over it, experiencing a brief flash of pain. I gritted my teeth, and applied first aid cream and a temporary pressure bandage, wrapping it all with the remaining gauze. Job completed; I stepped into the leather chaps and adjusted them to best hide the blood that had accumulated on my jeans.

During the whole procedure Steven sat on the table beside me without saying a word, staring into the nearby woods, perhaps not wanting to anger me again. His expression was blank and difficult to read.

"Okay. Let's hear it Steven. What's on your mind? Just don't try to tell me some witch is responsible for that nightmare we just left. That killer was real...too damn real and I have enough real pain to prove it. I mean, I felt the power in those arms. That was no "evil spirit" or any of that bullshit, this guy was as real as you and me Steven."

"Well, I ain't arguing that—but whatever it was, it was female. It had to be. You heard it and you saw the same things I did. You saw what she did to him? I mean I hated that little shit, but nobody deserved that. I ain't seen nothing like that. If you ask me, I think Rising Wolf might not be so crazy after all. It all makes more sense now."

I began to repack my bags as we talked. "Come on Stevey. All we have here is a killer who has heard all this crap and is using it to scare his victims; there's no other logical explanation. It might be a woman, yeah, but it's one big woman if it is, bigger and stronger than any I've ever seen before, and I think you might be right about the drug thing. That would help explain a lot of this, the strength and surviving those initial shots. That's another thing right there, someone had to be with him…her…whatever, someone was underneath that deck and took that body. I don't know how or who, but you're not going to tell me anyone could have withstood the punishment you dealt out and survive…that's just crazy. The only logical explanation is that more than one person was there tonight. We just missed them somehow." I think by then I was more talking to keep from thinking further about Jordan than to make a point. "And another thing, there are rarely, if ever female serial killers. It just doesn't happen."

"I'm sorry, Morg, I don't buy it." He shook his head and kicked at the gravel as he spoke. "There are too many things that don't add up. I think Rising Wolf is right. I'm just glad we got the hell away from there. If she was still around, I didn't want to be. Know what I mean? If she took all those shots and lived, I don't know if I ever want to see her again if I can help it." He turned away from me as if to hide. "This thing is, it's, evil in the worse way. We need some help with this one Morgan. I'm ready to put as much distance as possible between us and this killer. It's nighttime and that's when the old man said she traveled. Hell, she could be on our ass right now for all we know." He looked nervously in the direction of the nearby woods and I unconsciously followed his eyes.

I tried to explain it all again, perhaps more for my own benefit than his, "Look, dumbass, have you ever heard of body armor? With body armor someone could have taken those hits. They would hurt like hell and be black and blue for a month, but they would have lived. That would have explained some of the size of the bastard too."

His reply took a second or two, "Yeah, I never thought of that…maybe…that could be. Hell, I don't know! This is all too damn crazy. I'm going home and I'm going now. I don't like this stuff, especially when I'm not on my own turf."

I thought about what he had said for a moment, "Alright, but I need to go to Charleston first, there's a few things we're going to need. I'll meet you at the pasture in Valle Crusis around dark tomorrow night, if I don't find you before then. You know the place." It was a statement not a question. "We can plan on staying at the cabin up on the ridge until we get this mess sorted out."

"Alright. Sounds good to me." But he couldn't leave it alone. "Look, I know you think this is all too loony, but I believe in some of the old stories. I been listenin' to em' a lot more here lately. Sometimes they make sense, Morg. You know what I mean?"

"Look Steven, you've known me a long time, you know the show. If I can't feel it or experience it I am reluctant to believe it. I'll be the last one to tell you the laws of nature and man are correct and all knowing." I finished packing and leaned on the bike, trying hard not to let my frustration show through again. "I hate the very rules of logic damn it, but this stuff you're talking about just doesn't ring true. It may be so, but I'll have to see it for myself before I believe it. Until then, you're totally welcome to believe what you like. You believe what you want and I'll do the same until I learn differently."

That's what I said. What I didn't say was that my whole world was hanging by threads of sanity that I had been trying to weave back to something stronger for the last two years. The last thing I needed was something to come along and question things I knew positively to be real. It upset my whole precious balance, or imagined balance.

"Fine, but just so you know, I'm going right to Rising Wolf with all this by morning. That's what I have to do and you remember what you gotta' do. The book, don't forget to find that damned book. I think we're gonna' need it." He hesitated as he mounted his bike, then lightened his tone, back to the familiar, chiding lilt he was famous for; "Why don't we ride up as far as we can together? That way I can watch and make sure your puny Cherokee ass don't fall off that seat." He was making a good effort to change the subject and the conversation, seemingly choosing not to discuss further the events of the evening. I don't know if he did it for himself or me.

Either way, I took the hint and followed him over to the gas pumps. As we topped off our tanks, we silently watched huge night moths dart at the light, sacrificing themselves in their eagerness on the hot bulb; their lives liberated with a soft pop. Death seemed to come quickest when it was expected least. The night was clear, the air humid and clean. It seemed I could still smell the fresh salt water even though we were many miles away. The evening was warm and pleasant and hid all things, good and bad, with equal cover, yet changed nothing. There was something out there and I knew we hadn't seen the last of it as yet. I could feel it out there, waiting…stalking.

When Steven returned from paying for the gas, I spoke the same tired departure line we shared for years, "Keep it between the lines, Cuz. If you need to get a message to me, call Marilyn, I'll be talking to her soon." I hesitated, "One thing I been thinking though."

"Yeah, what's that?" He asked expectantly.

"You know, by morning they are going to have the FBI in on this. I doubt the local police are going to be very fast about connecting this to the FBI case but they will eventually. It's just a matter of time." I put on my gloves as we talked. "They might not realize it's a Federal case until mid-day. Anyway, the most time we have is a day or so, by then they will have found someway to place us at Jordan's. You know that little worm Smith is going to want to have another little "chat" with us. The moral of the story is; watch your ass and plan to stay under for a few days. If we don't find some answers and quick, these people are going to hound the crap out of us. They'll figure we have to know something."

I straddled my bike and continued, "If you're the Feds and we're the only link to the capture of this killer, you can bet we're bound to get a hell of a lot of attention. Serial killers are not at all popular in real life. They want this guy real bad and that means they'll want us real bad."

Steven kicked his motorcycle to life and slipped on his helmet, "Right! I'm sure our little buddy will mess in his pants if he figures out we were at Jordan's tonight." He laughed and I joined him. He was right; Smith was not going to be so cooperative the next time we met. That was about the only thing from the night I was sure of.

As we were about to ride away I added seriously, "No matter what the deal is, Cuz, you watch your ass, and you watch out for everyone else too. I'll be there as soon as I can. Whatever is going on, this "person…" I stressed the word for his benefit, "…plays for keeps and takes no prisoners. Be careful Stevey."

"You got it man, but don't forget you're not Superman either. You'll be closer to her than me; I'm going further north and just as fast as I can." He raised his middle finger in my direction before he added; "And incidentally, I thought I told you about that Stevey crap, Morgan."

I caught his use of the word "her" and ignored it, letting him enjoy the last jab, "Yeah, I'm really scared. I'll see ya' there Cuz." Anything else wasn't worth saying and, with that, we roared up the road together. Steven for his home, to the top of the Blue Ridge, and me to the marshlands of Charleston. It wasn't far up the road we separated, he to the north, me east, towards the ocean. I turned off on a smaller two-lane road, trying to safely increase distance and speed.

I tried to ride and clear my mind, to not think of my brother's death or what the future might hold for me. My leg throbbed solidly in the background but less and less painfully. As I rode through the night, nothing became clear with the passing of the miles. Nothing was as it should be. There weren't enough miles for me to ride to solve this one. Try as I may, I couldn't make sense out of anything I had seen or heard. No angle seemed quite right. The puzzle definitely had plenty of missing pieces, and I didn't even have a picture on a box to go by.

CHAPTER EIGHT

When I saw the first light of morning illuminate the dew by the road-side, I began to look for a phone booth. As I continued to speed along the road, and the sun began its slow upward journey from east to west, I marveled at the sight. It was easy to appreciate a beautiful sunrise, any sunrise, after the night of death.

I was still a couple of hours from Charleston when I found a pay phone at an all night Quick Stop. I borrowed the bathroom key and removed the bandage from my leg to redress the wound. I cleaned it and applied fresh gauze and tape which I managed to buy in the station. The surgical-like cut was healing nicely. There had been more blood than damage. I didn't get an answer to my phone call so I stopped again about an hour later and sixty miles closer.

I tried the number and, again got no answer. Then I realized she would already be at the shop at that time of the day. She picked up on the third ring.

"Roberts Cycles, may I help you?" answered the familiar female voice. I found a notable measure of reassurance in the tone.

"Hello, is this the Divine Miss M?"

"Well, well, well, Morgan. You decided to take time off from being off? What, didn't you think little old me could handle things around here while you were gone? You've only been gone one day for Christ's sakes."

"Marilyn, I have total faith in your abilities. If someone sent the Special Forces to invade while I was gone, I feel sure you would force them to send for reinforcements. What's going on anyway?"

"Well, you aren't going to believe this, but that worthless sales manager of yours sold three bikes yesterday. Beat his personal best. There's no living with him now. You know how he is, when he thinks he's on a roll. Right now he is an absolute pain in the ass."

"Like a dog in heat is he?"

"Yeah, but he's barking up the wrong tree here, bubba."

I laughed, "Well, I'm sure you can handle him. Just do me a favor and don't castrate him before I get back, sounds like we need to keep him around awhile longer. Incidentally, where were you this morning? I called you at home early and didn't get an answer."

"What is this, heh? Fatherly concern, or something else? You decide to change the terms of our relationship have you?" She kidded me expertly, knowing just which of my buttons to push, "Jealously is something I've never seen in you before."

"Ha ha, very funny. You know better than that. I don't care what you do, I was just curious that's all."

"Oh really? Then go ahead, insult me why don't you? I thought you still cared for me deeply. You're such a natural born charmer, Morgan Roberts! You know just what to say to turn a girl's head."

I smiled, picturing her face as she continued her rave in a thick Charleston drawl.

"If you must know, I spent the night with Robin. She had another big fight with her husband, who was out only God knows where, doing only God knows what, with God knows who. She called and asked me over and we spent the night drinking tequila and discussing how truly disgusting and flawed the male personality is. You know, the same conversation we girls always have when there are no guys around."

"You know, that's funny you mention that. I've always had a theory that was the main topic of conversation between you girls."

"It is! You're absolutely right." Her laughter was pleasant and light. "We girls always talk about you. You know what else? We even talk about how you look when you're not around to hear. You know, great ass, great chest, no brains that sort of thing. Speaking of which, where is that good looking cousin of yours? How's he doing? Does he miss me? And what in the hell are you doing calling me at such a God awful time of the morning anyway?"

Her conversations typically buzzed around from one topic to the next like flies on a dropped ice cream cone. Most people had a hard time following her and often mistook her manner for a lack of intelligence, usually a big mistake on their part. Marilyn, even when she seemed to be paying no attention, missed little or nothing.

"I imagine Steven's back in the mountains by now. We sort of ran into a little problem in Florida, Marilyn". I tried my best to hide the real worry I felt.

Her voice reflected concern, all kidding and prodding ceased. "What do you mean, "some kind of problem?" What's wrong, Morg? You don't sound right. You okay?"

"Yeah, I'm fine I just have a problem and I need you to help me with it, that's all, no big deal. I don't have time for a lot of questions, I need you to do some things for me and I'll try to explain it all to you later. How's that?"

"Sure. I mean this all sounds so mysterious, but sure, whatever you need." She hesitated. "You should know that by now."

"Yeah Marilyn I know, that's why you're the one I called." I had few really close friends in my life but those I did have were tops in their field. "Listen, I need you to pack some things for me. I'll give you a list of everything in a minute. I also need you to meet me with the truck, not the new one but the old pick-up around the back."

"You're kidding me. What the hell are you going to do with that old rust bucket?"

"Look don't insult my truck if you know what's good for you."

"Ooohhh, I'm really scared now, redneck. I wouldn't dream about messing with your truck."

"Yeah, right. You think maybe you could let me finish my conversation without interrupting so much?"

"Sorry, sorry, master. Go right ahead master. What else do you need boss?"

"Don't call me boss."

"I will if you keep acting like one."

I knew there was no use fencing with her, I always lost when I tried. "Just hush and listen. I'm going to need some spending cash in small bills. And while you're upstairs getting the other stuff I'm gong to tell you about, I want you to go into the back of my closet and push the latch in the upper right hand corner. The rear panel is a door that opens into a small alcove and there are some things I want you to bring from in there."

I talked for a few minutes, listing everything I thought we might need. As I finished, she could hold her curiosity no longer.

"Can I ask one question? Just one little ol' question?" I could imagine her gesture; her manicured fingers an inch or so apart. "Why in the hell can't you come by and get all this stuff yourself? Or do you just like ordering me around?"

"We'll talk about that when you get here." I hurried on before she could ask anything more. "You know the doughnut shop on Savannah Highway?"

"Yeah."

"Meet me there in an hour and a half." Then I continued, trying to sound casual, "Incidentally, if anyone calls and asks anything weird about me, or where I've been; you have no idea. I went out of town on a bike trip and you literally have no clue as to where. Got it?"

"Alright, sure, but this whole thing is beginning to sound like something I saw on the movie of the week, or was it Cops?"

"Funny."

"You're not pulling my leg or something like that are you?"

"Now Marilyn." I said, quickly changing direction and subject as best I could, "I'd be the last one to brag about sexual prowess, but if I were messing with those legs of yours, you would definitely know it!" I stuck to what I knew best; when in doubt—joke.

"I'm aware of that Morgan, my memory is not bad, just my attitude. I remember some things very well. Why do you think I put up with you as long as I did, anyway?" She laughed.

"You had me wondering there for awhile. Okay, that's enough of this sex stuff, get on with it! I don't have time to sit around all day and discuss your sexual reveries and my sexual prowess or lack of it. Jesus, what is it with you women today? Don't you think about anything else?"

"Nope...we've been barefoot, pregnant and stuck in the kitchen for so long, we haven't had the opportunity for much else."

"Fine...fine...just keep your mind on what I asked and hurry your pretty little bottom along."

"Now, that...that was a sexist remark."

"Yeah, so sue me. Now quit giving me a hard time and do what I ask. I need your help here."

"Yes master. No problem master. Please don't beat me again master. I'll be good, I..."

"Alright, alright! Enough already. One more thing, don't mention this to anyone, okay? Not even the dog in heat sales manager of ours."

"Of course not, are you crazy? If I told someone about this conversation they would come get you with one of those big butterfly nets and make you wear one of those stylish jackets with the arms that tie in the back. Then who would keep me in the style to which I have become accustomed? No one else will pay me as much as you do, and even if they did, they'd be too smart to let me con them like I do you. I'd have to find another patsy and start over from scratch, no thank you."

"Again, funny, very funny. You should start a late night comedy show like everyone else in the free world. I'll see you soon Marilyn." I started to hang up the phone.

"Morgan?"

"Yeah?"

"Be careful, okay?" Her voice was serious. She knew something was wrong even through all the kidding.

"Always, gorgeous, always."

I rode the rest of the way at a more leisurely pace in the warmth of the morning sunlight. Everything looked better in the daytime; things didn't seem near as imposing. The bright day was a welcome partner and soothed my nerves as I cruised slowly along, watching my speed, exhaustion crowding my edge. The last thing I needed was a speeding ticket. I topped off the gas tank and grabbed a soft drink to ease the thirst of fatigue. The traffic was light and I was able to make good time. It seemed cooler on the highway, with a light, northeast breeze at my back blowing me along. My tired body appreciated both the breeze and my brief rest stop. The short trip passed rather quickly and I was able to organize my thoughts a little better during the remainder of the ride.

The doughnut shop appeared on the left as I entered the outskirts of Charleston, I signaled my turn, and noticed my old red pick-up truck parked in the lot. True to the plan, there were very few cars or customers. Near my old truck, sat an old blue station wagon, and a carload full of kids was just leaving. The rest of the city must have already gotten their morning supply of doughnuts and coffee.

I coasted to a stop next to the old truck, pulled my bags off the bike and tossed them in the truck bed. I noticed that the bed was quite full and had been tarped to protect the contents. Dog's head poked through the driver's side window and looked towards me expectantly.

"Hey girl! What's up?" I inquired, as she wagged her whole body in answer. "Glad to see me are you?" I rubbed her head behind the ears.

"How many times have I told you about getting up on the driver's seat? Now get down, over on your side."

At the word down, she quickly moved into the floorboard on the passenger's side. She looked at me to make sure she had done the right thing. Dog had the ability to draw attention to her, even when she was minding her own business. Attention was something I didn't need today. "Good girl! I know it's hot; I won't be in here but a few minutes, then we'll go for a ride." At the word "ride" her ears poked up and she seemed satisfied and settled down in the floor to wait. I knew that no matter what, unless she heard me command otherwise, she would not leave the truck.

A few years after I first acquired her, or she acquired me, I left her in the truck while I went into a bar to talk to a guy who had an old Harley I was interested in buying. The bar was unfortunately frequented by some less than desirable characters. As a few of their semi-intoxicated patrons were retiring for the evening, they passed the truck and happened to notice Dog as she rested casually on the front seat. Both windows were open to allow the spring breeze to keep her cool.

They quickly gathered around, and of course, thought the sporting thing to do would be to taunt the animal—not a good move on their part. She must have sat there at first, patiently enduring their yelling and their nonsense; it was not her business what the crazy men wanted to do. The only thing that involved her was the inside of her truck and me. As far as she was concerned, if I was not there, she was in charge of the truck while I was away. That made her responsibility pretty clear-cut, at least from a dog's point of view.

I rounded the corner just in time to see what must have been the second person to question her responsibility. The first stood a few feet away, cradling his bleeding hand between his legs. The most recent recipient of her wrath was just withdrawing his hand from the driver's side window rather quickly. I could hear Dog's low growl of anger.

"Dog!" At the sound of my voice she turned and locked her eyes on mine through the rear glass of the truck; her body was rigid, ears up and waiting. "Excuse me gentlemen, may I get to my truck please?"

The guy who I had just purchased the bike from spoke from my side, "What the hell are you idiots doing? Get away from the man's truck, you bunch of drunks!"

The biker with his hand cradled between his legs complained loudly, "But Jesus, Jake, look what that damn dog did to my hand for Christ's sake." He held his hand up for inspection, confirming my suspicions. She had just given them a little nip to remind them who was in charge. I guess the luckiest part of the day was that Jake was a man of some influence. He tried to convince the nice gentlemen to allow my animal, and me to vacate the premises. As they debated the issue, I took the opportunity to do just that.

As I walked through the double glass doors of the doughnut shop, I knew Dog would be right where I left her no matter when I returned. I also knew, in all probability, the truck would be there too. Who needed a fancy security system? I had a hundred pound alarm alternative that worked better and was even portable to boot.

Marilyn sat in a booth to the left of the entrance. She smiled at me as I pointed to the counter with a questioning look. She shook her head from side to side and glanced towards the cup of coffee in front of her.

I went to the counter and ordered two chocolate covered and a soft drink, a great combination, the true breakfast of champions. As I walked towards the table, Marilyn shook her head in disgust.

"How can you eat such a nourishing lunch and intend to have an intelligent conversation? You're going to need some real food to hang out with me big guy."

"Yeah, like that coffee you're drinking is a lot better for you I suppose." I slid into the chair opposite her. "God woman, but you have great legs! Have I ever told you that?" Marilyn had on a rather short, bold red dress and Roman sandals. She looked as if she just walked off the set of a music video.

"I believe you have mentioned it once or twice in the past, yes." She responded with complete candor and no embarrassment. She was a woman totally at home with her sexuality.

Marilyn always seemed oblivious of the effect she evoked from her sexual opposites. She seemed that way, but I suspected a woman of her intelligence would most certainly be aware of her attributes. I think she was comfortable with her assets and basically just didn't give a damn about other people's opinions concerning her actions or her physical qualities. "Old Charleston breeding", premium education, and a unique gift of good, common, sense, had formed her into a woman to be respected. A lady of true grit and style that every woman admired, and every man seemed to secretly fear. The woman was one of a small select group of individuals that I termed friends.

"I guess you noticed I've done everything you instructed, your highness." She passed me a thick manila envelope. "Here's your money."

"Sure, I parked by the truck and checked it out on the way in. Look, I'm sorry I had to come on so strange. Something has happened, something just too weird to believe. I need your help. That's all there is to it." I paused and added, "I'm sure glad to see you." I grinned and met her beautiful green eyes with my own.

She smiled briefly in acknowledgement and turned her eyes down towards her cup, "Yeah, I know you say that to all the women in your life. Don't forget I know you pretty well, Morgan Roberts!" She paused to take a sip of her coffee. "It sure must be something strange for you to act so goofy. I've never known you to get excited about anything, and now you throw this crazy request at me in the middle of the workday. What am I suppose to think?"

Anyone else in the world, I would have never mentioned a word about the previous night's activities. Marilyn on the other hand, was a person whose opinion I respected, a quality rare in a woman of such beauty. I didn't feel that beautiful women couldn't be intelligent, it was just my personal observation that the two rarely went hand in hand. I thought Marilyn might be able to interject some logic into a situation, which defied all logic.

"Well, I do want you to listen to a short story, if you have a minute."

She rolled her eyes and addressed me with pretended venom, "You actually think you're going to have me gather all the weird things you ask for, pack your dog, your truck, and meet you in a doughnut shop in the middle of the afternoon, and not find out why? Have you lost your mind, Morgan Roberts? Who the hell do you think you're talking to? You're damn right you're going to tell me what's going on!"

"I intend to tell you. I…I just want you to know, that at this point, I don't understand a damned bit of what happened in Florida last night. This makes little to no sense to me, and I imagine it will make less sense to you, but just listen first, okay? It all sounds absolutely crazy, and hell, I was there. I don't know what to believe myself."

She opened her pretty green eyes wide in feigned excitement, "Ooh, this all sounds sooo mysterious." She added a convincing shudder for good measure.

"Just shut up and listen, smart ass." I told her. I left out nothing. I tried to remember every scrap of conversation and fact. I fed all the information into that beautiful head which hid a mini-computer just behind the bright eyes the color of pool table felt. As I talked, her expression changed from one of puzzlement to one of concern.

It took over half an hour and another large cola before I finished. I told her everything that happened from the time I walked into Myskyns, meeting with Steven and Agent Smith, to our timely departure from Jordan's house just hours before.

I knew I was falling behind schedule, and knew that schedule was very important, but I felt the need to talk the events through equally important. Marilyn's opinion and analytical brain could be very helpful. Plus, I've found if I tried to verbalize things to someone else, sometimes they made more sense. After I finished talking, I stopped and patiently waited, slowly sipping my drink. She took what seemed a very long time before she finally commented.

"This is the most incredible story I've ever heard. If I had heard this from any other person in the world, I would laugh out loud. You have got to be kidding me!" She shook her head in wonder, "I leave you alone for one damned day and you totally screw your life up, in just one day! How did you get in this crap, bubba? What the hell were you thinking?"

"It's really hard to explain, let's just say I have my reasons. That's really irrelevant now, just tell me what you think about the murders."

She was quiet again for a few moments before she continued, "Well, it sounds like someone, someone who knows the history and myths of the Cherokee, has decided to try their hand as a serial killer. He seems to be exploiting this myth and preying on victims who will be afraid of him. He probably enjoys that. Or maybe he's using the legends to justify the killings to himself in some way. Hell, who knows? I do know that this sounds like one sick individual and you do not need to be messing with him, or her, or whatever!" She held up her hand as I started to interject something. "No! You said you wanted my opinion and you're going to get it. And don't give me any crap about that macho bullshit. I know the kind of training you've had, big deal!"

She absently pushed a strand of baby fine blonde hair from her face, "I also know that someone this sick doesn't care. This killer will not be playing by any rules you know or recognize. This is some bad shit, Morgan dear. You mess around with this, and you could wind up dead too. I don't know what you can do at this point, and I don't really want to know, but I'll help in any way I can. But this whole thing sounds beyond you, me or anyone else for that matter."

I thought about what she said. "Well, I agree with you for the most part. I have no idea as to what I'm going to do, or not do. I do know I have to try something." I tired to sound confident. For her or me, I wasn't sure which. "We can't just sit around and wait for something to happen. Hell, the authorities are not going to let us do that. If they haven't shown up yet, they'll be around soon enough. That you can count on." I pointed my finger at her, remembering another point I wanted to make, "Incidentally, if they do show up, stick to the story; you know nothing about what I'm up to. I'll talk to you if anything changes."

"Well, hell! You better talk to me! Tell me what the hell you're doing and what's happening and I mean regular! I do worry about you occasionally, not often, but sometimes." She dropped her sunny smile and paused for a second. "I would like to help, Morgan. I just don't know how—I really don't, but I'm willing to do whatever you need."

"You can help the most by staying around and doing just what you normally do. Keep everything running as usual and watch my back while I'm gone."

"Just like always."

"Yeah, just like always."

"You got it, boss. What else?"

"First, don't call me boss. Second, I sort of needed you to do one other small thing for me, but you're definitely not dressed for it."

"And that is?" she asked with a childish, yet mischievously seductive, smile.

"The bike. I needed you to ride the bike back." That was the small factor that changed her from one in a thousand to one in a million. With all her other attributes, she could also ride or drive anything with wheels. Early in our relationship, when we had a "relationship", we often took road trips together on the bikes. No one could believe their eyes. They weren't used to seeing a woman, especially a woman like her, on the back of a motorcycle.

I continued, "I guess you could call Mike and he could…"

"Hell no, I am not calling that man for anything! I can ride just fine in this dress, thank you very much. If the tourists can't stand to see a little leg, they don't need to be visiting Charleston, right?" Her electric smile would have convinced any man of anything.

I laughed at the thought of her in the red dress riding the motorcycle home, and decided it might indeed be a sight worth seeing. "Okay. If you think you'll be fine with it, I will be. I just hope you don't cause any traffic fatalities."

"Yeah, right! Let's get out of here you big jerk." As she and I walked out into the hot early afternoon sun, I retrieved my helmet from the back of the truck and spoke reassuringly to Dog. As I handed Marilyn the helmet, I said, "You know I'm not what most people call an emotional person…"

"No kidding! I never noticed." She laughed.

"Well, I just want to say; I really appreciate all this, Marilyn, more than you know. I mostly just needed to talk about this and you were the first one I could think of. I didn't mean to get you involved."

"Will you get real? You, who never asks for anything? If you had called anyone else, I would have been really pissed." She looked into my eyes and smiled in such a way that made me wonder about things I shouldn't. God, it was difficult with her sometimes!

"Now?" She asked with a mischievous grin, "Don't you have somewhere to go and things to do?"

"Yeah. Yeah, I do. Thanks again, Marilyn." I watched as she hiked her skirt up, exposing a beautiful expanse of perfectly tanned leg to upper thigh. She casually swung that leg over the saddle of the motorcycle and forced her hair into the helmet. She started the powerful engine with a touch of one manicured nail and flipped up the faceshield of the helmet.

"Do me a favor, Morgan?" she spoke loudly over the idling of the big engine.

"Just name it beautiful."

"Don't get yourself killed. That would purely piss me off, you know? I don't like wearing black, except on a date, and I'd just hate having to do another resume and all that crap. You get offed and I will never, repeat never, forgive you! Got it, bubba?"

"Don't worry, I don't intend to. I'll call you okay?" I pointed my finger at the motorcycle and frowned, "And don't you even scratch the bike or it's your ass!"

"You wish, you pervert!" She dropped the bike into gear, raised her middle finger in my general direction and pulled expertly out into traffic. She smoothly accelerated and headed towards the Ashley River, her red skirt flapping in the wind like a banner, a very short banner. With any luck, she wouldn't cause more than an accident or two in the few miles back to the shop.

I got into the familiar old pick up and extended my hand to Dog. She raised her head to be petted and looked at me as if to question what was next, where were we going this time?

"Just like old times, girl. You ready to go home? We can get you out of this heat for awhile, anyway. What do you say?" She looked at me as if to speak, but offered no reply, other than the thump of her tail on the worn carpet of the cab floor.

The old truck of mine moved into the busy traffic of Savannah Highway, out of place among the new, shiny automobiles. We drove past the round Holiday Inn and crossed the Ashley River heading towards the I-26 interchange. As we drove from the city, I glanced over to my right at the Cooper River Bridge departing from the skyline of Charleston on its way to Mt. Pleasant. I watched as the familiar view of the city receded in the rear view mirror and, for just a second, I had a weird premonition that it might be the last time that I would see it.

I returned my eyes to the highway, and the tasks ahead, and headed north to the mountains. To the mountains, and home.

CHAPTER NINE

"Cow Paddy Pasture" was the name it had been given, by whom we never knew, but we all most certainly understood why. The ancient pasture was situated near the top of what we termed "the greatest motorcycle road in the world." A winding and rough road, filled with hairpins, cutbacks and banked turns, extending nine or ten miles, start to finish. The crumbling blacktop began in the valley and climbed steadily upward before reaching the peak of the mountain, guaranteed to increase your heartbeat as the altitude increased. It was a truly great ride to an even better reward, the majestic view from the top.

From the summit, you could look towards Banner Elk in the west, or back towards Boone in the east. The view from the pasture was one of the most beautiful sights in the world, our world anyway. The surrounding mountains protected the picturesque valley spread beneath them like a pastel painting by an old master. The valley was Valle Crusis, the "Valley of the Cross", and if there was a heaven on earth, it most certainly had to be there.

It was a small valley, just outside of Boone, near the heart of the Blue Ridge, famous for its beauty and antiquity. In the seventies and eighties, tourists began to discover it's splendor and regularly visited one of a few Bed and Breakfasts, which sprang up over recent years, or they visited the real live General Store. Of course, snow and harsh winter kept them away part of the year, or at least lost them to the local ski resorts.

The old store in the valley, Mast General Store, was a true general store of the past; complete with a cracker barrel, checker board and hard rock candy. In one place you could purchase anything from a plow handle to a good pair of work boots or a strong, hand made, oak rocker for your front porch. People in the "Valley of the Cross" still used their front porches for sitting, rocking and discussing the weather. You could always count on a friendly wave as you rode by the old, clapboard farmhouses, which still dotted the landscape. Other than the tourist traps in the bottom, very little had changed in the small, picturesque community in a hundred years or more.

Over time, as we made road trips to or from the area, we always began or ended them atop the valley, on that same cow paddy covered ridge. The tradition was time honored between Steven and I. To change would undoubtedly have brought bad luck, or at least that was the excuse we used. The pasture was situated on a 180-degree cutback and a mirror was placed on a tree at its apex to allow a view of on-coming traffic. The curves on the old road were treacherous and well represented a good test of any motorcyclist's capabilities. Recently, I had a tendency to ride the old familiar obstacle course with more respect than during younger days of foolishness and bravado. I guess, with age, one does indeed grow to respect the gift of life more and more. My average speed over the route had steadily declined over time, as had my nerve, and my youth. One good thing about the trek from bottom to top was that speed was not really necessary for fun. The road itself, at the posted limit, was enough to make most people wary, and rightfully so.

There was a small, graveled, parking area near the mirrored tree and it was there my old pick-up rested after the long drive from Charleston. The sun was gradually setting, and a soft evening glow was spreading over the view. The shadow of the mountain shaded it's interior, bringing early darkness to the valley. The sun had yet to set fully, but the lengthening evening shadow signaled the rapid approach of the night.

"Cow Paddy Pasture" was on a very large, very steep hill carved from the mountainside hundreds of years before, with plenty of effort and lots of sweat. True to its name, the pasture sported small piles of evidence from the day's occupants, who had probably retired to their stalls for slumber and rest from a hard day of eating. I managed to find a relatively clear spot and was lying on my side, with Dog resting near my outstretched legs. My mind was focused on the beauty in front of me, the sight as impressive as it had been the last time I saw it, and the time before that. Yet, my thoughts were elsewhere.

Dog growled low in her throat and turned in the direction of the truck.

"Yeah, I hear him." I then spoke in a loud voice without turning, "Boy, I guess it's true what they say about old age, even for you hard core Indian types. Your "sneaking up on people" needs work my friend."

"Alright, don't hand me that shit! That damn dog of yours let you know I was coming." Steven called back to me from the top of the hill as he stepped on the bottom strand and stretched the upper strands of the rusty barbed wire fence, just as my grandfather had shown us to do as children. He doubled his long frame and stepped through the opening he created. "How long you been here Cuz?"

"Half and hour or so. It took me awhile longer than I thought at the storage place."

I think he had on the same jeans I saw him in last, but he had replaced his black tee shirt with an identical, but clean, black tee shirt. The Harley emblem on the front was the only difference I could see. His scuffed boots kicked indifferently through the dried cow droppings, scattering them in his path, like the lumbering giant from Jack and the Beanstalk. An unlit cigarette dangled casually from his mouth. He carried a beat-up canteen in one hand, which he carelessly dropped, just above my resting-place, before walking past a few paces.

I watched, without speaking, as he folded his arms across his chest in a gesture I had seen a thousand times before. He turned slowly; looking from peak to peak, drinking in the small rolling hills and densely wooded forest that covered the vale like a blanket. He breathed slowly, deeply of the mountain air, and for a time, seemed to be lost to the view.

Several minutes later, he stretched his long frame opposite mine, "I give up asshole, how the hell did you hear me?" His voice filled with mock sincerity.

"I didn't really hear you, I heard the chain on that old Harley when you cut the engine up the mountain and tried to coast quietly. It might have worked if you had left the bike a little higher up, you would have had to walk an extra fifty feet or so, but I figure you're too lazy and fat to do that, correct?"

"Yeah, right. You're a lot louder than I am, man. At least you didn't hear me walking up to the fence, I always hear you coming fifty feet away. Hell, you couldn't sneak up on my mother in a tornado."

"All I know is I heard you, you big redneck."

Steven picked up the canteen and tossed it forcefully towards my chest, and I was just able to move my hands in time to catch it. "I thought we might need this."

I opened the old canteen and the smell of aged bourbon washed over me. I shook my head and tossed the container back nearly as hard as I had received it. "No thanks. I don't think that'll do me any good right now. You now, you go right ahead though. I'm sure your "Ravenmocker" probably prefers her Indian with a little Jack Daniels sauce."

"Why thank you, Cuz, don't mind if I do." He ignored my last comment, and tilted the container and drank deeply from its contents, then gestured above my head. "What's the pea shooter for?" Referring to the nine millimeter automatic dropped casually close to my hand.

I made no move to retrieve the weapon but responded "It's no pea shooter, dummy. Handguns have come a long way since that antique you carry around. I feel very comfortable with fifteen in the clip and one in the chamber. If that doesn't do the trick, we're in more trouble than we can handle anyway. Besides, if need be, I brought a few other personal protection items. They're in the truck."

"If I remember right, you were damned happy to have this old antique around not too long ago." He took another long draw from the canteen, and then asked, "You find the book or not?"

"Yeah, I found it."

When I made no further move to elaborate, Steven dropped flat on his back and gazed upward at the darkening clouds. We lay there as we had a hundred nights before. Neither of us spoke. Dog remained motionless at my side, already asleep. Her light, contented snoring was the closest sounds we could hear. We lay quietly for sometime, both lost in our own private reverie.

The night came slowly. The dark shadow of the mountain spread evenly from peak to peak as the sun finally slipped completely from view. The summit at our back prohibited our seeing it, but the sun disappeared as sure as it would rise. A symphony of crickets began and we watched as a set of headlights worked their way slowly up the incline. The car eventually passed by the road above us, the area briefly illuminated. The sound of the engine slowly labored out of hearing, climbing the remaining miles of curving incline before the road began it's downhill journey into Banner Elk.

Steven was the one who ultimately broke the silence. "Well, I told Rising Wolf about last night, about what we saw. You should have heard him. He's sure all the things he told me are true. When you see him, you'll be more apt to believe him, he's so convinced. I told him you and me was going to be staying at your grandfather's old cabin. He thought that was cool. Said it would be good to discuss the old stories in the council house on your Papaw's mountain. Just like the old days."

"Papaw" was a Native American word for grandfather, and nearly everyone, related or not, called my grandfather by that at one time or another.

"Ben plans to come over in the morning to see the book and "make plans" as he put it."

My property in the high mountains was set up in sort of a trust from my grandfather. Ownership had passed to me and after that, if all surviving family members perished, the property reverted to the ownership of the Cherokee Nation. My grandfather's father had built the log cabin, several outbuildings, and a traditional seven-sided council house. The structures all remained basically the same as they had for several decades. Little had changed. Over the years, I had used the property to get away from the world, when it became too much for me.

"I found the book." I said with little enthusiasm.

"Then what the hell is your problem? Even for you, you're acting strange as hell. What's up? Hell though it was, I know it's more than last night." He had his hands crossed behind his head as he watched the night clouds form, not looking at me at all.

"I went to the storage place to get the book, just like I planned. It wasn't hard to find, really. Anyway, this old book, and I mean an old book—it's nearly falling apart—turned out to be in a cardboard box. It was an old liquor box taped up, and on the side, my dad wrote, "the old man's stuff". It looked like a child's writing. The book was inside along with a bunch of other things."

"Okay, but you still ain't told me the problem Cuz."

"Oh hell, I'm not even sure myself what the problem is. It was something about seeing my old man's scribble on the side of the box. I didn't even look around at the other stuff in the storage unit. I just grabbed the box and got the hell out. It was just kind of strange that's all."

I had given up trying to understand things between my father and me. There was no way to explain what I myself did not, could not, comprehend. If it hadn't been Steven I was speaking to, I would never have tried. But something in me wanted help and he was the best person I knew to talk to about my past, as his and mine were so intertwined. He had been there. He knew, really knew what happened, unlike the worthless hordes of psychiatrists, who had forced their well-educated, pompous minds into my life. Steven was my brother, more than Jordan had ever been, both in blood and in heritage. If I couldn't look to him to help me understand, there was no one else.

I concentrated, trying to find words best to describe what I couldn't quite grasp. "I felt...I felt as if he was there, as if any minute he was going to jump from behind one of the boxes and start ranting and raving about me being there without his permission or something. I could smell the damned bourbon he reeked of it was so real. I felt I was back there all over again. I wanted to go somewhere and hide until he sobered up. You remember how it was. I got out of there so fast it was embarrassing. I was like a scared kid or something."

"Yeah, I remember how he was, and I don't mean any offense by this Morgan, but you got no reason to worry about his drunk ass anymore. He's gone and he ain't coming back."

"I know Steven, that's the whole point. I remember when my mother used to send us over to your house, or my grandfather's for the weekend, when she knew it was going to be especially rough. I used to lay in bed and think of her in the house, alone with him and what I knew she must have been going through. I hated him and I wished him dead almost every damn one of those nights."

"There you go again! I thought we talked about this same thing just last night, before all the shit hit the fan. You can't be responsible for the whole damned world, Morg. Things just happen man."

You couldn't have stopped what went down with your old man anymore than you could have stopped what happened last night. Why the hell do you put yourself through stuff like this? Thinking like that will eat away at your insides."

"I don't know if I believe that, Steven. If I hadn't gone away, maybe things would have been different. Mom loved that man. I don't know why—hell, nobody knew why. She was going to stay with him no matter what he did. I should have hung closer to home, at least for her sake."

The big Cherokee smiled, "And you really think that would have made any difference?"

"I don't know. Maybe."

"Maybe my big ol' hairy ass." Steven laughed that damned laugh of his; a deep bellow which seemed to echo for several seconds down through the valley and back again. "Sometimes you amaze me, Morg. You've been all over the damned world and been to more schools than I've driven by. You're as smart as all get out, and sometimes you still ain't got a lick of common sense. Look, I know I'm just an old mountain boy. I didn't even finish the tenth grade, but even I know you wouldn't have made a dang bit of difference. Again, don't take this wrong Morg, but your old man was on a short road to no good. I know cause my old man was on the same road. Nothing was going to change that. Hell, he had all the answers; no one could tell him a damn thing. I think even your grandfather knew that early on and he gave up on him, and if he gave up on him, I don't think your little narrow ass would have made your old man change his wicked ways."

I didn't respond for a long time…couldn't…the things he said were my own thoughts, at least some of them. I wanted to believe there was nothing I could have done. To make it easy for me to wash the responsibility of my violent past away, but it just didn't work for me. I was not sure why the events of my father's life and demise had chosen such a time to make an impact on me. Perhaps the problems we were facing, the problems I faced in the months up till then and my brother's violent death, stewed and bubbled the pent-up emotion all at once, freeing it with a jolt, some sort of shock or whatever. Perhaps it was the realization that I was now the last of my family, my immediate family anyway, and hell, it looked like someone was going to try to kill me as well.

"Steven, I know all those things. I'm not as stupid as you think. I've told myself those same things ten thousand times on hundreds of nights, but tonight is the first time I've really tried to deal with the situation. I'm tired of trying to forget what happened and not coping with it. Steven, my father sent mom to the store for beer, then he took one of those ugly, yellow, vinyl-covered kitchen chairs out into the front yard, carrying his ever present Jack Daniels bottle in one hand and his old twelve-gauge shotgun in the other. The son-of-a-bitch waited until she pulled back into the driveway so she could see him, then put the barrel of that old shotgun in his mouth and pulled the trigger with his toe."

My chest tightened with the familiar anger, which always visited when my mind came to this point of the tale. "She watched helplessly twenty feet away." My hands clenched at my side. "That son of a bitch!" My voice had faded to a venomous whisper.

I made a conscious effort to speak normally as I continued, "I've tried not to imagine the absolute horror she must have felt. The thought of her pain hurt me as much as anything else in my life ever will…more. That woman tried everything she could to save our poor excuse for a family for too many years. Hell, in the end, it finally killed her." I looked at Steven through the growing veil of darkness between us; "I should have been there Steven, not running around all over the world playing soldier. She needed me to be there. She never left us or stopped looking out for us. Never. Ever. It didn't matter how hard or tough things were, she stayed. I know it's insane to be thinking about all this now, but I can't help it."

Steven spoke softly, "Morg, I know how hard this must've been." He spread his big hands, "I mean I don't really know, hell, nobody could know for sure unless it happened to them, but I can imagine. I also know the kind of woman your mother was, she wouldn't have let you take the blame for this, think about it. She knew what she was doing, Morg."

He took another sip from the bourbon-filled canteen; "No one made her stay with your dad. She could have left him anytime, that's what God made divorce for. Your mother had to love something about your old man. She had to. She loved him for reasons only she knew. Maybe he was one hell of a man when she met him, who knows? The point is; she made her own decisions. Now you've got to make yours. Deal with this shit and let's get on with the problems we got right now. Know what I mean, dude?" He tried to hand me the canteen and I again shook my head.

"Yeah, I've thought all those things Steven. They just don't seem to help right now though, and they matter even less. Hell, they're dead. Jordan's dead. And someone's trying to kill half the people I've ever known in my life. What the hell am I supposed to do?"

"Do? I sure as hell don't know. Right now, the only thing we can do is take the book, let Rising Wolf read it and see if he can find some answers to this mess. I know you don't believe all this witch stuff, but right now it's the only chance we got. That's the deal. We gotta' play the hand. I ain't sitting around and waiting on this crazy bitch to pay me another one of her late-night visits. You know what I mean?"

"You're right. I know. I'm just getting a little sidetracked, I guess. We'll work it out. We always have." I said it with more confidence than I felt, then changed the subject in hopes of putting it all behind us. "In the meantime, I think we need to mosey on up to the cabin. It's going to be late when we get there, and we'll have to clear the road before we go up. The last time I was there, I dropped an old tree over the road to keep those damn curious four wheelers out. Why don't we put your bike in the back of the truck and you just ride up with me? You don't need to be driving, anyway, as many times as you been hitting that canteen in the last few minutes." I kidded him in an attempt to lighten the moment. "You know what they say about us Indian types and firewater."

"Oh, like who made you my old man all of a sudden, Mister-I'm-So-All-Fired-Perfect?"

"I never said I was perfect, asshole."

"Good thing."

"Just get that piece of crap motorcycle you left up the road and we'll put it on the back of my old piece of crap and get up the mountain, okay? Think you can handle that?" I rose and dusted off my worn fatigues. Dog woke to see what all the excitement was about.

"I think I can manage. One thing though, I need to go by the house and pick up a few things. I went straight to see Rising Wolf and I didn't have time to clean up or anything."

"As a matter of fact I was going to talk to you about that very thing." I smiled and sort of rubbed my nose, "We might have to be in that truck with the windows up and I was definitely going to mention the shower thing if you didn't."

"Very funny, very funny! I didn't have the luxury of casually driving up you know. Anyway, we can go by the house and I'll get some clean clothes and shower up at the cabin. You already got gas up there for the generator?"

"Yeah, it'll just take a bit for the hot water heater, but we'll have plenty of electricity when we need it." One of the few concessions I had made to modern convenience was to install lighting and hot water in the old log structures. The property was far away from electrical lines and I saw no fast approach of civilization. The answer to the problem manifested itself in the purchase of an industrial generator, which supplied power on demand.

Steven pushed his large frame to a standing position and continued, "You know the old man will be glad to see you. The folks haven't seen you since your mother's funeral. Mom has this thing about you, you know. She believes you're one of the few "decent" people I hang around with. Keeps thinking some of it will rub off I guess. She bugs me all the time to be more like you."

"Smart woman."

"Like hell! She just doesn't know what I know. But seriously, it'll be good for them to see you and you know she'll fix us something to eat. What do you say?"

"Sure, sounds good. It might make me feel a little better to be around family for awhile, but we can't stay long."

"Alright, let's get this show on the road."

With that, he totally caught me off guard with a trick we used to play on each other when we were younger. He dropped quickly to the ground and swept my feet from under me in a well-practiced move we had both learned early in our martial arts training. Caught totally unaware, I dropped heavily to the ground and he sprinted towards the truck with Dog growling and snarling at his heals.

"Dog!" I snapped as I struggled to my feet. She reluctantly stopped her chase and returned to my side. "You'll pay for that one Steven!" I dusted myself off, checking to insure he hadn't dropped me in a cow paddy.

"I guess there's someone besides me getting old!" Steven hollered back over his shoulder as he slowed down to a walk and rounded the curve to retrieve his Harley.

"Let's hope we're able to get older Cuz." I muttered under my breath, then addressed Dog who stood looking up at me as if I were crazy, puzzled that I would not allow her to pursue my attacker. "It's alright girl, he was just playing. It's okay."

I knelt and opened my arms as she buried her head in my chest, perhaps sensing my anxiety. I rubbed her briskly and she pushed her body closer to mine, loving the attention. "Don't worry girl, everything's going to be alright."

She wagged her tail and trailed behind as we walked up the steep incline towards my truck. I carried my gun and Steven's discarded canteen and turned for one last look into the valley now completely shrouded in darkness. The three-quarter moon and a multitude of twinkling stars supplied enough light to illuminate the valley contours. The houses in the valley sparkled with lights from living room windows as their occupants settled in front of their televisions or prepared for bed. Just another peaceful night in the valley, everything was right with the world, no different of a night than any other.

I found myself hoping it wouldn't be the last time that I would see the "Valley of the Cross." It was the same eerie feeling I had earlier when I left Charleston and I wasn't liking it very much.

I called over my shoulder, "Come on Dog, let's get up the mountain." I purposely didn't look back again.

CHAPTER TEN

She awoke to the sounds of the night. She never knew how much she missed them until they were taken away. When they imprisoned her, she could not hear the night. It was lost through the dense walls of stone. The agony in her chest had subsided. The flow of blood had slowed from a mere trickle to not at all, and the pain had ebbed away to a distant throb. Still, she would not travel. She would sleep again, building her strength and her emotion, for the next time.

There, in the darkness, she waited for her body to heal itself more completely, feeding on her anger and the need for revenge. She was only sorry she had not been allowed to finish the punishment. Even now, she felt the stirring in her lower regions and knew that her body soon would be crying for satisfaction, as her mind had cried the long years of her torment and imprisonment.

The events of the night before had given her more reason for hate. She had immediately known the men for what they were—had sensed it, as she had the others. They were part of the ones responsible for her great misery. A brighter sense of anger filled her as she imagined the way it would feel to meet the two again. Her dark mind rejoiced, as she pictured the way their cruelty and interference would be repaid. The thought of the joy she would feel when her flesh met theirs, brought her warmth and solace. The promise of ecstasy and delight filled her wicked thoughts. Fantasy became real in her, keeping her alive as it had for years.

She decided she would make the two wait for a time, letting their fear become great and their anger strong enough to taste. She wanted them to pay for the physical pain they had inflicted on her body and the cruel interruption of her pleasure.

There had been something different in the one, something she knew even he was not yet aware. She would have to be more careful when the time came for their final meeting. She had seen men such as he before. She felt a deep longing to sample the pleasures his mind and body would yield.

The others had been good. She had enjoyed their anguish and their suffering. She had relished their fear and feasted on their hatred at the end. They all hated her at the last, only then fully understanding what she was doing to them. She returned their hatred ten fold for what they had done to her. When they had given to her all they had to give, when she had sucked the last of the life blood from their mangled bodies, and drained their tiny minds of every sweet drop of emotion, then, their suffering and torment became the nourishment her tainted heart craved. They became feed for her twisted soul.

She could close her eyes and recall, with exquisite detail, every death since her escape. The torment she inflicted seemed to get better and stronger with each execution. She couldn't wait for the next visit, each becoming more intense, more fulfilling than the one before. The more agony and anguish she extracted, the more her pleasure. It was the blood lust again, coming just like before…before she was imprisoned. She enjoyed the killing, needed to kill…almost as much as she needed her revenge…almost.

But it was their coupling which offered her greatest reward. As her victims felt the absolute shame and humiliation she inflicted upon them, she reveled in their revulsion. She drank in their soundless cries for mercy as she drew them into her body for a final time. Their last hopeless emission was the payment she extracted. Payment against the debt they all owed! Payment for the wasted years of hunger and humiliation their kind had inflicted! She had not deserved such treatment at their hands! How could they, the poor, pitiful beings, ever hope to judge one such as she?

As the dark night passed, her hunger grew. She knew she would not be able to remain for too long and she knew, she would be forced to find another way to soothe the hunger—perhaps some small animal near the cave when she awoke. It would not be the same, but her strength must be restored. Her wounds must be healed; her body ready for the work yet to be done.

The morning sun began to creep into the dark, moist lair that was her temporary home. She had come to hate the light over the years. She hated the warmth, hated the very brightness of it. Her injured body slipped deeper into the recess, away from the torment she so detested. She would rest impatiently and long for the welcoming darkness through the long hours of the horrid day. Darkness had become her entire world; a world in which she ruled and none dare enter.

Her body shook with anger as she recalled the two who had indeed challenged her by entering her world without invitation. She smiled inwardly as she settled to rest. They had dared, yes, but they would be sorry, they would be very sorry.

She closed her eyes to sleep, and to wait for the night.

CHAPTER ELEVEN

Frank and Mary Waters were my aunt and uncle. Mary was my mother's younger sister and they both had the fortune, good or bad, to marry mountain boys from western North Carolina. My mother, Elizabeth, met my father in a grocery store near Asheville one fine spring afternoon, and from what I've been told, he swept her off her feet. I guess it was another of those, love is blind kind of things.

My parents were married six months later against the better wishes of my mother's parents who were of the well to do upper crust of local society. My father, a Cherokee Indian with few prospects and less money, was definitely not of a status which allowed marriage to their daughter. They were not at all happy. To their continued dismay, their younger daughter, Mary, met a friend of my father's and she also was "led down the garden path" by one far beneath her station. My grandparents were infuriated and cut both of their offspring off without a cent. As it turned out, they ended up losing all their money and died early on, leaving my mother and aunt with just what they were promised...nothing.

In the long run it would have made little difference. Neither daughter would be destined to leave her mate by coercion or misfortune. My mother remained with my father until the last violent seconds of his life, to the dismay of all who knew her. By the same strange token, my Aunt Mary would never leave my Uncle Frank.

Steven's parents were as different as dark and light, but you could sense when you were around them, how truly in love they really were. Over the years, they became the brunt of family jokes, as they rarely, openly said one kind word to each other. We all surmised they must be truly in love to speak to one another the way they did and not try slitting each other's throat on a nightly basis. The constant, good-natured bickering allowed them to survive years of a marriage filled with strife and turmoil, and still go on together, year after year. Occasionally, if you were really watching closely, you could spot moments of compassion and understanding between them…but not very often. They played their parts all too well.

We drove to Steven's parents house, well, I guess it qualified as a house. It had started out as a mobile home about twenty-five, or thirty years before. Uncle Frank built addition after addition, changing it constantly. It was difficult to determine where the old trailer had been assimilated into the structure. There were bedrooms, bathrooms, den and shop, all branching off from the original structure. Any decent architect would have been immediately and violently sick, but my aunt and uncle called it home and they were very happy there.

I saw my Aunt Mary sitting on the front porch of that "house" as we pulled into the driveway from the lonely winding back road near Banner Elk. She looked as if she were waiting up on late teenagers like when we were boys. She lifted her large body from her porch swing and gave a small wave of greeting as I turned the truck lights off.

"Morg, before you get out, I called ahead and told them about Jordan. I…"

"What?" I turned to him, "Steven, are you crazy? You can't tell them…"

He raised his hand, "Calm down. I told them he died and we're not sure of the circumstances yet. I didn't tell them we were there or what happened. I just kept it simple. They won't ask any questions you know that. We can tell them the whole thing later if we have to. I just thought

Ma would want to know about Jordan. I mean he was a little shit but he was her nephew you know?"

"Yeah, yeah, you're right." I paused, "Let's just keep the details to a minimum. I don't want to get anyone any more upset than we have to, at least not tonight. I'm just not up for it right now." I pulled the door open and Dog jumped out into the front yard.

"You got it, man." Steven got out on his side and walked towards the porch where his mother met him at the front steps and struggled to put her arms around her immense son. He accepted the gesture in the same fashion I had seen for over twenty years. He tightened his big frame and gritted his teeth, feeling embarrassed by the show of affection. It all ran so contrary to the image he tried so hard to cultivate, it was almost comedic. The porch light illuminated the discomfort in his face as he rolled his eyes at me from a good two feet above his mother's head. Mary was a surprisingly short woman to have given birth to such a giant offspring. The comical embrace proved the love I knew Steven had for his mother. He would have endured any earthly discomfort to spare her feelings. He had to feign embarrassment to remain in character for the world, but I knew what he really felt for the little round butterball of a woman.

I walked around the pick up, Dog trailing at my heels, about the time my Aunt broke her hold on my cousin (to his pretended relief), and rushed to hug me in the same way. Dog parked herself on the familiar porch as if she had lived there all her life, and had never left, dangling her front paws over the edge.

"Oh Morgan, I'm sorry. I'm really sorry." Tears rolled down her chubby cheeks and she hugged me tighter, her head buried just above my belly button. Mary wasn't very tall and over the years had acquired girth almost equal to her height. She had always been a firm believer that all ills could be cured with food consumption, preferably in large amounts and hopefully often. She continued tearfully, "My poor

Morgan. I just don't know what to say." She looked up into my face, her head tilted to the extreme.

I returned her hug, "It's okay Mary, I'm alright, everything is going to be fine, I promise." I hated to lie to her, but I didn't have much choice.

"Oh, I sure hope so, Morgan." she continued in her down to earth accent, "You've just got the darndest luck, and you're such a good boy. You know your momma was always so proud of you, she always said…" Her voice trailed off into sobs.

"I know, I know Mary. Everything will be fine—it always is. Jordan's gone now. Let's not dwell on it. Why don't we just visit for awhile, okay? I'd like that very much."

"Yes, that'll be more than fine." She dabbed at her eyes with a tissue she kept in her pocket for just that purpose and put on a brave smile. "You know, I just took corn bread out of the oven and I made some of those pintos you're so fond of, with ham hock and onions. I can just throw on some fresh biscuits."

"Who in the hell is doing all that jabberin' out on my front porch?" A loud voice boomed from the hallway. The screen door opened with a bang. "How in the hell is a man supposed to get any rest if people are doing all this jabberin' on his front porch? For God's sake woman, can't you keep it down? We got neighbors just five miles away and they want to sleep tonight!"

My Uncle Frank limped through the screen door, allowing it to flap closed in his wake, and it hurt my heart to see him. He walked with a carved dogwood cane in his left hand. His deep voice was strangely out of place in his withered body. His legs had been severely damaged in not one, but several auto accidents over the years. The accidents were inspired by excessive alcohol consumption, and had resulted in permanent loss of driving privileges and intense physical damage. A few years earlier, he had a major heart attack, also alcohol induced. His choices were quit drinking or live, he chose life and fought for it every day.

He looked at me and gestured with his cane, "How you boy? I sure ain't seen you in awhile. You been down there in that other Carolina ain't you?"

"Yessir, I've been living in Charleston for the last little while." I extended my hand and he took it. His ready smile brought back many memories.

"Yeah, I think little Stevey here said somethin' bout that, yeah, course he did. Course, we never see him around here much anymore neither." He turned his gaze on his son. "He's too busy chasin' tail and gettin' into trouble I guess. Right son?" His grin was lecherous and matched the wink he gave me. Steven didn't say a word about his father's use of his nickname.

"Oh, will you just leave the boy alone, Frank!" my aunt began, "You're always picking on him. It's no wonder he don't come around no more than he does, what with you giving him such a hard time and all."

"Oh hush up, woman. Don't you have somethin' to do in the house for God's sake? These boys look hungry, you gonna' feed em' or talk em' full?" He stamped his cane on the porch.

Steven laughed, "You guys are never going to change are you? Morgan didn't come all the way up here to hear you two argue. Now Ma, why don't you come on in with me and fix us something to eat while I pack some stuff? Morgan and I are going away for a day or two and we need to leave pretty quick."

"But Stevey, I just fixed you two a room and everything. You can stay here and visit with us. You can spend the night, okay?"

I put my arm around her and said, "Aunt Mary, I would love to stay, honest, but we can't. I've got some things I need to do and Steven is going to help me. I'll come back and stay real soon though, I promise. In the meantime, I sure would love to have some of those beans you were telling me about. The smell is driving me crazy. I'm as hungry as Steven when he's awake" I said just the right thing to make her happy.

Her face lit up. She showed her biggest smile and gave me a little hug for good measure, "Why sure. You just sit out here on the porch with your good-for-nothing uncle and I'll go in the house and whip you up a supper you'll never forget. How will that be?"

"I guess that'll be just fine, woman," my uncle interjected, "But when you gonna' quit jawin' about it and do it? For God's sake I hear my stomach growlin' and I 'spect everybody else can too. Let's eat already!"

"Alright, alright! You just be nice or you can fix your own supper, old man." She turned to me, "Now, don't you worry you just sit down in my rocker and have a nice rest while I go on into the kitchen, you hear? Just you be sure and don't listen to anything this old geezer tries to tell you. He doesn't know a darn thing he's talking about anymore. He's gettin' senile and mean as a copperhead to boot."

"You just watch your mouth woman." Uncle Frank called after her retreating figure, as she and Steven disappeared into the house. "Now boy, lets set a spell out here where there's some peace and quiet. Pull up a chair there."

I pulled over the worn cane back rocker and we sat beside each other on the old porch, rocking and watching the twinkling stars in pleasant silence for a time. I finally turned to him and asked, "How have you been, Frank? I haven't been up to see you guys like I should have, especially when you were ill. I'm sorry about that."

"That's no problem boy, don't you worry any about that. I'm gettin' along just fine." He twirled his dogwood walking stick between his fingers, resting it in his lap. "I feel better than I have in years. I just don't let on as such around you-know-who. If she thought I felt better she'd be meaner to me than she is now, and she's already down right hateful."

"Now Frank, who are you trying to fool with that nonsense? You know it would be impossible for you to find anyone else who would have put up with you all these years."

Frank laughed loudly in his deep baritone, the sound echoing from the surrounding woods. "Yeah, I reckon you're right enough about that, but don't you tell her I said it, you hear?"

His accent was a dead give away to the place of his birth. There was nowhere else on earth, but the deep mountains of Carolina or Tennessee, where such an accent could be heard. Over the course of my travels around the globe, I had gradually worn mine down to a faint echo, but I still caught hell from people in certain parts of the country.

Uncle Frank was full Cherokee. His dark complexion helped mask the pronounced broken veins in his nose and face, the sign of a confirmed alcoholic. He and my father had grown up best of friends and they had worked and drank together for more years than most could remember. I could recall very few weekends when the two weren't bickering and raising pure hell all over the highlands of North Carolina and Tennessee.

Frank pulled a yellowed, corncob pipe from his shirt pocket. As he placed it in his mouth, I noticed it was empty. His doctors had forbidden him to smoke, so he just sucked on the pipe as he had done for years. A half a century of habit was hard to break.

"You know, Morgan, I still never understood why you were always so all-fired hurried to get out of these hills. We would like to see you around more, sure enough. Your Aunt Mary worries about you all the time." He pointed his pipe at me, "Course, she frets about most everything at one time or another, but she cares about you boy, she surely does. I think she figures she owes it to your mother, God rest her soul, to look after you some. She wants to see you around more often and I 'spect I could stand it a little myself."

It took a moment or two before I could answer, but then I began, "I know, Frank, it's just that my life has taken me to other places that's all. I do miss the mountains, and I know I should get up more often, it's just that…well…"

"Boy, you got to stop thinking what you're thinking. I may be a slow old man but I ain't stupid. Your daddy ain't around no more, boy. There ain't nothin' for you to be a'scert of."

I was shocked by the insight of his words and as I started to interrupt, he raised his hand, "No, you just sit still and let me have my say. I ain't been able to talk to you for a spell and there's some things that need sayin'. Your daddy had his problems son, God knows we all do boy, but he was a good man. He had good intentions even if he never showed em'. He loved your momma and he loved you boys. Life just sorta had its way with your daddy and it wasn't always pretty. I know boy, cause I expect me and your daddy was about as close as two men could get and still be men, if you know what I mean." He laughed and raised one eyebrow, "Anyway, I just wanted you to know that your daddy sometimes did things on the spur of the moment like, and them things didn't always turn out to be the best, you know what I mean son?"

I hesitated as long as I could, hoping he would continue without a response from me. After a few moments I realized this was not to be the case. "Yeah, I know that, I guess I do anyway. It's just hard for me to understand that one last thing. It was something that always sticks with me Frank. I worry about it and I worry about Mom and what happened with her. I think I should have been there…I…I feel responsible somehow."

He stopped rocking and banged his cane on the floor. "Son, let me tell you somethin' real quick; I've seen men a whole lot bigger than you try to stop your daddy from doing things his way. I've seen em' all get seriously hurt tryin'. That daddy of yours was as stubborn as an old mule and mean as my Aunt Mildred, God rest her soul. They weren't one force on this here earth could have changed that. Lord knows, if anyone could have changed him it would have been your granddaddy and I 'spect he gave up a'tryin' long before you were even born. Yessir, that old man of yours was something else, I tell you."

He resumed his rocking and returned his cane to his lap, again twirling it slowly between his gnarled fingers. He then just closed his eyes and sort of faded away somewhere in his mind, as if remembering scenes from his past that only he could know. He had memories of a man that I never really knew and whom now I would never understand. I was almost jealous of his memories. Maybe they could help me deal with the past that wouldn't let me alone. My son-of-a-bitch of a father managed to keep a hold on me even from hell.

The wrinkled Indian sat quietly on the porch, bent over with age and the effects of his life. His body had become old and frail since I had seen him last; the heart attack only the most recent of his body's betrayals. It seemed his sickness had done little to dampen his spirits. I seriously doubted anything could hurt the intrinsic pride of my Uncle Frank. He was another good man grossly misunderstood by his peers.

I could hear my aunt singing some old gospel tune from the open kitchen window and the occasional banging of a pot or the clank of plate against plate as she set the table. The peacefulness of their mountain home was as I remembered it, serene and, somehow soothing, in it's every day predictability. There were rarely any surprises; meals were always the same time, as was bedtime and waking. The routines were set firmly with the passing of the years. Even with their constant bickering, it was a relaxing environment.

Frank stopped his rocking, opened his eyes and looked at me, "Okay boy, enough of these problems from the past. You can't do nothin about 'em. You gotta' cept that and put it behind you. What you gonna do about the killing problems you got right now?"

"Excuse me sir?" I asked, jolted from my reverie by his frank question and abrupt change of thought.

"Look, you two might fool that lady in there with your story about what killed your brother, but you ain't gonna' put nothin' over on me. I know what's been hapnin' with the people of the tribe. These here killins' been going on for months now, we all know about em', not the women folk as such, but most of us old-timers anyway. There's been plenty of talk in the council about it too, I tell you that. Somebody's been killin' our people all around and I think that somebody musta visited your brother." He poked the side of my chair with his cane. "Now, you stop tryin' to fool with me and spit out some truth, boy. What you gonna do?"

When I got over my initial surprise, I figured he probably knew more than I did and so I answered honestly, "Well, I really wish I knew, Frank. At this point, I don't have any answers, only more questions than I know what to do with. Steven seems to think Rising Wolf can shed some light on the problem, I don't know."

"You know, sometimes that boy of mine does have some sense. I think you got no choice, boy. Somebody's a'killin' our people and if anyone can help, that old medicine man is the one." He pointed at me with the tip of his cane, "He's the last of his kind, boy, you mark my words. There's others around, sure, but not like him. When he's gone, they'll be a lot goes with him that's for damn sure. I can tell by the look in your eyes you ain't believin' nothin' I'm sayin' to you, but I think you're wrong boy." He looked away towards the nearby woods, "I really do."

"Whether I believe it or not, it seems like I don't have a whole lot of choices. Ben and this old book he had me dig up, are the only chances we have. I have to listen to him, it's the only road we've got."

"You're right on that sonny." He returned his cob pipe to his shirt. "Now, you just take a little advice from a senile old Indian, you give what he's got to say a chance son. There's a lot more to life in these here mountains than you know, with your big city learnin and all. There's a lot that ain't in no schoolbooks. In the old times, they was some sure nuf' powerful shaman could do things people would never believe nowadays. You would'a had to be there and seen it. Remember boy, they ain't nobody knows everything, ain't none of us no different." He leaned forward in his rocker and lowered his voice, "Now I hear your Aunt Mary a comin'. We ain't gonna' mention any of this in front of her, you hear? You just think on what I said a spell and maybe you'll figger it out."

"I will Frank. And Frank…"

"Yeah, boy?"

"Thanks for the talk about my father, it helps. I needed to hear it."

"I sure as hell hope so son." He gave me a nod. "I sure as hell do."

Mary called through the screen door, "Alright, old man, if you boys are ready, I got supper on the table. Steven's already sat down so I would hurry if I was you." She giggled, "My that boy can eat!"

We all moved into the kitchen and enjoyed the country dinner my aunt had prepared. She heaped food on my plate until I felt ready to explode, and the meal, of course, was great. Her reputation as a cook was somewhat of a local legend and subsequently Frank claimed that as the number one reason he had wed her. Mary sat a plate for Dog on the floor as if she were family. Dog growled at Steven when he pretended to take it away and we all laughed.

The time we spent at the table was relaxing and familiar. I had been there for a thousand meals it seemed and, at least for a time, it brought back the better days from my youth. I had eaten at their table more than my own, often escaping from my father's wrath to visit with them. We laughed and joked as we used to in years past. The meal was a welcome respite from the previous day's events.

After we finished dinner, we retired to the den. Steven brought out his duffel bag of supplies and sat it by the door. I noticed he had also brought along his shotgun case and I briefly glanced at my uncle and saw that he too had registered the addition to the supplies. Frank averted his eyes and didn't acknowledge the gun.

"Well, even I will admit, boys, that weren't a bad meal at that." He winked at me careful Mary couldn't see. "I guess you do have a few uses after all, woman." I felt sure he was sidetracking her so she didn't notice Steven's luggage.

"And if you want to keep eating, you better keep civil about my cooking, you crazy old Indian." She punched him playfully in the arm. "You want Morgan to think I don't feed you? I don't know why I even put up with you sometimes, I really don't."

"Don't let her kid you boys, she knows well why she puts up with me. She's just not likely to say in front of you young fellows, that's all. Might make her a little bit embarrassed if you know what I'm sayin." His mischievous grin confirmed his meaning precisely.

My aunt's face colored with embarrassment and she giggled like a schoolgirl before she chided him back, "Yeah, don't you wish? He sure talks a good fight; anyway, least he talked a whole lot about it before he married me. Lately it ain't been one of his favorite topics so to speak."

We all laughed at the uncomfortable look on my uncle's face. He first pretended great displeasure at her remarks but then joined us in our laughter, his loud voice dwarfing us all. It was a memorable moment, as we all stood around their living room on that warm summer evening, laughing together. It made the problems of the past seem slightly farther away, not quite as important as they had seemed just hours before. I knew, however, that the problems hadn't gone away, they were just postponed.

Before my aunt and uncle could move to their seats, I quickly interjected, "I can't remember the last meal I had like that, Aunt Mary. I'm sure whenever it was, it was probably right here. I really appreciate it. I didn't know how hungry I was until we sat down."

"Why thank you Morgan, you've always had the nicest manners." She cast a look at Steven as he towered over her. "Not like some people we know."

Again I got to watch the big giant squirm uncomfortably, "Oh Ma, you know that's not true. I talk about your cooking to everybody. Just ask Morgan here, he'll tell you."

"As much as I would like to get him in trouble Mary, he does compliment your cooking all the time, and look at the size of him. You sure did something right." Her face beamed with pride and I knew I had again somehow managed to say the right thing. It felt good seeing her smile.

"Anyway, I guess we should be going. Steven and I still have to drive to the cabin tonight, so we'd better go before it gets too late."

"You sure you boys can't stay? I could get you up early in the morning and fix you a big breakfast."

My uncle interceded quickly before I could reply. "For God's sake woman let these boys go on their way. Can't you see they got more to do than hang around here with us old folks? They might have some women up at that old cabin for all we know. Do you boys? You don't maybe have an extra one for an old geezer like me do you?"

"Oh, you old fool!" Mary elbowed him in his ribs. "You wouldn't know what to do with some young girl anymore! You'd probably have another heart attack just trying to figure it out. Okay, if you boys won't stay, I've sorta packed you some goodies to take with you. I'll go out to the kitchen and get them together. I'll meet you boys out by the truck. What don't you fellas see if this old codger has enough spunk left to walk you boys that far without me prodding him along? If he can still think about young girls he don't need my help."

Frank pointed at her with his unlit pipe, "You just go get their food woman, and we'll see who gets there first."

Steven retrieved his stuff on the way to the front door, slung the bag over his shoulder and carried his gun case in his free hand. He followed behind his father patiently as he hobbled slowly towards the door, working carefully at each painful step with his cane. Little groans of effort passed from his lips and I knew there was agony in the old man's frail body, but neither Steven nor myself made any movement to assist him. We both knew that was not the right thing to do. Frank still had his pride and nothing was going to take that from him. That was about all that he had left, that and Mary's love.

We walked out into the front yard and stopped just short of the truck. Dog left her place on the front porch to join us.

Uncle Frank looked up into the summer sky and commented without turning to us, "Sure is a pretty night. Nights like this makes you relaxed—maybe a little too relaxed; make you forget things; take things for granted. Nights like this you have to be 'specially careful. Know what I mean, boys?" He turned and looked at his son as he spoke, "You two take real good care of each other, you hear? There's a lot can happen to two fellas like you on nights like this."

His meaning wasn't lost on Steven. He looked at me and I nodded my head, indicating his father knew the truth. Steven answered him, "We know Pop, but remember we ain't boys anymore. We'll do what we can and we'll be careful, I promise."

"I know you will, boys." To him we would always be boys. "Hell, I used to tell your daddy all the time Morgan, you two together can be pure hell-on-wheels. I'd hate to be the one to tangle with the two of you that's for sure. Just remember two things; don't forget where you boys came from, or where your people came from. There's more to our folks than most people know and you best not forget that."

"Yessir, I know." Steven answered seriously.

"Good, just don't either of you forget. Then there's the second thing."

"What's that Frank?" I asked.

"Ain't nobody perfect, Morgan, there ain't nobody perfect." He looked at me as he spoke and I knew he was telling me more than it seemed. "You remember that, Morgan. All we can do with what God give us is try our best. It ain't always gonna' be the right thing, but you do what you got to at the time. Just don't look over your back and try to second-guess yourself. Life just won't work for you if'n you do."

The screen door screeched open and banged shut as my aunt came out of the house.

Frank muttered under his breath, "That's enough of this kind of talk boys. You just mind what I said and it'll turn out right."

"Here you go, I put lots of food in there." Mary's arms were loaded with two large bags. Steven took them and put them in the back of the truck. "If you guys are going up to your grandfather's old cabin you probably need some staple goods. There's even some fried chicken I fixed for yesterday's lunch and Mister Prince Charmin' here wouldn't eat it. I threw a few other things in there too."

"What do you mean wouldn't eat? I had three pieces, I can't help you made enough to feed all of downtown Boone!"

"Oh, hush up. You boys need anything else, you just come on back and I'll fix you up. They ain't much for a lonely old woman like me to do around here except take care of this ungrateful old fool. I enjoy cookin' for somebody that really appreciates it."

Steve said, "Yes ma'am. I'll come back and see you in a day or two and maybe my all-fired perfect cousin here might come too." He had just dropped the tailgate on the truck to roll his motorcycle off the back and into the log garage beside the house.

"Need some help with that, Stevey?" I asked from the front of the truck.

"No, and don't call me Stevey!"

Aunt Mary interjected, "But Stevey it's your name, sweetheart."

"No Ma, my name is Steven, remember, not Stevey. That's some little boy's name. Don't help him out any. He gives me a hard enough time as it is."

She laughed as she turned to me; "We sure miss you around here Morgan. You will promise to come back? Even for just a short visit?"

"Yes ma'am. I promise I'll come back and visit before I go back to Charleston. But only if you promise to fix me one of your pecan pies."

She beamed, "Well I can surely do that."

Frank had remained quiet during our conversation. He stood nearby on wobbly legs and stared at the stars. When Steven returned from the garage, Frank finally spoke, "It sure is a pretty night, or did I already say that?"

"Yessir. I think you mentioned it, yes." I extended him my hand and he took it, his grip still firm despite his maladies. "Thanks for having me over Frank, I appreciate it. It felt good to be here."

"You'll always be welcome here boy, you know that." He squeezed my hand harder still, "You just mind what we talked about and everythin' will be just fine."

"Yessir." I answered him and walked over to hug my aunt goodbye. As I did, I saw Frank catch his son's eye.

They both gave a slight nod to each other before Frank spoke; "You take care of your cousin, son, and you listen to your heart." Then he turned towards the porch and called over his shoulder, the same thing he had said to us all our lives; "Boys, don't do anything I wouldn't do." He paused for effect, giving us a wicked smile and a wink. "And if you do, name it after me." He made his way slowly to his old porch rocker and settled in with a sigh of effort I heard all the way across the yard.

Steven gave his mother a final, short hug just before he entered the cab of the truck.

"We'll see you later, ma."

I glanced into the back of the truck to make sure all was ready and opened the driver's side door for Dog who jumped up and took her place between us. I think she liked when I had a passenger; it was the only time she was allowed on the seat.

After taking my place behind the wheel and starting the engine, I backed around on the drive and threw my hand up towards my aunt and uncle. Frank had gotten up from his chair and stood beside Mary as they returned my wave.

I said to Steven, "They're amazing people, your folks."

"Yeah, I know." He said softly, so softly that I almost didn't hear him. Then he turned to look into the darkness out the side window.

As the beams from the headlights illuminated our path, I caught a glimpse of them in my mirror by the red glow of the brake lights.

They were standing arm in arm waving goodbye.

Chapter Twelve

The ride to the cabin was quiet and uneventful. Neither of us felt much like talking. We drove south, twisting and turning our way up and down mountain after mountain, each seeming to go on forever. My grandfather's property, or my property I guess, was off of State Road 261 near a peak in Pisgah National Forest called Roan High Bluff, elevation 6267 feet. My parcel was actually on a slightly smaller peak adjacent to the higher mountain and had been the home of Cherokee for many years. We left Banner Elk on 19 east, passed through Elk Park, then crossed briefly into Tennessee before coming back into North Carolina. We picked up a small mountain road, State Road 143, and followed it through Glen Ayre. The small town boasted only a single gas station and a few stores. The gas pump stood isolated and alone in the weak light from a nearby pole. We passed by and drove further into the night.

My grandfather's father had acquired the remote property well over a hundred years prior. No one was actually sure when, or how, the land came to be owned by my family; it had been that way for so long I guess the story was lost. Perhaps it may have been one of the many stories my grandfather never had time to tell me before his death. Cherokee had been there long before white men came. There were burial mounds, shards of broken pottery and arrowheads all over the mountain. I grew up on that mountain—well for the most part anyway.

We reached a vaguely marked side road, State Road 1343, and began
our serious up hill climb. Gooce Cove Road started out as a state maintained gravel road, serving a few dilapidated old farmhouses. It gradually
worsened, narrowing, strewn with rocks and gullies and eventually, we
rounded a curve to find the "official" road ending in a pile of gravel. The
road continued but became little more than a path along a dry
streambed, nearly impassable in the thaw of springtime and requiring a
four-wheel-drive vehicle the rest of the year. The road followed the path
of the creek bed occasionally breaking off along it's own ancient course
for reasons long forgotten by everyone but the mountain, washed away
by time and nature.

Dog sat on the seat between us and watched the road as if she knew
exactly where she was going.

I often thought that, soon, I was going to have to explain to her that
she wasn't human. I would have done so sooner but I wasn't sure how
she was going to take it, and didn't want to hurt her feelings.

Steven spoke first, breaking the silence that had settled between us.
"Thanks for going by the house. It meant a lot to the folks, you know.
They don't get many visitors anymore and they really wanted to see
you."

"I enjoyed it actually. I never expected your dad to know so much
about what was going on, though. He sort of surprised me with that. He
said the elders have been discussing the killings for some time and he
guessed what happened with Jordan. I didn't go into any details, he just
knew already."

"Pop always was good at guessing things. Hell, I never could get away
with anything. And anyhow, I'm sure he's been talking to Rising Wolf.
He never mentioned any of this until tonight so I'm as surprised as you
are."

We had long since abandoned the air conditioner in favor of the crisp
outside air. The deep shaded forests in the higher altitudes were always
cool after the sun went down, even in the heat of the late summer. The

wind blew comfortably through the cab carrying with it the familiar fresh smells we had both grown up with. I kept our speed down to stir less dust and to avoid large boulders that occasionally appeared to slow our progress. Dog had her nose up high and was enjoying the air in her fur. She moved her head from side to side occasionally to better catch the breeze from the open windows.

"When we get to the cutoff, we'll have to get out and lock the hubs into four-wheel-drive. I cut down an old pine tree, felled it right across the road, but we can hook it to the front and just pull it to one side. We'll leave the road open for Ben to come up in the morning." I turned to him, "You did say he would be here in the a.m. right?"

"Yep."

"Probably take most of the morning to get here you think?"

"Hour or two I reckon." He added absently, pretending it meant nothing, "Morgan…you know he won't be drivin' himself don't you? He still doesn't have a driver's license."

"I know, and yeah, I know who will be driving. I'm not stupid. It doesn't matter; I've got to see her sometime or another. Might as well be now. There's nothing really wrong between us Steven." I down shifted to get better traction as the road got worse in one spot. "I mean we don't hate each other or anything, at least I don't hate her. We just couldn't stay together; it's as simple as that. Hell, she probably doesn't even think about it anymore. Last I heard she was planning to marry some lawyer or something."

"Shit." He snorted.

I looked at him, "Shit? What the hell does that mean?"

"It's bullshit, that's what it means."

"What the hell are you talking about Steven?"

"Don't play stupid with me, Morg. You know as well as I do that fell through. Hell, I think I might have told you myself."

"Look Steven, this is the last I'm going to say on the subject; I've got no problem with Kathy alright?" I shook my head and smirked, "You know we've been friends since we were little. Just because she and I have had a few personal problems over the years doesn't mean we're not friends anymore." I hesitated for a moment, trying to be sure of what I was going to say. "I just never explained to her what happened in Fayetteville." My voice betrayed me again, showing emotions when I wanted most to hide them. I saw him turn his head towards me out of the corner of my eye, but I kept my gaze on the twisting road.

"You should have." His tone revealed more than his words. He was angry with me for not coming to him with the story. That was the first time he even hinted that it bothered him.

"I know that Steven." I looked at him; "I just couldn't okay? I had to deal with it myself on my own. I couldn't talk to her—to you even—anybody. If I did I would have screwed things up even worse. I needed, hell need now, to sort things out in my head. I have problems I've got to deal with and I couldn't do it around anything from my past. I have to start over Steven. I've got to leave what's past, past."

He turned his head away, "Yeah."

He knew basically what had happened, I told him that much from my jail cell in Fayetteville, but I never told him why, or went into any detail. I tired again to explain, "Steven, I had to do it alone. Only I could...can, work things out in my head. I mean it's my head that's screwed up here. Mine alone. It's taken a lot of time for me to sort things out. I'm getting there, but I'm not there yet. At least I was before all this stuff started." I banged my hand on the wheel in frustration. "Now I have to deal with this new crap on top of everything else."

Silence settled again between us.

When he didn't say anything for awhile, I finally asked, "Do you understand any of what I'm saying here Steven? At all? Or am I just talkin...finally, and I realize too late, but talking, to thin air?""

"Yeah Morgan I do get what you're sayin', sorta. I mean, I think I do anyway. "

I tried a smile, "Good, that's all I can ask."

"I mean hey, you're not the easiest guy in the world to understand anyway"

"Oh, yeah. Look who's talkin; the epitome of the hard faced Indian. You've never confessed an intimate emotion deeper than your love for the new Harley Evolution frame in 87."

"Hey, I am an emotional giant."

"Giant, maybe. Emotional, no. Anyway, I'm glad you get what I'm sayin. I'll work things out. Things will be…good."

"Good." he mimicked me. "All that's well and good, but you're still an asshole for not telling Kathy all this shit—and me, especially for not telling me."

"Yeah, but I'm your blood kin, you have to let me get away with things like that. If not, I'll tell your mother. Now stop making such a big deal over this Kathy thing, alright?"

He snorted, "Me make such a big deal of it? Will you listen to yourself? But if that's the way you want to play it, fine with me." He faked a serious tone and added, "You think we're going to have weather tomorrow?"

I laughed, "Yeah, I think there's a good chance of it. Listen, I'm sorry okay? I get a little carried away sometimes about certain things, and I'll admit she's one of those things."

Steven didn't reply. He reached behind the seat and pulled out his canteen. "Now that we got all this soap opera bullshit out of the way, you ready for a drink? I mean correct me if I'm wrong, isn't the property we're on yours? If there's any po'leece around they ain't got no say so here."

"Well, I think I might be persuaded to have a slash or two. Purely for medicinal reasons you understand and because I know how you hate to drink alone." I laughed, "Sorry, I always wanted to say that." I dodged a rock in the road and Dog almost fell off the seat. "I guess you're right, there can't be any law enforcement types within twenty miles of here. Hell, I don't know of any people for twenty miles around. That's one of the reasons I like this place so much, it gives new meaning to the word privacy."

I paused and took a sip from the ancient canteen, and handed it back to Steven. When the open container passed by Dog's nose, she jerked her head away as if she had been slapped. She sneezed and tried to shake her head to clear her nose of the bourbon smell.

Steven and I both laughed and Dog looked at each of us as if we were crazy. We laughed like I hadn't in years. Laughter is indeed sometimes the best medicine. It acted as a soothing balm for abrasions of the spirit.

As the laughter died away, we reached the intersection of my "driveway". The old pine tree I had cut in the spring covered the roadway. It's needles had all turned brown and fallen away from the branches and it looked strangely out of place, barren and lifeless amidst the lush summertime green of the forest.

I pulled in until the front grill of the truck almost touched the fallen tree, then backed up slightly and cut the lights. I retrieved my flashlight from the door pocket and stepped out calling for Dog to follow. She jumped from the seat and trotted off into the woods to do her duty. I closed the door and turned to Steven, "Let's have that firewater again Stevey. That's some rank stuff but it sort of grows on you."

"Look Morg, you're gonna call me Stevey one too many times and then you won't do it again." He tossed the canteen at my head, slightly harder than I would have liked.

"You know, you're a lot of talk for such a big man, cousin. You think you're man enough to hook the logging chain to that old pine while I pull it out of the way?"

"I think maybe I can manage that. If I can't I'm sure you can probably teach me, according to my mother, anyway."

"What can I say? She's such a smart woman your mother, she knows you got the brawn in the family and I got the brains. She's just a realist, that's all."

"See, now who's stupid?" He faked seriousness, "She's not no realist, she's never sold houses for people in her life."

"Sometimes, Steven, you have the strangest sense of humor. Well, the stupidest, anyway." I shook my head and laughed, "It's even hard for me to figure you out."

"Well, at least I have a sense of humor." He handed back the canteen after wiping the opening dramatically with his sleeve. "You know, they say you can catch stupid, just like the flu. It sneaks up on you when you're not looking, bites you on the ass and then just never leaves. You better stay on your guard man, or it'll get you." He held his hands apart. "Hell, you've just had more practice being smart than I have that's all."

I took another long swallow of the warm liquor, tasting charcoal from the filtering and the oak of the aging process "Knowledge has very little to do with real life, my friend. You could be a rocket scientist and still not have common sense, as you have been so gracious to point out to me in the past."

"More or less, yeah." He took the bourbon back and took a big swallow as I continued to rant.

"No one is really smarter than anyone else Steven. They just know different things. That's all. For instance, you know that old Harley of yours better than anyone else in the world. As far as the rest of the world is concerned, you're an absolute authority, a genius when it comes to that bike."

I took the Jack Daniels from his hand and had another shot myself. It was getting better, and smoother, with each swallow. "See, it's all relative, and if someone really was smarter than you, so what! Would they be happier than you? Live a better, more fulfilling, life than you? Hell no! Knowledge may be power, yeah, but it doesn't make a shit difference in the end. You think you buy one more second of life, when your time is up? Just because you know the theory of relativity or algebra? Uh uh, nope, no way, I think not…you're dead just like everybody else, end of story. End. Period. Dot."

"There you go again, analyzing everything from your most righteous soapbox. You lose me, Morgan, when you start talking shit like that. Can you go slower next time, teach? I'm just a slow old mountain boy. I can't follow all that school book learnin."

"Now, that is bullshit."

"It's the truth."

"Oh shut up already! Let's get this thing off the road and get the hell up the mountain."

I retrieved the rusty chain from the floor of the truck and held the light while Steven wrapped it around the truck and the tree. Dog watched us from ten feet away, supervising to insure we completed it to her canine expectations.

The quiet of the night air was lost when I started the engine and shifted into reverse, easing the tree to one side. The remaining dry, dead branches shattered audibly as it slid across the ground. Brown pine needles fell like rain.

Steven stowed the chain and opened the door on his side. He looked at Dog expectantly. When she didn't get it, he called to her, "Well, get in already."

She looked at him, as if to ask who the hell he thought he was, and just stood there. I decided to intervene in the battle of wills and called: "Alright, get in here, Dog." She bounced over past Steven, not acknowledging his existence, and jumped onto the seat beside me.

My cousin got in the truck mumbling under his breath, "Damned Dog, acts just like you, hard headed, stubborn."

"What?"

"Oh nothing, nothing. I was just talking to myself, that's all."

I laughed and turned the wheel towards the steep dirt road leading up to the cabin. In the beam from the headlights I could make out small bushes that had sprouted in the center of the old road. Grass too, had taken hold along the roadside and spread, slowly and surely, as high as the truck hood in some places. The deserted roadway didn't get enough traffic to keep it clear.

The road had been carved into the mountain by hand a hundred or more years before. I suspected a harnessed horse had been the only horsepower around. Over the last several years, I had done some repair to the road; dropping in gravel in the worst spots to fight the erosion; cutting trees that had been allowed to grow too close, but it really didn't do much good. Without someone living on the property full time, it was a war of the elements that I could never hope to win. The forces of time neither rest nor sleep.

From the foot of the mountain to the top was four long miles of narrow, twisting road. The steep incline followed a series of cutbacks to make the climb possible, as straight up was out of the question unless you were a bird or crazy. In the daylight hours you could look over the side and see where you had just been on the 180 degree turns. It wasn't as scary at night because you couldn't see over the edge to know how much trouble you would be in if you went over. The red pick-up barely fit on the one lane, or path we called a road. Tree limbs occasionally scraped against the hood and top of the old truck and Steven frequently had to pull his arm in the window or push a branch from our path.

He looked at me and said, "You know, we could do some work on this old road, if we have some extra time."

"Yeah. In our spare minutes, we'll get right on it Steven."

"Asshole."

"Yeah, it does need some work, but I sort of like the road like this. You're right though, there are a few limbs that need to be cut that would make it less of a bitch. I've been away for too long."

"That's for damn sure." He whispered under his breath. Still, I heard the comment and knew he meant for me to. I said nothing.

We climbed the mountain at a snail's pace, the truck trudging along in low gear with no strain or hurry. Within the first mile, we jumped three rabbits and a number of squirrels and by the second, a huge raccoon walked slowly across our path, seemingly slow and unconcerned. Dog growled softly from where she sat by my right shoulder. She watched carefully as the masked animal completed his journey across our path and strolled off in the dark as if we weren't even there. His eyes were briefly visible off to my side window as we passed. They looked like two red dots in a sea of empty black. The large trees of the surrounding forest blocked out the light of the moon and left only the narrow strip of stars immediately overhead for illumination.

I decided the time was ripe to ask Steven a few questions I had postponed until the "right time", "Let me ask you Steven; suppose, just suppose now, I had the slightest doubt about this old Indian tale. I don't, but just suppose I wanted to know more about it. Tell me, about this "Ravenmocker" stuff.

Steven hesitated, yet didn't start giving me a hard time for asking as I expected. He dropped all pretense of playfulness, suddenly very serious and earnest, as if repeating a lesson learned in a classroom. "Well, to tell the truth, I don't know a whole lot, but I do know what a Ravenmocker is. I'm sorta' surprised you don't remember. I know you heard about it when we were kids."

I didn't tell him how hard I had been trying to forget everything about my past life that I could.

"I've been spending a bunch of time over the last few years listening to all the old stories and legends that I could. I just wish I had done it sooner, when there were more people alive to tell them. My old man is right about one thing, he always says that Rising Wolf is the last of his kind. You have no idea how right he is."

"Yeah, he can be persuasive."

"Damn right he can. Now, don't interrupt me when I'm talkin'."

"Sorry."

"Yeah. Anyway, the old Shamen kept their secrets very close to their hearts. They told no one. Over the years, there were less and less people interested in the old ways. History, myths, legends, and the old formulas died with their keepers." He sounded confident as he spoke of something he knew and loved. "Hell, Morgan, when the Cherokee tribe was driven from this land and put on the reservations, their children were forced to go to schools run by whites, who taught them their heritage was wrong! That it was a bad thing! They were taught to hate everything the "Real People", the Cherokee, stood for. They were told only the way of the white "civilized" race was proper, that their customs and beliefs, those of the Cherokee, were sinful and wicked. Hell, they beat them, they washed their mouths out with soap, or worse, if they even dared to speak Cherokee!" His voice betrayed the frustration and anger he felt with that part of our people's history. It was anger shared by any knowledgeable Native American.

"You can see why the legacy of the Shamen was hard to keep. The main way they carried on was with the thousand or so of the tribe who stayed here in the mountains and fought to keep their homes. I mean, they eventually lost out too, but they kept more of their heritage. Hell, now I'm doing the same kind of preachin' you do." He pointed his finger at me, "You know if you get me started on this shit, I'll talk about it all night and you don't want to hear it."

"No Steven, I want to hear it, honest. But tell me, how does this tie in with this "Ravenmocker" business?"

"Well, what I'm leading to is; I never will know as much as I should. I know some legends and history but I don't know crap about the sacred formulas. That stuff's way out of my league, we're going to have to talk to Rising Wolf about that. I know about the Ravenmocker though. I know that story well. Most Indians do. Purely because it's one of the best known legends, if for no other reason. The stories were the same with all the tribes. The Iroquois, the Catawba, the Seminole and others all had the same tale. A "Ravenmocker" was the most dreaded wizard, or witch, in the history of our people." He paused just long enough to light a cigarette. "This thing could change shapes and fly like a bird." Steven used his hands as he spoke, unconsciously giving motion and illustration to his words. "It preyed especially on the sick, the old and the young ones and ate the victims, always the heart if nothing else. Rising Wolf told me they absorbed the life force of their prey and lived that much longer with every victim, adding their years to his own. He said that when they found the victims, the heart would be missing, but there would be no scar where it had been." He smiled, "Scary as hell, huh?"

I didn't know if he was serious or not.

"Yeah, it is." I didn't comment one way or another about the truth of the myth. "You think somebody else could maybe...I mean anybody could find this out if they tried hard enough, right?"

"Morgan, anything is possible, but yeah, I guess someone could find out about the old legends if they wanted. Like I said, this thing is no big secret; a lot of people have heard this stuff, but just the old people seem to pay any attention to it anymore."

He stopped for a moment as if thinking about what he had just said; "It's a damn shame, really. I'm telling you, Morgan, there's more in our past than you know. The Cherokee were a truly great people, they were probably the closest thing to a perfect lifestyle in the history of this country, but you'd never know it." He shook his head. "It's sad man, that's what it is, it's sad."

"Listen Steven, you were the one who told me earlier I couldn't change things, to let them alone. Now listen to you. I know how you feel about this, but that was over two hundred years ago, you can't change it now. You got to get off this and live in the today's world cousin, because that's all you have. I'm sorry, but that's the deal." Maybe I sounded a little sterner than I intended.

"You know sometimes, Morg, you really piss me off." He startled me by slamming his big fist on the dash so hard I felt it through the steering wheel. "You need to start listening more and stop figuring you got every answer to every problem in the whole damned world."

He continued sternly, and I was surprised as he rarely showed any emotion so vividly. It was probably as close to anger as I had seen him in a long time. "I don't give a damn about trying to do something about it now! I just want somebody to admit what they did, that's all! Just once! I want somebody in some civil rights press conference or some other bullshit like that, somebody to stand up and ask Mister Perfect All American, how come they killed entire races of people and took their homes from them in the name of their all important white progress? How come they ordered soldiers to kill women and children? Ordered them to burn their homes, destroy their property? How come they allowed the torture, rape and mutilation of the most peaceful people their almighty powerful God ever created?" He was really fired up. "Jackson was as big a mass murderer as Hitler and they put his face on a hot damned twenty dollar bill for Christ's sake!"

My huge cousin turned toward me, his chiseled features animated, voice loud and full of emotion. His eyes burned and he was sort of eerie looking by the dashboard light. "And Morgan, you know what the worst part of the whole mess is? Do you? Nobody knows about this shit! That part of the history books was never written. People still believe the Indians were all bad guys' just cause they saw 'em in the movies that way! I mean, we know all about the terrible deal the black man got— every little detail. Just turn on the damned TV set, it's still on every night. Poor colored folks, my big ol' hairy butt! Big freakin' deal! The big difference is they're around to tell about it. No one is around to tell the Indian's story, nobody ever was and nobody ever will be. That's the real bitch of it all Morgan!"

Steven folded his massive arms, and abruptly dropped into silence. He turned his head away from me. I could rarely remember him ever speaking that many words at one time in our lives. Several quiet minutes passed as I continued to maneuver the truck up the mountain until I finally braved the silence between us, "I'm sorry, Steven. I really didn't mean it the way you took it."

After a minute he shook his head, "Hell, I know that. It wasn't directed at you anyway Morgan. It's just this screwed up situation we're in that's all." He changed his tone and smiled, "I really had you going there for a minute right?"

"Yeah, you scared me, I suppose. I'm not used to hearing an even vaguely intelligent argument from that mouth and you were sounding fairly literate there for a time." I laughed and asked, "What the hell did you do with that canteen anyway?"

He laughed and passed it to me after taking a large swallow himself. Dog kept her head pulled well away from its path. "We're almost there, right?"

"Yep, right around this next bend it'll level out to the old cabin."

True to prediction, the headlamps revealed the faded gray logs and tin roof of the small cabin nestled between large oaks. The other out-buildings were only faintly visible in the nearby woods.

I cut the motor and the lights, slowly rolling near the cabin entrance with the truck out of gear. We were immediately surrounded by the complete and utter darkness, and total quiet of the mountain retreat. A "quiet" found in few places on earth. I had discovered no other place like it in my lifetime, and I knew I never would.

I pulled the lever to open my door, "Let's get out guys, we're home." And I knew in my heart, I meant just that.

CHAPTER THIRTEEN

The home of my grandfather, and his father before, was almost completely hidden by forest. The cabin and outbuildings had been built in harmony with their environment, and trees grew unmolested right next to the structures. Few trees in the immediate area had been felled for construction and those that had been cut had replaced themselves with the passing of the years.

The majority of the logs were taken from the surrounding mountainside, maybe where the road had been cleared, then transported to the building site. Traditional Cherokee structures were primarily made of logs. All Indians had not lived in tepees. In fact, the popular myth only applied to the nomadic tribes of the western plains who followed herds of animals as a means of survival. The most common homes in the eastern mountains were cabins formed from logs and thatch. The Cherokee Indians tended to be a more stationary people and their structures were more permanent.

The main cabin was the largest structure, serving as primary living quarters for two to four, depending on how cozy you wanted to be. To the rear was a smaller building used for storage, and that was where I had placed the generator and a store of supplies, enough for many months, maybe a year.

A small stream flowed within thirty feet of the front door, just to the right of my parked pick-up truck. The gurgling cascade of the mountain stream seemed loud in the quiet night air as Steven exited and closed the heavy truck door. Dog rushed off into the woods to explore as soon as her feet hit the ground. On the opposite side of the stream, hidden from sight by the trees, was a traditional seven-sided council house, an asi, or "hot house", and another smaller cabin with living quarters. The rushing water was crossed by a small wooden bridge leading to a pathway, which stretched through the trees for forty or fifty yards to the other buildings.

"Man, I haven't been up here in a spell." Steven said, "I almost forgot what it was like. I'm telling you, if I were you, this is where I would be all the time."

I looked around, "Yeah, I do like it—it's home I guess. Don't forget you're welcome to stay here. You know where the key is."

"I've thought about it before, believe me, I just never have the time to come up here and I feel sorta funny about it anyway."

"What do you mean you feel funny?" I asked as we walked around the cabin towards the rear building. "My home is your home Steven."

"Well, I don't know how to explain this Morgan, and it come out right."

"Just say what's on your mind, Steven, That's always the easiest." I retrieved the key from over the hand made door.

"Well, It's just that this is sort of a special place. Your grandfather lived here. He built most of it. The great thinkers and shamen used to meet here and "sit down together", talking and telling stories of the old days. My old man used to tell me about it all the time."

The wooden door squeaked on rusty, also hand-made hinges. I used my flashlight to find the generator and started the small motor. "We'll let that run awhile and the water will be nice and hot in a few minutes." I moved around to the front of the main cabin and settled on an old cedar bench beneath an oak tree. "I still don't understand why that stuff makes you not want to stay here, Steven. I mean, my grandfather and those other guys were just people like you and me and they're all dead and gone anyway. What's the big deal?"

He looked sort of strange for a second. "That's just it Morgan—they're not dead and gone—at least unless we let them be. But that's the problem, Morg. I don't think you can totally understand it, I mean we just don't think about it the same way. The other night in the bar, I sorta tried to explain it to you. It's that...well you don't."

"Look Steven, just spit out what's on your mind." I was unaccustomed to him "skirting" around any issue and I was growing quite impatient.

"Well, you just don't understand how important this kind of thing is. I don't mean you don't know all about the forest and the land that's not it; you just don't know very much about your own people. It's hard to make you understand things like this because you never really cared about them." He hesitated, "At least not lately." He held up his hand cutting me off when I tried to interrupt, "I know you did at one time. I remember you used to love to listen to your grandfather and Rising Wolf talk. I remember when we used to stay up late to listen to their stories, then things happened and you just drifted away."

He paused and looked at me for comment. When I said nothing, he continued, "I'll give you a good example—Rising Wolf. Even now you call him Ben and not by his Indian name. There was a time when you never would have thought of doing that unless he asked you to, you know what I'm tryin' to say?"

I took a minute before replying, realizing I had thought very similar things just a night or two before. "Yeah, I know what you mean, Steven. I just haven't given it much thought over the years. I have in the last few days though. I'm not sure when it stopped being so important to me, but it did." His words hurt, but they were the truth. "I can't argue that. I just didn't see a need for it I guess. I was trying for a new start and that stuff just reminded me of my old life. I guess I related it all together in one tidy little package, if I forgot about my past, I could forget about everything else."

The night sounds of the woods were a familiar backdrop for our conversation. I realized how much I had missed them in the months since I had been away from the mountain.

Finally, Steven spoke, "I tell you, Morg, while we're talking about this I need to ask you a favor."

"Sure Steven, what's on your mind?"

"No matter how it goes against your grain, or how stupid things sound to you, I want you to promise me you'll keep an open mind about this whole mess. I know you don't believe the same as I do, and I don't expect you to, but I want you to trust me on this. I don't want you to try to rationalize everything like usual." He again held up a hand to silence my attempted interruption. "No, now just listen for a minute. Rising Wolf is a great man. He demands respect and I aim to see he gets it from both of us. If you have a problem with that, we'll talk about it later. Just listen before you condemn, know what I mean?"

"You mean for me to keep my mouth shut."

"Yeah, that's exactly what I mean." His eyes met mine, his expression hard and determined, leaving no doubt of his conviction.

I wondered to myself why he was so intense about Ben. He undoubtedly had gotten a lot closer to him in the year or two I had been gone. I had never seen him so concerned about another, enough to say so anyway. "Alright, I promise. I wouldn't do anything to insult Ben…Rising Wolf, you know that."

"I know that Morg, it's just that I want you to understand things better and you're going to have to listen to do it. That's all I really want, okay?"

He left his place near the stream where he had been standing and moved closer to where I sat on the hand-hewn bench.

"Morgan, this place here," he gestured with his arm, "is special. It has great magic and power. I can smell our history here like it was still alive.

I know he was your grandfather and that's what he will always be to you, but he was more than that—much more. There are many stories and legends about Screaming Eagle. It is said by many that your grandfather was gifted with special powers and he is still greatly respected among the elders. He will never be forgotten among the Cherokee. They speak his name like he was a God or something. I'm not sure you appreciate how really important that is, Morgan. Until you do you will never understand me, why I feel funny about coming here alone, or anything else about this whole crazy mess."

"Alright, alright." I held up my hand like a Boy Scout. "I promise to listen and give all this a chance. Hell, I really don't have any choice anyway. Not all you seem to think is true, Steven. I know more and understand more than you realize. I just have to experience things first-hand before I can believe totally, that's all. It's not so confusing. With me it's no different with most organized religions; I don't believe them either, because I haven't experienced what they preach for myself. If all this proves true, fine, then I know it for fact, but I have to find out for myself. All we're really talking about here is faith, and I don't hand that out very freely anymore because I don't have very much of it left."

I kept talking. I felt like I couldn't have stopped if I tried. It was as if his words had opened a gate I couldn't close "Steven, faith in the old ways, or faith in anything else, wouldn't change the things that have happened to me or make them any better. I've given up on all that crap, and I just put faith in what I know, mainly me, because what I do, is what effects my life. I'm not interested in what's right or wrong by someone else's yardstick. If I'm a good person or a bad person, it's not because of laws or religion. Life made me the person I am and that's what I live with every day." I looked at him and it seemed it was his turn for silence, "Contrary to what you might think, I respected my grandfather more than any man I have ever known. I respect Ben "Rising Wolf" and I respect you, Steven, but that doesn't mean that I'll accept what you tell me as gospel. To me, that's not what life is all about. I have to experience it for myself for it to be real."

I stood up and paced on the porch, nervous with the turn of the conversation. I wasn't planning on saying things so close to my heart. They sorta just came out. "One of the things, the only real thing I learned from all the shit I had been through, was that I had to do things for myself; see things for myself or it's all bullshit. It's not that I don't believe or respect the old ways of the Cherokee, or my grandfathers beliefs, or yours, I just need to find them on my own. I promise I'll listen and learn, but I can't promise I won't make my own decisions in the end. I'm sorry but that's the way it is, cousin." I stopped and looked at him for a reply.

He turned away and walked back to the edge of the stream, crossing his arms in front of his chest. "That's fair enough, I guess." He paused for a minute before continuing "You know, funny thing is sometimes you sound more like a Cherokee than anyone I know!" he turned back to me. "Maybe you have been paying more attention than I thought."

"Maybe so." I decided to change the uncomfortable subject while I could, "How about we stop all this heavy conversation and get the damned truck unloaded?"

"Sounds possible, I guess I could really use a hot shower and another round of JD before bed."

"You can say that again, the part about the shower I mean."

"You just open the door and I'll start carrying stuff in, smartass."

I unlocked the front door of the main cabin and reached inside to flip on the light switch. Everything was just as I had left it the last time I had been to the mountain retreat, even though months had passed. Time stood still on the mountain.

The central room, indeed the entire cabin, was sparsely furnished. The only decorations were several ornamental or symbolic artifacts that my grandfather had placed on the walls decades earlier. There were "medicine wheels" hand made to protect from the unknown; rawhide covered wheels with special colored beads representing different stages of life. In all the bedrooms he had fashioned similar items called "dream catchers". Their job was to catch dreams as they blew through the air, trapping the bad dreams until the morning sun destroyed them with its light. The good dreams were caught in the small crystals in the web-like center of the wheel and trickled down the attached feathers to the sleeping form in the bed beneath.

These and other objects adorned the walls; some of their functions I was not even sure of, but I had never removed them. They were part of the inheritance from the man I had loved more than any other. I could never take them down. Contrary to what my cousin believed, I understood my grandfather better than he thought. Even though I had been very young when he passed away, I still thought about him often and related more to him than my parents.

Steven spoke from just behind me, interrupting my reflections, "Well, it's going to be pretty damned hard for me to carry my stuff through this door with you standing right in my damn way. Do you think you might could maybe move the hell over?"

"God, are you impatient or what? Sure, sure, your highness let me move for heaven's sake." I made a short bow and waved my arm across the entrance. I went out to the truck to retrieve my bags and various necessities I had decided I might need.

"Dog! Where are you?" I yelled into the dark forest from my place on the front porch. I heard a rustling of brush and a splash from about fifty yards upstream and she came running into view as fast as she could move. She came flying by me and made a playful turn, stopped at my feet, and looked up at me to see why I had called her. Her body dripped water in small puddles by her paws.

"Well, I hope you're pleased with yourself. Now you're all wet and you won't be able to come in for awhile." I reached down and patted her head, and she immediately flopped over onto her back to have her stomach rubbed. "Uh uh, nope, I don't have time for that. You're having such a good time; you go play some more. I've got work to do and I don't like wet dogs. Go on, beat it." She wagged her tail and headed upstream through the woods.

I removed the tarp from the back of the truck just as Steven arrived to help.

"I put my stuff in the small bedroom. You're staying in your grandfather's room, right?"

"Yeah, I've got a few things stashed in the wardrobe and closet. I like that room better and I have more space in there. You want to help me with some of this stuff?"

He let out a low whistle when he saw the implements of destruction I had asked Marilyn to bring from my gun closet. I had two twelve gauge "riot guns", two converted assault rifles (fully automatic, illegal but very effective), two handgun cases which contained 44 magnums, and plenty of ammunition for the lot. I also had a few small wooden boxes of surprises that I had thought would be better to have than not. I still wasn't sure what, or who, we were up against, but the next time we met I fully intended to be better prepared than the last. I didn't want any surprises I couldn't possibly overcome.

Steven said, "And to think I was making fun of your little gun earlier. I thought you intended to use that to protect us. Man, we could stand off an army from here. It'll be just like the tribe hidin' out after the Trail of Tears."

"Well, I don't know about that, but I want to be able to sleep at night, at least sleep a little better. Let's get this stuff into the house."

We made trips until everything was properly stowed. I got us a couple of cold sodas from the cooler I brought and we sat on two ancient rockers on the rustic porch. I looked at my watch and it glowed 1:30 a.m. It had been a long day and night.

Steven seemed to read my thoughts. "I don't know about you, cousin, but I'm tired as hell. I believe I best go inside and get my shower while

I've got any energy left at all. You think one of us needs to stand guard tonight, maybe in shifts?"

"No, I don't think there's any way in hell anyone could find us here tonight, not as fast as we got here and as far removed as we are. No one even knows about this property but close family and I pay the taxes and keep the title in such a way, even Uncle Sam would have a hard time tracing it to me, I mean quickly anyway. I don't think we have anything to worry about tonight."

"I wasn't worried about the law, Morgan."

"I know that, Steven, but even your so called Ravenmocker can't find us this soon. No way in Hell. I think we can rest easy tonight. It might be different tomorrow, but for now I think we're just fine. Dog will let us know if we have any unannounced visitors, she's damned good about things like that."

"Okay, cousin. I'll take your word for it. I think I'm going to try and catch some shut eye after I clean up. You want me to leave this canteen out here with you?"

"Yeah, I think I might borrow a little bit more of that rotgut, thanks."

Steven handed me the canteen and turned to enter the house, then stopped and turned back, "Morgan...I...Well it's good we're together again" He looked at me seriously, "I know it's for a shitty reason but at least we're going through this mess together. I just wanted to say that and that's all I'm going to say about it." Like me, he wasn't very good at expressing emotion. "See you in the morning."

"Good night, Stevey." I called to the retreating figure, smiling at his uncomfortable attempt at familiarity.

His voice called back, from inside the cabin, "Don't call me Stevey, damn it!"

I laughed to myself and removed the top from the canteen, then took a long swallow of liquid fire. Dog returned from her exploration and collapsed with a heavy sigh near my feet. The soft rush of the mountain stream masked some of the normal night sounds but still, a symphony of crickets played in the background with an old woods owl in the lead.

I missed the mountains. It was as simple as that. I had searched the world over and I knew I would never find the absolute peace and serenity that was in the very air atop the high peaks of the Appalachians. The Charleston area was one of the most beautiful spots in the world, but only in the mountain place my family had lived for generations, was I able to find solitude. It was strange, in that it seemed solitude without loneliness. It was solitude of healing and self-preservation. It was something I could not quite understand but didn't question, I just accepted it, even took it for granted when I was there. It was undeniably home, mind and spirit. I should have lived there but I just couldn't.

The problem with living in the mountains was the memories and the ghosts of my earlier life. They were always waiting for me when I lingered too long or thought too much. They were around every bend in the road, every turn of the path, haunting and following me everywhere. After the death of my father, I left the mountains. I had to get away. I came for visits, but they were always just that, visits. I knew I would be leaving before the ghosts of my past came back to remind me of all the mistakes I made…the trouble and the pain. I had been running from those ghosts for years and I was about to be forced to come face to face with them, like it or not. Freedom of choice had been taken from me by the recent turn of events. To make things worse, I knew, the next morning I would probably have to face another ghost from my past, a beautiful ghost, but a ghost just the same.

Kathy Walker, Old Ben's granddaughter, had been a playmate and friend through most of my life. We played together as children, learned together in school, and shortly after that, we became something more, much more. I think that we were destined to be together intimately all along, and were just too close to see the truth.

We became lovers and lived together off and on for a number of our "formative" years, I guess you could say. We broke apart periodically for whatever silly reason we might find to fight about, but then always ended up reunited. I used to joke about it with her all the time. I would tell her; I loved her more than anyone I had ever known. I just couldn't live with her. The joke held a lot of truth for us both. I would say, more than either of us cared to admit.

When my father died, I came home for the funeral and Kathy was there as she had always been, helping me through the tough parts of my life. She listened patiently while I complained, offered advice, held me when I cried, and welcomed me again into her bed. I thought for sure we had separated for the last time, that I would get my shit together, that we would finally marry as we had always planned. She even quit her teaching job and returned with me to the base in Fayetteville to live. But, of course I was wrong. Just, as I was been wrong about many things, well confused might be a better word. It sure as hell beat "mentally unstable".

Just when I thought I had come to terms with my life and could deal with my past, my mother passed away. I realized I hadn't dealt with anything. I was like the little kid with his finger in the dike trying to hold back all the emotion that threatened to break through, to drown me in it's wake and unfortunately it did just that.

When everything did explode, I lost more than Kathy. In one ironic turn of events I lost my Army commission and career, Kathy, my mother, and my desire to live in the mountains. I never even had the chance to explain things to Kathy and honestly I didn't try very hard. I took the coward's way out and ran away to Charleston. Just like always.

I took another deep drink of the Jack Daniels and realized that the next morning life would present me with the opportunity to face that particular failure head on, like it or not. There was no where left for me to run.

As I sat there in the early hours of the morning, I reflected on the mistakes of my past and wondered what she was thinking at that moment in time. She had to know the day would bring us together again and I tried to imagine what she might say or do. Was she anxious? Hurt? I quickly gave up that train of thought as to my knowledge, no one had ever been able to predict what she would ever do from one minute to the next, God knows, I had never been able to anyway. Kathy had the ability to defy all rules of logic and she acted totally on her own set of values and ideas. She looked to no one for approval.

I remember once, when we were very young, my grandfather had confided in me, "That girl has fire in her heart to match her beauty. She will not be one easily tamed and you would do well to remember that. Your grandmother was such a woman, both are of the same cloth that formed the great Cherokee women of our past." My grandfather was definitely a very wise man. He knew a great deal about everything and evidently much more about women than I did.

I tossed the canteen aside, deciding I had enough bad taste in my mouth for one night. I rose from the rocker and stepped out into the clearing by the stream. I looked up at the bright stars gleaming in the deep ebony of the summer sky. They flickered silently from their positions like diligent sentinels of the heavens, unconcerned about the troubles and cares of the creatures beneath. It was like standing beneath a planetarium dome. There, far away from the lights of any city, darkness was complete. The brightness of each star and planet were visible like no other place on earth. It made one feel somehow smaller, problems less intimidating and life somehow shorter, and more precious.

I surmised I had been without sleep for far too long and turned to the cabin. Daylight would come soon enough and worry was worthless, it wouldn't change a damned thing. I was so tired I couldn't think straight. Exhaustion worked better than any sleeping pill. That and half a bottle of Jack Daniels anyway. I walked around to the rear building and turned the generator off for the night.

"Alright Dog, I guess you're dry enough to go in now." I pointed to the house and she trotted obediently inside with me. I softly closed the door, so as not to wake Steven, and walked through the darkness into the bedroom that had once been my grandfather's. I turned back the covers on the bed my grandfather's father had made by hand over a hundred years before. Dog settled at the foot, totally at home and content just to be there.

Just before I closed my eyes for the last time that night, I wondered not about Kathy, or Ben, or Steven. My last thoughts were of that horrible smell and a glimpse of a figure from the depths of hell. A killer who took the life of my younger brother with no apparent remorse or pity as I did nothing but watch. I wondered what or who the killer could be and I wasn't really sure I wanted to find the answers.

As I finally dozed off, I found myself silently thanking my grandfather's spirit for placing the "dream catcher" over the headboard of the oak bed. I hoped that, just for the night at least, I might have enough faith left in my doubting heart for the ancient charm to catch the bad dreams hiding in the darkness and waiting there for me. The way things were going I had enough nightmares in my life already.

BOOK TWO
"Ada'Wehi'Yu"
(A very great magician or supernatural being)

"In ancient times the Cherokee had no conception of dying a natural death. They universally ascribed the death of those who parished by disease to the intervention or agency of evil spirits and witches and conjurers who had connection with the Shina (Anisgi'na) or evil spirits."

John Haywood
Natural and Aboriginal History of
East Tennessee, 1823
267-8 Nashville

"Murder is murder and somebody must answer, somebody must explain the streams of blood that flowed in the Indian country in the summer of 1838. Somebody must explain the four thousand silent graves that mark the trail of the Cherokees to their exile.

...Let the Historian of a future day tell the sad story with its sighs, its tears and dying groans. Let the great Judge of all earth weigh our actions and reward us according to our work."

Private John G. Burnett
2nd Regiment, 2nd Brigade
Mounted Infantry
On the Cherokee Indian
Removal of 1838-1839
December 11, 1890

"Thou shalt not suffer a witch to live."

Exodus 22:18

CHAPTER FOURTEEN

I knew it was past dawn by the light coming through the window over my bed. I had tossed and turned and remembered looking at the clock last around 5:30. It was Dog that woke me from the fitful sleep I finally managed to find. Her deep, throaty growl somehow penetrated my exhausted slumber. I could hear her, and I knew she was trying to tell me something, but I wasn't awake enough to make it out. As she grew louder, I forced myself from the depths of sleep, understanding, at last, that that something was wrong. I saw her standing by the bedroom door looking towards the front porch. Her body was tense and rigid. Her eyes fixed on the door. She glanced back towards me briefly, then resumed her growling and staring towards the sound. Something was outside that should not have been.

I slipped from the bed wearing just the old gym shorts I had put on the night before, retrieved the nine millimeter from the bedside table and pulled back the slide, injecting a round into the chamber. My head was still filled with the cobwebs of sleep as my brain tried to catch up to my adrenaline level. I moved as quietly as possible stepping around Dog as I went. Her eyes remained fixed on the front entrance. I gave her the hand signal for "down" and she flattened herself on the hardwood floor, ears up and ready for my next command.

The window beside the door revealed nothing within immediate view. I glanced to the clock by the bed, 7:08. The sun had yet to burn away the misty fog and it floated thickly through the forest like a lake covering the undergrowth. The moist haze dampened sound and limited sight as I tried moving closer to the window for a better look.

Steven's door was closed and I assumed he was still asleep. Whatever Dog heard must not have been very loud or I felt certain Steven would have been awakened. We never had unplanned company on the mountain. I seriously doubted Ben and Kathy could have arrived so early, having to travel from Cherokee to Roan High Bluff. The trip would have taken several hours. It was possible, I just thought it was much too early.

I slowly moved my hand towards the barrel bolt on the door and gradually, very softly, slid the bolt from the catch. The doorknob turned smoothly and quietly, and I gently began to open the door with my left hand. I held the powerful handgun ready in my right.

The thick morning fog and the mesh screen of the door kept me from seeing much in the surrounding forest. The trees were so thick around the cabin; very little morning sunlight seeped through the deep foliage. The screened door opened outward, and for the life of me I couldn't remember the last time I had oiled it. I was afraid it would make too much noise if I tried to ease it open. After some debate, I decided the best course of action would be to exit quickly and take my chances. For a moment I thought I heard the soft rustle of fabric against fabric, then…nothing. Dog hadn't moved a muscle. I motioned for her to stay, mentally counted to three and turned my back towards the door, cradling my gun in both hands. I inhaled deeply and jumped against the screen door, almost tearing it from the hinges. I rolled my body out onto the small front porch, quickly scanning left to right, panning with the gun as I moved. On the right side of the porch, sat the origin of all my trouble, and in more ways than one.

The early morning haze painted an eerie, soft background. The dew-covered, emerald green of the forest was muted, and somewhat out of focus. Sitting ten feet away from me, in one of the old rockers, was a vision from the distant past, like a painting on a museum wall. In the chair sat the most beautiful woman I have ever seen, her long black hair cascading down her back, thick and luxurious, the color of a raven's wings in the early afternoon sun. Glistening drops of moisture had settled in her hair adding a silky shine. Her body was cloaked from neck to foot with an old Indian blanket; its deep red and blue pattern a startling contrast to the surrounding soft pastels. As she turned her face slowly, regally, almost arrogantly, in my direction, I observed striking features with a smooth complexion the color of an old penny. I was being afforded the rare pleasure of viewing a true Indian princess from years gone by, full of beauty and grace. I slowly lowered the weapon to my side and the vision spoke to me, breaking the spell she had cast upon me.

"Are you going to shoot me now, Morgan Roberts?" Her voice was low and musical, filled with just a touch of mischief.

I replied hesitantly, "No, Kathy, I think I'll spare you just this one time." I looked down, suddenly embarrassed at the gun in my hand, and stuck it in the waistband of the shorts near the small of my back. When I realized it wouldn't hold the gun, I placed the weapon on the wide, porch rail. "What are you doing here so early? We didn't expect to see you until around ten or later. You must have gotten up before the sun."

She responded in the same even unhurried tone, "Well, neither one of us could sleep, so we got up around four and just drove on up." She looked towards me, but not at me, as she spoke, "Grandfather stopped the truck about a hundred yards down the road to get some things from the woods he needed and I decided to walk up ahead. He still won't drive on the road, but I convinced him to drive the rest of the way up when he's finished." She looked away, "I wanted to see you alone before we drew a crowd."

"Great, that's just great," I replied, not sure if I meant it or not. She kept her face averted and it allowed me to review the familiar profile I hadn't seen in nearly two years. The distinctive cinnamon skin could only have belonged to a full-blooded Cherokee. Her coloration accented the features of her face, which might have been called plain or average by some without the proud badge of her heritage. The long black mane of hair and the beautiful dark eyes added to her beauty. She may not have been attractive to all the men in the world, but she was to me. Of course, I may have been a little biased.

The uncomfortable silence was broken as Steven came onto the porch, gun in hand, rubbing sleep from his eyes, "What the hell's going on? Can't a guy get some sleep around here?" He had obviously heard her before he exited the living room. He joked and held his gun loose and relaxed by his side. "Hello, Kathy. What's up?"

"Good morning, Steven." She smiled as she spoke her tone much more friendly with him than me. "If you must know, I got here a little ahead of Grandfather; he'll be along in a minute or two, I suppose." She looked at him with a steady gaze telling him something he wasn't hearing.

"You two must have got up before the chickens to get here this early. What are you trying to do, get yourself shot or something?"

She ignored his question and asked one of her own, "Steven, I love you and all that, but don't you think I came ahead of my grandfather for a reason?"

Steven hesitated, "Okay…sure…" He looked from her to me and back again before it finally sank in. "Oh yeah, sorry. I think I'll go turn the generator on, and get dressed. I'll just use the back door? How's that?" Somewhat embarrassed, he continued, "Morg, you want me to take this worthless dog with me and get her out of the way too?"

"Yeah, I think she could use a trip out back," then to Dog, "Go with him girl." She rose without question and followed Steven as he closed the door in their wake

I stood in the same spot as if rooted, unable to move or speak, or make eye contact with Kathy. Not a single word of what I planned so carefully to say came out. I didn't know how to begin.

Kathy rose from the chair, removed the old blanket, folded it methodically, and placed it in the seat. She turned and slowly walked towards me across the porch, stopping in front of me, our bodies almost touching. She raised her head slightly to look into my eyes; her moist brown orbs sparkling like amber crystals. Memories flooded my mind, her proximity and the familiar look caused me to recall way too much of our past. The familiar scent of her perfume washed over me, light and sensuous. Her look softened somewhat, and then she, matter-of-factly, slapped me hard across the face. I saw her open hand coming and could have easily stopped it, but I didn't. I knew the stinging force of the blow was going to leave a small imprint of her fingers on my cheek. It was that hard a slap.

She looked at me with a blank expression before turning back to her chair. Without speaking, she picked up the blanket and wrapped it around her again. She sat back down as if nothing had happened.

"Thanks," I said, reaching up to rub my cheek, purposely and prideful, waiting until she looked away before I did.

"You're welcome." She replied. I thought I saw a very slight smile on her profile. "You damned sure deserved it."

"No argument there."

At that moment, I heard an awful scraping noise from just around the first curve of the road. A second or two later, a late model Ford Bronco came into view. The truck hesitated and bucked, and would abruptly come to a stop every fifteen or twenty foot, before lurching ahead with a great rushing of the motor. I turned to Kathy with a questioning look.

She responded, "I said I convinced him to drive, I didn't say he was any good at it." She smiled and continued, "Don't think this gets you out of anything, I fully intend to finish our little conversation."

"I have no doubt about that." I rubbed my face and tried to smile, "I sure hope we speak in a different language the next time. I don't think my body can stand much more of your talking to me the way you have been lately."

"Don't try to be cute with me, Morgan." She countered, just as the Bronco came to a sliding stop, bare inches from the rear bumper of my old truck.

An old man, instantly recognizable as a Native American, exited the truck with a dramatic flourish. Ben "Rising Wolf" Walker was a Cherokee Indian medicine man, or "shaman", perhaps the last of a breed. He was about five feet seven, one hundred fifty pounds, with a face like badly tanned leather and hair the color of gray sweat pants. Nobody knew for sure how old the man was and he wouldn't tell, and it was always best not to push Ben on anything he didn't want to say.

He slammed the truck door, walked to the front of the vehicle with his hands on his hips and mumbled something in Cherokee I couldn't understand. After a time, he kicked the left front wheel of the truck with exaggerated venom and it seemed to make him happier.

During the little escapade, Kathy turned to me and asked, "Do you have a TV up here that works?"

"Yeah, but it only gets Asheville and Knoxville, and those two stations aren't very plain. Why?"

"You'll see soon enough."

Ben turned from his attack on the truck and walked towards the porch. He wore faded black jeans, boots, an old white dress shirt buttoned to the neck, and a string tie. In one hand he carried the traditional insignia and tool of his trade, an old gourd medicine rattle. His long gray hair was tied back in a ponytail, the rawhide strips hanging down his back woven with beads of red and yellow and white.

"Morgan, it's been a long time. How are you?" His voice was strong and confident; it never wavered in my memory.

I took his hand and the grip was as strong as I remembered. "Just fine sir, and you?"

"Very well, thank you for asking." His response was polite but he seemed distracted. He spoke, not in the typical Indian fashion people constantly stereotyped, but in a slow, well thought manner. He did, however, limit his words and his use of needless adjectives or adverbs. He preferred the basics of language, but not because he wasn't aware of the use; I heard some remarkable things stated by the man. Ben still considered English his second language and he always would, but he just liked things simple. He was very well read in English though, even other languages. I had heard him quote, verbatim, some of the great minds of the past, Plato, Suzuki, even Nietzsche. Behind the mask Ben presented to everyone, was a very intelligent mind, perhaps the most intelligent I had ever known. He was not easily fooled and there was little he didn't know something about. Still, it was a different kind of knowledge he possessed. Perhaps that was his special gift. His knowledge was as basic and simple as the rest of him.

Steven came around the corner and greeted the old man, "Good morning, Rising Wolf." He came forward to shake his hand and I marveled to myself at the respect in his tone and manner.

Ben shook his hand and said, "You smell like whiskey." He cast a sideglance in my direction. "You both smell like whiskey."

Steven lowered his eyes like a kid caught with his hand in the cookie jar. "Yessir, I know." I couldn't believe what I was seeing. I expected him to lower his head and kick at the dirt at any moment. Some giant he was. Perhaps Steven had changed even more than I thought.

"Good, that means you can sweat it out later in the "asi". For now, I need two things. One, I need for you," he pointed at Steven, "to go to the hot house and prepare it for later. We will need some wild parsnip from the forest and wood for the fire." Steven nodded as Ben turned to me; "Do you think I might be able to borrow your television? I have already missed the early part of Good Morning America." He smiled at me and his expression made me think of that of a child for an instant, "Did you know Tom Selleck will be on in the second hour today?"

"No, I sure didn't." I tried not to laugh.

"Yes, should be on in just a few minutes." Then as an aside, he whispered, "You know I don't know about you, but I really miss Magnum

P.I. I think they took it off the air much too soon. Watching the reruns is just not the same."

"Well, to tell the truth, Ben, I never thought much about it, but of course you can use the set. The reception may not be too good, but you're welcome to it."

"That's all right, I already know what everyone looks like." His voice was serious but I knew he was being funny. His sense of humor was as different as his intelligence.

"Come on in and I'll hook you up." I said, smiling at his remarks.

"Also, I would like to see your grandfather's book."

"Yessir, I'll get that for you as well."

Steven left immediately to do the things Ben had instructed. He stopped just long enough to retrieve his shirt and boots from the bedroom and he was gone. I turned the television set on for Ben and he settled in front of the small picture. Kathy stood just outside the door and watched her grandfather through the screen. She hadn't said a word since his arrival.

I went to my room and retrieved the book from the dresser. The old leather-covered manuscript was wrapped in a piece of heavy black cloth. The book was thick; the pages dry and brittle with the passing of time. I had looked inside when I first retrieved it; the age-yellowed pages were torn and smudged in places and the writing in the older sections had almost faded away with the years. I couldn't read the manuscript, of course, but I could almost feel the care and research that had gone into its creation. I had no idea how old the book must be, but it appeared to have been written by three or four different hands, the last recognizable to me—my grandfather's.

I carried the old book almost reverently into the living room where Ben sat, engrossed with a weather report for the greater Denver area. When I started to speak, he held up his hand for silence.

I looked to Kathy who first glanced at her watch, then held her fingers an inch apart, asking me to wait. I sat down in the chair beside Ben and learned that the day would be beautiful and clear, in Denver anyway, and then Joan Lunden told us, "in the next hour" a leading child psychologist would advise us on how to deal with temper tantrums in two-year-olds. Immediately after, the snowy screen image on the small set changed to a woman telling us how wonderful it was to find relief from feminine itching; if we would only buy her product we could find out for ourselves.

The commercial came on and Ben immediately extended his hand for the book. I gave it to him and watched as he carefully removed the cloth and took the book in his hands without opening it.

"You know, it's very rare for one shaman to read the works of another." His tone was respectful and subdued, "We have always been very careful to keep secrets even from our own kind. I want you to know that I respect this work of your grandfather's and will return it to you as soon as we have finished." He looked seriously into my eyes, his old wrinkled face concerned and anxious.

"That's okay, Ben. I didn't even know about this book until Steven told me about it. You have every right to read it; I'm sure my grandfather wouldn't have minded."

I got an impression, by the fleeting look that touched his features, that I had said something wrong, but I didn't have a clue what it was. I quickly tried to repair the damage, "I mean he never really said who he intended the book to go to anyway, he died so suddenly. I guess my father just packed it away and forgot about it."

He stared down at the tattered manuscript, tracing invisible lines on the worn, leather cover with his aged fingers. Someone on the TV tried to sell us fabric softener, using a little teddy bear to get the point across.

"I think maybe we will get it back to the one he intended when we are finished." Then before I could respond, Good Morning America resumed and he again turned his full attention to the set, his old, wrinkled face deep in concentration. His expression changed so quickly I couldn't believe we were having a conversation just seconds before.

Kathy motioned from the doorway and I followed her out as she walked off the porch and stopped a few paces from the stream.

"It's useless to talk to him while his programs are on. You can catch him during commercials, but other than that you just have to wait." She laughed at my expression and continued, "I can tell you've been away from him too long. He's still lost in his own little world sometimes, but that's just the way he is. People think he's crazy as a loon, until they need something from him. After a while, you learn to just go along with him and it works out much better that way, believe me. I don't think he's ever going to change." She turned from me and stared at the rushing water of the stream, "Just like some other people I know."

She had left her blanket on the porch and I noticed she wore jeans, a faded denim shirt and soft suede boots. Her jet-black hair reached below her belt. She hadn't changed. She was still as beautiful as I remembered, and just as feisty.

The cascading murmur of the mountain stream sounded as loud as a busy highway in the uncomfortable quiet between us. I searched my mind frantically for just the right thing to say, and lamely came up with, "You look really great Kathy." Not too good I admit, but the best I could muster at the moment.

She looked at me for a second or two, the look on her face confirming I had failed to find the right phrase, then she replied, "Yeah, well, there are more wrinkles everyday, but I suppose I'm older and wiser. Isn't that what everyone says about age?"

"I don't know about wiser, but I'm definitely older anyway, and getting older by the minute. I guess that beats hell out of the alternative." I picked up a hand full of rocks and began tossing them into the water. I was acting like a twelve-year-old but I couldn't stop myself. "How have you been? Still teaching? I heard you were going to get married," trying too hard to casually work in the last remark.

"Boy, if you're trying to be subtle you're failing miserably." At least the comment brought a faint smile to her lips. "Yes, I'm still teaching at the high school, but we're out for the summer. I don't start back for a few weeks yet. Yes, I thought about getting married, even said yes, then changed my mind. That's my prerogative, you know."

"Yeah, it always has been." I said it, and regretted it almost immediately.

"Right," she smirked, "look who's talking. In answer to your next question, no, I am not still in love with him…I don't think I ever really was. Anymore questions?"

"As a matter of fact, yes."

"Well forget about them." She stepped close to me again. I could smell the light flowery scent of her perfume. She looked up at me, "I do not intend to begin explaining my life to you. And do you know why?"

"I think I've got a good idea, yeah," I replied, holding her gaze as best I could.

"Damned right, you have a good idea." Her brown eyes blazed with anger, an anger I had caused. "I have no intention of telling you anything until you start explaining some things to me." She shook her head; "Not that it's going to make a bit of difference. I mean, we can be friends until this is over." She raised her voice; "You don't have to explain what you did. I know you obviously don't care to. If you did, you would have had the common courtesy to explain it to me two years ago when you shut me out without a word."

She poked me in the chest with her finger, a little harder than I would have liked, "You put me through hell, left me high and dry with no explanations. I mean, what the hell was I suppose to think, Morgan? I thought you had finally lost that damned chip you've been carrying around half your life and then everything just fell apart." She stepped away from me, leaving a few feet of dead space between us. "Now, I need to know how we're going to proceed from here. We have to work together. We can be cordial and deal with the problems at hand and just be "buddies" like we used to be. You just have to tell me how you want to play it, Morgan." She pointed to me as she talked, "You've got to make a decision, and I know how you just hate that, but hey, life isn't always fair." Her icy stare challenged me; almost daring me to question what she had said.

"Look, Kathy, I fully intend to explain everything to you, just give me a little time, okay?" I shrugged, "I'm sorry. I'm sorry about everything. Hell, I'm sorry for things you don't even know about, but I can't lay it all out for you right this very minute. I mean this is not exactly the best time and place." I couldn't touch her eyes with mine. I found a pine tree over her right shoulder and stared at it—something I hated when others did it to me.

"Morgan, with you there's never a good time or place to talk about things. There's always something in the way. Just let me tell you this, I know we've got some very important things going on now, but I'm telling you, and only once; I will not go another night without you explaining to me what the hell happened! If you don't find time in your busy schedule to tell me today, then I'll assume you're never going to and that will be that. I won't ever bring it up again. I will, however, continue to believe that you are the biggest asshole I have ever known. How's that for a deal?" Her look left little doubt to her seriousness.

I finally managed to meet her eyes; "I think that's fair enough."

We continued to stare at each other for several moments, neither of us backing down. Then one of us, and I wasn't sure which, cracked just a slight smile. The smiles grew bigger until we both laughed at the absurdity of the situation.

I finally spoke to her, "Damn, woman, you could always bring out the weird side of my personality."

"Morgan Roberts, every side of your personality is weird." She laughed until she remembered something and then her expression changed somewhat abruptly, "Morgan, I'm sorry about Jordan. I really am." Her brown eyes softened and glistened with a familiar light I realized I still loved and probably always would.

"Yeah, me too." I resumed tossing rocks into the stream. "It's funny, you know how I felt about the little twerp, but his dying really shook me. Something about his death—maybe it's because I was there and couldn't prevent it, or maybe it's this whole screwed-up situation. Hell, I don't know. I'm confused. I can't accept anything that has happened in the last few days and I'm mad as hell someone would kill him so easily for some insane reason that he didn't even know. Something about it bothers me in a way I don't quite understand." I paused for a second and something about her eyes told me she was remembering what the death of my parents had brought about in me. Deep behind those brown orbs was the faintest touch of fear, perhaps apprehension, and that hurt worse than anything she could have said did.

"I understand what you're saying Morgan. I don't understand all this killing anymore than you do. The whole thing is really weird; especially when Grandfather knew all this stuff was going to happen beforehand. The fact that he predicted this whole mess made it that much crazier. I don't know what's real and what's not anymore."

I leaned on the fender of my truck and crossed my arms, "Well, let me tell you this, whoever killed my brother was real. That son-of-a-bitch is more real than anything I've ever seen. It was no myth. I've not seen anything like it in my life. I have no earthly idea where to go from here."

"Morgan, I don't think anyone could know at this point. I do think you need to let Grandfather read the old book and see if it holds anything that might be a clue. If there's anything in there that will help; he'll find it. He'll try to help anyway he can, this whole mess has a lot of people really concerned."

She moved closer and leaned beside me on the truck, but not close enough for our bodies to touch. "There has been much discussion about this up here over the last several weeks. The more deaths that occur, the worse it gets. All the tribal elders keep coming to visit grandfather for advice and it bothers him that he can't supply answers. Of course, the younger people don't believe in him anyway, but they are just as upset, that's for sure. As more and more people hear about the killings, talk and conjecture spread like wildfire. Somebody has got to do something about this, and soon. Everyone is afraid the killer will come back to the mountains and they don't know what to do. They have no faith in our illustrious government or the local police force, such that it is. They have nowhere to turn, so they just sit, wait and worry. Grandfather got tired of that and sent Steven to find you and the book in hopes of uncovering some answers. He had no where else to turn. For the first time, I honestly think he's questioning his own abilities and his faith."

I saw the worry etched in her features.

"No one else can see it, but I do," she continued, "and I don't like it. I hope he finds something to stop this madness for all our sakes." She looked away and almost whispered, "Especially for him."

"All I know is this asshole is going to pay for what he's done if I have anything to do with it. I'm tired of this shit already and I've only known about it for a few days. The question is, where do we go from here?"

"Well, well." She almost smiled, "Listen to Mr. Macho here. What happened to that "show no emotion" oriental crap you're always spouting?"

"Time changes lots of things." I said it too quickly, and without thinking.

"Yeah, you're right." Again, her voice nearly a whisper.

The silence between us again lengthened. Kathy turned away, her voice becoming suddenly cheerful and light. She had the ability to flip a switch on her emotions and it was a trait I greatly envied. "Well, grandfather gave me a list of things that he thought we might need. I think you should run down the mountain and pick them up. That will give him time to see what's in the book and Steven time to do his penance. What do you think?"

"Sure, I need to make a phone call or two. You want to ride down with me? It will give us time to talk."

"Are you kidding me? If you think I'm going to pass up the opportunity to find out why you screwed up both our lives, you've lost your mind. Hell yes I'm going with you!" She glanced down at her watch before she continued, "Look, it's almost time for a commercial break, I'll go inside and tell him we're going. You go tell Steven." She spun on her boot and headed towards the cabin without waiting for a response, knowing I would comply.

"God you're a bossy woman!" I called after her.

"Yeah, but that's one of the things you love most about me and you know it!"

I chuckled to myself and turned away. The funny thing was, she was right.

CHAPTER FIFTEEN

The pick-up truck rattled down the steep incline in low gear, the worn engine complaining at the snails pace necessary to control our descent down the mountainside. The sun rose higher in the morning sky, bringing with it the blue for which Carolina was so well known. Something about the smell of the misty woods suggested a possibility of an afternoon rain as the deep green of the forest passed by inches from the open windows, so close you could reach out and touch tree branches. Kathy leaned her head slightly out the passenger window, and looked over the edge at the steep drop of the road before us. The deep cutbacks twisted and turned like garland around a Christmas tree. Without them there would be no way to get a vehicle up the mountain. The sweat of my ancestor's brow, a couple of mules and a drop bucket had carved the road.

"I like it better going up and down at night; then you can't see how far you'd fall if you screw up."

Kathy spoke for the first time since our departure, pulling me from my thoughts. I laughed at her joke and for a time we settled into comfortable small talk as if nothing had happened between us—how was her job? Mine? Normal, almost meaningless things, staying well away from the subjects at hand. I knew her and I knew she was dancing around something and I knew what that something was, but I just sort of followed her lead as she rambled.

After a time we settled back to silence as the brisk morning air blew freely through the cab and seemed to demand a respectful silence for the pure pleasure of the experience. The moist air was like a cool caress, touched with the lingering musk of the morning dew as it evaporated and rose from the undergrowth. The trees around the truck sometimes looked as if they were growing from the mist that completely hid the forest floor in low, shady spots. It was almost cool enough for a long sleeve shirt, but not quite. It was the kind of mountain morning that made you appreciate life more and your problems less. The peacefulness washed over your soul taking at least a portion of your mortal concerns as it went. It was hard to be worried or stressed when you were traveling through a living post card; the sights, sounds, and atmosphere better with each turn of the road.

In the mountain forest there were no horns, sirens, sounds of the highway, hustle or bustle. Here there were only the safe, quiet sounds of the deep woods. Animals scurried from our path as we approached. The trees were filled with birds of all kinds, their calls distinguishable in the early budding of the coming day. The robin, finch, bobwhite and the occasional call of the whippoorwill, echoed through the forest along with the determined tapping of a woodpecker. My grandfather used to say there was nothing more beautiful than an early morning cardinal perched on a blossoming dogwood tree. I remembered my grandfather, and his words, most on such mountain mornings. He and I had walked every inch of that mountain together. Those times were the most pleasant ones I remember, and such mornings, unfortunately, hurt my heart in a faint and far off sort of way. I looked at Kathy and smiled and she smiled back, still not saying anything and that was all right with me as I turned back to the rocky, bumpy road.

Dog rode in the bed of the truck and moved from side to side, catching the breeze in her fur. She growled or barked at the occasional mountain squirrels in the nearby trees if she thought they were too slow moving from the path of "her truck". Before Kathy and I left, I fed Dog a quick breakfast and tried to get her to stay behind and it did little good. Dog remembered Kathy, of course, and as they played and jostled each other, I knew there would be few places while she was around that Dog wouldn't want to follow along. Dog had found her "puppy" playmate after a two-year separation. It had taken the big shepherd a moment or two, but as soon as Kathy spoke, she went right to her and almost knocked her down trying to get in her lap as she had done as a pup.

As I watched them play, I caught myself laughing for the first time in days, for the first time since the whole nightmare had started with Steven's visit to Charleston. I hadn't seen Kathy since before "my trouble" and subsequent discharge from the Army. I knew I had hurt her and I knew I never meant to but that didn't matter. In the end, there was only me to blame despite the assurances of my Army "shrink" otherwise. We are all victims or our actions and I, most assuredly, was a victim of mine.

It was only when I watched Kathy and Dog play together before we left, that I realized just how much I had missed her. Her laughter touched me in a place long forgotten, from a time when I was another man, in another lifetime.

I tried to concentrate on my driving instead of my past, as I carefully maneuvered the narrow curves of the rocky dirt road. Kathy watched me as her long black hair blew out the window. I could see it fluttering softly behind like a banner as I glanced in her side mirror. She had leaned her head back on the seat and closed her eyes, allowing the morning breeze to wash over her like a shower. She and I had grown up together playing and running through the forests of the Appalachian Mountains. I knew her love of the forest was probably more intense than mine, maybe even greater than Steven's.

With Kathy, it had always been more of mythical love than it was respect. Steven and I had both grown up respecting the woods and the power, the rewards and the dangers to be found within. We hunted and explored with our fathers, our friends, and alone. Kathy was different;

she actually preferred to walk through the woods by herself, shunning company on occasion. She definitely knew the forest and could survive if she had too, but she never really cared to learn all the things about the forest, the hidden aspects or the adventure. She preferred to love the woods just for the incredible beauty they held. She felt the forest was a continuously changing painting we had been given to exist within. With her it was a gift, and I think that is why she had always been so active with ecological issues over the years.

Once again, it may have been the Cherokee in her, that caused her to love the land, which had been literally stolen from her people, nearly two hundred years past. Whatever it was that pushed her, she believed in fighting to keep the mountain land clean and pure, untouched by the greed and uncleanness of modern society.

Kathy was very active in local political issues and was chairperson of numerous committees representing the beliefs of both Cherokee and non-Cherokee in such matters. To her, it was the responsibility of all humans to protect the world and maintain the precious gift for future generations; she didn't give a damn about what one's skin color might be. She was never hesitant in vocalizing her beliefs and reasoning to anyone who questioned her motives or actions. She had acquired the reputation of being a well-educated, very outspoken young woman. Within the political tribal functions she had gained much respect and was thought of very highly by the current governing officials and elders of the Eastern Cherokee. It was not unusual for Cherokee women to hold positions of power within the tribe, at present or historically. Kathy accepted her heritage, worked hard for herself and her people, and was generally happy with life. I envied her for that.

Such thoughts made me again realize the sacrifice she made on my behalf when I had asked her to leave her mountain home and move with me to Fayetteville, North Carolina. When she agreed to move with me to Fort Bragg, and try once again to work things out, I was shocked. I think I might never have asked had I even remotely thought she would say yes. If nothing else, I would never doubt her compassion for me at that moment in our lives. She had to love me to leave her paradise, and she had said "yes" without hesitation and done just that.

We had been very happy for awhile, happier than I had ever been. I had finally dealt with the deaths of my parents and was committed to resuming the road my life had taken, or so I thought. I had all the tools to be happy, and once again, I blew it. My life, as it had done time and time again in the past, took a radically different, and most unexpected, turn.

After my mother's funeral, I returned to Ft. Bragg and altered my living arrangements, moving off base to allow Kathy to join me. We settled into the normal day to day routine of the happily married couple, only with the absence of ceremony and a license.

Kathy interrupted my thoughts, "Well, at least it's a pretty day."

I looked at her appreciatively and commented, "Yeah, in here anyway."

She looked at me with a smirk and shook her head; "Boy you haven't changed, have you? Still think lines like that get you by with anything, do you?"

"I wasn't trying to "get by" with anything, I was just paying you a compliment that's all. God, talk about ungrateful! I was just trying to be nice."

"You want to know how you can be nice?"

"Yeah, yeah I do."

"Fine, then you answer a few questions for me."

With some hesitation, I replied, "Okay, shoot." I turned my head straight ahead, suddenly feeling the need to pay more close attention to the winding road in front of me.

"First question; why didn't you try to see me after all the trouble and explain to me what you did and why? Don't you think that was unfair as hell?"

I tried a smile, perhaps making one last unconscious, though valiant I thought, effort to change the subject, "That's two questions."

"Don't try to be funny, damn it! I don't think it's funny now, and I especially didn't think it was funny then. You think you can answer these questions without the comedian in you coming out, or not?" She was growing irritated with me again and that was not a good thing.

"I'm sorry, I didn't mean it to be funny. I was just trying to lighten the mood, that's all."

"Alright, my mood is now lightened. Can you answer the question?"

I let a few moments pass as I pretended to give the sharp curve I was navigating my undivided attention. I used the borrowed time to try to formulate a way of telling her one of the most embarrassing experiences of my life. Time didn't always make things any easier.

"Look Kath, I know what I did was shitty, but I had good reasons, at least to me, anyway."

"That's the point, Morgan, I just wanted to know why you got into trouble and then turned me away. I mean for God's sake, first I hear from a friend why you're late coming home; you've been arrested by the MPs and placed in the guardhouse and not allowed any visitors. I was told you had an "altercation" with another officer which would probably result in your court martial and all I got from you was a goodbye note!"

"Look, I told you I was sorry, what else can I do?"

"How many damn times do I have to ask, for Christ's sake? Just tell me what happened! It's as simple as that! I want to hear it from you."

Dog listened to the rising tempo of our voices, following our exchange from face to face with her head as if watching a tennis match.

I took a deep breath and purposely lowered my voice, "Okay Kathy, I'll tell you the whole thing, but I want you to promise me something first."

"You want me to promise you?" She sighed with exasperation, "Well isn't that just dandy?"

"Do you want to listen or not?"

"Fine, fine." She held up her right hand, "I do so promise."

I stopped the truck, turned off the ignition and faced her, "Come on, let's get out."

We both exited the cab and I went to the rear of the truck, dropped the old tailgate and positioned myself with my feet dangling over the edge. Kathy didn't join me; she walked a few feet away and sat on the steep bank by the truck, her back resting against a large red oak. Dog dropped heavily at my feet.

"I will tell you everything, but I want you to promise to listen to the whole thing without saying a word until I'm finished. I've only told this story to one other person, and I was forced into that. I know you don't understand, and I don't know if after I tell you, things will be any different, but I'll try. Okay?"

She nodded a silent agreement.

"That day I got up like always and went to the base. We had some jump training scheduled for that morning and I was observing some of the new recruits we had in the platoon. I had spoken to one of the new guys earlier on a couple of occasions. He was Vietnamese but came here early, years ago when he was about two. He joined the Army, then the Airborne, for the same reasons that a lot of men do, he wanted to prove he was a man, and to serve his country. Except with him, I think there were more reasons."

I stared at my boots as I talked, "He was shy and withdrawn, and had probably been that way all his life. I knew that America must not have been such a good place for a Vietnamese kid to grow up the last twenty years. He had to be blamed by a lot of people for things he had nothing to do with. I think he joined the service to prove he was part of things, to make people accept him as an American. I didn't know for sure, but I had gathered as much, speaking to him the few times I did. It was difficult to tell what he was really thinking; I couldn't ask him things, as I wanted. He was basically afraid of me. He was an enlisted man and I was a Captain, those hierarchy lines are hell to get around. Anyway, this fine sunny day I pass by and find that asshole of a Colonel, Jacobs just giving this boy pure hell in front of the full platoon."

I looked at Kathy, "I don't know whether you remember or not, but this is the same nitwit I had already had several run-ins with. That big son-of-a-bitch thought he was king of the world and always wanted everybody to know it."

Kathy said, "I remember him. He was that obnoxious guy in a drunken stupor who cornered me at the party in the officer's club that first week we were there, right?"

"Yep, one and the same. Anyway, I was used to people dressing these guys down; hell, I did it myself. It was all part of the process, the "army way"; you broke them down, then built them back up again as a team player. Bragg wasn't as bad as basic, at least not normally, but that kind of stuff still went on."

"This time, Jacobs was giving this little guy a really bad time. Of course, he was giving him crap about the most obvious things. He was telling him his people had killed his friends, even though I knew he wasn't even in the Army during the Vietnam War. He told him that he had no right being in the United States Army and should just save everyone a lot of time and trouble and just quit. Nothing really out of the ordinary, I guess; I just didn't particularly like it that day for some reason or another."

"I was walking with a couple of NCOs I knew pretty well, at least well enough to comment in front of them, as we stood and watched Jacobs screaming at the little guy at the top of his lungs. He towered over him by at least a foot and the poor kid seemed to shrink even smaller with every passing minute. From where I stood, I could see tears forming in his eyes as he tried to maintain his best military bearing. I asked the men if this had been going on for long. They looked at each other before they replied, and finally admitted Jacobs had been riding the kid non-stop since he arrived."

"I know you never knew or cared for the military, but that's not really what the whole thing's about. It was assholes like Jacobs that gave the service a bad rep, so I decided, foolishly I admit, that I would intervene. I don't know why, I just did. I mean, I even knew at the time it was not the right thing to do, but I stood there and watched as long as I could and then I walked up and politely asked if I might interrupt for just a moment."

"Jacobs stopped his raving and turned to me, obviously pissed off that I had the gall to interrupt his fun. The poor kid looked like he could have kissed me. Anyway, I asked Jacob if I might speak with him a minute and he decided to change his target. I guess he figured if I had the nerve to intervene, as a superior officer was giving some peon hell, then I deserved some of the same. I don't think it ever occurred to him that I might take offense, I don't think it ever occurred to me, really, but when he started shoving his finger into my chest and screaming at me, something snapped. I don't understand it to this day, so I can't really explain to you what happened next. The whole thing was so out of character for me, it didn't make any sense. It still doesn't."

I hesitated, getting to the hard part of the story, unsure how to continue explaining something I had yet to understand myself. "I asked him nicely to quit poking me with his finger and he sarcastically assured me that he would do what he damned well pleased, I was just a Captain and he was a Colonel and that was the deal, period. He shoved his finger even harder and put his nose almost to mine, and then...well...I..." I paused for a moment in my story, and the surrounding noises of the forest suddenly seemed quiet, as if the entire mountainside had stopped to listen to my tale of humiliation. I glanced at Kathy and she was looking patiently at me, waiting for me to continue, but she didn't say a word.

"The next thing I knew something inside my head said; reach up and just break his finger. It was just that simple. I don't know why, I didn't even remember it as a conscious thought. It just came into my head. I felt...angry...only anger like I had never felt before in my life...it was rage...blind rage. One minute he was yelling in my face, the next he was holding his injured finger and looking at me with pure hatred and disbelief. He told me I was going to regret what I had done. He dropped back and aimed a roundhouse kick at my head. Jacobs always thought he was a tough Karate guy, you know the type. I saw the kick coming and easily could have done several things to stop it peacefully but I didn't. For the same reasons I don't understand, my mind said hurt him and that's what I did. Almost without thinking, I shifted my weight and kicked his support leg hard, right in the kneecap. I heard the cartilage shatter and I regretted it as soon as I did it, but..." I once again looked at Kathy, "...but, in a strange way—in a way I didn't want to admit—it felt good—and it only fueled the anger. I know it was wrong, but I was glad I had hurt him. I wanted to rip his heart out right there on the tarmac. Something came over me I hadn't felt before. I remember looking down into his face as he lay there on the ground, holding his knee with both hands and moaning in pain, I remember him looking at me and I remember smiling, and I said, "Whoops." That's all I said. Then I just did manage to turn around and walk away."

I stopped and looked at Kathy and admitted something I had yet fully to accept myself, "I think I would have killed him, Kath. If he had said one more word...I...I...don't know what I would have done. The anger I felt was so great, my hands shook and I could think of nothing else but putting them around his throat as a way to make them stop. It was all I could do to turn away." I shook my head, "Of course, when the witnesses testified later to what I said and the way I looked, it sort of sealed my doom. To make a long story short, I screwed up big time. I was arrested and formal proceedings were announced and things just got worse from there."

Kathy didn't say anything, but from the look in her eyes, I knew what she was thinking. I got off the tailgate and walked aimlessly around the rocky road. I kicked a rock with my boot, aiming it towards a tree by the road and missing badly. I wandered slightly ahead of Kathy's resting-place and turned my back to her, looking up the old road we had just came down.

"A couple of months passed while I waited for the court martial and the rage came again and again. During those months, I couldn't stop myself from attacking a shrink and hospital orderly on two separate occasions. The anger would come from nowhere and just…just consume me. There seemed nothing I could do about it—no way I could control it. It was strange, Kath. Anyway, they appointed me this lawyer type, a pretty slick guy really. We talked about what happened, about my life, my past, my father and my mother's death, and he decided to plea bargain."

I hesitated once again, this time purposely not looking at her. I kept my head turned away, "The bottom line; I was offered an honorable discharge if I would undergo six months of psychiatric treatment and voluntarily resign my commission. I said yes. I couldn't deal with what I felt that day, it…it scared me…it still scares me. It still comes and goes even now. It makes me think crazy thoughts and do crazy things for almost no reason." I looked back to her, "I mean it's a lot better now and I think I've got a handle on it…but…" I let the rest trail off. It seemed to me after I completed the embarrassing revelation, all sound in the forest stopped yet again, just like on the old cowboy movies when the bad guy walked through the swinging doors of the saloon.

"As for that lame note I sent you, it was all I could manage at the time. I was upset with myself, and I didn't want anyone to know what was going on, not even you Kath. I had too much pride I guess, plus you know all the things I've always said about psychiatrists. I hate those bastards, and I was right too, they are a bunch of sanctimonious hypocrites."

"That's about the size of it, I did what they asked. I didn't want to drag you through all that bullshit. Maybe I was wrong to send you the letter and not see you, but at the time I wasn't thinking real straight, obviously. When I got out of their nut house, I moved down to Charleston, away from the people I knew the best, and just started my life all over again. I haven't even thought about these things…at least not very often." I tried my best to make the lie sound convincing.

I turned to her, looking into her brown eyes and trying to read her thoughts, "Kathy, the one thing I do know, the one and only thing I'm positive about is; I never meant to hurt you. I'm very sorry. I know that doesn't mean anything now, and this whole mess probably sounds like a crock of shit, but I can't change the things I did. Believe me, I would if I could. I don't expect you to forgive me, I just hope that we can at least be friends. I don't have too many of those, and you've been closer to me than anyone for so long, I don't want to lose that, too. I know I've blown any chance of us being anything more, but please, just forgive me enough to stay around when this whole thing is over?"

I walked up to where she had been sitting and looked down at the top of her head. She didn't look up to meet my eyes; she just extended her hand to be helped up.

As I pulled her to her feet, she looked briefly into my face and quickly moved past me towards the truck. I thought, but I wasn't certain, that she might have been trying to hide a tear.

She called over her shoulder, "Will you please call that dog of yours and get in the damn truck, we haven't got all day, you know." She opened the door on her side and slammed it dramatically, not looking towards me or commenting in any other way.

"Dog!" I yelled, and she came running from the brush she had wandered into on the up hill side of the road. "Get in." After she jumped up into the cab, I slid behind the wheel and moved to start the engine.

When I couldn't stand it any longer, I turned to Kathy and asked, "Well?"

Without looking away from the road ahead she responded, "Drive, just drive, okay?"

We rode the rest of the way down the mountain in silence.

CHAPTER SIXTEEN

Marilyn answered the phone, like always, on the third ring. "Robert's Cycles, may I help you?"

"Yep, sure can. What's up?"

"Yessir, what can I do for you?" Her voice kept a courteous but impersonal tone.

"Alright, what are you up to, gorgeous?"

"No sir, he's not here right now. Can someone else help you?"

I paused before I replied, finally understanding, "Someone's there right? The FBI?"

"Yessir, that's right." She replied brightly, "We do indeed carry that parts line. Would you like to place an order?"

"Is it a little dweeb of a guy? Polo glasses, GQ look?"

"No sir." She used her best customer service voice.

"Okay, can you call me back when they leave?"

"Sure, I would be more than happy to do that sir. What's the make and model of your bike?"

I could see her in my mind, pencil poised over the composition book she took all her notes in, "If you can call me back in the next fifteen minutes or so, I'll be here;" and I gave her the number of the pay phone. As I spoke, I could see my truck where Kathy sat patiently waiting, Dog nuzzling her through the open back window. The glass of the phone booth was dirty, the floor littered with cigarette butts and trash. An empty soda can was beside the phone, a couple of bees humming around the opening.

"I don't think that will be a problem at all sir, I'll get right on it and you should have your part within the week. I'll call you as soon as it gets here, okay?" She dripped southern charm and I knew the guys watching her had to be eating it up.

"Did I ever tell you, you're as smart as you are sexy?"

"Why thank you sir, its just part of my job." Her voice hinted at humor, but I knew the people with her would never notice.

"Alright Beauty, I'll talk to you in a few minutes."

"Very good sir, and sir..." she paused for effect, "...have a nice day."

"You are such a smart ass," I said, and hung up the phone.

I returned to the truck and told Kathy about the FBI. While I waited for the phone to ring we talked about the day, the weather, nothing important. We had driven to Bakersfield, and the nearest phone, maybe twenty minutes away once we reached the main paved road. It was a small mountain village on the southernmost tip of Pisgah National Forest. It was a small town, not much more than a few stores, gas station and a barbershop, but it was the closest civilization to the cabin.

The phone rang and I managed to answer it before the third ring, "Yeah," I said into the receiver.

"Hello, is this 1-900-Dial-a-man?" Her voice was husky and deep. "Do you have something in a 42 long, say six foot, blonde, blue eyes? You know the type, no brains but pure hell in the sack?"

"Will you stop with all this sex stuff? You trying to embarrass me, Marilyn, or just make me jealous?" I chuckled into the phone.

"That'll be the day! How's it going, Morg?"

"Not bad, Marilyn. We had some visitors, did we?"

"Yeah. It was just great! I got to play my dumb southern girl part and you know how I love that. "What-little ol' me? No, I haven't the foggiest idea where that Morgan is. You know he never tells me anything any-more! I just don't know what I'm going to do with him." She feigned a syrupy, southern accent. "I just batted my eyes, played the dumb blonde thing to the hilt and leaned over every once in awhile so they could get a better look down my blouse. I just know they're in the car right now telling each other how obvious it is why you hired me. They probably think you're a leech." She laughed, "And I guess they're pretty much right if you think about it."

"Okay, don't start, I don't have time for any of your crap right now. What's the deal?"

"Yessir, master. I'll just tell you right now, master." And she moved from her kidding voice to her serious business voice. Her mind remembered each detail like a good homicide detective. "There were two guys, Agents Davis and Anderson. Anderson was big; six four, two, maybe two hundred-twenty pounds, not real bright, wore scuffed wing tips and sat in his chair and did nothing but listen and stare at my chest."

"Can't say as I blame him there." I interrupted.

"Excuse me, but do you want to talk about these guys or my tits?"

"Now that's not a very fair choice."

"Look, you're the one that's in such a hurry. The other guy, Davis, was pretty sharp, almost as big, but not nearly as stupid. Dark hair, heavy northern accent, maybe Boston, definitely Ivy League type, I would say he was probably a Yale man. They both had on dark blue suits and button down white shirts. They looked sort of like matching book ends."

I started to interrupt again.

"Hush now. They wanted to know if I knew where you were, said their boss needed your help with a very important investigation. I tried the "Oh my how impressive! What do you ever mean?" more of the slow southern bell routine, but I didn't get very far. They were pretty closed-mouthed about the whole thing. Then they started with all the questions; When had I seen you last? Would you call in? Did you go away like this very often? Did I know if anyone was with you or did you mention where you were going? Of course, they harped on that one. This guy Davis kept trying to trip me up, so I just got dumber and dumber as the questions just sort of overwhelmed poor little old me."

"That'll be the day." Before she could respond, I interrupted again, "I hope you didn't over do it, if this guy was as good as you say…"

"Will you give me a break here? I said he was sharp, yeah, but he is a man, after all. It's not like he's intelligent or anything a woman of the world can't handle. I mean get real!"

I cleared my throat impatiently.

"Alright already! Anyway, they stayed for awhile, asked a few questions around the shop, and that was about it. They wanted to look through your things upstairs."

"Oh that's just great."

"Don't worry. I said; "You know I don't really know a whole lot about law stuff and all, but didn't I see on TV where you needed some kinda' paper thing to do that, some kinda' legal thing, wasn't it a warrant or something like that?" They sorta' looked at each other and rolled their eyes and shook their heads. It was really kind of fun."

"Look Marilyn, you've got to take this seriously."

"Alright Morgan, I was just picking at you. For God's sake can't a girl have a little fun?" She snorted, "When they got ready to leave, they gave me this number of the regional headquarters in Charlotte they set up for their investigation. Their boss is this guy Smith you told me about and he's already in Charlotte. They wrote down a message I was supposed to give you if you called in or showed up, I guess they figured I was too stupid to remember it."

"Boy, if they only knew."

"Wow, that sounded almost, just almost, like a compliment—anyway, that's the way I'm taking it." I heard the rustle of paper as she continued, "The note basically says to call Smith at the number given. He says to tell you that he knows you can help each other. He has information that he feels sure you will find helpful and he's willing to exchange information, no strings attached."

"Yeah, right, I really believe that shit."

"Sounds to me like he really needs to talk to you though, doesn't it? The note says that he'll be available when you call anytime, night or day. If he's not there, he will have someone patch you through to him." She paused for a moment, "I think you should call him Morgan, this thing is getting really out of hand. I think you need help on this one, big guy."

I didn't answer her. I let the silence build.

She finally broke the standoff, "Okay, Mister Macho Superman, but you aren't invulnerable, you know. I'm not there to take care of you and we all know how much you need taking care of. You want me to come up?"

I looked towards the pick-up where Kathy had taken Dog off the back. They were playing ball by the grassy roadside. "No, I've got people here who can help me, I think. Look, don't worry, I'm going to call him just to see what he has to say. You just hang around there and mind the store, I promise I'll call if I need anything."

"Okay Morgan, but just be careful, alright? And don't brush me aside and tell me you will, because I know you won't. Is Steven still with you?"

"No. He's back at the cabin with an old friend of the family who's trying to help."

"Be sure and tell him I said hello, and don't let anything happen to him either. I sorta' like that guy."

"What the hell is it with you two for Christ's sake? I'm not a match-maker here!"

"Calm down Morgan, if you're jealous, just say so." Sometimes I think she lived just to needle me.

"I'm not jealous, damn it! I've just got more important things on my mind than your love life."

"Well, excuse me all to hell. You just go right ahead and get killed then, see if I care. I won't even miss you when you're gone."

"Liar." I replied with a laugh.

"Okay! Get off the phone now. I've got a business to run here in case you've forgotten. Somebody has to work around here and it's usually me. Sure as hell ain't you."

"Alright." I paused, "Thanks again, gorgeous."

"No problem. Keep your head down and call me when you can."

"Bye, Miss M." I cradled the phone and walked out to where Kathy and Dog were wrestling. Kathy was losing.

She looked up as I approached, "Well it's about time, I was beginning to wonder if you were going to be on the phone all day. My clothes were going out of style." Her smile was infectious and unexpected.

"At least you're giving me a hard time, that's an improvement anyway. Now, where's this list of things we're supposed to pick up?"

She handed me a scrap of paper with the list.

I read the short list and looked at her inquisitively, "I don't get it, what's this stuff? One bolt of black cloth, one bolt of red cloth…?"

"Look Morgan, I know you don't understand everything my grandfather does, but you need to humor him on this. It's important to Steven and it's important to him, and that means it's important to me, Okay?" Her brown eyes were beautiful as she defiantly met my gaze. "Even if you don't believe it, I want you to promise me you'll listen, at least listen, to whatever he has to say. If for no other reason, I want you to do it for me. Do you have a problem with that?"

"No, I don't have a problem with that." I held my hands up in surrender. "Hell, Steven had the same exact conversation with me just last night. You two must think I'm a total asshole."

She looked at me like she couldn't understand my point, "Well…yes. Doesn't everybody?"

"I guess we better go shopping, it sounds like I'm outnumbered on this. I'll agree to anything that gets you off my back."

We visited a few of the local stores and managed to get the items on the list rather quickly. As we walked back to the truck I told her, "I need to make just one more fast phone call. It'll only take a minute."

"Oh that's just great, you really know how to show a girl a good time Morgan. It's good to see you haven't lost your touch. I'll just wait in the truck with Dog; at least she seems to have genuinely missed me." She smiled at my expression, "Don't worry, I'm just kidding. We haven't been apart that long, can't you take a joke anymore?"

I returned the smile, "Sure, it's just that I wasn't sure what terms we were currently on, if you know what I mean. I don't know if you're going to slap me again at any moment or what."

She ignored my remark and turned serious, "Look Morgan, whatever problems you and I might be having, we can work them out later. This thing that's going on, this killing of our people, is much more important than our "terms" as you call them. I'm not forgiving you or anything so drastic, so don't get your hopes up. We need to work together on this and we can't do that if we're fighting. I say we just forget about the whole mess for a little while longer." She put her hands on her hips, "Doesn't that make sense to you?"

I smiled brightly before I could stop myself, "Sure, I mean yeah, I think you're absolutely right. I've got no problem with that."

"Good, now wipe that silly grin off your face and go make your phone call, I haven't got all day." She turned quickly and her long black hair whipped around behind her. I silently admired the way her hips swayed beneath the denim as she walked to the truck. She was still one hell of a woman, a little cocky, but one hell of a woman.

I dialed the number Marilyn gave me and it was answered quickly, "Agent Mooney." No hello or courtesy, so I knew then that it was a dedicated line. They had already established themselves pretty well in Charlotte.

"Agent Smith please."

"He's not here. Who's calling?"

"Morgan Roberts."

"Hold on."

I couldn't tell if he recognized the name or not. I held the phone for at least two minutes until Smith came on the line.

"Agent Smith here." His voice sounded far away and I suspected I had been patched through to a car phone.

"Fred old buddy, how in the world are you? You know I've missed that cheerful voice. You just can't imagine how much."

"Hello, Mr. Roberts. Once again, I find your attempts at humor severely lacking." I could almost envision his look of distaste and I could hear the frustration in his tone.

"Well, Fred, it would help if you actually had a sense of humor." I kept my voice light. "Now, what can I do for you?"

"I need you to come in for questioning. We know you were at your brother's house the night he was killed and I need to ask you some questions. I need some answers Mr. Roberts, and I need them immediately. Where are you?"

"Uh uh, Fred, that's not the way it works. See, you tried that hard line shit once, didn't you learn anything?" I said, purposely pushing him to see how much he would take.

I heard only the quiet buzzing of the phone line as he hesitated, "Look Mr. Roberts, we need your help. This whole thing has gotten totally out of hand. I know you're involved in this and I suspect you've got something planned yourself with regard to our..." he paused to search for the word, "...our mutual problem. Look, we don't think you're involved with the killings; we've checked out your whereabouts for the other murders, but I need to talk to you about the night at your brother's."

"I'm glad to know you're at least smart enough to know we haven't killed anyone—at least not yet anyway."

"Now look here..."

"Uh uh, Fred. Don't start. I'll hang up. Come on now talk fast I don't want to talk long enough for you to trace this call."

"I know you were there the other night and I'm sure you must know things about your brother's killer we don't." He said it like it hurt to admit it. "I need to talk to you about those things. If I have to, I'll put out an APB on you and your cousin. I'm very serious about this, Mr. Roberts."

"Look Fred, you really need to pay better attention. I do not respond very well to threats from assholes like you and if you want my help you better wise up and soon. Your time is running out here."

"Alright Mr. Roberts, what are your terms?" He was huffy and abrupt.

"Well, for starters there's always the all important question; what's in it for me?"

"Really! Mr. Roberts…"

"No, no, no. You better watch it Fred, I'm thinking real hard about hanging up on you."

I knew he was really steaming as he continued, "Alright. I believe you're probably a vengeful man, Mr. Roberts. I suspect you want this killer as bad as we do now. I propose an exchange of information. I would be willing to discuss certain aspects of the case with you in return for your explanation regarding the night of your brother's demise." He paused, "Does that sound agreeable to you?"

I hesitated as if to consider his proposition, having already reached a decision before I ever made the call, "I think it might be possible, yes."

"Good, now if you would be so kind as to tell me where you are I'll dispatch a team to pick the two of you up."

"No thanks. I don't think so."

"Excuse me, but I thought you said my idea was acceptable?"

"Part of it was, the first part, but if you want my help you're going to have to come to me, and without half the FBI trailing behind. You know what I mean?"

"But that would be highly irregular."

"Hell, half the world's irregular Fred. What's that got to do with any-thing? Look, I'll agree to meet with you and one other agent, only one, and it will be in a place of my choosing. That's the deal, take it or leave it."

He hesitated so long, I thought for a moment I had lost the connec-tion. "Alright, what do you have in mind?"

"I would assume since you have already been to the mountains, you must have an idea where Grandfather Mountain is, right?"

"So you are in the mountains. I suspected as much."

"Now pay attention Dick Tracy, I don't want you trying to get cute with this thing. I am in the mountains, but I can promise you if I don't want you to find me, you and half the United States Army could search for months and not find a clue, get it? Now listen and don't interrupt anymore. I hate that." I continued quickly, "You, and one other Agent, drive to Grandfather Mountain's main gate, buy an entry pass, go up the mountain, and park at the visitor center. There, you follow the hiking map they give you and take Grandfather Trail to Macrae Gap. Don't bring anyone else. If you do, I assure you I will be in such a position to know immediately and this will be the last time we talk for awhile, understand?"

I moved ahead before he had a chance to answer, "Good. You two fol-low that route to a place off the main trail called Indian House Cave. At this time of year there should be few people on that part of the mountain. I'll meet you there in the cave. But don't forget that if you try anything different from what I have outlined, you will not see us. I'm telling you, my cousin and I know these mountains better than most and you won't have a chance in hell of finding us, got it?"

"Yes, I believe so."

"Great. Now Fred, let's allow this as a sign of faith. You be honest with me and I promise you I'll try to help you if I can." I thought I was maybe being too hard on him and decided to lighten up a bit. "One thing Fred, are you in pretty good shape?"

"Of course!" He answered huffily.

"Good, because the trail you will be hiking is not an easy one. I picked it because it will allow me to be able to watch you. I suggest you wear some good hiking boots and ditch your designer suit. It's going to be hot when you start out, but it might get cold on the summit so be prepared, better bring along some water too. It'll take you about and hour and a half from your car to me. Any questions?"

"Yes, but are you sure all this is necessary? I give you my word if you come down and talk, we can work something out."

"No. I've heard promises from government men before. Your kind has been telling lies to us Indians for too many years to count easily. You do this my way or we don't do it. Will you be there at noon tomorrow?"

"Mr. Roberts, I must tell you I know all about your past—about your little...how shall we say this...psychological problems."

"Good for you." I betrayed nothing with my voice.

"Well, I just wouldn't want you to do anything...well, rash."

"Up yours Smith."

"Surely you under..."

"That's enough Smith. I'm through talking to you. Are you going to be there or not?"

"Yes, Mr. Roberts, we'll be there."

"Good. Fred, have a nice day you hear." and I quickly hung up the phone just as he started to say something else.

Kathy spoke to me as we pulled away from Bakersfield, "Okay, hot-shot, you want to tell me what's going on?"

On the way back up the mountain, I filled Kathy in on all that had happened since the crazy nightmare began. I started with Steven's phone call to me and ended with the one to Smith. She had already heard most of it from Steven when he explained things to Ben, but she encouraged me to repeat them to her again. I knew that she was trying as hard as I was to understand the strange things that were happening. She gave me what little information she had, and ultimately I realized neither of us understood what was going on, or why. The thing we both agreed on was that we needed help and more than we had readily available. It appeared the only source possible for answers to the riddle was sitting in my grandfather's cabin watching television. I wasn't so sure that was an encouraging thought.

CHAPTER SEVENTEEN

As we crested the last hill, I saw Ben sitting on the front porch, peacefully rocking as if he had not a care in the world. The sun had risen above the treetops and light filled the clearing around the isolated cabin. Billowy, white clouds moved quickly across the sky as a strong, cool wind blew through the mountain pines, pushing the trees back and forth with a slow rhythm. It was hard to imagine the world having problems on such a day, and in such a place.

Kathy and I discussed our options on the return trip and it was a tragically short discussion. For the moment, all we could do was listen to what Ben had to say about the book and wait for something to happen. I called to Ben as we left the truck, "How was Tom Selleck?"

"He looked good, and guess what? He's agreed to do a "Magnum" movie, I found that interesting but disappointing. That means he's not bringing the series back to television and that's a shame. I really wanted to see Magnum in something new."

Kathy noticed my puzzled expression and commented, "Grandfather refuses to go to the movies. If it's not on television he won't see it."

"That's right." Confirmed the old Indian, "I will not be caught in a theater with hundreds of crazed people if there's a fire. It would be disastrous. Most people are crazy anyway, and fire makes them totally unpredictable."

"He also won't go near shopping malls, department stores or any-where there's a crowd, no matter how often I try to talk him into it. I don't know what I'm going to do with him."

"You don't have to "do" anything with me. I'm a grown man and can take care of myself. I will go or not go wherever I please. That's my right, isn't it?" The old shaman sounded indignant or pretended to anyway. "I don't need to visit a department store. For what? I have no desire to see a "blue light special" and be trampled to death by a shopping stampede. Besides, if I wait long enough, all the good movies will be on television, and I buy whatever I need at the general store. And there's always the Television Shopping Network."

Kathy laughed, "Oh no! You remember what happened last time? Not a chance."

I kept silent.

Ben interjected seriously, "We agreed not to speak of this anymore. Did we not?"

"You did."

He put his arm around my shoulder and turned me away from her. "It's time for some food, don't you think so, Morgan? Even the old need nourishment."

Kathy wasn't going to let him get away with it, "Yep, he did it. He called them. Of course, he used my credit card and without asking. He would never have a credit card himself and be further enslaved by soci-ety, as he puts it, but as soon as he saw something he wanted, bingo! He sure decided he needed one in a hurry…mine."

"Enough! Kathy, go in the house. I'm hungry and I would like some-thing to eat. I'm an old man and would appreciate proper consideration."

His tone was pitiful and pleading, a true master at work. I couldn't help but smile.

"I can't make it any clearer. It's positively cruel for you not to feed me. Don't you think so Morgan?"

"Excuse me, but I'm not about to get in the middle of this. I'll just sit here and mind my own business."

"Fine, I'll just sit with you. Kathy, you can go inside while we talk." His tone suggested that it was his final word on the matter."

His granddaughter thought otherwise. She winked at me, without him seeing her.

"Sorry, Ben, but I have to ask one small question; what was it you ordered anyway?" I smiled at his sudden discomfort.

"It's not important really." He flipped his hand as if to brush the topic away.

Kathy grinned, "Come on now, if you don't tell him, I will."

"I already told you, it was because he was part Indian." He spoke to her sternly, but I knew his anger was feigned. "Didn't I tell you that several times already? Why is that so hard for you to understand? If your mother were around to see the way you treat me, she would not be happy I assure you. Why is it that the whole world manages to treat me with respect, with the exception of my only grandchild?"

"Don't try to change the subject." Kathy stood defiantly with her hands on her hips and a smirk on her face. "Are you going to show him or not?"

He looked at me with dismay, "I needed a new watch, mine was broken and…"

"Quit stalling and just show him."

Ben mumbled something under his breath, then reluctantly extended his arm and pulled back his sleeve. He wore a shiny gold wristwatch, with a full-length picture of Elvis on the face. The King's hands indicated it was 10:15.

I couldn't help myself. I laughed and Kathy joined me. I don't know if she was laughing at him or my expression, as I tried to contain myself.

Ben interjected a smile, "It's a good watch, keeps perfect time."

Steven walked up just then, puzzled and curious at our behavior; "Did I miss something funny?"

"Don't worry, Steven, we were just admiring Ben's watch, that's all."

Steven smiled, "Oh, you mean his Big E watch? I've seen it. Wouldn't mind having one like it myself."

That started the laughter all over again.

Afterward, Steven and I unloaded the bags from the truck and stowed them away. I showed Kathy the things Aunt Mary sent up and she went into the kitchen to prepare an early lunch.

Steven and I returned to the porch and sat with Ben. My cousin pulled an old cedar bench next to the porch and propped his feet on the rail as he lit a cigarette.

Ben asked him, "Have you prepared the asi?"

"Yessir. I got the fire going and I gathered some wild parsnip just like you said. Everything is ready."

Ben seemed to think for a moment, then addressed me, "You know when I was young, I helped your grandfather build that small cabin, the one on the other side of the stream. These other buildings have been here as long as I can remember. I believe your great grandfather built them, oh, I would guess over one hundred years ago." As he spoke, he stared into the forest towards the other structures on the far side of the stream. His eyes took on a far away look. "There has been great magic worked here, many times over many long years. I just hope this place can help us now."

He seemed lost in his thoughts and Steven looked at me as if to encourage my silence. We just sat quietly for a time. The stream rushed in the background as Dog sniffed along the side of the porch and gradually worked her way into the brush downstream, following in the wake of some previous explorer long gone.

Finally Ben turned to me, "Morgan, I want you to tell me everything that has happened in the last few days. I would like to hear everything you can remember."

So, for the second time that morning, I relived the happenings of the previous seventy-two hours. I tried as best I could to recall every detail.

As I spoke, I began to feel as if I should just record it as much as I was repeating myself. First Marilyn, then Kathy, and finally Ben all listened as I recalled the chain of events that led to Jordan's demise. Ben stopped me several times and asked questions about the killer when I reached certain parts of the story. He had me review the strange condition of Jordan's body several times, and asked probing questions concerning my somewhat limited description of the killer. Steven sat and smoked cigarette after cigarette without comment. I knew Ben had already extracted all the information he could from him. I seriously doubted a criminal investigator could have done a better job of interrogation.

When I finished, he commented, "It is indeed a strange tale, but it's not something I am surprised about. The Ravenmocker has returned just as I thought. This is bad, very bad indeed." He paused and added under his breath, "And I hope it doesn't get worse."

Steven glanced at me as if to try and judge my reaction and to encourage me to keep my mouth shut. I ignored his look and asked the question on my mind, "Ben, couldn't it be someone who's familiar with the Cherokee myths? Surely other people are aware of these same legends?"

"Yes, I suppose that's possible," he conceded, "but I don't think that's the case now."

"Perhaps you can help me better understand." I kept my tone respectful, not doubtful, "Can I ask why you think it's a "Ravenmocker" and not a human, everyday type killer?" Steven glared openly in my direction at that point.

"That's a good question, Morgan."

I glanced at Steven and winked at him. He casually reached to rub his nose with his middle finger, sending me a message that Ben couldn't see.

"I can answer you, but I before I do I want to ask you a few questions of my own. First, if we're not talking about the demon from our past, how do you explain the ability of someone to withstand Steven's bullets and live? How do you account for the absence of a body, as if the killer just flew away? You yourself said you saw no weapon, but saw injuries that could only have been inflicted by a weapon. How are these things possible?"

I thought for a moment and then admitted, "I don't know how those things happened, but there would seem to be some logical explanation."

"Why?"

"Sir?" I asked, truly confused by his question.

"You say there must be a logical explanation, why?"

"Well, there has to be a logical reason for those things. Such things can't just happen. I mean, no one can just fly through the air. Maybe the killer was wearing a bulletproof vest or something when Steven shot him, and maybe his weapons were hidden from view. I don't know."

"So let me understand what you're saying, Morgan. What I'm suggesting is contrary to the laws of science and man that you have come to accept as your belief. Is that right?"

I answered after a brief hesitation, "Well, that's not exactly the way I would have put it, but yes, that's about right, I suppose. I mean, I don't necessarily believe science is always right, but it's the closest thing to explaining why things are, what they are, I guess. It's what I've learned in every school I've attended and it's what the rest of the world seems to believe. Things like you're suggesting are just hard for me to accept unless I see them for myself. I'm sort of hardheaded that way. I don't mean any disrespect, that's just what I believe."

"Morgan, I thought..." Steven began.

Ben held up one hand and silenced him. "Your words are words to be considered, Morgan. I understand and respect your convictions and your beliefs. I understand your "hard headedness" as you put it. You forget I knew your grandfather well, and if you know it or not, your grandfather was the most stubborn man I have ever known. There is one thing I want you to consider however; just because scientists can't prove or explain something, doesn't mean it can't be so. I myself know of many things man's precious science and logic cannot explain."

"Yessir, I suppose you're right about that."

"Yes, I know," he continued with a smile, "I sometimes hate being right all the time. It can be such a burden."

I laughed, "I can see where that might be a drag, yeah. Of course, I never have that problem. I make enough wrong decisions for the both of us."

"Oh, I never said I always made the right decisions, I just said I was always right." His wrinkled face broke into a grin.

I smiled, "Okay, if you say so, but I'm still a little confused. I still have to see this "Ravenmocker" for myself once again before I can believe what you're telling me."

"I understand, Morgan. I wouldn't respect any man who would give up his convictions so easily. I would, however, like for you to think about a few things for me. Do you think the scientists of the world have always had the knowledge? What were these things before science came along and gave them a name? Light existed long before Einstein ever formulated the equation; it just didn't materialize with his discovery. Light was always there, it never needed science to prove its existence; it just was."

Ben shifted his seat to a more comfortable position and continued. Steven remained quietly on the old bench and listened, the ever-present cigarette smoke drifting slowly towards the treetops and the blue sky above.

"When I was a small boy, the idea of a man walking on the moon was much harder to accept for me than the idea that a Ravenmocker might exist, but yet it came to be. Everything is relative, Morgan, the white man and the Indian just think in two completely different ways. To the Cherokee of the past, the belief in ghosts and witches was as real as your belief in the aircraft you've been aboard. Can you imagine how hard it would be to convince a Cherokee of a few hundred years ago such a thing could be possible?" As I started to interject my thoughts, he held up his hand, "I know what you're thinking. You're thinking that the difference is the rocket ship is tangible and the belief in spirits is only in the mind…correct?"

"Yessir, something like that."

"By the same token, to the early Cherokee, the spirits were very real. Our people were raised in the belief that all things were part of their world. They saw proof of their myths all around them. Their faith made them real. Don't you see? The same way that people's belief in the bible makes God real to them, or the same way people believe in the Buddha. I think you would have a difficult time trying to convince a Christian that Jesus Christ didn't exist because his life has no basis in scientific fact. Yet these things are no different from what I'm telling you. The myths of our people were very real in our past, and they could become very real again. That's what I want you to try to remember, Morgan. Things can be very real and very deadly, even when you don't believe in them. You can die just as easily by the hand of something you don't believe in, as something you do."

He finished speaking and looked intently into my face as if searching for something there. I sat for long moments and tried to digest what the old man said. He had an eerie gift of choosing just the right words, and I had forgotten his ability to cut right to the core of things. Ben could always find a way into the heart of anyone he wanted to reach. His knowledge and intelligence, combined with his uncanny feeling for the human spirit, made him a scary man to be around sometimes. If he ever turned to TV evangelism as a way of life, the whole world would be in big trouble and he would become very wealthy.

After a few moments, he rose slowly to his feet. "I think it would be a good time to eat, don't you? It will be wise to allow such talk to rest for awhile. We can eat and then we can retire to the asi for a time. The hot house cleanses the mind as well as the body. Don't you think so, Steven?"

Steven rose from the bench and answered him, "Yessir, I think it'll do wonders for me, and I can't wait to see what it does for Morgan." His knowing smile was a little unnerving, in light of the fact I had no idea what he was talking about.

"I'm sure he'll do just fine," Ben commented and then turned to me, "Have you ever been in the sweat house when parsnip is used to cleanse the spirit?"

"Well sir, I can remember being in the asi only once; my grandfather and some of his friends allowed me to tend the fire during a meeting when I was a small boy, but I don't remember them using any parsnip."

"It isn't used all the time, just when there's a special need for purity of thoughts and spirit."

Steven chipped in, "Yeah, you'll see, cousin. It'll be "educational" as you call it. Right up your alley." His tone turned sarcastic, "But I don't want to say too much about it, because I know you'll want to "experience it for yourself" and all that sort of thing."

"Smart ass." I hated it when people used my own words against me.

Kathy had evidently been standing in the doorway for some time when she spoke, "Well, if you fellows have solved all our worldly problems, we can eat anytime now."

I answered, "You and Ben go right ahead, I need Steven to help with the generator before we go in. We'll be there in a minute or two."

"Suit yourself. Grandfather, your food's on the table. Now what are you going to complain about?"

I heard Ben answer her as they retreated towards the kitchen, "Just give me a minute and I'll think of something."

"I'm sure you will," Kathy replied as they headed for the kitchen.

I spoke to Steven as we walked to the rear of the house. I told him about the phone calls, my conversation with Agent Smith, and our planned meeting for the following day. He listened briefly and agreed with my tentative plans.

On the way inside I commented, "Incidentally, Marilyn said to tell you hello."

"Imagine that."

"It sure surprises the hell out of me, but then again, she's always had this thing for stray dogs and street bums. I guess with you she gets a little of both."

"It could just be my hick-mountain-boy charm at work," he said with a conniving smile.

"If that's all it is, you're in deep trouble with this one, let me tell you."

"We'll see."

"Alright, Stevey, let's eat. I'm starving all of a sudden." I held up my hand before he could offer a smart retort, "I know, don't call you Stevey."

Kathy and Ben had started without us.

CHAPTER EIGHTEEN

The "asi" was the Cherokee equivalent of the sweathouse, or hot house, found within the cultures of almost all the Indian tribes of early America. It was generally a small log building, chinked with clay, sporting a sloping shed roof. The one on my grandfather's property was about twelve feet square and only high enough to allow sitting or reclining.

Steven started a fire earlier in the center of the small building, and had placed a couple of flat rocks into the fire. The flame had burned down to coals, and pine knots had been gathered which I knew would be placed on the flat rocks to blaze up and heat the structure. The knots produced a hot fire but very little smoke. The small door stood ajar, and I noticed a stack of what I assumed were wild parsnip roots stacked by a stone bowl.

We finished our meal and Kathy stayed behind to walk Dog in the woods. Ben sat near the entrance of the "asi" and used the stone mortar to grind the root with a pestle. "Why don't you two sit for a spell, while I prepare the parsnip. I think afterward, it would be good for us to go to the water before our sweat bath."

"Going to the water" was a Cherokee term for entering a stream with purification in mind. The procedure was thought to cleanse the body and spirit, and I knew it was often done prior to any ceremony or council. I didn't remember a whole lot of my grandfather's teachings, perhaps because I purposely chose not to, but I had retained a little.

As Ben ground the roots, Steven and I stripped to our underwear and stacked our clothes on nearby rocks. We were on the opposite side of the water from the main cabin and some thirty yards upstream. The stream made a slight inward bend close to the asi and council house before flowing swiftly and coolly down the mountain. Moss covered rocks, placed decades earlier, covered a natural dam which created a small pool near the asi.

I finally broke the silence and asked Ben, "Okay, I give up. What do we do with the parsnip?"

Ben answered, "I grind the root, combining it with water from the stream." He demonstrated as he spoke, "When it is mixed, we pour it over the hot rocks inside. The vapors help cleanse your body and your mind. From the way you two smelled when we arrived, I would think this will be good for both of you." He glanced at Steven.

Steven laughed at my expression of doubt; "It'll work—that is if you're able to handle the vapors that long. It's one of those separating the men from the boys kinda' things."

"Okay, I'm ready." I said it with a great deal more assurance that I actually felt.

"Well, let's see how long you keep thinking that, Cuz."

Ben tapped the pestle against the mortar as he finished; "Now Steven, it's not that bad. Morgan will do just fine. Why don't we enter the water now?"

The old man removed his clothing down to his boxer shorts. His skin was like old leather, but his body seemed remarkably well preserved for his age. Of course, I had no idea what his age was. My best guess was he had to be very near eighty, but his mind showed no effects of the years.

We entered the stream together, and even though it was late summer, the water was still cold. My breath caught in my chest as I lowered my body into the water to waist level. It was sobering and invigorating. I remembered the frigid feel of the stream in the winter, and in early spring when the thaw of the mountain snow fed the water, increasing the current as well as dropping the temperature.

Ben suggested we follow his lead as he faced the sun and ceremoniously dipped himself under the water seven times, in the traditional manner. I looked at Steven, who nodded his head. When I hesitated, he made hand gestures and gritted his teeth at me until I decided I better do as he wished. I shrugged my shoulders thinking, what the hell, and followed suit. I felt sort of ridiculous, but the water felt fine after it lost its edge. We remained in the stream for some time, talking and discussing the weather, the mountain, anything but why we were really there.

Ben splashed water on his face as he rose, walking towards the bank, "I think it's time we retire to the asi. I will not be able to stay with you long as I need to continue with your grandfather's book, but I can stay for a time."

We left the water and entered the cramped enclosure. The temperature in the asi was already extremely hot and the moisture on my body never had time to evaporate, it just changed to sweat. As Ben closed the door behind us, we were plunged into near darkness. A weak light bled through various cracks in the clay chinking and the faint glow of the coals allowed us to see only dim outlines of each other. Ben took one of the pine knots and placed it on the flat rock nearest him and a quick blaze of light brightly illuminated his face as he squatted by the fire. As the blaze died down, he poured some of the parsnip onto the rock. The small room was immediately filled with a sharp pungent odor, not unpleasant, but extremely strong, almost overpowering. It reminded me of the military "gas mask" training I had during basic, when we were forced to remove our masks in a room full of tear gas.

Steven spoke, and I could make out his face but not his features. "Morgan, I got a crisp five dollar bill says I stay in here longer than you. You interested?"

Caught up in the moment, I responded, "Anything you can do, I can do better. Why not make it ten big spender?"

"Okay, what say loser has to wash the other's vehicle?"

I heard old Ben chuckle softly in the darkness of the asi. I was enjoying taunting my cousin. It was something we had done all our lives. Such childish wagers reminded me of our younger years when we either bet or dared one another on what seemed an hourly basis. Anything from; "I dare you to jump that creek on your motorcycle," to; "I bet you I can drink more tequila than you without throwing up." It was with those dares and bets that we had grown together; even in losing, we always won something. It was a way to make fun of life, to answer it's challenges with impunity and I knew Steven had been thinking of those same bets when he made his light hearted challenge.

My eyes were already stinging from the astringent odor of the wild root. I moved to a sitting position, crossed my legs, and closed my eyes against the smoke of the pungent concoction before responding bravely, "You know my truck is a lot bigger than your motorcycle. I hate to take advantage of you like that, but I will mind you, I'll just hate myself for doing it."

"You just hate yourself all you like, but you'll leave before I do. When you're outside coughing and trying to breathe in all that nice cool air, I'll still be here."

"We'll see," I laughed in his direction but I didn't open my eyes.

Ben's voice interrupted our childish attempts at humor, "If you young men have finished flexing your muscles, might we continue our discussion of the problems at hand before I have to leave?"

I heard Steven reply, sheepishly I thought, "Right, sorry about that, but he gets carried away sometimes."

"I get carried away?"

The old man laughed and the sound seemed somehow out of place in the darkness of the hot house. "Its good to see you've kept your sense of humor. I suspect we will need all our laughter before we next have to face the Ravenmocker. There will be no time for laughter then." His words took the humor from the air and left behind only parsnip, smoke and concern.

I took that moment to ask a question I had been holding for just such a time, "Ben, I've talked with Steven about this already, but I would really like for you to tell me what you know about this Ravenmocker myth." I spoke slowly and reluctantly, not wanting to draw anymore of the harsh fumes into my lungs than I could help. I felt tears pooling up in the corners of my eyes and tried to close them tighter.

Ben described the evils of a Ravenmocker, and the resemblance between the Cherokee legend and the similar stories of other tribes. He spoke of the same things Steven had mentioned; the ability of the witch to take different forms, to absorb the lives they took into their own, and their tendency to prey on the young and feeble.

"They could supposedly fly through the air in a fiery shape and made the cry of a diving "Ka'lanu", or raven, from which their name was taken. The Ravenmocker, "Ka'lanu Ahyel'ski", was the worst evil the Cherokees knew. Hearts filled with dread at the mere mention of the name. Parents were fearful for the children of the village when the "asigi'na", or devils, moved in the night. There were a few who could kill them, but only a few. It took a very special magic and they could only be killed when they took their true form to feed."

In the pause that followed, I asked without thinking; "Surely, if such a thing existed today, we would know about it. There is no way such a killer could hide in today's society for any length of time."

Ben asked without hesitation, "How do you know this?"

"What? That we would know about them?"

"Yes."

"Well, something like this would be all over the news for one thing. It's just a matter of time and we'll be reading about these recent killings in line at the supermarket."

"That may be so, but I believe this Ravenmocker is real and is killing for a reason. A reason I can't even guess as yet, but this killer is not the same as the old ones. This killer doesn't care who knows about the killing. It is almost as if the witch wishes everyone to know, and that is very unusual. It disturbs me." His voice changed slightly as he continued, "It was always the way of the witch to hide, to work their evil under the secrets of darkness. They were hard to find and even harder to kill. At the time of the legends, the Ravenmockers were known to exist for hundreds of years." He breathed deeply of the parsnip, "They could very well be with us today, hidden within our midst as they have always been."

"I still think it would be front page news by now." Somehow I managed to speak through the haze with much more confidence that I actually felt.

"How do you know it hasn't already been "front page news" as you call it?"

"Sir?"

"Well, it seems every time I pick up a newspaper or turn on the television, I hear of a young boy or girl missing. What do you think happens to those children on those milk cartons? How many of the old and homeless do you imagine go unaccounted for every year? I think our society would be an absolute paradise for a Ravenmocker. They could hide forever, preying on the young or the discards of society." The reality behind his words gave me an odd heavy feeling in the pit of my stomach." Does this really sound so unreasonable to you?"

It didn't. Unfortunately, it sounded very reasonable, just not very logical. I found myself ignoring the discomfort I experienced with each gulp of air. My eyes burned, but I ignored them too. I still didn't believe in the old myth, but I found myself beginning to question my own certainties and the security of our world against such a threat. If something so crazy could exist, the people of the America had created a perfect environment for it to thrive. The conversation was moving in a direction I didn't like. I couldn't afford to begin questioning my own values and beliefs at that point in my life. My emotional foothold was precarious at best.

"I guess you're right about the possibility anyway, there would be no way to say for sure. Again, I'd have to see such a thing for myself to believe it." I just refused to accept such things were possible.

Ben spoke from the misty darkness, looking almost like a demon himself in the frail light and the haze of the smoke. "This "Anisgi'na", has the ability to blend into any environment and remain hidden, that's how it survived so long. I have read reports of the Spanish explorers from the De Soto expedition of 1540, who lost troops in unexplained abductions and later found their mutilated bodies, with the same type injuries the Indians described. You see it's not just the Indian people who have experienced these type killings. These demons could have came over on the Pilgrim's boats or they may have been here all along. They could be as old as man could, older maybe. There are some stories that suggest that they even bred mankind as their fodder. All such secrets may have been lost when the white man forbade the teaching of our old ways. Any knowledge of the time before is therefore priceless and must be maintained at all cost. This old book of your grandfather's, for instance, could not be purchased for any amount of money, and I would gladly give my life to keep the words within it alive."

I felt embarrassed by his words. He genuinely meant what he said, and to me, the book had sentimental value, yeah, but that was about all. I never understood just how important the old manuscript was until that moment. I don't think I understood how really important my grandfather was either, until then.

In the hot smoky confines of the log and clay structure, I found myself questioning a lot of things all at once. Thoughts, usually just past the edge of my consciousness, nagging questions that never really went away, washed over me. Maybe the whole "society" bit, with its rules of logic, law, and decorum, was not the only answer. Maybe there were other ways of life equally as good, equally as right. The option of these other lifestyles was taken from us just after we were born. From that moment, someone was always telling us what was right and wrong. Before you knew it, real freedom of choice was taken away, never to be seen again. Of course, by then we thought all the decisions we made were actually ours. Of course, they never were.

What disturbed me the most was the thought that if the things Ben said could be correct, then perhaps all the things I had been putting so much "stock" in lately, might not be so right after all. The idea was too much for me to handle. If such thoughts were possible, then everything I had learned and worked for all my life was a farce.

Suddenly I'd had enough. I had to get out of the asi. The stinging vapors had seeped into my lungs, my skin, even into the very depths of my mind. I had to get out.

I threw open the door and rushed out into the clean mountain air by the stream, gulping cool, moist air and coughing up the remains of the painful smoke still in my lungs. I could feel my heart beating much faster than it should have been and my hands shook when I held them in front of my face. Sweat ran from my body in little rivulets and I watched as the sandy area under my face was painted with little drops of my perspiration. I put my hands on my knees and inhaled as deeply as possible. I could hear Steven laughing from the confines of the asi, but I didn't give a damn.

After a moment, I felt a soft hand on my shoulder. I turned to find Ben standing by my side. Sweat dripped from the ancient shoulders and chest, and a single drop of moisture hung precariously from the tip of the regal nose of the old Indian. He smiled, "Don't worry my son. I know what it is like to feel the questions. I have always felt them. They will always be there."

I stood and looked at him, trying to figure how he could possibly know what I had been thinking within the dark confines of the asi. However strange it was, he seemed to know at least part of what I had felt.

"Even though Steven has been down the same path you have just taken many times, he has never seen the power at the end as you have. Men strive all their lives to realize the true meaning in living and most die unfulfilled. A rare few find themselves, and only a few others are ever given the opportunity to do so. You have been given the opportunity and what you do with it now lies in your hands, and in your hands only. No one can find the way for you Morgan, but sometimes, if you look carefully, someone may help you find the right path for your journey. Quite often, that someone is the one you would expect the least."

I was confused, no longer about the Ravenmocker; my confusion ran much deeper than that. "But Ben, how can I give up everything I believe in? Because that's what we're talking about here, isn't it?"

"Is it?"

"Oh hell, I don't know anything right now. I was in trouble long before this whole nightmare started. I thought I was dealing with my problems but I was only kidding myself. I just don't know anything anymore—what's right? What's wrong? Who the hell knows?"

"Good." His steady smile was disarming.

"Good? What's good about confusion?" I was trying as best I could to understand.

"At least you're now asking the questions." He began to slip into his clothes as he talked. "At least your mind is trying to tell you there is another way for you. I will tell you something Morgan, something I could only say to you and no other. Your grandfather searched his whole life for the answers just as you are doing now. Many times, I heard your grandfather termed, "different", sometimes crazy even. He was not crazy but he was, however, very different. He was very..." he hesitated as if trying to find the right word, "...special. You have a lot of his same qualities. I can see them in the look of your eyes at times."

I thought quietly to myself and walked around in a small circle by the stream as my heartbeat and breathing returned to near normal. I didn't know what to say. I tried, "Thank you, I'll take that as a compliment, I guess."

"And well you should, he was a very great man, your grandfather. Now, you go to the water and wait on your cousin, for all his bragging I know him, he will be out within the next two minutes, wait and see." He turned to walk towards the main cabin.

I called after him; "Ben!"

He stopped and turned back to me.

"Did my grandfather ever find the answers he was looking for?"

"Only he would know for sure, Morgan, only he and no other." He turned and disappeared silently into the woods.

I walked to the edge of the flowing water and stepped into the coolness. I felt the smoothness of river rocks under my bare feet and waded further into the stream. The chilly water offered immediate, soothing relief to my body and I closed my eyes, trying to force my mind towards emptiness. I was too confused to think clearly and didn't want to think at all. I ducked my head under the frigid flow, the water working it's magic on my stinging eyes.

About sixty seconds later, true to prediction, Steven burst from the asi, coughing and cussing. He coughed loudly, began to speak, stopped to cough again, then finally managed, "I forgot to tell you, just before I parked the bike..." he coughed again, "...I ran through a huge mud puddle and a pile of horse shit." He laughed and ran into the water near my side, entering the final bit in a smooth, shallow dive, knifing under the quick flow of water.

He surfaced, blowing water in a steady stream in my direction. I heard his labored breathing as he tried to replace the tainted air in his lungs with clean air. Faint, schoolyard tattoos covered his upper torso; crude blue etchings on red-brown skin.

"You cheated! You smoke those damned cigarettes and your lungs are already in such bad shape they don't know the difference!"

"Look, a win is a win in my book. You gonna' welsh on the bet?"

"You know better than that."

"Good, and don't think I have forgotten about the ten bucks either. I can buy a lot of cigarettes with ten dollars, and I intend to smoke every single one in front of you. What do you think of that?"

"I hope you choke on them, that's what I think."

We walked onto the bank and lay down on the bed of pine needles to dry before dressing. The sky had become darkly overcast while we were in the asi and a storm was rapidly approaching just as the morning air suggested it would. The tall trees began to dance back and forth as a strong wind blew across the mountainside and down the ridge. It was going to be a bad storm, nothing uncommon in the high mountains in the late summer.

"What did Ben say when he followed you out?" Steven asked me as we dressed.

"Nosey as hell aren't you?"

"Yeah, so?"

I hesitated before replying; thinking that if I waited long enough, he would lose interest in the question. He didn't.

"Well?"

"He just said he was going back to the cabin to read, that it would probably take him awhile, and for me to wait for you, not to hurry back."

"Really?"

"Really, Steven! You want me to write it in blood?"

"Alright, alright." He held his hands up as if to ward off an attack. "No big deal, okay?"

I didn't say anything right away, but walked towards the ancient seven-sided "council house" nearby. It was a small enclosure shaped like a stop sign, with an opening in the middle of the roof for smoke from the center fire to escape. The old door creaked on ancient, leather hinges and the rush of outside air blew little dust devils about the still room. I stopped in the doorway, reluctant to enter for some reason.

Clouded sunlight trickled down through the circular opening, softly illuminating the room and its contents.

Seven vertical support logs held the ceiling of overhead beams. Various masks and withered-feathered headpieces adorned the poles. The walls sported stretched hide drawings of the tribe's past, and scattered in a circular pattern throughout the room were thickly woven fabric chairs with log supports. Their fading colors, once bright and crisp, were worn; the cloth tattered and frayed. In the center of the room was a carved out section of earth surrounded by stones, blackened with fire from many long years of use and the leaves of a previous fall. Near the stones was a small cooking table, complete with pot and ladle. Gourd water dippers hung from various places around the council house walls. The room smelled dusty, damp and old like an old chest of drawers left in the rain for the garbage man. Nothing had been touched in the room for over fifteen years, it was as my grandfather had left it, and nothing had changed and yet, everything had changed. Time had left its mark on the old room just as it did each and everything in life. Nothing and no one was immune to its altering caress.

Steven stood just behind me, as we looked around the dusty room without speaking. I could hear the wind outside the door growing stronger by the minute. A heavy rain was coming for sure and soon by the sound of things.

Steven spoke in a harsh whisper, like a little boy in church. "Can't you just feel the age here, man? It's like going back in time, Morgan. Some of the greatest minds of our tribe have stood in this very room."

I was quiet for a minute before replying. "Ben told me my grandfather was as strange as people tell me I am. He told me that I reminded him of my grandfather." I wasn't looking at him, I was looking at a hide drawing I suddenly found very interesting.

"Well, you're in good company then," he replied. "Your grandfather was a great man."

"Yeah," I spoke softly, "I'm beginning to understand that more and more."

I moved back outside leaving Steven to close the door to the council house. Leaves and small twigs twisted and danced in little whirlwinds. Small saplings bent grotesquely in the draft and the sound of the wind was so strong it covered even the loud ripple of the stream.

Without turning, I asked, "Are you sure Ben is going to be able to help Steven? Do you really believe all this stuff? Really? I need to know the absolute truth okay? I need to know just what you honestly think, nothing else." I tried to keep the sense of urgency I felt out of my voice. After years of questioning my own sanity, filled with self-doubt, I needed someone to help me understand what to believe.

He looked at me, stepping closer so I would have no way of misinterpreting his words. His face was serious and concerned. "Yes, Morgan, I believe it. I know it sounds crazy, but I believe it." He looked for my response and when I offered none, he continued, "Is that what you want to hear?"

I made no comment. Instead I yelled into the wind, "We better get back and check on Kathy. It would be just like her to stay out in the rain, and I don't want Dog all wet again."

I started running just as large raindrops began to pelt the roofs of the log buildings. Within twenty feet, it became a steady downpour, soaking me to the skin. I never looked back for Steven, but I could hear his heavy boots splashing right behind me as I ran through the pouring rain towards my grandfather's cabin.

I could never remember being so confused in my life.

CHAPTER NINETEEN

We sat on the front porch of the old home as the summer rain came down in buckets. Wind blew the steady downpour in sheets. Leaves and small branches were torn from the trees as if it were early fall. We heard the loud crack of a breaking pine somewhere off deep in the woods, somewhere behind the cabin.

Through that long afternoon that stretched into early evening, we remembered. We relived the past with words, laughing at the good things and passing quickly over the bad. It felt good to be with the friends of my childhood again and I felt myself relax for the first time in a long time. My earlier concerns slipped away for a time. My life in Charleston was planned and as emotionless as I could make it. With Steven and Kathy, I was myself for the first time in a long time. I knew we weren't children anymore, but it still felt good to relive the past, especially when the present wasn't so nice.

Ben had retired inside early in the day, closing off the cabin so he could read in peace. He said it was bad enough to miss his television shows, he was not going to try to read with us in the room, babbling and annoying him. Dog kept trying to sneak off the porch without me seeing her. She would scoot ever so slightly towards the end of the porch farthest from my view, and I would call her back just before she made the final plunge off the edge. She loved the place as much as I did and she wanted to run and play through the woods, not sit on the porch.

When Ben finally finished his reading, Steven and I had our chairs leaned back and our feet propped on the rail. Kathy was sitting in the old rocker, which was once my grandfather's, when Ben called for Steven.

My cousin moved quickly to his feet and inside. His speed, for a man his size was uncanny, on the rare moments he chose to exhibit it anyway. He returned a few minutes later and stepped into the diminishing rain and towards the bridge without saying anything.

"Where you going Stevey?" I yelled.

"To do what I'm told, asshole! And don't call me that again." He yelled the last over his shoulder as he disappeared from view into the tree line on the far side of the water.

I looked at Kathy with a puzzled expression.

"Don't ask me, you know as much about what's going on as I do, probably more."

I shook my head, "You know, it's really strange the way he acts around your grandfather. I've never seen him this way before, it's kind of weird." I snorted, "I've never seen him show respect for anyone but his parents."

"Yeah, it's strange but I sort of take it for granted now. It was sort of a gradual thing; he just started showing up more and more, spending all the time he could with grandfather. Of course, I think grandfather secretly likes the attention and I know he's pleased when anyone takes an interest in the old ways. It makes him feel good when someone from our generation actually cares about our history."

She shook her head and smiled, her deep amber eyes soft, "He really gives Steven a hard time, but I know he is happy because it goes beyond just him and Steven. It's something bigger than that. It's sort of hard to explain, but he feels the more he passes on the knowledge, the better off things will be after he's gone. He knows he's the last real shaman and that bothers him." She paused, "I mean, think about it; generations of shamen die with him if he finds no one truly able to carry on. Morgan, for him it's the weight of a hundred worlds. He has tried his best to accept it, but he still keeps trying, keeps looking and hoping to find someone to carry on tradition." She looked into the darkening forest where Steven disappeared, "I don't suppose he will stop trying to save our past until he has become part of it himself."

I said nothing. The tone of her voice suggested our conversation had upset her in some way I hadn't expected. I had no intention of chancing further damage to our already shaky relationship with unwanted and untimely questions. Silence was sometimes the best medicine.

Nearly half an hour later, Ben walked out onto the front porch carrying the old leather manuscript in his hands. "Have you enjoyed your afternoon's discussion? It was amazing I could read anything with all the laughing and loud talk going on out here." His face was so serious I wasn't sure he was kidding.

"Oh grandfather, you heard no such thing. We kept our voices down."

"You see? You see Morgan?" He pointed his finger at her, his expression stern. "See how she always challenges me? I tell you, it is amazing the lack of respect I receive from my very own family members." He smiled and I knew he had been kidding her the whole time. "It's a travesty, that's what it is, a travesty."

"Oh, be quiet. Where did you send Steven off to, anyway, if my asking is not disrespectful?" Kathy inquired with a mischievous look on her face I easily recognized.

"I sent him ahead to start a fire in the council house. I feel it best we talk in there." His statement was more serious. He wasn't kidding any longer. "I have a story I must tell you and it doesn't have a happy ending."

I asked too quickly, unable to contain my curiosity, "Did you find out how the murders are being committed?"

"Not exactly, no. I have found out why they are being committed but it's a long, sad story, a tale which I think will best be served in the council house." I started to interrupt and he silenced me with a gesture,

"Please don't ask more of me until I have had a chance to tell you the whole story. I think it's necessary for you to understand the occurrences surrounding the myth, as well as the myth itself. I want you to hear what was happening to our people at the time because it has a great bearing on the story."

"Sounds reasonable enough, we're ready. Would you like to go now?"

While we walked, the rain tapered to a steady drizzling mist. The night air was almost cold. The wet mountain forest smelled so clean and familiar, like no where else on earth. It could never be duplicated. Kathy wore her jean jacket over her shoulders and walked close beside me without speaking. Ben showed no evidence of being cold; he just walked slowly and patiently through the mist, following the trail towards the council house. I noticed he carried the book underneath his jacket to protect it from the weather. Dog trailed along behind, happy to be off the porch at last.

As we approached the council house, the soft, yellow glow of fire was evident through the open doorway. The damp misty rain softened the normally harsh light of the blaze. Steven had a fire going and had taken all the log chairs outside and dusted them for use. He hadn't bothered with the rest of the room—it would probably have taken days to clean properly. Still, he had stirred the dust and little particles danced around in the firelight. Smoke rose thickly from the burning bark of the damp logs. The fire felt good after the short, wet walk from the cabin and we huddled around the fire in the chairs, enjoying the warmth it gave while watching the dance of the flames.

Ben's face remained passive. He hadn't said anything since we left the porch. We sat without speaking for several minutes, just listening to the pop and crackle of the fire and watching the shadows dance along the walls in the firelight.

"I want you to listen very carefully because there is more here than just an old myth to be told. Our people have gathered together like this for century after century, and sadly, that too is a thing of our past. Things are not what they once were, and they never will be again."

He paused and looked at each of us in turn, perhaps to stress the importance of what he was saying.

"It is important to me that young people like yourselves listen to stories such as this one, to try to preserve what you can and carry these things into the future with you. If someone does not step forward to shoulder such responsibilities, our history will truly be lost forever."

The light from the fire illuminated the wrinkled face of the old shaman and I saw him in a way I never had before. He had an air of sadness about him, mixed somehow with the wisdom of the ages. He looked old, but he still projected a sense of power and knowledge that was comforting and inspiring.

"For you to understand what has happened I feel you must know everything about the time it all began. It was the most difficult time our people have ever faced and it is one of the reasons this story has been overlooked for so long." He nodded his gray head towards me; "It is through the efforts of your grandfather that we are able to know what happened at all. We would be totally lost in the darkness now if he had not left us even this dim light from the past." Ben paused as Steven added another log to the fire.

"I haven't found all the answers we need to fight the Ravenmocker or how this terrible situation came to be. I don't yet know how to change things. Maybe, after you hear the story, together we can come up with a plan to stop further killings. All we can do is try, nothing more."

And so Ben told us the story. It must have taken a very long time, but it didn't seem so. The Cherokee have always prized the art of storytelling above all others. The stories were their only means of preserving the teachings of the elders, the only way for the young to learn, and their primary form of entertainment. In the long run, that was why the art of storytelling was the most respected in the tribe. In these days of books, movies, television, satellite dishes and the Internet, the art of storytelling has been sadly forgotten for the most part. It is rare to find one who still practiced the art well—as it was meant to be.

Ben "Rising Wolf" was a master storyteller. Never in my life have I listened to anyone able to paint such vivid pictures in my mind. His words flowed freely and smoothly, mesmerizing us and transporting us through time. It was tainted with humanity and touched with the personality of the storyteller and that "human touch" made it all the more real somehow.

On that cool, rainy night, on the side of my grandfather's mountain, Ben took us back into the past. The smoky room vanished, the sound of the rain and the fire dissipated. We were on-lookers transported through a time machine and we became lost to the magic of his words.

That was the way that night began, with Ben telling us a story.

CHAPTER TWENTY

When the white men came, they brought with them gifts for the dwellers in the land of the mountains. They brought many things for the Indians of the New World; they brought greed, torture, rape, murder, and disease in abundance for all. They brought measles, mumps, rubella, chicken pox and plague. These were the only things they ever "gave" the proud people who occupied paradise. They never gave anything else; they just took, and took, and took until the Indians had nothing left to give but their lives. Quite often, in the end, they took those as well.

When the savages began dying by the thousands, the settlers deemed it "God's Will". He was punishing the savages and they were his chosen instruments. Their God told them it was right to take the land from the heathen, to allow the savages to perish by the disease they themselves brought. Thus began the most horrible and most ill reported era in the history of the United States.

The Cherokee, like all other Indian tribes of early America, were forced into treaties they never wanted. Their land was slowly whittled away from them, beginning with the first signed treaty in 1721, and continuing to the treaty, which ultimately called for their removal in the Summer of 1838. Over that period, of slightly more than one hundred years, the Cherokee were forced, or coerced, into participating in almost two treaties per year. The previous treaty always forgotten, honored

only by the Indians anyway. New ones were written when something
was discovered of value that mistakenly was left the Indians by a previous treaty.

Then, in the spring of 1828, the worst possible thing in the world
happened to the Cherokee people. One little event changed the destiny
of the people and decided the deaths of too many tribal members to
count. A small Cherokee boy, playing in the waters of Ward Creek, happened upon a small gold rock which he later sold to a white man. The
fate of the Cherokee people was sealed forever with that one little trans-
action. Ultimately, Washington decided it would be in "the best interest
of the country to forcibly move" the entire Cherokee Nation from their
homeland. This action gave their lands to the rising number of white
settlers who had decided they were more deserving of the territory than
the savages who currently lived there.

In the northwest portion of what is now the state of North Carolina,
there was a small village of Cherokee residing near the Hiwassee River,
opposite the present town of Murphy. The village was called
"Gu'lani'yi", "Village of the Long Hair People." In the late winter of
1837, the people of the village were vaguely aware of the order to move
them to the west, but they had more pressing problems at the time. It
had been a cold, hard winter for the people of the tiny, isolated village.
They were more concerned with finding food for their children than
they were the crazy things the white man might do. The Indians had
lived in the same location for many years, and had heard the stories of
their fathers and grandfathers about their homeland.

When their tribal ancestors arrived in the territory, they discovered a
peculiar people living near the area of the Hiwassee. They were white
people, with "moon eyes", albinos, who could not see in the daytime and
made their homes in the darkness of cave-like structures. Over time, the
Albino people vanished, not to be seen again in the high mountains of
the Appalachians. But in the little village by the Hiwassee, one
remained, one very special, lone survivor.

The people of the village allowed her to stay on the opposite side of the river far upstream from the settlement. They avoided contact with her for they all knew she was a witch, but they let her remain, and tolerated her practice. When crops were bad, or game was scarce, the people went to her for help. They paid her with blankets, beads, whatever she asked for, and in return she would bring the rain or the game back to the people. The people didn't like the witch, but they needed her great power. As generations of the village passed, they distanced themselves more and more from the old witch. They found the need for her services less and less, and the people grew more afraid of her and her dark magic. Her power was great and her potions and formulas strong. Over the long years, the woman never aged, which especially scared the villagers.

As the harsh winter of 1837 continued, the worst nightmare the Indians knew came true for the little village. People vanished, the old, the young, and the sick. The people knew well the legends of the "Kalanu Ahyeliski", or the Ravenmockers that flew in the night to steal the hearts from people. The hearts of their victims would be removed from the bodies and eaten by the evil ones, adding their remaining years of life to their own. Where the heart had been taken, no scar would be left behind, but the heart would be missing from the body just the same. It was not unusual for the Ravenmocker to eat more of the body, but the missing heart was a sure sign of who or what, the killer might be.

The problems with stopping a Ravenmocker were many, perhaps the biggest problem was the demons only took on their true appearance when they were devouring their victims, and it was only then that they could be destroyed. The remainder of the time, they could be anyone; they could be the brave in the next cabin or an old grandmother who tended the fires at night. They hid within the villages of their victims for years, and they were rarely detected until it was too late. It was extremely hard to kill a Ravenmocker. Only a certain few possessed enough spirit to even try, for it was well known that if a shaman tried, and failed, his own magic could come back and kill him instead.

In that small village, the people began to suspect the presence of just such a demon. The elders consulted with the shaman who confirmed their fears. Victims turned up in the woods or in the nearby stream. Their bodies were horribly mutilated, many of the body parts missing, and always without a heart. These killings scared the villagers even more, because they were different, even more brutal than those they had heard about in legends and campfire talks. Within a few weeks, more little ones turned up missing for they were the favorite of the Ravenmocker. Frequently their little bodies would be found floating in the stream, mutilated in such a way that they were hard to recognize even by the unfortunate parents. The taking of the children was not something that could be tolerated by the people. And so it was, the shaman of the village came upon a plan, a way to find the terrible beast killing their young ones.

The shaman of that small village was very powerful in his own right. He had learned his craft well and developed his knowledge over many years of patience and practice. He gathered from the forest the necessary herbs and barks he needed, and retreated to his dwelling to prepare a strong medicine to aid his people. After that, they waited…and waited. They waited as the snow continued to fall and the villagers continued to despair. They waited as old people and children vanished with each new moon. The people began to wonder at the plan of the shaman and grew worried.

When word reached the shaman of a sick child in the village, he quickly rushed to the bedside and discovered the small one sick with fever and beyond all his powers. The shaman returned to the chief and told him of his plan, and what must be done. As bad as it would seem, the child would more than likely become the next victim of the Ravenmocker. Nothing would alter that. The shaman proposed to introduce into the child a potion, which would allow the dogs of the village to track the body. In this way, they would find the evil one and stop the reign of terror. The chief was wary and asked, "How could this be so if the Ravenmocker flies through the air with the child? The earth will not hold the scent." The shaman assured the chief that his medicine was strong and, promised they would be able to find the evil one.

The chief reluctantly agreed and called the parents of the unfortunate child to the council house. There, they discussed the idea with them. Their dismay at the unavoidable death of their child was great, but eventually they saw the wisdom of the decision, especially when the shaman told them the potion would bring a peaceful sleep to the little boy who suffered unbearably with fever. The mournful parents knew their great sacrifice was necessary for the good of the village. That night, the shaman did as he had planned; he administered the potion to both the boy and the dogs. He recited sacred formulas to kill a witch and to bring about death, and any others he thought might help with his fight.

The next morning the child was missing from the cabin of his parents and they were filled with sorrow. The people heard nothing in the night, yet he was gone before the first light of morning. The chief summoned the shaman and a party of the strongest warriors was chosen to follow the dogs and they followed all day long. No trace of the child was found.

The people were disappointed and grew disturbed with the medicine man's failed magic. The old shaman insisted they first cross the stream and try the opposite side before he would accept defeat.

Almost immediately, the dogs pulled from their handlers and charged off upstream. The dogs followed a trail for less than an hour and finally arrived, of course, at the home of the white witch. The dogs had pulled up short as the men of the tribe arrived and would not cross the threshold of the old cave.

The Cherokee people believed an animal pure white in color was sacred, and must be respected. So, as the men met outside the home of the witch to determine the next step, few were willing to enter the enclosure to find the Ravenmocker they thought to be inside. As the elders discussed the problem, the men around the cave found traces of blood in the fresh whiteness of the new fallen snow. They searched the surrounding area and began to turn up the remains of their missing family members. They found a half eaten arm, withered with age, limbs of various sizes and states of decay, heaped in piles, carelessly tossed behind the cave. Bodies, seemingly yet untouched, lay nearby in a dead-fall of pines, almost preserved in the winter cold and frost. They knew they had found their killer. The unspeakable horrors they found were proof the worst nightmare known to the Indians waited in the cold darkness of the cave.

After some discussion, the father of the sick child agreed to enter the enclosure. He drew his bow and notched an arrow, and slowly crept towards the door of the stone enclosure. He vanished from view of the anxious crowd, and almost immediately the sound of the man's screams echoed from the darkness. The villagers pulled back in alarm. The shaman came bravely forward.

The old medicine man called upon his most powerful formulas, sealing the doorway with his magic. As he performed the ritual, a course female voice spoke to him from the cave, lightly mocking his actions, "Do you think you have the power over me old man? Do you dare challenge one such as I?"

The old shaman stood his ground even when the body of the man was tossed from the cave into the snow, bloody and limp, like a corn husk doll. The medicine man did not stop his incantations. The voice from inside grew angry, cursing the old man and his efforts, promising unspeakable acts upon the villagers. The voice demanded they leave her immediately or suffer her wrath. The old shaman ignored her threats, knowing if she was speaking to him of such things; his magic must be working.

The remaining warriors gathered around the doorway with drawn bows, ready to send a hail of flint arrowheads into the body of the

Ravenmocker if she appeared. The wise chief knew the spells would not restrain the evil one for long. He sent runners back to the village and the entire village returned, every man, woman and child. They brought a crude cart used in the fields and instruments for digging and chiseling and the chief sent them to find a seal for the cave.

The old shaman continued to work his magic, hour after hour, as the long day wore on. The men continued to hold their bows at the ready, their arms shaking with effort. They knew something must be done, and soon. Night was coming and they all feared the darkness when a Ravenmocker was near. They knew the power of the medicine man was great, but they thought even he would not be able to stand in the way of the great strength possessed by the evil witch.

As the sun neared the treetops, the villagers returned. They had found a large oval boulder near the edge of the stream and with great effort, moved it to the cave. The entire tribe worked frantically to roll the stone into place. The curses from within grew to a fever pitch, describing in great detail the harm the Night Goer intended to inflict upon her captors. The people were afraid, but the chief and the medicine man assured them, and pushed them to hurry and position the stone over the enclosure. As the large stone neared the entrance, the shaman stood bravely in the opening, cursing the white witch to remain imprisoned until they could find a way to kill her. From the darkness of the cave, two red eyes blazed with hatred into his. He could just make out the whiteness of her face in the rapidly dimming light. As the darkness of the night came closer, she moved nearer the doorway ready to strike.

The oval stone inched closer and closer, partially covering the opening and still the old man stood bravely in the pathway, slowly speaking his formulas, cursing the demon to remain inside. It was all he could do to hold the wicked stare, which met his. Hatred for him and the villagers poured over him like water from the stream. The witch moved ever closer to the doorway, the sickly whiteness of her face shown like the underbelly of a fish and, as he watched, her features began to change, to shift to a face of evil as he never imagined. The witch altered and her body grew larger. The words coming from her wretched throat became harsh and gruff, dwarfing the sound of his voice completely. The evil one cursed the villagers, their chief, and especially the old shaman. The people trembled even as the stone was rolled into place sealing her within the cave. She promised vengeance on each of them. She swore they would suffer, as would their children and their children's children. They heard curses in languages they did not recognize and other terrible sounds from behind the large stone. The stone vibrated as mighty blows struck it from within. The villagers, even the warriors, retreated in alarm, but the large rock held. She would not escape, or so they hoped.

Throughout the long night, the people held council outside the cave as the witch continued to chant and curse them in languages they did not know, but well understood her meaning. It seemed one could hear even through the stone. They knew that she could not be allowed to live for she would never forget what they had done to her.

With the coming of the morning light, the sounds from within the cave lessened, finally growing silent. The chief placed guards at the prison he had created for the demon, and had the stone cutter from the village chisel warnings and symbols into the stone at the shaman's direction. For weeks, they met in council and struggled to find a solution. The shaman had felt the power of the Ravenmocker and he knew that he would not be able to kill one such as her. Her power was too great. It was greater than anything he had ever felt before.

Weeks of council became months, and with the coming of spring, the chief reduced the guards on the cave to two. The village slowly returned to normal. The people tried to forget the horrible cold winter and their wicked tormentor as the warm April sun warmed their faces. The Cherokee of old accepted the supernatural as easily as they accepted sunrise and the sunset. It was all part of the "one" of their life in the mountain wilderness.

During the first weeks, the guards reported that on some nights strange stirrings and sounds came from behind the stone. As time progressed, the sounds gradually lessened and finally stopped altogether as April gave way to May, and the spring became the summer of 1838. The Ravenmockers attack on the village was the worst thing that the people had ever experienced. They could not imagine anything more terrible. Until...the white men came.

As part of the so-called Treaty of New Echosta, devised by Washington bureaucrats and President Andrew Jackson, the Cherokee were forcibly removed from their homes effective May 26, 1838. The treaty was of course fraudulent, but that didn't matter. President Jackson appointed General Winfield Scott the task of rounding up all the Cherokee and placing them in stockades until they could be moved onto the "new" Cherokee land in Arkansas and Kansas. White men poured into the mountains like waters of the great ocean and the people were driven from their homes at gunpoint with just the clothes on their backs. Looters followed the army and before the families were even out of sight, their homes were in flames and their possessions divided among the white settlers. The graves of their ancestors and family members were unearthed to steal whatever valuables might be buried with them. Any resistance was met with brutality. Men, women, and children were beaten and driven like cattle into stockades where hundreds died of starvation and poor living conditions. In October, after months in the stockades, the 11,000 people who were forced onto the overland route, were herded into 645 wagons and marched halfway across the United States in the dead of winter, many without shoes or blankets. The people of the tribe died at a rate of ten to twenty per day during that long treacherous journey. In the history of the United States there has never been a more cruel act condoned by the American people.

When the movement was over, and the horrible "Trail of Tears" was at it's end, over four thousand of the most peaceful people ever to live, died horrible deaths at the hands of the United States Government. Fortunately, not all of the Cherokee were captured or removed. A party of 1046 Indians fled to the high mountains under the leadership of the great chief, "U'tsala", or "Lichen". They made their headquarters amid the high peaks near the headwaters of the Oconaluftee River and from there, defied the best efforts of General Scott to kill or capture them for month after month.

That small remaining group of the proud Cherokee nation fought the elements, starvation, and the forces of the U.S. Government. It was only through the efforts of Colonel William Holland Thomas, a great friend of the Cherokee, that they were eventually successful…to a point. They were allowed to remain in their mountain home on a tiny reservation, a mere fraction of what was rightfully theirs.

When the little village of "Gu'lani'yi" was destroyed, most of its people were lost on the horrible "Trail of Tears". Some actually made it to the west, and quite a few fled to the mountains and joined "U'tsala". The old shaman of the village happened to be one of the remaining bands of eastern Cherokee and ultimately told the wise chief what happened in the small village on the Hiwassee. The great chief took the matter seriously, and immediately dispatched warriors to the dangerous cave near the burned out village. They later returned and reported the cave just as it had been—the stone slab still sealing the demon within. No sounds were heard from inside. The leader of the Cherokee decreed that all his people must know of the evil so future generations could be made aware of the great force imprisoned in the cave. They must never forget.

As the years passed, and the problems of the eastern band became many, the people did forget. The story dimmed. It became an old wife's tale, then eroded to legend and finally, over the course of time, just a faint, forgotten myth.

With the years, the remaining members of the village, and the old shaman, died and were also forgotten. Some told the story to their children, but later the young were forced to attend white man's school where they were told all their history and beliefs were false. They were forced to forget what their elders told them and to turn against their own people and history. As the years wore on, fewer and fewer were around to remember what had happened in the winter of 1837 on the banks of the Hiwassee. Memories faded and died with the people. And yet...

Deep within the forest of northwest North Carolina, near the rapidly flowing waters of the Hiwassee River, close to the burned out remains of what was once a peaceful village, there was one who would never forget.

She remained there, where they left her...and she waited.

Chapter Twenty-one

When Ben finished the story, he stood and wandered about the smoky interior of the council house. His expression was empty and withdrawn, as if the telling was an emotional drain. During the tale, his voice traveled lightly over the words, graceful and clear. As he spoke, I listened and could almost feel the world he created with his words and gestures. His face shifted from one expression to another and his hands followed his words, speaking his anger and his anxiety at the appropriate places in the story.

The story changed him as he told it—it changed him in a way I can't describe because I couldn't understand it myself. He seemed to become more alive somehow, bigger than life, reliving the past with his thoughts and words. His eyes filled with a fire sparked by pride and reverence for deeds of his ancestors and a longing for something he would never know. The sound of his voice made the whole story easier to accept for some reason. I guess it was the way the old man related the story from my grandfather's book. I knew, regardless of what the actual truth might be, Ben genuinely believed in the tale. I had known old Ben for as long as I could remember, and may have met smarter men, but not many. When he obviously believed so strongly, the whole insane mess seemed almost plausible…almost, but not quite.

I still couldn't believe such a thing could happen, that a "Ravenmocker" could actually exist. But then again, totally condemning the idea due to my lack of knowledge would be stupidity, at the very least arrogance. Until I had the opportunity to personally check the immortality of my brother's killer, I couldn't accept such a crazy explanation. It just wasn't logical and logic dictated everything I did and believed in—it was one of the last "rocks" I had to cling to. Logic always seemed my best way to prevail over the anger. It was my only guard, and I wasn't giving it up easily.

I knew I would have to be careful of my reaction in order not to offend the old Indian in any way if at all possible. He was one of the few men alive I actually respected. I figured the best thing, would be for me to keep quiet and word my comments and questions carefully.

I glanced to Kathy and Steven as they both sat gazing into the fire, lost in their own interpretations of what we had heard. For the first time, I noticed the tears in Kathy's eyes. In the red glow of the firelight, her cheeks had taken on a golden coppery sheen glistening with fresh tears and the emotion she wore too close to her heart. In the lights and shadow of the firelight, I could only guess, but I knew she was too lost in her own thoughts to be concerned with mine.

Steven had leaned back into the old canvas chair; a cigarette dangling unlit in the corner of his mouth. He stared out of the fire hole into the night sky above. He seemed to be watching the smoke as it danced it's way up the tunnel of moonlight and disappeared through the circular opening. At that moment, with his long black hair trailing down nearly to the floor, he seemed every inch an Indian warrior of old. His eyes were set in a hard expression I couldn't read, anger, maybe confusion…I could only guess at the rest. If he wanted to be, Steven could be as unreadable as a French menu and I hated him for it sometimes. People accused me of having the same personality trait, and I hated that too.

I think Ben's voice startled all three of us as he finally spoke again, "There is something else I must tell you."

Something in the way he said it made me feel ill at ease. We all looked at him respectfully, waiting for him to continue. "I believe the

Ravenmocker is back among us for sure, that goes without saying, but there is something else I sense. It's something I have gathered from the stories I have heard of these killings, but I can't prove it." With a nod of his head, he gestured to me, "Morgan, you remember the way both of you described the body of your brother?"

I glanced at Steven who was now paying very close attention. "Yessir, I remember very well."

"Your description is not unusual. From what I have gathered from the tribal grapevine, the other killings have been similar. All the bodies were found in the same manner. Something about the story suggests to me a much greater problem which we have not discussed."

I looked at the old man, trying to guess where he was headed.

"I believe the Evil One is breeding."

Steven finally broke his silence and asked for us all, "Sir?"

"I believe that is the only explanation for such behavior. I can not say for sure. She may think she is the last of her kind and believe she needs to procreate or perhaps she thinks it is appropriate punishment, these things I don't know, but I do sense she is joining with her victims. She may be trying to reproduce more of her kind into the world. As I have said, no one can know for sure the reasons for such a demon's wicked deeds. A Ravenmocker can be evil purely for the sake of evil."

Kathy spoke from her seat across from me, "Then that means this witch must be dealt with as soon as possible."

I looked at her somewhat surprised with her comment. I knew she felt very strongly about the Cherokee and the beliefs held by that band of people, but she was a well-educated woman. She had gone to one of the better colleges in the south, and graduated with honors. She had to know that such a story could have no basis in fact. I was surprised she would be so easily taken in by an old myth. I wondered if perhaps she was just trying to appease her grandfather.

Steven addressed her, "That's not the question, the question is how? What the hell can we do about it? If she couldn't be killed before, what can we do now?"

I couldn't help myself. I had to interject, "Steven if the killer is the same one, and we don't know that she is, surely you realize things have changed. I mean these people of the village didn't have automatic weapons or C-4 explosives. Somehow or another, this asshole apparently survived the shots from your gun, but that doesn't mean she can't be killed, for Christ's sake." I mentally kicked myself when I realized I was actually going along with the story they were buying so readily.

"I still believe this is something real here. Something we can defend ourselves against."

"Oh, she can be killed." Ben spoke and we all turned to look at him expectantly. "The legends say that she can be killed if the conditions are right. There is a poem by a modern Cherokee poet who writes of the stories and myths of our past. Part of a poem she wrote concerns the Ravenmockers. If I remember right it goes:
"The wise ones knew what to do,
For Ravenmockers can be killed for seven days
Once they have taken their guise to feed
And someone has seen them as they are"
The words hung in the air for a moment or two before Steven finally asked, "But what does that mean? I don't understand."

The old man's voice was becoming raspier the longer he spoke. I knew he must be getting tired. "Well, if someone who believes in her, sees her in her natural state, as you two did, that person can kill her within seven days. If she is not killed within seven days then she cannot be killed. Her reign of terror will continue." He looked at Steven and me with steel in his old gray eyes, "We can't allow her to live and we can't allow more of her kind among us again." He gestured with his hands, "If they were ever gone."

"But how can we kill her if we don't know where she is? And if we do find her, how exactly do we kill her?" Steven was showing signs of frustrated anger himself—something I had somehow miraculously managed to avoid.

"That I don't know. Perhaps we can come up with a plan. There are some things I can do for you tomorrow to help you prepare before I return to the reservation. There are many there that will also need my help, so I must go back. She could strike there anytime. I feel she will be returning to the mountains very soon."

I asked, "What makes you think that?"

"Well, her killing draws her ever closer. I think she began her work at its farthest point in order to finish here where it all began. It is here that she will find the most knowledge of her legend and therefore the most fear. She feeds off that fear, cultivates it like a plant, and harvests it when it is the ripest."

Kathy asked, "Grandfather, I can't understand what chance we could possibly have against a murderer like this. I know you have no respect for them, but don't you think the FBI is better equipped to handle something like this? I mean even if this really is a Ravenmocker, they seem perhaps better suited to stopping her than we are."

"There is some truth to what you say, yes, but they will not catch her. They will not catch her because they do not understand what she is and would never listen to such an explanation. They would be so sure of their own logic; they would totally disregard the possibility of the old legend. The myth would not be something they would listen to, let alone accept." He paused and looked from her to me, "Isn't that so Morgan?"

I was sure he directed the question to me for more than one reason. I was momentarily embarrassed that he seemed to sense the doubts I myself held about the validity of his story. "He's right Kathy, these guys are not likely to listen to anything like this. They would think we were totally crazy and probably figure we were just trying to hide something. That's the way their warped little bureaucratic minds function."

"But you're going to see them tomorrow right? What could it hurt to at least try? All they can do is laugh right?"

"I know Kath, but…"

"Don't start with me Morgan Roberts!" She threw her hands in the air angrily, "You always do that for Christ's sake! You can at least feel them out about it can't you? You at least speak to them about it. You're being as ridiculous as you think we are."

"Kathy, I fully intend to speak to them about it, I promise." She had seen right through me, which didn't really come as a surprise to me. "I've already thought about it and I think we will at least tell them. They aren't going to believe any of it, but I'll tell them, okay?"

"Okay." She looked at me suspiciously, perhaps disappointed that I had given up the fight so easily.

What I had not told her, was I still believed my theory that someone knew the same stories we had just heard, and that person was using that knowledge to further some warped ideas of their own. Even though I had accepted the fact that such a thing could possibly exist, I was not ready to give up everything I ever believed, in order to accept a myth hundreds of years old…and told so many times it was worn away to near extinction. One brief glimpse of a shadowy figure, and a small gash on my leg, wasn't going to convince me that a Ravenmocker was alive, well and on the loose. I decided to stick with my plan and just go along with them and their beliefs concerning the supposed ghost from the tribe's past.

I knew Ben believed in the truth of the story. Steven told me even before he heard the story he believed it, and it seemed Kathy had also been drawn into the spell, or maybe not. Hell, I never had an earthly idea what she was thinking at any one time. She was just too hard to read. She generally read me as easily as a quick lunch menu. I could only hope Agent Smith and his boys had come up with something that might shed some light on the killer's identity, at least some light of substance rather than fiction.

"It's late." Ben interrupted my thoughts, "I'm old and I'm tired. I think it's time we all got some sleep."

"Of course." I answered, "Let's go back to the cabin. You can sleep in Papaw's old bed and Kathy can sleep in the spare room. Steven and I will share the couch. We'll sleep in shifts tonight anyway."

Steven caught my eye and nodded his understanding. He went outside briefly and returned with an old clay urn filled with water, which he poured over the smoldering fire. The flames gave a last dying hiss, and thick smoke rushed to escape towards the night sky. The rain had tapered off during our long stay in the council house. No stars were visible in the cloud filled sky, but I sensed the rain would move away by morning. We walked back to the main cabin in silence with Dog following obediently behind. The mountain air was still and very cool, the woods strangely silent in the dark dampness of late evening. Kathy and I made some sandwiches, and after an impromptu supper, she and her grandfather got their things from her truck as Steven and I cleared the kitchen.

A little later, just before Ben retired to bed, he came and sat down briefly on the old sofa and motioned for us to join him. "I know I've talked so much tonight that you're tired of hearing my voice, but there is one other story I must tell you." He held up his hand and smiled tiredly, "Don't worry, it is a much shorter story, but one I think you need to hear and I think tonight it is especially fitting. In times like these it is very easy to give up hope, to forget what's really important. It's easy to accept defeat when one thinks there is no other way out. I also know that you all three have probably heard this tale before, but it has a particular bearing on the things we have discussed tonight. So please listen for just another few minutes and then I will keep you awake no longer." He looked at each of us in turn as if to insure he had our undivided attention. The old shaman again transformed into the master storyteller.

"You remember I told you of when the white men came to drive the people from their land in the summer of 1838? Well, the soldiers came upon one particular family in the wilderness, the family of "Tsali", or Charley, as he came to be called. Charley, his wife and brother, three sons and their families were all driven from their homes at bayonet point. They were forced to march towards the waiting stockades, and they were beaten and prodded for the amusement of the soldiers. Charlie's wife became the center of attention, with a bayonet being constantly shoved into her back until she repeatedly fell and was beaten. Charlie decided he could allow the abuse no longer. Speaking in the Cherokee language which the soldiers could not understand, he encouraged the others to await his command and then to turn on the soldiers, seizing their weapons from them, and then to run for their lives.

During the scuffle that ensued, a white soldier was killed, whether deliberate or accidental no one knows for sure. Charley, with his family and his small band, escaped into the mountains and joined with the Indians who remained behind. There, they defied all efforts to remove them from the deep mountains. General Scott took the incident as a personal insult." Ben leaned further back in the cushions and took a deep breath. I could tell he was exhausted. His voice faded to a quiet monotone.

"As the months passed, Washington became disillusioned with the ability of anyone to remove the remaining band of Cherokee, and Scott was ordered to withdraw. He was ordered to reach a treaty agreement and to leave the remaining Indians alone in the mountains. A civil war was brewing and the country suddenly had more important things to think about than a bunch of starving, diseased Indians. General Scott sent the most trusted friend of the Cherokee, Colonel W.H. Thomas to the tribe with a proposal. He proposed that if they would surrender

Charley and his family, they would be allowed to live in peace and the white soldiers would leave their mountain home."

"When Charley heard of the proposal, and before the acting Chief could decide, he marched into the nearest encampment of white soldiers and surrendered himself in order to save his people. General Scott, in an effort to further humiliate the tribe, forced a detachment of Cherokee prisoners to shoot Charley and his entire family, only one small boy was spared the wrath of General Scott. The killings were uncalled for, and unordered, but were of course of no consequence except to a "bunch of Indians." He shook his head sadly. "As you know, the story of Charley and his great courage and sacrifice is told and retold. This story is proof positive of the strong spirit that flows within the people of the Cherokee. This same blood, this same spirit, is part of everyone in this room...everyone." He looked at each of us and his eyes seemed to sparkle as I had seen them do in the firelight of the old council house, "This is something to be proud of and we must always remember Charley and his supreme sacrifice. We owe a dept to Charley and his family, for it is only perhaps through his act that we are all here today."

He stopped as if thinking what to say next, "These problems we are facing are grave ones, but we will find a way to overcome them. Our people have faced more difficult things in the past and have survived. We, here, must do the same thing. I don't know how, but I know we must. Do you understand me?" His sat forward in his chair as if to better make his point, to insure we all heard what he had said. When we didn't answer he continued, "It was not a hypothetical question, do you understand what I am trying to tell you?"

I responded for us all, "Yessir, we do." Such a story would touch the heart of a statue and even the most hardhearted had to see the beauty in the immense sacrifice of Charley for his people.

"Good, I truly hope you do." He smiled a tired smile, his eyes almost lost against the wrinkled cinnamon skin, "If so, that is the most important thing that has happened here tonight. Everything else pales beside this knowledge. The Cherokee, the "Real People", will always, must always, continue to find a way. A way to keep the tradition alive, our history alive. We must not perish, for our fathers, and our father's fathers, all fade as we do. The Cherokee have no real written history, most of the knowledge we have, has come through the Storyteller, from one generation to another."

He shook his head and hesitated before continuing in a soft voice, all at once sounding his age; "The problem now is finding a generation that cares less about the Internet than our heritage."

I had never heard old Ben sound more earnest or concerned. As I glanced at Steven I was surprised to detect a look of respect...actually more of awe. For a moment, his expression reminded me of a true believer in an evangelist's audience

"You young people must find it within yourselves to make it happen. You are the last hope for the future of the Cherokee and it will be a harder time for you than it was for me."

I wasn't quite sure what he meant by his last statement, but I was deeply touched by what he said. I vaguely remembered the story of Charley from my youth, but the true meaning of the story was lost to me until his moving re-telling of the tale.

Ben bid us all goodnight and finally retired to his waiting bed. Kathy followed within a few minutes, leaving Steven and me to plan.

I turned to my cousin, "I think we should stand guard starting tonight and every night from now on. We can do it in shifts and Dog can sleep on the porch with us. I'll take the first shift. How does three on, three off sound to you?"

"Fine I guess." He stretched and yawned, his big hands almost touching the ceiling of the cabin. "You sure you don't want to sleep first?"

"No, I'm too wound up now anyway, and you sure as hell need the beauty sleep." I then added more seriously, "I think you better keep your shotgun near the couch. We still don't know what, or who, we're dealing with here. We don't know how much time we will have to react. We could have only seconds, so I want to be well prepared." I thought about it for a minute and added, "As a mater of fact, I don't think we should travel anywhere from now on without carrying serious firepower along. I'll check and load both assault rifles and put one by the door and keep one outside on the porch."

"Sounds good to me, I'm so tired I'll fall asleep in two minutes. You wake me if you hear anything okay?"

"You got it cousin."

"Morgan, one other thing." His smile was a different one this time, more uncomfortable, "…thanks."

"For what?"

"You know…" He shrugged his giant shoulders, "…for hearing Rising Wolf out, for not saying everything that I know is on your mind. I know you're having a hard time with this, but Rising Wolf really believes. Your respect for him means a lot to me."

"Look Steven, I've known Ben for a long time myself. I'm not faking respect here. He and my grandfather were best friends. I truly respect him more than anyone I know. I never intended to insult him, or his beliefs, I just…"

"Our beliefs." He interrupted me.

"His beliefs Steven. They may be his, yours, Kathy's I don't know. I know they're not necessarily mine."

"They're yours. You're just too stubborn to admit it."

I felt my temper rise just a touch too sudden, "Look Steven, just because I have the same skin color as yours, doesn't mean I have to believe as you do. It's my choice, damn it! Not yours or anybody else's".

Steven, perhaps knowing me better than I knew myself, held his hands apart and said, "Hold on there Cuz. I'm not giving you grief. I just don't want us to miss anything because we can't see what is right in front of us."

I took a deep breath and released it slowly, "Yeah...yeah.... I know." This time, it was I with the embarrassed smile; "Sometimes I get a little carried away." After a moment I added, "Steven, if I have reservations, which I admit I do, I'll discuss them with you, in private. I don't intend to express my doubts or questions to Ben. You should give me enough credit for more sense than that. What's between us, stays between us." I paused, "Steven, I'm not saying I don't believe any of this, I'm just saying I don't know what to believe, that's all. Right now, I haven't heard or seen anything to change my mind. When the time comes, maybe I will. All I know is something totally crazy is going on here that I don't pretend to understand. If there's any answer, I'm ready to try at this point, if I believe it or not." I turned away before he could reply, " Now, go to sleep. I'll be waking you soon."

As I opened the door to leave and as he stretched out on the couch, I called over my shoulder in a teasing voice, "Goodnight, Stevey."

I quickly closed the door on his rather vulgar response. I was sort of disappointed though. For some reason the little joke didn't seem quite as funny as it usually did.

CHAPTER TWENTY-TWO

She had traveled far during the night and it had worn her down more than usual. Perhaps it was the wounds from which she had yet to fully recover, perhaps it was just exhaustion. It was rainy and the wetness felt good against her skin. Of course all the things in the world once absent to her felt good after being removed from them for so long. There were no stars out to guide her way, but that was fine, for she knew her way.

She had been sure her prey would be asleep in their beds, but she could make out a light from one of the windows near the front of their house. She knew they were inside for she could feel the closeness of one of "them". She had come to know the familiar stirring in her gut very well. Her evil heart began to beat a little faster, her breathing quickened as it did every time just before she paid one of her "little visits" on the cursed ones. Even though she wanted to hurry, she made herself wait, made herself take her time—prolonging her need—making her gratification that much more rewarding when it finally came.

As she silently approached the front door of the house, she heard muted voices from behind the walls. She could sense two of them, a woman of no consequence, and one of the men. She could feel him…she had been drawn to him like the rest—like a hungry vulture to a long dead carcass. She heard the masculine voice from inside and her heart beat faster still and she moved yet closer. The boards on the old porch creaked under her weight and she paused for a moment to insure no one had heard. She filled her lungs with the clean night air, savoring the anticipation, exercising the patience she had learned through long years of practice until she could wait no longer.

She raised her mighty arms, sharply striking the doorframe with all her strength and was quickly inside before either could react. The old woman meant nothing to her and, with a quick blow from her powerful forearm, she bounced the old hag off the nearest wall and into unconsciousness. She was careful not to hurt her too badly, as she usually needed the women alive…at least for a time. It was often only through the pain of their loved ones that she could truly touch the heart of some of the stronger men.

For a few, it was the only way…but always…always she found the way to make them suffer. She felt the old man strike her across the back with a stick of some kind. She turned quickly to face her attacker, anticipating the normal fear in his eyes as he took in her ghastly appearance. Her true appearance was normally enough to push many of the weaker of them over the edge.

In this one, instead of the normal shocked expression of disbelief, she was briefly disappointed when she saw no immediate fear. The man showed only anger as he raised his arm to attack her again. She intercepted his next blow and threw him across the room, furniture and lamps shattering in his wake and hers, as she followed him across the cramped space.

The man rose shakily to his feet, looking even more frail and weak than she first thought, but he still somehow managed to stand arrogantly against her yet again. She struck him hard across the face and inwardly cursed herself when she saw fresh blood fly from his broken nose. It was too soon for that kind of damage and she altered her plan slightly. As he moved to attack her, she effortlessly folded her big arms around him, drawing him to her like a favorite lover. His face was close to hers and she could smell an inner sickness as she bent to administer the first dose of her potent poison. She felt his thin body go instantly limp in her arms just as she dropped him to the floor like an unwanted doll. The strong poison worked quickly and she knew he was aware of everything that went on around him, yet would remain unable to move any part of his body for hours. She was free to do with him as she liked and when she liked.

She rose to stand over his body, and as she did, she noticed him following her with his eyes. She saw the hate in his gaze, and laughed out loud at his pitiful expression. The strange sound of her laughter, unnatural and evil, filled the quiet stillness of the room. The pure stench of her floated in the air like a heavy cloud.

The old gray-haired woman rested against the wall where she had been tossed, showing no signs of waking. She grabbed the woman casually by one leg and pulled her alongside her husband until their faces were just bare inches apart. She saw the man's eyes look at her and if looks could kill, she was sure, even her seemingly immortal life, would be at an end. As he strained to see his bride, she turned his head so he could better view what was to happen to the one he loved. Her touch was remarkably gentle as she did this. She savored the sight of them both lying at her feet…awaiting the pleasure of her vengeance.

She looked into the eyes of the old man again, letting his hate filled gaze drink in the hate of her own. The difference in this one was he knew about her. She could sense it in the way he looked at her. He knew just who she was and why she was here. He was the first to know about her and the first who would understand the great punishment to come.

She smiled wickedly and then began screaming her rage, maniacally—moving about the room as she did—destroying all as she went: furniture, lamps, and pictures from the walls, until there was nothing in the cabin untouched or undamaged. She made her way back to the old couple on the floor.

She moved her face close to that of the old man, inches away, knowing the smell of her, the look of her so close, would bring revulsion and fear, sure of her power over the mortals by that time.

Instead she saw something else, something she had yet to see in the others: defiance, yet something more. She saw rage, maybe even pride. But she saw no trace of fear. And that made her even more angry.

This one would not be easy.

She stood again, just as the old woman began to stir. When the old man heard the sound of his bride, the look in his eyes finally changed, just as she had known it would. As she moved closer to the old woman, moved to kneel over the silver haired hag, his eyes pleaded then. Oh yes…then he pleaded. And that is when the fear began. That is when she felt the first of it…tasted it upon her lips like hot blood and warm flesh. Just as real and almost as satisfying.

Then, and only then, there in the shattered, darkened interior of the remote cabin, at the foothills of the mountains she once called home, she began her long night's work.

It would be a long time yet before the coming of the dawn.

CHAPTER TWENTY-THREE

"Morgan...Morgan."

I felt a soft, familiar touch on my shoulder, waking me from sleep. Steven had earlier relieved me from my watch and I replaced him on the couch for some much-needed rest. When the time came for us to change again, it was all I could do to keep my eyes open. The events of the previous days had an exhausting effect on my mind and body, more than I cared to admit.

"Well, are you going to wake up or sleep all day?"

I looked up into the beautiful brown eyes of the Indian princess who stood over me. "Sleep all day sounds good." She smiled that knowing smile of hers, sort of a cross between a smirk and the beginning of a laugh. I always found her smile touched me and for some reason always made me want to return it—even if I was upset or depressed. She used it right in the middle of an argument, sometimes diffusing my anger, sometimes not, but that particular smile had always disarmed me in one way or another. I tried a weak, sleepy one of my own in response, partly at the memory and partly at her.

I sat up, rubbing sleep from my eyes, and asked, "What time is it, anyway?" My throat was scratchy and parched and my voice horse and gruff.

Kathy handed me a steaming cup of coffee. "It's just after seven. Grandfather and Steven are already outside. They just came and asked me to wake you. They're out by the stream."

I placed the cup of coffee on the table. The wooden floor was cool and smooth beneath my bare feet. I briskly rubbed my hands through my hair to bring myself fully awake, then stretched my arms high above my head. The joints creaked and popped in the quiet of the still room, the effects of many years of physical abuse. I guess it wasn't really the age of the vehicle, it was the miles and how they were traveled.

Kathy laughed from her place in the chair across from me. "My aren't we getting old? I hope you feel better than you sound."

"Not really." I picked up the hot mug and folded my feet beneath me as I sipped the contents. I noticed she had added the appropriate amounts of cream and sugar and snickered at the observation.

"And just what may I ask, is so funny all of a sudden?"

"Oh nothing…nothing, just my own private thoughts if you don't mind. I can have those, can't I?"

"Suit yourself."

"What's for breakfast?" I asked with a another smile.

"Nothing."

"Nothing?" My smile faded.

"That's right, nothing." Her expression was mischievous and hard to read.

"Does that mean nothing, we don't have anything, or nothing, you're not fixing anything, or nothing, I have to fix it myself?"

"None of the above, but since you've brought it up, I will not be expected to fix your meals just because I'm a woman you know."

"Oh yeah, that I definitely know. Do you really think I would be stupid enough to make such a statement to you of all people, Miss Emancipated-Woman-of-the-World? I may be a slow country boy, but I ain't stupid."

"Good for you. Maybe you're not as dumb as you look."

I waited on her to continue and when she didn't, I tried once again for an answer to my question. "Well?"

"Well, what?" Her smile was wicked and taunting, she was enjoying herself at my expense. "What about breakfast?"

"You're not getting any."

"Why not?"

"Because you're fasting."

"Oh really, and why am I doing that?"

"Because grandfather said so, that's why."

"Of course. Any particular reason, if I might be so bold as to ask?" My stomach was growling and I was in no mood for riddles.

"Sure you can ask, but you can save time by going outside and asking him yourself. I've already told you they're waiting for you Sleeping Beauty."

"Alright, I can see I'm not going to get anywhere trying to talk to you anyway." I took a last sip of the hot coffee and reached for the boots I had placed beside the couch in the night.

"Maybe, maybe not." Her tone was taunting.

"Well, at least you left some chance for compromise."

"Maybe, maybe not."

"Oh, hush up, woman. You know sometimes you really get on my nerves." I chuckled as I laced up my boots and rose to walk out the door.

"Ditto," she replied her face void of emotion as she looked up into mine.

Before she could react, I quickly leaned down and placed a kiss on the end of her regal Indian nose. "Give me time and I'll wear you down, girl."

Without changing her expression she said, "You're going to have to work harder than that."

I smiled and called over my shoulder as I left, "Maybe, maybe not."

I heard her say, "We'll see, smart ass."

The morning was beautiful and still. The forest floor and the majestic trees were still wet from the storm and the dew. There was no trace of rain in the sky, but at high elevations that was subject to change at any moment. The sun was already peeking from behind the thick wall of trees, mixing with the patches of crisp blue visible through the deep forest growth. Birds sang loudly in the quiet of the morning as Dog came running from somewhere in the woods to greet me.

"What's up, girl? Where have you been?" I rubbed her briskly as she dropped to her back, encouraging my attention. I knelt beside her, pulling on her paws and playfully grabbing her snout with my hand. She growled back at my attack.

"What? You think you're a bad ass now that you're so big?"

I grabbed both her ears in my hands and shook her head back and forth. She snapped at my hand as I withdrew it, lightly enclosing it with her sharp teeth. I let her hold the hand in her mouth for a moment as she growled her pretend anger. I smiled at the big animal, knowing she could take my hand completely off by just closing those powerful jaws. I reached my other hand up and lightly thumped her big black nose. Her mouth immediately released my hand and I stood, "You're a good girl Dog, I think I'll keep you around awhile." Her tail wagged as she moved in quick circles around me, jumping and playing, ready for my next movement or command. I hadn't seen her so playful in months. The mountain air must have agreed with her.

"Come on girl, let's go see what's up."

I noticed Steven standing at the edge of the stream near the bend. Ben was sitting on the bank just behind him and they spoke quietly together. They stopped speaking and turned to me as I approached.

Ben spoke, "Good morning Morgan. It's a beautiful morning isn't it?"

"Yessir, it is. I guess every morning is a good morning if you live to see it."

He laughed and agreed, "Very true indeed. Did you sleep well?"

"Yessir," I answered as I stretched again, " just not enough. Good morning Stevey, what's up."

"You are, if you keep calling me Stevey." He changed his tone and nodded towards the old shaman, "Rising Wolf is preparing a formula to help us. We've just been waiting on you to start. Think you can work it into your busy schedule?" He indicated the materials spread on the bank of the stream, which I hadn't noticed before.

There were pieces of the black and white cloth I had purchased the day before. On the black cloth were seven beads of the same color, the white cloth contained a like number of red beads. Near them was a tube fashioned from the bark of a birch tree, a gourd water dipper and the small mortar Ben had used in the asi the day before. The bowl contained some paste-like substance I didn't recognize.

"Perhaps Kathy has told you I requested we all fast until this evening. This is necessary to improve the effectiveness of the formula. It should increase our chances of killing the wicked one and fasting helps clear and focus the mind. This afternoon, when you two have returned from your meeting with the FBI, I will take additional measures to safeguard the cabin where you sleep. We only have to fast until then. After that, I have to return to the reservation. There is much yet to be done there." His expression was sad, and he looked older and tired there in the morning light. "I don't know when the witch will return, but I expect it will be very soon."

I looked briefly at my cousin who gave a slight nod of his head. "Okay, what do you want Steven and I to do?"

"Since you two are the primary beneficiaries of the formula, you must both enter the stream, but only to hand length. Then we will perform the ritual."

As the old shaman knelt over the bolts of white and black cloth lying on the stream bank, Steven and I removed our boots. While I struggled with my socks, Steven told me that besides being necessary for the ceremony, the bolts of cloth were considered ancient symbolic payment for the services of the shaman. Ben, already bare footed and shirtless, stood over me as I struggled with my laces, "Your cousin is perhaps more familiar with the formulas so he can translate anything you don't understand. He has learned the Cherokee tongue very well and in a short period of time."

I turned to Steven in amazement and blurted without thinking, "No kidding! When did this happen?" I didn't really mean for it to sound like I found it amusing but it came out that way. I knew I had perhaps gone too far when Ben interrupted before Steven had a chance to answer.

"I think the fact that Steven has shown enough respect to understand our language speaks well of his desire to learn. You could do a lot worse than to learn from him a respect for the old ways." He looked at me sternly, "The ways of your grandfather."

Then, I think he realized he might have extended too much in the way of a compliment and took steps to correct his error. "But again, just because Steven has learned the language doesn't mean he has accomplished any great feat. Small children accomplish the same thing even as they begin to walk; it isn't a big thing. Your cousin has a lot yet to learn himself."

Steven gave me a look that told me he was not at all happy with me. Again, I had managed to put my mouth in gear before my brain had a chance to catch up. I wanted to add something in the way of redemption, but before either of us had a chance to speak, Ben continued his lecture.

"You will notice the two colors of fabric, the white and the black. The white represents goodness and prosperity, and the red beads symbolize success and the two of you. The black is something else; the black represents the evil one. It is the color of death, of bad tidings and of coming demise." Ben bent to pick up a bead in each hand, in his right a red bead, in his left, black. The old, gray-haired Indian turned and waded waist deep into the rushing water, unmindful of the coolness or the pants he still wore.

Steven elbowed me painfully in the side and said, "Okay big mouth, walk into the water, but just ankle deep, right near the bank, that's what's meant by "hands length". Just keep your mouth shut and watch Rising Wolf and try to learn something." His voice was low and serious. I stood quietly as he suggested, slightly embarrassed by my earlier untimely outburst.

Ben turned to the east, facing the bend in the fast moving stream. He extended his arms over his head, holding the beads between thumb and forefinger. The old medicine man began to recite in the language of the Cherokee, the sound of the language soft and melodic in the stillness of the early morning. Steven, apparently having forgiven me at least for the moment, translated his words softly under his breath. I didn't understand the meaning behind all the phrases, but then I never expected to. The more I heard, it seemed the less I understood. Once again I noticed, as I had the night before, the majestic transformation which seemed to occur when Ben became caught up in the great magic of his people. I understood why Steven was developing such a strong belief in the power of the shaman. His words were strange and mysterious, full of grace and strength and when the old man spoke, he was indeed "Rising Wolf", and the forest rang with the power of his speech;

"Listen! Now I have come to step over your soul. You are of the Ravenmockers. Your name is Night Goer. Your spittle I have put at rest under the earth. Your soul I have put at rest under the earth. I have come to cover you over with the black rock. I have come to cover you with the black slabs, never to reappear. Toward the black coffin of the upland in the Darkening Land your paths shall stretch out. So shall it be for you. The clay of the upland has come to cover you. The black clay has lodged there where it is at rest at the black houses of the Darkening Land. With the black coffin and with the black slabs, I have come to cover you. Now your soul has faded away.

It has become blue. When darkness comes your spirit shall grow less and dwindle away, never to reappear…Listen!"

The last word was shouted, his frail arms raised skyward, startling a pair of robins who had been sitting in a nearby tree. They flew up into the sky with a flutter of wings and a rustle of leaves. I turned to Steven but he shook his head, indicating a need for continued silence. Steven resumed translating as Rising Wolf turned to us and addressed the "Su nikta Gigage i", the "Red Bead."

Steven spoke softly under his breath. "He is invoking blessings upon us, calling for the power of the stream, "Yu wi Gunahi ta", the "Long Person", to aid us, to cloak us in the red colors of success. He is asking the "Long Person" to use it's power to raise us to seventh heaven, where we will be secure and safe from our enemy."

The shaman shifted his gaze to his left hand, concentrating on the black bead as Steven continued to translate. "Now, he is bringing down curses upon the Ravenmocker. He is using his power, and the great power of the water, to cast a curse of death over the evil one." He listened quietly for a moment; "These curses are very powerful and very rare. I have never heard any of them before. I've only heard about them."

As the old man finished, we watched as he used the water gourd he had clipped to his belt, and poured water over his head. Seven times he dipped into the cold water, and seven times he rubbed the water over his head and shoulders. Afterward, he moved from the stream and stooped to dig a small hole on the bank. He placed the black bead in it and used his heel to stomp dirt into the hole, covering the bead of the Ravenmocker with earth. Thus, he condemned the "Evil One" to death, to return to the earth.

Ben retrieved the remaining six black beads and pushed them into the tube along with the paste I saw earlier. Steven told me Ben made it by grinding seven earthworms together. They were thought to eat the soul of the one cursed. The tube also contained a splinter of a tree struck by lightening, which the old Indian retrieved the day before when Kathy had left him to search in the forest. He would return to that same tree and bury the tube at the bottom among the roots. That was the last act necessary to complete the formula.

I remained quiet as Ben "Rising Wolf" walked away and disappeared into the deep forest, his movement unnaturally quiet and ghostlike. I never even heard a leaf move. He had not spoken a word after finishing the curse. Steven told me that there was a brief formula to be recited when Ben reached the lightening struck tree. Once that was completed he would return. That part of the ceremony would be done in private.

I turned to my cousin to speak, but before I could, he stopped me with an angry outburst.

"Real good job, Morgan—for a minute there I thought you weren't satisfied with putting just your foot in your mouth. Why'd you have to get him pissed at me for Christ's sake? I really want to thank you for support, Cuz. Just do me a favor and don't do me any more favors, alright?"

"Sorry Steven, I just spoke without thinking first. I didn't mean to start anything. It just came out, that's all." I started to lace my boots.

"What, you think it's crazy that I learned to speak Cherokee? I may be a hick mountain boy, but I can learn things, you know." He looked away from me, "I might not be as smart as you, but I ain't stupid."

"I know that, Steven, I just didn't know you felt so strongly about all this stuff. I was just sort of surprised, I mean you didn't tell me you learned the language."

"Like, when was I suppose to tell you? I haven't seen you in almost two years, I guess I should have sent you a postcard or something. Anyway, I tried to tell you earlier how much this stuff means to me. I'm just not real good with my words like you, I guess. All this stuff is leaving us man, and there's nothing anybody can do about it." He paused long enough to light a cigarette, "I started thinking about that, and after awhile, I figured somebody needed to listen to some of the old ways while people were still around to tell. The more I thought about it, the more I thought I might be that somebody. I'm not the only one, but they ain't very many around anymore who really give a shit, you know what I mean? If not me, then who?"

I thought for a moment and looked into the face of my big cousin. His long black hair was still pulled into a ponytail, his amber face unusually serious and intense. He felt strongly about what he was saying, I knew then for sure. Once again, I felt myself envying another's intense feelings about something. It had been so long since I myself had been touched, really touched by something, that I had forgotten what it was like. I was glad for him, but selfishly sad for me and sorry for the things I said to him.

"Steven, I'm glad you feel that way, I really am. I think it's right for you to feel so strongly about something, I even sort of understand." I paused, "It just took me a while to realize just how committed you were, I guess."

"Damn, here we go again. I didn't mean to start no heavy conversation or anything—let's just drop the whole thing." He asked, changing the subject, " You ready to head over to Grandfather for our meeting with the Feds?"

"I can hardly wait." I began to walk back towards the cabin, away from the spot where Ben had entered the woods.

Steven spoke from my side, "How are you going to play this anyway?"

"Well, I haven't got the whole thing completely figured out yet, but I sort of have all the basics. We can fine-tune the rest when we get up on the mountain. If we leave now, we'll have time to get up Profile Trail a full two hours before they have any chance of being there. Maybe we should have gone up earlier, but I don't think so, I don't think these guys are going to try to pull anything, at least not right away. I think now they're just anxious to hear what we have to say and they'll probably play it more or less on our terms, at least to start."

We returned to the front porch of the cabin where Kathy sat in the same chair that she had the morning before. She looked up to greet us.

"My, my, doesn't this look like old times? You two strolling through the woods together, pretending you're at war with the rest of the world, plotting this, plotting that…it's a wonder we have any chance at all." Her tone changed to one more serious, "Hell, you guys have been playing this same game since you were kids, only this time it's for real cowboys. I don't give a good damn what either one of you think or believe, you two better pay close attention to what's going on around here. If you two get hurt, I'll not be very happy about it. I'll tell you that right now. Furthermore, if I find out you get killed just because you were careless, I will not cry at the funeral and I will not forgive you. You hear?"

"Yes, ma'am." I thought the stern expression she put on was a nice touch.

Steven laughed out loud; "I can remember when you played cowboys and Indians, just like we did. I seem to remember, before you turned into Miss Goody Two Shoes, you used to play the same games and do just fine. You remember back when we were a whole lot younger, and you thought you were really a boy in disguise? If I remember right, you used to wrestle pretty good, for a girl, anyway."

"Steven don't you ever again use the phrase, "for a girl, anyway", in my presence." I knew, as soon as he said it, he was in for trouble. "If you do, I will not be responsible for my actions. You may be two feet taller than I am but I don't fall for that act you put on for the rest of the world. I'm not afraid of you, just because you're the size of a small house and look like twelve miles of hard mountain back road. I don't care. I may be a woman, but I think I can take care of myself good enough to deal with the likes of you—you big redneck Indian."

Steven started to argue and I thought it would be a good time to jump in and try to save what remained of my badly injured cousin, "Okay guys that's enough for now. Ding! There's the bell ending the first round. Steven, why don't you and I go inside and pack a few things we might need for our little afternoon stroll up the mountain."

As I pushed Steven through the open doorway of the cabin, I heard Kathy laughing as she commented, "You guys are never going to change, never...never...never."

CHAPTER TWENTY-FOUR

Over the years I may have lost sight of many of the teachings of my family and tribal history, but the most important things never faded completely. The people of the Cherokee have always been as one with the deep forests of the high country. At no time in history was there such a bonding between people and earth. The ancient Cherokee didn't consider themselves apart from the life of the forest—they were part of it; the animals, the trees, the great waters; these things were all portions of the "whole". A deep respect and love of the land allowed the Cherokee to become a peaceful and prosperous people. Children learned of their land from the time they were born and never stopped learning until they were returned to the earth in death. Their schoolroom was the forest and their teacher, Mother Nature herself. Steven and I attended that same school, just centuries later.

We had the privilege, in my opinion anyway, of being born into families, which still maintained a tremendous respect for the mountains. My father may have not given a damn about the rest of his heritage, but he loved the outdoors and respected the power and the great beauty there. He had many faults, but he and Uncle Frank both grew up running all over the mountains of the Carolinas and Tennessee. They spent more time with a roof of stars overhead instead of the more conventional type. That legacy, the love of the outdoors, was at least one good thing passed to me by my father. Unfortunately, I had very little else to thank him for, but maybe that was enough.

I learned to walk tripping over the branches, sticks, and roots scattered across the forest floor. Before that, I crawled out the front door of the cabin (or so I've been told) whenever someone forgot and left the door ajar. As the years passed, Steven and I were allowed to follow along with our fathers, exploring the mountains by their side, hunting, fishing, and hiking. I recall those times well and remember them warmly, as I was too young to yet understand the many faults of my father. During those early years, and only then, I regarded him with an admiration and awe that only the very young, or the very naive, can exhibit. The inexperience of youth blinded me to the problems he had then, the drinking and the beatings. He may even have been a good guy at the time. It's too late now for me to find out any differently.

As my cousin and I became teenagers, there was nothing anyone could do to stop our "little adventures" into the wilderness. We started exploring the land around our homes, and as we grew older, our circles of exploration grew larger. By the time we had our driver's license, the entire Appalachian Mountain Range became our "hood". By the time we were seventeen, we had managed to trek a large majority of the Appalachian Trail. In the summers of our youth, we would enter the forest, and stay gone for weeks at a time, with nothing but a knife, packs, and maybe a rifle or shotgun.

Over the years, the mountain forests became our home. We both had many reasons not to want to linger in our normal households, so the forest became our retreat. In the forest we found freedom, solitude, and the ability to control our own destiny. We didn't have to ask anyone for a damn thing, and everything was ours for the taking. By the time we became adults, we were as comfortable in the woods as most people were in their living rooms. We were rulers of our own peaceful mountain kingdom.

The plights and turmoil of the inner cities were far away and meant nothing to us. Where we lived, there was no crime, no senseless murder, no rape, and no gang warfare. Where we lived, there was no television, billboards, automobiles, anxiety or stress. Where we lived, there was only the peace of a misty spring morning or the indescribable quiet and tranquility of the first winter snowfall in the high mountains. Where we lived, there was no time or need, for racism, for greed, or for hate. In the high mountain paradise that we called home, there was only time for learning about the real beauty of our world. You could learn a lot about the forest when you lived as we did, but more importantly, you learned about yourself.

Within our mountain world, we learned the ancient ways of the warrior, and added a few twists of our own. We explored every inch of the wilderness within reach, and saw and did things very few men have the desire or the ability to do. Steven and I learned all these things together, and I was as confident in his abilities as I was my own. I guess it was only natural that I ended up in the Special Forces. From those years, I learned the best ways to apply my love and knowledge of the forest and kill people while I was doing it, a perfect product of the U.S Army. I believed, at the time, it would be good for me. Maybe I was right, maybe not. But, it was for these reasons, I chose Grandfather Mountain as our meeting place. It was our home ground and we were both as comfortable there than as anywhere.

The Indians named Grandfather Mountain for its resemblance to an old bearded man lying on his back, the profile sharply defined by the peaks and valleys along the crest. The mountain had become one of the top tourist attractions in the South and the mile-high swinging bridge, museum, and wildlife habitat were only part of the draw. The main reason for the popularity was the spectacular views from the summit. The preserve was privately owned and covered over 3000 acres in total. Two of the mountain's nine trails were designated National Recreation Trails, and subsequently, in the last several years, hikers and climbing enthusiasts flocked to the mountain almost daily. Long before it had become popular to do so, Steven and I had explored and climbed almost every inch of the huge mountain. When I chose the mountain as the meeting place with Smith, I knew there would be few people on the profile of the mountain, yet there would be plenty of tourists where he and his partner would be forced to embark. I thought this might force him to be more honest and, if he was foolish enough to try anything on the mountain, Steven and I could take a few steps into the woods and vanish, quickly and easily. I didn't know how much training Smith and his partner might have in such areas, but I knew it wasn't enough to compare to ours.

We parked the truck in a small shopping center just outside Banner Elk, and hiked the remaining short distance across the intersection of NC 105\184. Normally a permit was purchased at the small ski shop near the base of Profile Trail, the route we had chosen to access the mountain, but we made no such purchase. The fewer people who knew we were there, the better.

Profile Trail began at the base of Grandfather and followed a rather easy route of about two and one half miles before joining with the much more difficult Calloway Trail near the summit. The higher up the mountain you went, the fewer people you found. Near the top, all trails were strenuous, treacherous and difficult. Paying an admission fee could access Calloway Trail, and the others, and driving to the visitor's center near the swinging bridge but for obvious reasons, this was not a good choice for Steven and I, but it was a damn good thing to force on Smith. From the top of the mountain's peaks, we could watch his arrival and see if he had anything tricky in mind. Hiding places and escape trails were endless. If you were as familiar with the mountain as Steven and I, they could bring in an entire army and it would be difficult to find us. Our ancestors had proven that same fact to General Scott a few centuries before, and in the very same mountains.

Steven and I traveled light; he had a backpack and I carried only a small daypack. They were less for supplies than to hide the weapons we brought. Steven's pack contained one of the twelve gauge riot guns, I carried my handgun and plenty of ammunition, and of course Steven was never without his big .45 automatic. The shotgun was hard to hide with the butt sticking out of the pack slightly, but it went unnoticed by the tourists we happened to run across. The real worry was the park rangers who occasionally wandered the trails. If we ran into any of those guys, we were going to have a hard time explaining the weapons and the lack of hiking permits. We both carried water and jerky, never taking the woods for granted. No matter how well you thought you understood survival in the wilderness, you had to be prepared for the harsh lessons nature kept in waiting for people with such foolish arrogance. Dangers on the high peaks were too numerous to count, steep drops, flash flooding, rockslides, wild animals…the list went on and on.

It was about ten o'clock when Steven and I stopped for water at Shanty Spring, a point just below where Profile Trail intersected Calloway Trail.

Steven asked, "What time are those guys supposed to get to the visitor center?"

"I told them to be at the gate at noon. That means they should reach the cave around one thirty. I thought I would backtrack towards Macrae Peak and see if I could spot them coming. You can sort of lag behind here and make sure no one tries to sneak in on us from the eastside trails." I topped off my canteen. "I don't think Smith will try anything, but we can't be sure. By one o'clock we'll meet back at Indian House Cave. That will give us time to set up and wait for them."

"Sounds good to me."

We hiked the remaining short distance to the intersection of Profile and Grandfather Trails. Steven turned towards the east, following the trail towards Calloway Peak. At 5964 feet in height, it would allow him to view all the trails on the eastside of Grandfather, Daniel Boone Scout Trail, and Cragway Trail.

Before he got out of sight, I yelled after him, "Watch your ass, Stevey; don't take chances with these guys."

He turned to me just as he reached a huge rock on the uphill climb, "Who the hell are you talking to? You mind your own business and I'll mind mine. And don't call me Stevey you asshole!"

I showed him my middle finger, laughing in response, then quickly moved over the rocky terrain of the well-marked trail, heading west. I made good time moving at a quick pace which both Steven and I had used for years. The pace was probably faster than most would have considered safe, almost a jog. My grandfather had once told us the ancient Indian warriors ran almost everywhere they traveled, even in the deep forest and over high mountain trails. The trail I followed shifted from steep rocky slopes to deep forest trail, snaking over the exposed roots of twisted pine trees and between rocks and boulders that were constantly sliding and shifting on the side of the big mountain. Frequently, the trail called for hand over hand climbing or relied on ropes or ladders to help over the more difficult sections. Even with the climbing aids maintained by the Forest Service, the trails were not for everyone. Every trail on the mountain, with the exception of the entrance trail, was rated as "strenuous" and I had seen a horde of tourists who should have paid attention to the warnings and never did.

Even though the morning had started out bright and blue, the skies had begun to darken and swell, as Steven and I had made our way through Banner Elk. Another storm was coming and that would work in our favor. The weather would keep most hikers off the mountain. The Park Service advised all that would listen to stay off the mountain in bad weather. Many hikers died on one of the high peaks from falls, lightning strikes, exposure, and even heart attacks. The mountain regularly had some of the region's most severe weather. Electrical storms were not uncommon, nor were winds of over 100 mph. In the winter, with deep snow and sub zero temperatures for months at a time, climbing or hiking the huge mountain was only attempted by well equipped parties of experts or lunatics.

On our way up the entrance trail, the only people we saw were coming down as fast as they could. A few turned to look at us like we were crazy for ascending the mountain under such conditions. I imagine Steven's appearance prohibited any smart comment they might otherwise have made. Traveling with someone of my cousin's size and appearance held at least some advantages.

I passed the cut-off that led to Indian House Cave and continued on the trail towards Attic Window Peak. The trail wound up and up in a series of cut backs, the narrow path surrounded on both sides by huge rhododendron, thick and green in their summer glory. The sky was misty gray and the air slightly cool as I reached the "Window", almost 6000 feet above sea level. Near the summit, I was forced to slow my pace, pulling myself over large rocks onto the highest point of the peak. From the high perch among the huge rock outcroppings, I could see the slightly smaller Macrae Peak. I chose a guarded point from which I would be able to see anyone who followed the trail towards me.

I stood on the top of the high rocky cliff and slowly turned, taking in the panoramic view. I was so high up the mountain; I literally looked down into passing clouds. The darkening sky and rapidly forming rain clouds mixed with thick fog and shrouded the surrounding valleys from view. As far as the eye could see, mountain after mountain stretched in all directions, their number seemingly impossible to count. Their peaks visible above the haze, their bases buried—it looked as if they were floating on air. The valleys of mist separated the mountain ranges one from another, yet blended them together as one endless sea of beauty. The view was too much for mere words. It was a pity that people went their entire lives and never saw such a sight. The majestic mountains were a sure way to put a little humility in your life. In a way I didn't quite understand, it always made my problems seem smaller and less important somehow. Even with the terrible things that were happening, I felt the strings of my soul loosen just a little.

At that high altitude, and without direct sunlight, the temperature plunged rapidly. I took time to remove a jacket from my pack and put it on, then quickly rechecked the slide and clip in the automatic I carried in the small of my back. Attached to my pack were several extra clips of ammunition. I squatted on my haunches, settling my eyes on the next peak, and waited. To me, the waiting was always the hardest part.

An eagle traveled by my line of sight, just above the tree line. There was less than twenty feet between us when he passed by, majestic and deadly, searching the mountainside for lunch. He was so close I could see the glassy glint in the small marble eyes, the eyes of a predator elite. Even in the absolute stillness of the mountaintop, he passed by as quietly as the moon, his wings moving slowly and soundlessly. I watched him as he effortlessly drifted with the air currents coming off the side of the huge mountain, making it look so easy. Suddenly, without warning, he fell from the sky, straight down, diving like a fighter plane, disappearing briefly into the mist and the heavy brush just below where I sat. Seconds later, he reappeared with a small squirming body clutched in his mighty talons, perhaps a ground squirrel or small rabbit. As the furry animal twisted in futile effort, the great bird of prey passed out of sight, returning to a hidden nest perhaps. The laws of survival were never better illustrated, both the brutality and the beauty were equally important. Without light there would be no darkness, without death there would be no life. It all made sense in a very basic and poetic way.

I was startled by voices just beneath me, and I moved back against the rock face of my hiding place about twenty yards from the blazed pathway. Two young men came into view sporting climbing gear and talking to each other, never suspecting anyone was around.

"Well, hell, you went out with her, what did you think?"

"I think she was one certifiable bitch that's what I think. All she is, is a prick teaser, buddy; you better not try man, I'm tellin' you."

"But I gotta' man, I just gotta'. Have you seen the ass on her? I gotta' make a run at that, man."

They climbed to within feet of me, continuing past without noticing.

"Well, don't say I didn't warn you dunce. That chick is only giving it up for guys with lots of money and you don't have any."

"You willing to put your money where your mouth is hotshot?"

"Look, if we don't get the hell down this mountain before the rain hits I ain't gonna' even be in the mood to take your money. Let's move more and talk less."

As they passed from view, I heard them continue to bicker their way over the peak, their voices fading away as they descended. I wasn't happy with myself for allowing them to get as close as they had without hearing them sooner. Maybe Kathy was right, maybe I was getting too old for this kind of shit.

Long minutes passed as I watched the opposite peak. The sky got darker, the wind colder until, finally, I saw two figures struggle onto Macrae Peak. Even though I knew they had no chance of seeing me, I moved against the face of the cliff. I raised my binoculars, knowing there was no sun to glint off the lens and alert them. Sure enough, it was Smith and another agent. Smith seemed to be struggling to maintain pace with the other man, who was much bigger and was leading the way over the rough trail. They both had on light clothing, and it appeared they at least had the good sense to wear hiking boots. I gathered they had not, however, brought along any warm clothing, if they had they would have been wearing it. I watched them for a few minutes to insure they were alone, then began my gradual retreat along the trail, backtracking my earlier route.

When I reached the blaze marking the fork towards Indian House Cave, I turned off into the deep woods following the narrow trail. The cave was about two hundred yards or more down a slippery pathway and had once been the home and meeting place for the Cherokee, who dwelled on and around the mountain, hence the name. The woods were full and dense in full summer foliage. With the overcast sky, it was as dark as twilight under the thick branches. The old cave came into view, the steep rock overhang cutting sharply back into the rock of the mountainside. The cave was large and rather open, the ceiling as high as thirty feet in the front tapering to only two or three feet in places. Like most caves, the walls were slick with moisture.

I gave a short whistle and Steven spoke from overhead. "I'm telling you, Cuz, when this is all over, you and I gonna' have to work on your sneaking around stuff. I heard you coming when you left the main trail."

"Yeah, right. Bring your ass down here where we can talk." Steven was perched atop the overhang of the cave forty feet or more over my head, almost hidden from view. I would never have seen him at all unless he wanted me to. He was good, much better than me, although I would never tell him that. He was too cocky as it was.

Steven came down and I told him of our approaching guests. He had seen no one on the mountain during his exploration of the East Side. We briefly discussed the best way to handle the situation and agreed it would be better if Steven returned to his lofty seat until we had a better handle on what was going down.

"Fine, but I wish you'd make up your damn mind, Morgan. Come down here Steven, go back up Steven. What? Don't you think I got better things to do than climb up and down that damn cliff all afternoon?"

"Look, I'm doing you a favor, big guy. You yourself said you were developing a gut, and I admit in this one instance anyway, you're right. It won't hurt you to hustle up there, now go on."

As he struggled up the steep embankment he called over his shoulder, "You have always been a bossy shit you know that Morgan. One of these days you're gonna push too hard."

"Just shut up and climb fat guy…just shut up and climb."

I removed my daypack and placed it on a nearby rock, then moved my gun to the right front pocket of my jacket, and settled in to wait

once again. I was anxious to hear what Smith had to say, curious to see
if he knew anymore about the killer than he had just a few days before.

It was hard to believe that only a few days had passed since the three
of us had met in Myskyns Tavern. I sat on a cold mountainside awaiting
a pending rainstorm far removed from the cobblestone streets of
Charleston. I knew I should have missed the city but I really didn't. It
felt good to be "home" again. I had been kidding myself for too long.
Charleston was probably the best city I had ever lived, but it wasn't
really home. The sea gulls of the bay were nice but they weren't eagles.
The Cooper River Bridge was tall as hell when you crossed it, but from
where I sat it would seem constructed of Popsicle sticks. No, I had been
kidding myself into believing I didn't miss the high mountains. Like
Dorothy said, "there's no place like home."

I heard the rustle of a pine bough and the scrape of a boot against
rock from the woods behind me just as Steven gave a light whistle from
above. It seemed our company had arrived.

CHAPTER TWENTY-FIVE

The two men emerged from the rhododendron bushes sweaty and angry, Smith, by far, in the worst shape. He was winded, flushed, and not in a very good mood. He wore designer jeans, scuffed and torn in several places, newly bought hiking boots, and a once clean Rugby shirt. I guess it was his idea of what the fashion conscious hiker should be wearing. He had a canteen attached to his belt which clanked against his side with an empty sound, his water obviously already consumed.

The big man accompanying him was something else entirely.

He had on worn, but starched fatigues, a light sweatshirt, and combat boots. I looked at the boots and could tell they were old but well cared for, they still bore evidence of a proper shine beneath the rough exterior. His manner suggested ex-military turned federal agent. Although somewhat out of shape at the moment, it was clear he had not always been that way. If I had to guess, I would have said he was a man who would hate for that to be brought to his attention, and the forced mountain hike had done just that. His breathing was labored, but not nearly as bad as Smith's, who was leaning over and holding his knees, trying to catch his breath. The big agent's clothing was not torn or dirty, but he was just as pissed, I could tell. I made myself a mental note to pay him close attention.

"Gentlemen, so nice of you to drop in. Can I get you fellows a drink? Nice cup of coffee perhaps?"

Smith was still bent over, but his breathing was much improved. He stood with an effort and struggled to speak, "Very…funny…Mr. Roberts. If this was your idea of a joke, it's not very funny. I don't appreciate this. My God man! It's freezing up here, it's about to storm at any moment and you send us on a rock climbing expedition. I don…"

"Sorry you're not pleased Smith. The trail you came in on leads right back down, why don't you just turn and leave if you're not happy? Makes no difference to me." They were in my element and Smith was smart enough to know it.

The other agent spoke for the first time, his voice harsh and angry. "Don't you just wish asshole? You think…"

"Hanks!" Smith snapped, then spoke to me again, "No, that will not be necessary just yet Mr. Roberts. We came here to encourage you to return and speak with us in a more relaxed atmosphere. Surely you can see, we cannot have a meeting here on the side of this mountain? I think we would all be much more comfortable if we went back down together and talked. I assure you, if you cooperate, no charges will be filed against you."

"Charges? What charges are you talking about Fred?" A brief flash of anger crossed his features at my use of his name. It was one thing to call him by his given name when we were alone, but another entirely in the presence of a subordinate. I kept my voice calm and relaxed, reclining against a slanted stone wall of the cave, hands in my jacket pocket.

"Well, leaving the scene of a murder, interfering with a federal investigation."

"Up yours Fred. If this is all you've come to say, I'm out of here." I turned my back on the two men and began to walk into the forest just past the entrance of the cave.

"Like hell you will!" The gruff voice of the second man combined with the familiar sound of a gun hammer being cocked. It seemed I could feel the gun's touch against my back. I didn't move a muscle; I just waited and listened.

The slide action of a pump shotgun being cocked is singularly familiar. The sound came from the cliff overhang above us where Steven had
positioned himself allowing a clear shot of both agents.

"In case you don't know," I spoke without turning, trying not to
show the anger I felt at having a gun pointed at me, "that was the sound
of a twelve gauge pump shotgun in the hands of someone who knows
how to use it. Call off your dog, Smith. Your boy here is about to take a
full load right in the head. I'm only going to tell you once." I shrugged
my shoulders, "We can ditch your bodies within one hundred yards of
where you stand right now and walk away and no one will ever find
you, that's a promise. Neither one of you mean shit to me or the guy on
the hill with the gun." I heard the hostility creep into my voice despite
my best efforts otherwise, more harsh and demanding than I had
intended.

Smith hesitated for a few moments before he replied. "Holster your
weapon Hanks."

"But…"

"Holster your weapon damn it! I'm the agent in charge here, now do it."

I finally turned, "That's not going to work either Smith."

"What do you mean?"

"Well, you've already proven at least one of you can't be trusted, and
you know what they say Smith, a general is totally responsible for his
troops. I want you both to lay your guns on that flat rock over there by
the entrance."

I saw Hanks look of anger. "Like Hell! You ass…"

"Hanks! I'll not tell you again. Do what he says."

With a supreme effort of will, Hanks slowly walked over and placed
his weapon on the smooth flat rock, and moved to walk away.

I interrupted; "The back up gun too, big guy."

Hanks turned and gave me a look of pure hatred. He raised his pants
leg and retrieved a small automatic from his ankle holster.

I turned to Agent Smith, "Next."

"Mr. Robert's this is highly irregular. We are not accustomed to surrendering our weapons. It's against agency policy."

"And I'm just a highly irregular kind of guy, Fred. Hell, people tell me that all the time." I removed my hand from my jacket pocket exposing the weapon I held in my hand all along. "Agency policy doesn't extend into these mountains—never has."

He briefly glanced at the gun and slowly walked over and placed his weapon on the rock by those of his partner. As he turned to walk away, I prompted, "No back up Smith?"

"No."

"That's funny," I said shaking my head, "I believe you. Now, why don't you two gentlemen have a seat right over there." I indicated another large stone against the opposite wall. "Steven, why don't you come down and meet the nice gentlemen? I think it's extremely rude of you to stand up there and point your shotgun at them like that. Why don't you come down here and do it?"

"Sure thing." He disappeared and I didn't hear a leaf move or a twig snap. He was there one second and gone the next.

"Mr. Roberts do you think we can get down to business now?"

"I think that might be a good idea yes. Are you going to introduce me to your friend here or not? I think that would be the polite thing to do."

"Name's Hanks." The big guy spoke and his aggravation showed. For some reason he had taken a disliking to me and he wasn't trying to hide it.

"Is that the first name or your last."

"Just Agent Hanks to you Roberts."

"My, but we got up on the wrong side of the bed this morning didn't we?" I for sure did not like the son-of-bitch by then.

"Don't push your luck Roberts, I ain't no Army shrink you can fool with your bullshit problems."

I felt the anger come for me then. It sank teeth into my flesh and waited, nibbling but not yet biting down hard. I looked at Smith and ignored Hanks entirely, "I see you decided to dig a little deeper into my file."

Smith responded "It seemed necessary, yes."

"Well, now that we have no secrets from each other, I'm sure our relationship will proceed rather nicely from here. What can I do for you Fred? Let's cut the bullshit and get to the point."

"If you don't mind I would rather wait until your cousin arrives so I don't have to repeat myself."

"We wouldn't want that now would we? But you don't have to worry, he's standing right behind you."

Both agents turned to where Steven leaned on a nearby tree just feet from where they sat. I could tell by the stunned look on their faces that they were amazed to see him there. They had of course heard nothing of his approach even though he had to come down from the cliff through the thick undergrowth, which covered the hillside. The effect was disarming on them to say the least. I guess no one likes to think they can be approached so easily, especially when you are an FBI agent.

"Good afternoon gentlemen." I noticed Steven had slipped back into his good 'ol boy facade.

Agent Smith answered for them both, "Good afternoon Mr. Waters."

I interrupted, "Now that we've gotten past all the pleasantries, can we get on with it?"

"Yes, of course." Smith pushed his wire frame glasses up onto his nose, seemingly having regained his composure and with it his haughty manner. "Mr. Roberts we want to talk to you about what happened at your brother's house the other night. We know you were there and we want some answers."

"How do you know we were there?" I knew they would find out, I was just curious as to how.

"You were so kind as to leave a nice print on a burner knob of the stove and Mr. Waters left a matchbook on the patio table outside."

Steven spoke from his position on the tree, "So?"

"The matchbook was from the bar with the strange name where we had our meeting in Charleston. You were both there and we know it. Now if you would be so kind as to tell us what went on that night, I think we can work things out." He leaned forward intently, arms on his knees.

"What do you mean work things out?" I asked.

"Well, I think we might be able to exchange some information about the killer. Surely, you're both interested in who is killing your family members. We're not saying, mind you, that we are prepared to tell you everything, after all, you no longer have a security clearance and this is a federal matter."

Agent Hanks took the opportunity to interrupt. "That's for damn sure! They don't give security clearances to psychos." He snickered.

The jaws of anger gripped me tighter, the teeth piercing my resolve so quickly it scared me. I could sense my hands shake as they clenched into fists seemingly on their own. My heart beat faster and I felt the overwhelming desire to hurt. Evidently watching me closely, and before I could react, Steven exploded. He called my name and tossed the shotgun to me and I managed to catch it somehow. He grabbed the relatively big man by the collar of his sweatshirt and jerked him off the ground. He rammed the agent into the tree he had just been leaning on. I heard the air rush from his lungs and the grunt of pain as he hit the tree. Agent Smith jumped to his feet and I shook my head and motioned for him to sit back down.

Steven was pissed, and in that frame of mind, he would have scared any man alive. "Listen to me shithead, that is my cousin and you will show some respect or I will beat you into dog food and feed you to strays. Do you understand asshole?" With each word he shoved the man hard against the tree again and again. For a second, I almost stopped him. I knew the psychological effect his actions were having on the agent. Hanks, the "big bully" type, always bigger than everyone around him, always physically stronger, was probably used to pushing people around, not being pushed around himself. Steven had picked the man up like a rag doll and held him with little effort despite his futile struggles. I knew Steven wasn't seriously hurting him, but the guy was going to be sore for days afterward. I guess things had been sort of building with Steven and this jerk had unfortunately been the one to set him off.

Hank's face was red and angry. He was tougher than I thought, most men would have been just scared, and I made another mental note in my imaginary file on Hanks.

"You ain't answered me yet boy. Didn't you hear my cousin tell you we could just leave your ass dead or worse on the side of this here mountain? Don't you get it shithead? Didn't you see Deliverance boy?" His accent was heavy as he leered in the agent's face: "You do have a purty mouth boy."

I couldn't help myself, with the Deliverance line I had to laugh. That of course made Agent Hanks face all the more flushed.

Agent Smith could stand it no longer and finally interrupted, "Really Mr. Waters that is quite enough."

I figured I better intercede, "Okay Steven you can let the man down now. I think he's got the message."

"No, I don't think he does Morgan." He let go of the man's collar and before he hit the ground he caught him by the shoulders and once again held him against the tree. "You apologize to my cousin boy."

Through clenched teeth the big man replied, "You go to hell."

"Okay, Steven that's enough." Fortunately my own anger had faded with Steven's actions. I still wanted to hurt the guy myself but I no longer wanted him dead.

"No, it's not Morgan. I'll let him go when he apologizes, not until." His voice was stern and even, I knew there would be no arguing with him. I had heard the tone before. I watched his big hands tighten on the man's shoulders. Each massive hand completely covered the sockets and I could tell by Hanks quick change of expression that it was a painful hold, one he had never felt. Hanks tried to knee Steven in the crotch, but Steven just turned his hip and the attempted blows fell harmlessly.

"How about it asshole? I don't think you meant to insult my cousin did you?" His grip tightened and Hanks face grew white.

I don't know what hurt him the most, my cousin's hands or the short words that he forced from his lips. "I'm sorry." The words came out like spit.

"I know." Steven let go without warning and the man landed on his ass at the foot of the tree. He glared at Steven's back as he caught the shotgun I threw back to him. Steven winked at me without the two seeing him, displaying a wicked little smile. I smiled back, thanking him for what he had done in the only way I knew how. Steven knew what had happened to me in the Army, but I never really talked to him about it. I would like to think he understood why, and at that moment, I was sure he did.

I moved to try to interject some calm into the situation, "Okay Smith let's get down to it, what you got?" Hanks slowly returned to his position near Smith, rubbing first one shoulder, then the other. I made another note to insure neither one of us turned our back on him. He wouldn't forget his afternoon anytime soon.

"Were you or were you not in Florida the other night Mr. Roberts?"

"We were."

"And what time did you arrive and when did you leave?"

"We arrived in the late afternoon, five or five thirty, we left just before ten."

"Who was at the house when you arrived?"

"Just my sister-in-law, Lori."

"When did your brother arrive?"

"About forty-five minutes later." I noticed that whatever his faults might be, Smith was a good interrogator, an art in itself. His questions were clear and concise and he didn't bullshit around. I wondered briefly if I might have misjudged the man in any other areas.

"Were you and your cousin in the house at the time of the killings?"

"No."

Hanks, having regained some of his courage and cockiness, snapped, "No? No? We already know you were there…what the hell do you mean no?"

I didn't address the man; I ignored him again, determined not to let him push me to violence as he was obviously trying to do. I directed my answer instead to Smith. "As I was about to say before I was interrupted, we were on the patio by the pool before everything started. We went inside just after my sister-in-law was killed and just before my brother died." I kept my voice level and monotone, revealing nothing but details.

"What time did the killings occur?"

"Nine thirty…nine forty, I guess."

He leaned forward, his voice betraying the urgency he felt. "Did you see the killer?"

"We did, but we didn't get a very good look I'm afraid, just general overall shape and size."

"What happened to the killer after the murders?"

I gestured to where Steven and his shotgun leaned on a tree. "My cousin here emptied two clips from a forty-five automatic into him, so he got mad and left."

Hanks yelled, "What? You're crazy if you expect us to believe that shit!" He jumped from his seat with his words.

I smiled and stepped forward. I had about all I could take from him. I had control of myself this time. I moved to within a foot of his face. Steven started forward, "Uh uh, cousin, everything is just fine. I can handle this."

I turned back to Hanks, his eyes blazed. I wondered what it was he didn't like about me. I really didn't give a damn, I was just curious. The sanity question raised its nasty little head again. The whole world hated lunatics, after all, and I guess I wasn't too high on Hanks list. That, combined with the color of my skin, may have offended his tender, WASP ego.

Smith spoke to Hanks; "If you do not sit down and cooperate I will send you back to the car to wait. I can handle this alone if need be."

I never moved my eyes off Hanks. "Let me say this just once Agent. I don't think I like you at all…in fact I know I don't. You got two options here, one, listen to what Fred here is telling you and keep your mouth shut, or two, don't. It's as simple as that, but I tell you one is a painful decision and one isn't." I felt my anger rising—still in the cage, but waiting for another chance to escape and ravage. It made me uncomfortable. It was the same feeling I had when all my trouble started a few years before. I fought within myself to control my temper, keeping it inside as best I could…hide what I was feeling from the words I was saying. I was not about to give him the satisfaction of stealing the last frail dominion I held over my emotions. "I'm tired of your mouth and I'm tired of you. One thing though, you might want to recall what my cousin here did to you just minutes ago."

I paused a minute, deliberately putting my handgun in the pocket of my jacket then withdrawing my empty hand so he could see I no longer held a weapon. "He is indeed a big mean SOB, but where we come from he is considered nice compared to me." I moved my face to within inches of his. "Get off my case. That is the first, and only, time I'm going to warn you. Please, don't make me angry Hanks. You wouldn't like me at all if you made me angry, trust me."

I saw the turmoil in his eyes and thought for just a moment he was going to try to strike me, but the moment passed. He turned and moved to his seat. "Someday Roberts, someday." He muttered under his breath.

"I'll be waiting Hanks, but hurry okay? I hate long engagements." I turned to Smith, having dismissed any threat from him entirely, knowing if he moved on me in any fashion, Steven would stop him instantly. "Okay Fred, I think it's our turn for some answers, don't you?"

"I still have more questions Mr. Roberts."

"I'm sure you do Fred, but this was supposed to be an exchange of information as I understand it. I haven't seen anything from you yet. Tell me about the killings Smith, what did the autopsies show?"

He hesitated, then gave a little shrug and began; "Well they all were pretty much the same, your brother was slightly different."

"You can't…" Hanks began.

Smith cut him off. "I'm handling this investigation, I'll decide what I can or can't do."

He turned to me and continued, obviously irritated with his colleague, "We have the best people in the country on this. It's got everyone in turmoil, and it's all we can do to keep the doctors from publishing papers concerning what's happened. When this whole thing is over, you can bet they will."

"What's so different about these killings?"

"Everything. The bodies of the women found bore relatively normal mutilations, if you can call that kind of thing normal, but it was an entirely different story with the male victims."

"And?"

"Well, the bodies were discovered…were…well in an obvious state of physical arousal shall we say? The effects seem to diminish after a time. In addition to a strong sexual stimulant in the bloodstream, the chemists have found another toxin, which evidently causes immobility. The best scientists from around the country have not been able to isolate or identify either drug. They have been trying for months now and have come up with nothing, other than the theory that we are talking about two separate injections."

"Injections?"

"Yes. The toxins were injected into the victims all in the same manner, through a wound over the heart area. It would seem that the victims all share the same bite marks in that same location."

Smith was smoother than I thought. "Yeah, I noticed the same thing on Jordan."

"But the cause of death was different with your brother Mr. Roberts, it would seem he died of a broken neck."

"I know. I saw it happen." I washed all emotion from my voice.

Hanks spoke up, "And you did nothing to stop it?"

I turned to him and remarked coldly, "No, I didn't."

Smith continued before Hanks had a chance to comment further,

"We found traces of blood at the scene that were not your sister-in-law's or your brother's, we haven't yet identified the blood type. We found traces of the same type blood both in the living room and the exit foyer."

"Odds are, it was mine. The killer attacked me just before Steven opened up on him the second time. He cut me with some kind of extremely sharp blade, sliced me across my left thigh. I couldn't identify what kind of weapon he used." I paused, "You didn't find any other blood types, in the pool or on the deck?"

"No."

I thought for a minute, pacing back and forth in front of them. I stopped and looked at Smith, "There's something else—something you're not saying."

"Yes there is. In all instances we have found no traces of the killer, nothing had been left behind, no blood, nothing, with the exception of the toxins in the bodies and some strange gel-like substance found on the male victim's genitals. Believe it or not all the victims seem to have experienced ejaculation just prior to death. Very strange, very strange." He shook his head, "I know it sounds impossible considering the duress that the victims must have been under, but the fact exists, the autopsies were all conclusive on that point."

He stopped and looked to me for a reaction. When I exhibited none, he continued, "The wounds inflicted coincide with a weapon as you have suggested, very sharp, almost of surgical precision. The killer must also possess amazing strength." He gestured towards Steven. "Like your cousin here for instance. That fact confuses the matter even more as very few, if any, women could possess the power to inflict such damage. The whole thing is crazy. We have very few leads and you two are our only hope right now." He held his hands apart; "So you understand why it's imperative you tell us everything you know about the killing?"

I looked at Steven and he nodded, "Okay Smith, I'll tell you what we saw, but don't interrupt. Hear me out. Like the things you've told me, it might not make too much sense to you, but it's what happened as well as we know."

I related the events of the night of my brother's murder. I told him everything I could remember. He interrupted on occasion to ask specific questions and asked Steven a number of times to relate the same things, hoping to gather additional details. I left out the involvement of Rising Wolf and my grandfather's manuscript. I told him the reason we went to see Jordan was to tell him about our conversation with the FBI and we had both felt it was something better told in person. I told him of the legend we heard and my theory that someone knew about it and might be using that knowledge to justify the continued killing spree.

Hanks had remained quiet and withdrawn during the long discussion. He spent his time alternating between staring into the woods, sending me dirty looks and avoiding Steven's gaze completely. He was not happy his superior was freely exchanging information with two known criminals, one of them a certified lunatic.

Smith asked, "You sure you can't provide any kind of description?"

I thought for a moment and answered slowly, describing what I thought I saw the best I could. "Well, the killer was very big, I've already told you about the smell. He, or she, seemed to be wearing a cape of some kind, very thick, opaque. I thought I saw long blonde, almost white hair, and like we told you, hard as it was to believe, it sounded like a female voice when Steven shot the guy. As for the weapon; when I saw the hands move to my brother's head, then again when I was attacked, there appeared to be claw-like weapons of some kind attached to the fingers—like ninjas used in ancient Japan. I can't say for sure."

Hanks evidently could stand it no longer. "Oh for God's sake will you listen to this? Smith they're bullshiting and you know it! This is a lot of crap...witches, monsters...demons and now ninjas for Christ's sake! I say, let's run these assholes in and find out what they're not telling us. Hell, they could be the ones. They were there, they admit it."

Smith replied calmly, "But they're not. We've checked on the whereabouts of both Mr. Roberts and Mr. Waters during the previous killings and neither could have committed the murders." He spoke like a teacher to a spoiled pupil.

I looked at Smith; "Well thanks a lot for the vote of confidence Smith."

"Just doing my job Mr. Roberts."

"I know, I would have done the same thing." The situation was becoming sort of scary. I felt if I stayed around much longer, I might even come to like a few things about Smith. He was still a dweeb and an asshole, but at least he knew his job.

"I still think we should run these guys in. This whole thing is ridiculous. They're into this up to their eyeballs and you know it."

"What you think, you are free to note in your report. Agent Hanks, I suggest since we are near the end of this meeting, you should go ahead back to the main trail and wait for me there."

"But..."

"That will be all, Hanks."

Hanks moved to retrieve his weapons and I stopped him by saying, "I don't think so Hanks. Smith here can bring your guns when he comes up. Don't worry, there's no big bad wolf along the trail for you to worry about."

He looked at me with open contempt. "I wasn't thinking about shooting no wolf Roberts."

"I know, but I think we'll all feel much safer if you leave without them just the same. It would get kind of boring taking them from you twice in one day."

As he turned reluctantly up the trail he said, "You're gonna' get yours Roberts, you wait, and I'll be there to help when you do."

"We'll be seeing you I'm sure, and Hanks…"

He turned from the rough trail.

"It was so nice to meet you." I smiled my best smile. Steven laughed loudly, his voice echoing down the side of the mountain.

Hanks said, "Screw you Roberts." Then he turned and left, making his way noisily along the trail. I was damned glad to see him go. He brought out a side of me I didn't care too much for.

I caught Steven's eye as he nodded my way and moved to a point, which allowed him to watch the retreating figure. I knew Hanks had no chance in hell of doubling back without my cousin knowing.

I turned to Smith. "Fred, you mentioned you guys had all these doctors in a uproar over this whole thing. I sort of find it hard to believe they would get so worked up over a few chemicals they can't identify. Is there something else you're not telling us?"

He hesitated, then seemed to reach a decision, "You're right. There are a few things I haven't mentioned about the killings." He took on a dramatic, exaggerated whisper. "If the newspapers were to get wind of this, it would cause big problems for our investigation. You two will not discuss this with anyone. In fact, I would prefer you keep it between ourselves if you don't mind." He looked at us as if he expected as answer. When we kept quiet, he continued anyway, "It seems that all the male victims, with the exception of your brother, shared the same peculiar…how can I say this…mutilations? All the victims were missing both heart and brain, no traces of either organ were found in the bodies."

Steven shifted closer behind me. I had a funny feeling in my stomach, but I kept my face blank as I asked the question, even though I already knew the answer. "What's so strange about that? Surely that is not all that uncommon?"

"True, there are quite a few cases of such occurrences, but that's not the problem. The skulls were literally shattered with superhuman force and the brain removed, even that is not unheard of, but the heart...well that is where we have a strange twist. The victim's hearts were removed from their bodies with no trace of a wound, just a small bite mark. The chest cavity was left empty, but the chest itself showed no visible way for it to have happened. All the surrounding organs were undamaged. It is impossible by all medical standards of which we are currently aware. Whoever is killing these people has the hands of a master surgeon and a knowledge far beyond the best medical minds in the world today."

Steven cleared his throat and I knew his eyes had to be boring into my neck. I knew what he was thinking.

"Needless to say," Smith continued, "all these experts are begging us to do everything possible to take this killer alive. To further complicate matters, we're trying to play it that way. They say the techniques are priceless." He gestured again with his hands, "So you see, this whole thing is just one big mess. Up until this point we had absolutely nothing to go on, your information at least gives us a starting point. I think your idea concerning the motive and identity of this murderer may be the best we have at the moment. It's the only thing we have, really. Of course, the idea that such a creature could come from a legend, what did you call it, a Ravenmocker? That such a thing could exist is ludicrous. Surely you know how crazy this sounds? No, someone is using this legend to scare people. I think you're right about that."

He looked at me for a response. For some reason I didn't feel like talking anymore. I just wanted to be done and off the mountain and back to my family home as soon as possible. This whole situation was rapidly becoming something I wasn't comfortable with any longer. I needed time alone to think.

"Thanks for the information Fred. I believe you had better be leaving now if you're going to beat the rain."

"Alright Mr. Roberts, where can I reach you?"

"You can't, I'll reach you, I have the number."

"But Mr. Roberts, surely you understand now that I need to be able to speak with you?"

"We're still going to play this my way Fred. I give you my word; if we run across anything I feel will be of value to you, I'll call. Now, why don't you pick up your guns and get going?"

He started to say something more, but changed his mind, "Alright." He retrieved the weapons and turned towards the trail to leave. He didn't offer his hand as he left and I wouldn't have taken it if he had.

"One more thing Fred."

"Yes?"

"You don't have to go back by the way you came. There's a much easier trail that skirts the bottom of the ridge called Underwood Trail; it's blazed yellow. You can't miss it, just look for it about a hundred yards further on the main trail."

"You mean we didn't have to come the terrible way you had us come?" A slight edge of indignation returned to his voice.

"I just wanted to see what you were made of I guess." I turned my back to him. "We'll be seeing you Fred."

He muttered something under his breath and wandered up the trail. As he passed Steven he spoke, but I didn't hear what he said or what Steven answered.

After he was gone, a deep roar of thunder rolled over the mountain crest. Steven turned to me and asked, "Well, what do you think?"

"I think it's time we got the hell off this mountain, that's what I think."

CHAPTER TWENTY-SIX

The rain never really did come. It continued to threaten as we worked our way down the mountain and into Banner Elk where we parked the truck, even began to drizzle once or twice, but the big rain never materialized. That happened quite often across the Blue Ridge, threat but no reality.

We didn't talk much on the hike down. I was lost in the things we had heard, my insides in turmoil, struggling to keep faith with all the things going wrong around me. I searched my mind to find logical explanations for the strange things Smith told us and I couldn't fathom who, or what, was doing the killing. I still wasn't buying the idea of a three-hundred-plus year old woman killing people all over the country.

Steven had been especially quiet after he tried unsuccessfully to discuss the details with me. After a few tries, and my bad tempered responses, he finally gave up and left me to my own thoughts. He didn't try to talk to me again after that.

When we entered the truck he asked if we could go by and check on his parents since we were so close. After he promised we wouldn't have to stay "but a minute", I realized what an ass I was being and agreed. It wasn't Steven's fault I was confused as hell, that honor went to some dark figure as tall as he was, meaner than a rattlesnake, with the hands of a surgeon and a hard-on for my family members. Well, I guess technically speaking that last part might have been a bad choice of words.

I turned to Steven, "Hey, let's stop by the sandwich shop on the way and pick something up, I'm starved."

"No go. We're fasting until tonight remember?"

"Oh yeah, I forgot. Do you have any idea how long this thing is going to take Rising Wolf?"

"Nah, hour or so I reckon. He told me earlier that he has a plan to help safeguard the cabin. I hope the hell it works." He politely rolled down the window as he lit his cigarette, the smoke disappearing out the opening.

"No shit. Let's at least stop at a convenience store for a soft drink. We can drink right?"

"I suppose so. A cold beer would be even better, too bad this is a dry town."

"I guess we could ride back towards the store at the crossroads, they sell beer."

"Nah, we better not. Rising Wolf is in a hurry to get back to the reservation and I still want to go by and see the folks. Let's just stop at this little store here and grab something fast."

I pulled into the convenience store and we purchased a couple of soft drinks and continued on our way towards Uncle Frank's. I began to feel better and was even glad Steven suggested going by. Seeing the two of them might help bring the whole thing into a better perspective.

Steven looked at me and laughed, "You know I don't think we exactly made friends with that Hanks guy. What do you think?"

"No, I think you're right about that. I don't think he's in danger of falling in love with either one of us." We turned off the highway into his parent's driveway.

"Well I gotta' tell you though, I was beginning to wonder if he was ever going to apologize. It was all I could do to hold that big, son-of-a-bitch over my head like that and still look cool. Another minute or two and…" Steven stopped mid sentence and I caught a strange look on his face as we rounded the bend to his parent's house. He was out of the truck before I even understood what was going on. It was only then, that I noticed the front of the house.

The complete doorframe was destroyed; glass lay all over the front porch. Steven made his way towards the opening at a dead run. I threw the transmission in park and grabbed the shotgun off the rack, pumping a round into the chamber, and I arrived inside just seconds behind my cousin.

Steven stood in the center of the living room where we both had spent many happy hours over the years. The room was in shambles. No furniture was intact, no glass left unbroken, and of course, blood covered everything I could see. Flies swarmed in clouds. The oddly familiar odor of stale blood and death hung heavy in the air, and yet, another smell lingered beneath. The awful stench was not as strong as it had been the night of Jordan's death, but it was there—and it could have only come from one source.

On the floor, at Steven's feet, lay what remained of his parents. I would have given anything to be able to have stepped into the room ahead of him. Had I gotten there first, maybe I could have prevented him seeing what would undoubtedly stay with him forever.

The bodies were not even identifiable from where I stood. The room was drenched with the blood of my aunt and uncle who lay side by side, even in death. Steven stood without moving, like a statue in the park. I was afraid to speak, afraid that any words might set off an avalanche I didn't want to see. I didn't let my emotion get the better of me; I quickly moved room to room insuring the killer was not still on premises. When I had completed the circuit of the house, I returned by way of the kitchen and got a glimpse of the opposite wall of the living room hidden from earlier view by the fireplace. I moved closer to inspect the white plaster wall, stepping further into the other room to speak to Steven. My words caught in my throat.

The giant Indian had dropped to his knees beside the bodies of his parents. He made no sound as he slowly reached to close the open, staring eyes of the woman who had brought him into the world. Knowing how he must feel, I kept my mouth shut, waiting. The giant, whom I had seen fight six men at once and win, gently brushed the gray, blood-caked hair from her wrinkled face before turning to his father's body.

Frank had been left in a similar state as Jordan. His pants had been torn away from him, but evidently enough time had passed since the killing that Steven was spared the indignity of seeing his father's body in a state of sexual arousal. There was no doubt he had suffered the same treatment, all the evidence was there, but the effects of the toxins had worn off. He pulled the constantly present Harley T-shirt from his body and draped it over his father's private parts. His father's head had been turned towards the body of his wife as if the sightless eyes had struggled to see her one last time before the finality of death. Above his eye's, there was too much damage to describe; the top of his head and Mary's had been completely shattered. It was too much to hope that the powerful blow to Frank's head had been administered before the other atrocities had been committed. The frail bare legs peeked grotesquely from the edge of my cousin's shirt. Even the huge shirt could not hide all the damage done to my uncle's body.

Steven rose and turned to me. He said nothing. There were no tears in his eyes but there was great pain. I could never remember, in our entire lives, ever seeing my cousin cry. If his great pride could withstand the effects of this terrible carnage, I knew I never would. I opened my mouth to speak and nothing came out. Steven shook his head slowly from side to side. His expression slowly migrated from one of great pain and sorrow to anguish; slowly working it's way towards anger and finally arriving at hate. At that moment, if he could have confronted the killer, human or not, he would have made someone pay for what they had done. Having known him for years enabled me to read feelings others may not have caught. Normally his face betrayed little or nothing of what he felt. His expression then, as he stood over the mutilated bodies of his parents, in the room that had been destroyed in their struggle to live, left little doubt. He was ready to kill someone, and only God could help anyone who got in his way.

I retreated two steps backward and motioned for him to follow me. He walked towards me, confused at what I might have wanted. I nodded towards the once white wall and followed his eyes as he took in the bizarre spectacle. There on the wall, written in bloody dripping letters, were three words. The words, though badly written and somewhat hard to decipher, were clearly recognizable. I saw a look of confusion creep slowly over the face of my cousin. Scrawled on the plaster wall, in the blood of his mother and father, were the words, "SOON THE SON".

Those three small words seemed to reflect a perverse pride in what had been done. They also seemed to deny the idea of a mythical killer, at least to me. How could a witch, three hundred years old, learn to write English?

Steven replaced his automatic in the small of his back, and before I could react, he snatched the shotgun from my hands. He directed the barrel towards the wall and the loud retort of the shotgun blast filled my ears. In the small room, the magnum shells caused my head to ring, as he pumped and fired again and again. The plaster wall disintegrated into a cloud of white dust and chunks of dry wall. At last he pulled the trigger on an empty chamber, the firing pin echoing a loud click in the sudden stillness of the room.

He turned and spoke for the first time since we entered the slaughterhouse that had once been his home, "Follow me Morgan." He spun on his heels and headed towards the back of the house As we entered his bedroom, he put his hands into his tight jean pocket, and then tossed me a key, "Do me a favor, go load my bike on the back of the truck. I need to get a few things out of here."

"Steven…"

"Let's not talk right now Morgan. Just do this one thing for me okay?" His voice was tight as a drumhead.

"Alright." I could think of nothing to say anyway, so I turned to do as directed.

By the time I completed the loading of the big Harley, he returned and tossed a well-stuffed duffel bag into the truck bed alongside his bike. "Wait here." He commanded before walking quickly toward the shed, which served as the garage. A moment later he returned with a five-gallon gas container in each hand. He sat one container on the front porch and disappeared into the house with the other before I had time to ask what he was doing. Two or three minutes later the empty can came sailing through the front door. I finally understood what he was up to. He emerged from the shattered doorway and grabbed the full can and began dousing the outside walls and porch. I rushed to intercept him.

"Steven what are you doing?"

"What does it look like I'm doing?"

"You can't do this…"

"The hell I can't Morgan. Now just let me be." He looked at me with an undisguised fire in his eyes. "You just wait by the truck." His voice was level but forceful. "You got nothing to do with this that way."

"Steven think about what you're doing. There may be important clues inside that the FBI can use. These guys may not be great, but their crime scene crews are top notch. That writing alone was more than they've had to go on so far, and you've already destroyed that. You can't do this Steven!" I grabbed him by the arm and turned him to face me. The look he gave me made me hesitate. I almost stepped away, but I held my ground. I did move my hand from his arm however.

"Screw that Morgan. I will not have some stranger cut up my mother and father to help them with their precious investigation! They're not going to find anything anyway. You know that."

"No I don't, and neither do you. I can't let you do this Steven."

He dropped the gas can and removed his cigarette lighter from his pocket. Perhaps to calm his nerves or perhaps to buy time, he calmly lit a cigarette before he spoke again.

"Morgan, I'm only going to say this once." He pointed his finger at me. "I love you man, but you ain't going to stop me. Don't try me on this one, Morgan. That's my mother laying in there on the floor, you'd better think about what I'm telling you cousin."

He held my gaze, our faces only inches apart. I searched the dark brown eyes that so much resembled my own, looking for the truth in his words. What I saw there made me realize what I was asking of him. I had no right to interfere. This went beyond anything that had happened up until then. It was Steven's decision to make, not mine. Besides, I didn't like the look in those eyes. Steven and I had trained and fought together for many years. I had seen all his tricks, his strengths, and I knew what his weaknesses were. I was better trained in the martial arts than he, which generally allowed me to more than hold my own, but today something told me to let it go. Something behind those brown eyes warned me to respect his decision, to honor his choice. I think he may have really fought with me then if he had to.

"Please Morgan. I got to do this." The hard brown orbs softened a notch or two.

I thought about it for several long seconds and finally reached a decision, "If that's the way you want it Steven. I'll stand behind you, but they're going to know who did this."

He shrugged his shoulders as he removed the plastic from the paper of his cigarette pack. He smiled slightly; his way of saying thanks, and stepped further away from the gasoline soaked house. He placed the flame from his lighter under the paper, which caught immediately. He hesitated, only an instant, before tossing it onto the trail of gas. Light blue flame raced across the short distance between the house and us and seemed to jump the last few feet. The heat reached us in a quick rush as the fire whooshed into existence. Intense heat radiated towards us in waves and thick black, smoke danced skyward as the blaze engulfed the house.

Within minutes, the structure was blazing out of control as we stood side by side and watched it burn. Thick, black smoke bellowed upward. The roar of the flame and he loud cracking and popping of the burning dwarfed all sound. We watched as the front porch we helped build the summer of our sixteenth year, first tilted and then fell in on itself in a shower of sparks. I placed my hand on Steven's shoulder and he turned to look at me.

"We better go. The fire department will be here any minute."

"Yeah, I know. You go ahead, I'll be right there."

I returned to the truck, started the engine and looked through the dust-covered windshield at the lone figure silhouetted against the bright firelight. My cousin stood with his feet spread apart, hands on his hips, his immense, bare back towards me. As close as he was to the growing blaze, I knew the heat must be immense, yet he just stood there and watched the remains of his life burn. I wondered what was going through his mind.

Finally, he turned and walked swiftly to the truck, opened the cab door and slammed it in his wake. "Let's get the hell out of here Morgan."

As we pulled away from the house and I caught the reflection of the roaring inferno in my rear view mirror, I had a quick flash of just a few short nights before. I remembered doing the same exact thing, but in my mirror had been my aunt and uncle, arm in arm, waving goodbye to us. It was somehow fitting that was the last time that I saw them alive.

We moved onto the main road and headed away from the fire. Within a few miles we passed a fire truck, siren blazing, lights flashing. I moved respectfully to the side of the road allowing it to pass before we continued.

I struggled within my mind, trying to find words…something…anything to say, frustrating myself when I could not. I, who always had something to say, could find nothing to honor such a great loss. I tore my eyes from the road and looked to my cousin who had evidently been looking at me for some time. To me at least, his face displayed the deep hurt he must have felt. I tried to speak and stumbled meaningless over a half formed offering of sympathy, which came out worse than if I had remained quiet.

Steven smiled weakly and finally spoke, "Thanks Morgan, I already know." He turned his eyes back to the road and I did the same. After a minute or two of silence he spoke again, "And thanks for understanding."

But I didn't understand anything anymore.

CHAPTER TWENTY-SEVEN

When we pulled in the driveway, we found Kathy playing ball with Dog and Ben rocking on the front porch of the cabin. Steven got out of the truck before it had even fully stopped.

Kathy commented on his bare chest, "What's the problem? Those bad old FBI guys steal your shirt?" She began to laugh and then cut it short after catching the expression on his face. Steven walked right past them and spoke not a word to either.

Kathy turned to me, "What's happened Morgan?" Her face showing only concern.

"Nothing good I'm afraid." I told them what happened to my aunt and uncle. I had just begun telling them about our meeting with the agents when Steven returned. He had donned a new shirt, freed his long black hair and woven a single braid into it just in front of his left ear.

"I'm going up to the crest. I need the hike and I need to be alone for awhile." He directed his statements to no one in particular, just stared at the ground at his feet. He then turned his attention to Ben, "I'm sorry Rising Wolf, but I have to go."

Ben looked at Steven for sometime before finally commenting, "I understand. This is a very bad thing that has happened, son. Life is full of bad things, but life is at the same time full of good. You must accept the bad as well as you can, in your own way and in your own time, but then you must move on to the next thing. I am sorry for you and your grief." He placed his hand on Steven's shoulder, "When you return I will not be here. What has happened emphasizes the need for my services further down the mountain. Before I go I will do what I can to help, but I must leave you two." He paused and smiled warmly, "I wish you well, Steven Waters."

Steven nodded, "I wish you well, Rising Wolf." Then he turned away. Kathy stopped him before he got more than a few feet. She looked up into his face, her neck tilted up just like Aunt Mary's had done two nights before in order to meet the big man's eyes. "You two take care of each other. You know Morgan here isn't capable of taking care of himself so I'm counting on you."

He somehow managed a smile and gave her a quick hug, lifting her from her feet. He turned to me. "You know where I'll be." Then he turned and left the cabin at a brisk jog, heading further up the mountain, shotgun in one hand, canteen in the other.

I finished telling Ben and Kathy the details of our meeting with the Federal Agents told them about the autopsies and the limited information they had to go on. Kathy was extremely interested, as I had been, concerning the details of the medical findings. When I mentioned the removal of the heart, I looked to Ben expectantly, but he made no mention of it. I expected him to comment when I told him about the writing on the wall, but still he said nothing.

Ben remained silent as I finished the story. Kathy looked respectfully to her grandfather. Finally the old man spoke; "It is just as I thought. The things these people have told you support the legend. The "Su na yi eda hi", the "Night Goer" has definitely returned to take her vengeance. It would appear she has already come home, and I'm afraid many more will fall to her evil before she is done. I must finish our business here and return to the reservation as soon as possible." He looked at the sky; "Night is not far behind."

Kathy shook her head sadly, "I feel so sorry for Steven. He was never one to show affection but there was never any doubt how he felt about his parents. This is going to be hard for him on top of everything else. You can tell it has already affected his thinking."

Ben commented, "Yes, I'm afraid you're right. You too noticed his hair? It's good you haven't forgotten everything I have taught you young lady."

"Excuse me? I always remember what I've learned, I may not show it, but that's a woman's prerogative too I believe. But, yes I noticed. That's one of the reasons I'm so worried."

"I don't think Steven needs you to worry about him. He's very strong in more ways than one. His spirit will mend, and the challenge we are facing may do more to help him than we ever could. It will help occupy his mind while he grieves."

I interrupted, "Excuse me, I don't mean to ask crazy questions, but I think I missed something here. I don't understand about Steven's hair. What's the big deal? I've seen him wear it down before." I was confused by their discussion.

Kathy snorted. "Boy, I'm telling you, send you off to the city for a few years and you forget everything you left behind don't you?" I had a sneaky suspicion she referred to more than my question. "Didn't you notice the way he was wearing his hair? The single braid in front of the left ear?"

"Yes." I still didn't get it.

Ben interrupted. "The hair is worn that way to signify a warrior who will accept or give no quarter in battle. It is a signal to his enemies that he is dangerous and warns that he will fight until he dies. Nothing will change his attitude or alter his chosen course of action. When Steven next encounters the witch, he will immediately attack with no mercy and will expect none in return. To Steven, nothing else will matter in his life until his hand has killed the enemy or she in turn kills him. Everything he does now will be towards the killing of the evil one. Only the thoughts of her death will fill his mind, there will be little room for anything else. Maybe this will block out the feelings his parent's death have brought." He hesitated, "No, I think Steven will be fine for now. It will be later, when all is said and done, that he will mourn."

I again felt a loss. Once more, the people around me, my people, talked about things I should know of, but didn't. I couldn't relate. I felt like an outsider. These people were still my family, my friends, my tribe, but they shared something together that I had chosen to give up. Even Steven seemed to have realized the importance of his heritage and was taking it more seriously than I would ever have believed. I had not kept the faith. I had allowed life to lead me away from where I belonged and I kidded myself into thinking it was the best thing for me. I told myself such things were ancient, outdated, that they had no place in today's society. But, I was growing less and less sure of my decisions.

Ben interrupted my thoughts. "You two come with me. I will show you what I have done while you have been away."

Kathy and I followed Ben to the closest edge of the cabin where he indicated a sharpened stick he had driven into the ground.

The pointed end projected upward and away from the house, towards the surrounding forest.

"I have placed these arrows outside each corner of the cabin as well as the corners of the council house. If the Evil One indeed pays you a visit during the night, these arrows will fly into the air and come down upon her head. They will not kill in themselves, at least not right away, but will further weaken her efforts and further reinforce the need for killing within seven days." His voice softened and slowed, "If she does not die within the seven days then I must pay the price, but it is worth the chance. Now, if you two will stand in front of the cabin and remain silent, I will prepare the necessary formula. Kathy, would you be so kind as to translate for Morgan?"

"Yessir."

Kathy and I stepped away from the old man as he drew an ancient pipe wrapped in a black cloth from the small pack at his feet; he also withdrew a worn tobacco bag as well. Kathy told me it was filled with a

"I know it is hard for you to understand a lot of the things I have forced on you in the last day or two. I'm sure to you it sounds like the ravings of a senile old man." He held his hand up as I tried to interrupt, "No, don't insult me by pretending otherwise. I fully understand why you feel the way you do. These things we have spoken of, the things that are now happening within the tribe and to your family, would be hard for anyone to believe."

"I know that everything you have been taught directly contradicts the things I have asked you to believe and I could never fault you for honoring what you feel to be true. Throughout the history of the Cherokee, it has been our hardest battle to uphold our history and traditions against the so-called progress around us. From the time our children were forced into the white man's schools, they have been taught their beliefs were barbaric, uncivilized, with no place in "proper civilization"." He shook his silvery haired head slowly; "I could never blame the children for accepting these things because that is what they were taught. Over the years, the numbers of us who have struggled to uphold the old ways have dwindled. The effort wears a man down over time, as it has me." He smiled sadly, "As it did your grandfather."

His voice seemed to reflect the exhaustion of his years and the hopelessness of his situation, "Your grandfather was a very great man. It's hard for me to convey to you just how important his contributions were to the people of the tribe. Even now you can see where we would be without his great foresight for instance. But even though your grandfather was accomplished, he was very troubled. He well knew, many years ago, the few remaining Cherokee were fading into the pages of the history books."

As he talked, we watched a tiny brown squirrel climb a nearby tree. It sat on a high branch and chattered at us.

"I have been fortunate in recent years to see a rejuvenation of interest in the old ways. The young people of the tribe who once turned away, grasping the ways of modern society as their own, seem now to be questioning their decisions. They are beginning to see the many problems within today's society, the poverty, racial hate and unrest, the senseless killing of young people by other young people, the graft of the politicians. They seem to be asking genuine questions of themselves and their past. Your cousin Steven is a fine example of what I'm speaking of—you yourself know that it was not long ago all he cared about was drinking and carousing. Now he has taken a renewed interest in his heritage. I only hope such interest is not too little too late."

The intense sadness of his voice touched me and I felt a lump form in my throat.

"Even now, so many things have been lost, so much knowledge washed away with the blood of our people, never to be recovered again."

He tried a weak smile, changing the direction of his words, "I am very sorry your grandfather, my great friend, is not here to see such interest among our young people, and I am very sorry he is not here to see what a fine young man you have become."

"I know you've experienced some difficult times Morgan, and I know you're still greatly troubled by what has happened. I can see it in your eyes. I have an obligation to your grandfather, one of the few things he ever asked me for and I must fulfill it. He told me there would come a time such as this for you. He knew, even when you were a boy, you were special. I strongly feel had he not died when he did, your life would have been greatly different, but perhaps it is better in the long run that it was not." He held his hands apart, "Remember; it is only through hardship that we learn our greatest lessons, and with the continuation of life that we learn to apply what we have learned."

"As bad as it may sound, we are only born to die. Our lives here are very short and we must accomplish many things while we can. The most important of these is to live, nothing more. I understand you have spent a great part of your life studying and learning, but have you given any thought to why? Society would generally have you believe that only through following the prescribed guidelines; believing in the laws of

science, following some organized religion, can you possibly reach ful-
fillment and be truly happy."

He stopped and looked around the forest for the moment. The sound
of the water, the wind in the trees, the chattering of a squirrel, filled the
void. A cardinal landed on a twisted branch of a nearby dogwood tree,
oblivious to our presence. I remained respectfully quiet, trying my best
to understand what the old man was trying to tell me.

"Morgan, living is the only thing. There is nothing else. That bird
there has never been to school a day in his life, never learned what fork is
proper to eat with, never cared about the whims of fashion or the many
interpretations of right and wrong, yet it sings it's happiness from every
treetop. He doesn't care about such things, yet his life is full and he will
die just as we will and we will all leave with the same things...just the gift
of life, the joy of having lived, and the final rest of death." He turned to
me as he continued, "I don't mean to be so confusing, but time is short,
and I have so many things to tell you. In a nutshell, I want you to try to
understand that sometimes it's best to accept things around you as life,
without asking so many questions. Just because some scientist hasn't
found a way to justify something doesn't make it any less real. Life is real
and it is all that matters. Live it for what it is, and don't question the reasons why." He smiled, as if sensing my confusion, perhaps reading it in
my eyes.

"The people of our tribe were able to do this before the white man
came with their ideas of right and wrong, never thinking what they
were destroying might be more important than themselves. They didn't
understand the ways of the American Indian, so they proclaimed them
barbarians and destroyed them. It's as simple as that. Don't make that
same mistake Morgan. I think one of the reasons you're now so confused is you know in your heart things aren't right. I think deep inside
you, the spirit of your grandfather lives. He's telling you that the time
has come for you to take a leap of faith, and such a leap must be made
alone. It's the kind of journey no one can make for you and one for

which no map exists. You must find the way within yourself. Everything you need is already there waiting for you, this I promise." He paused and asked, "Do you understand what I am saying Morgan?"

I hesitated, wondering if I should lie and say yes. "Honestly, no, I don't understand it all, some maybe. It upsets me, some of the things you have said."

He did the strangest thing then, he smiled. "Good...good. That answer makes me happier than anything you could possibly have said. If you thought you understood everything now, you would be wrong to think so. I wouldn't expect you to. If I could tell you exactly, make you understand exactly, I would, but I can't. The things I am trying to convey can't be told to another. The things I have told you are only meant to offer you a way of finding your own answers within yourself. The answers are different for everyone and the answers are the same for everyone. Some day you will understand, but until then, just try to look at everything with an open heart and an open mind." His voice turned stern, "This killer is very real and demands that we see everything as possible, if not, it will mean our deaths. Do you understand this Morgan?"

"Yessir. I understand that very well."

"Outstanding. I feel I have accomplished something." He gestured toward the path to the cabin, "Now, we must go. We have things to do. I have duties elsewhere, and I think you need to help your cousin. As I told you earlier, he has the heart for these things but his mind has not yet been opened. I know you may feel as if your mind is betraying you, but that's just the door opening...the start of your inner journey." He gave me a reassuring smile; "I wish you the best on your journey Morgan Roberts, and I will be there as long as I can to help you find your way."

The look on his wrinkled face confirmed his words. I saw true compassion in those tired old eyes, true understanding of my plight. I felt close to tears, tears of gratitude—he had given me something I desperately needed at that moment…hope. I may not have understood what he was saying, but at least I knew there might be a light at the end of the tunnel of confusion I had been traveling for most of my life.

"Thank you Rising Wolf. I will not forget the things you have told me. That is something I will promise you." I used his Indian name for the first time in years. It wasn't a conscious effort on my part, it just came out.

He smiled, "That's all I can ask of you, Morgan. That's all anyone can ask. Now, don't you think we should head back? I'm sure you still wish to spend a moment or two alone with my beautiful granddaughter, or has that interest changed for you as well?"

I gave him an embarrassed look and retired. "No sir, I don't think that ever really changed."

He laughed, "No, I didn't think so. Would you care to walk with me back to the cabin?"

I rose and offered him my hand to help him up. "It would be my great honor." His withered old hand firmly clasped mine as he pulled himself upright.

We walked back through the same forest, but it was somehow different on our return journey. The birds sang just a little brighter, the air was a little cleaner, the forest greener. Things hadn't really changed in those few minutes we talked, but they sure seemed different somehow. I was still confused, but I felt a little better about things.

At least for the moment anyway.

Chapter Twenty-eight

Ben waited in the truck while Kathy and I returned to the cabin to retrieve her overnight bag. As she came from the room she slept in, I moved to take the bag from her hand, always the errant knight, tarnished maybe, but still trying.

"No thanks, big guy. This is one lady quite capable of carrying her own bags, thank you." She moved her bag to the hand opposite me and stood smiling up at me. "You know I'm still royally pissed at you Morgan."

"Yeah, I kind of figured as much. Just give me some time though, I'll wear you down." I smiled back, trying to put as much sincerity into it as I could.

"Think so, huh?"

"Well, I'm going to keep trying anyway. Can't blame me for that can you?"

"Well, no. That's at least one thing I can't blame you for, I guess."

"Ouch."

"Sorry, but you gotta' take your medicine sometimes. You know what I mean?"

I moved closer to her, my tone more serious. "Look, I know we don't have much time here, but I have to at least say I'm sorry one more time. I promise you…"

"Morgan, I don't care to hear another promise from you. If you apologize just once more, I think I'm going to throw up on those nice boots you're wearing. All these "I'm sorrys" from someone who never used to believe in apology is sort of disgusting. You're confusing me. Can't you at least be consistent?" Her smile turned mischievous, "Or is this just another one of your ploys to get back into my good graces? Maybe into my panties even? Either way, I'm just not in the mood right now. So can we just skip this for awhile? I really don't think there's any need in discussing it, this isn't the right time or place. When this whole thing is over, we'll talk about it, okay?"

"Well, I guess you told me, huh?" I don't know if it was my feigned look of pain that got to her, or just plain amusement, but she laughed at me anyway. To my surprise, before I could do anything about it, she rose on her tiptoes and kissed me lightly on the lips.

"Look Morg, I didn't say no did I? Why don't you just put all that suppressed sexual anxiety into keeping you and Steven alive long enough for me to come back and slap you again? Wouldn't that be fun?"

"For you, maybe, me…I'd just as soon we talk it out the next time."

She turned on her heel and walked towards the door of the cabin.

"Well, at least this way you'll have something else to think about until you see me again, huh? I wouldn't want you to take me for granted or anything."

"I don't think there's any chance of that." I moved to open the door for her, our bodies almost touching. She placed her free hand on my arm.

Her voice changed, her eyes filed with genuine concern, "Morgan, I want you to be careful up here. This whole thing really scares me." I knew from her manner she was speaking the truth, she wasn't kidding around any longer. "I know you and Steven have always thought you could fight the world together, but this is different. I don't want to see you dead, either of you."

"And you think I do?"

"This isn't funny Morgan. I'm afraid for you, I'm afraid for grandfather, and I'm afraid for the other people who may be the targets of this crazy lunatic. I don't want to see anymore people die." She turned away, "This madness has to stop, and I'm not sure who can stop it. This witch, or whatever she is, has left another Trail of Tears all the way across the country, right back here to the mountains where it all started." She dropped her voice until she was almost whispering; "I don't want any of us to be a part of her trail Morgan."

I placed my hands on her shoulders and turned her to face me. Her upturned face hinted at tears hiding in the corners of her dark eyes. "Listen to me, Kathy, I know this whole thing doesn't make a lot of sense, hell, I'm more confused now than I was a few days ago, but it's going to end. I promise you, if this maniac comes after us, we're going to be ready and waiting. I know your grandfather thinks this thing can't be killed, but whoever, or whatever this may be, I've got a few things in mind that will help. You know I don't lie, and I'm telling you Steven and I are going to stop this asshole."

Even as the words left my mouth, I felt my own doubts, but I tried my best to keep them from betraying me to Kathy. She needed hope, and I wanted to be the one to give it to her, just as she had done for me so many times in our past. "We've already talked about it, and as soon as I get Steven off the top of this mountain, we're going to do everything we can to get ready for tonight, tomorrow night…whatever night, but we'll be ready this time. Trust me Kathy, just once more, okay? I won't let you down this time." For a moment I couldn't believe the words, the promise I was making that I couldn't possibly be sure about. Then I realized that if I didn't fulfil the promise, it wouldn't matter…I would be dead. The dead didn't have to keep promises.

I don't know if Kathy realized the same thing or what possessed her, but she gave me a look that I will always remember. She moved her hand to lightly touch the spot she had slapped just the morning before. "Thanks Morgan." Just those two words, that was all. Her eyes danced with a familiar light that I hadn't seen in years, and had thought I would never see again, but it was there for a brief instant. I know it was...or maybe I hoped it was. Then she turned from my casual embrace and exited the door before I could do or say anything else.

I followed outside and watched as she patted Dog goodbye, and without saying anything more, got into the driver's side of her Bronco and closed the door. I looked at Ben who sat beside her and he gave me his best, wrinkled smile and raised his hand. I returned the gesture and looked through the windshield at Kathy. She just looked at me for a moment and finally smiled the peculiar smile that I had come to love and hate with equal fervor. She spoke and I read the soundless words from her lips, "be careful" and the white truck began to roll backward. I felt Dog lean against my leg and I moved my hand unconsciously to rub her head. Kathy waved to me after she completed turning the truck around.

I replayed the conversations I had with both Ben and Kathy as I went back into the cabin and took a long hot shower. The steamy water flowed over my tired body as I tried to figure what Kathy really had on her mind, and, as always, I decided I didn't have a clue.

After I dressed, I removed one of the magnum handguns from the gun stash and strapped it under my arm with a big, leather shoulder holster. I retrieved one of the assault rifles and loaded it, taping an extra clip to the one already in the weapon adding immediate, extra firepower if needed.

The sun was just starting to go down on what had been another shitty day in paradise. I went to the kitchen, poured Dog some dry food, and prepared some sandwiches for Steven and myself. After the forced fast of the day, it was all I could do not to wolf mine down, but I decided to wait, and contented myself with munching a slice or two of the lunchmeat. I wasn't in any hurry. I wanted to give Steven the time alone that I knew he needed. I remembered the pain of my mother's death and the mixed emotions I had experienced with the death of my father, but I was at least spared the horror of finding them as we found my aunt and uncle. I think one of the reasons I wasn't in any hurry might have been I still didn't have a clue as to how to help Steven deal with their deaths. I was still trying to cope with similar demons of my own, and I wasn't sure I could be of any help to him.

After I completed all the pretend work I could find, I called Dog and we started up the obscure trail that led to the crest of my grandfather's mountain. The trail, even though overgrown with weeds, was still easy to see even in the fading afternoon light. By the looks of things, it was going to be a clear night on the mountain. I could hear a bullfrog from the nearby wet of the stream and small animals scurried from my path into the surrounding brush as I approached. A few times I had to call Dog back from giving chase as we made our way up the gradually sloping hill. The old trail was dramatically different from the trails of Grandfather Mountain. It wound through the forest, through a meadow, several clearings, and occasionally returned to follow the stream, but it was all easy going. There were few rocks or roots, only a steady gentle slope to follow. It was about a mile from the cabin to the pinnacle of the mountain.

The top of the mountain was a place I remembered well from my childhood. I remember the nights I was allowed to spend with my grandfather, and the pleasant walks we would take to the top. All along the way he pointed out different things in the world around us and answered a young boy's unlimited questions with endless patience and understanding. I learned a lot from those walks and the ready talks, but I had come to realize I was only scratching the surface of knowledge inside the head of that old shaman. After the recent talks with Ben, and the tales of the past, I was sure I really had no idea how important he must have been in his day. He always had time to spend with me and always talked to me as his grandson. He undoubtedly had a different face for other people.

I remember when I was very young, maybe nine or ten, I was allowed to stay over with my grandfather. I think my dad was on a drunk and my mother jumped at the chance to get me out of the house. It was late winter and while I was on the mountain, a fierce winter storm blew up. Everything was covered with white. Snow blanketed the forest in drifts of two to three feet and temperatures plummeted to near zero, turning it all to ice in the night. At that time, my grandfather had yet to install the luxury of indoor plumbing. An old outhouse stood thirty or forty yards from the main cabin, well away from the stream. All the beds in the house had chamber pots beneath them for nighttime needs and thus the need for freezing trips to the outhouse were minimized. For some reason, I found the idea unpleasant, perhaps knowing that I would have to clean up after myself in the morning. I don't really remember. Sometimes the mind of a ten-year-old has ideas that seem preposterous later on.

That particular cold night, I had the unfortunate need to attend to the calls of nature around one or two in the morning. I recall huddling under the cold sheets attempting to force myself back to sleep. The room I slept in had a fireplace with only a faint glow of dying coals. The air was cold, and I knew the hardwood floor would be the same. I also knew that the outside temperature would be much, much colder. Even so, the alternative was something I just couldn't face at the time. So I forced myself from beneath the warmth of the covers and slid into the cold jeans beside the bed. I had slept in my socks, but my boots were still cold as I struggled to push my feet inside. I tried to keep my actions as quiet as possible, not wanting to wake my grandfather.

When I stepped from the rear door of the cabin, the bitter wind assaulted me like a wave. The snow had stopped and the virgin whiteness glistened and gleamed like diamonds in the bright moonlight. Pine trees were draped with solid white blankets, lower limbs stretched to brush the ground. The absolute quiet of that snowy night will always remain fresh in my mind. The sound of my footfalls in the deep, icy snow seemed so loud I felt they could be heard for miles around. The journey from the cabin to the old wooden outhouse and back seemed unbearably long and cold to my ten-year-old mind, but I eventually made it back to the log structure. I dusted the snow from my clothes as best I could and made my way quietly to my room.

The fire blazed with warmth; new logs had been added and the bed had been turned down to allow the heat to warm the sheets. A towel had been placed over the ladder-back chair at the bedside and an extra blanket had been draped across the bottom of the bed. I quickly dried my cold feet with the towel, jumped beneath the warm covers, and stared into the fire for a long time until I finally fell asleep.

I never mentioned the night to my grandfather or he to me, nor do I know to this day why I remember the night with such clarity or why it stayed with me so long. The lessons I learned from my grandfather were frequently like that. Sometimes it was only later that I realized I had learned anything at all. That starry winter night my grandfather allowed me to venture out into the coldness of the world on my own. He allowed me to make my own decisions for my own reasons and never questioned me even though I was very young. I could never imagine my mother ever having allowed such a thing, but he had. I could picture him standing by the window of his room, perhaps watching me struggle through the deep snow…not interfering, just watching. If I ever have children, I hope I will be able to apply the same type wisdom and caring.

I smiled to myself, recalling the night from my childhood, walking the same trail we shared together many times in those early years. As Dog ran along ahead of me, I wondered if things would have indeed been different had he lived longer. I wondered if he would have been able to stop this killer of his people. Most of all, as I trudged further up the mountain to find Steven, I wondered if I would be able to.

CHAPTER TWENTY-NINE

The sun was just beginning its decent as I reached the summit. Dog was somewhere behind me chasing a squirrel and I thought a little activity might calm her down, so I just let her run. Through the trees, I saw the flickering of a small fire. Steven must have planned to stay awhile.

The mountaintop had been cleared for a home site hundreds of years before; no one knew for sure how long it had been. All that remained was the stone foundation, crumbled down in most places, and a huge fireplace with no chimney. It had fallen in decades before. The ancient home site was a place I frequently visited in my youth. We came up and sat around campfires built in the broken down fireplace. The first time I remembered coming to the place was with my father many years before Jordan was born. He was an all right guy then, my dad, or so I thought.

It was where my grandfather brought me to show me the sky and to talk about the history of the earth, the stars, and the moon. He told the Cherokee legends of how it all came to be and, although I only vaguely recall those stories, I recollect those nights with clarity. Stars were uncountable on those evenings as the soothing, steady voice of my grandfather blended with the crackling and popping of the fire. To my young ears the meaning of his words was often lost, but the calming effect was always welcome and that's what I remembered the most. In later years, when I desperately searched for escape from my home life, he was my solace. When he died, the deserted mountain home became my "Fortress of Solitude." It was much more "home" to me than the one I had, no matter how hard I tried to believe otherwise.

Over the years, Steven and I camped at the old home sight whenever he came with me on one of my frequent visits to my grandfather's. When we started to drive, we cut school and sneaked up whenever we could. During our teenage years, it was a great place to visit with the young ladies; the moonlight view seemed a natural aphrodisiac. There were many reasons, but if I were ever to build a home of my own, that summit would be the sight.

Whoever owned the old house in a previous century must have cleared the surrounding area for crops of some kind; there were no large trees within a fifty-yard circumference. Tall grasses, blueberry and blackberry bushes and wild flowers blanketed the whole area atop the mountain. In the spring and summer, butterflies danced among the yellowbells and dandelions by the hundreds. Long-legged grasshoppers jumped as high as a man's head as I startled them with my passing. The vastness of the summit view promoted a sense of openness and spoke of the immense size of the world we lived upon. As far as the eye could see, mountains rolled one upon another like waves of a mighty ocean. It was a place that seemed to lessen the seriousness of any problem, made them seem small and less important. If there was a God in the heavens I think people felt closer to him somehow, on the top of a mountain.

Steven sat near the small fire, smoking a cigarette. His back was to me, his face turned towards the rolling mountain peaks to the west, and yet I knew he heard my approach. For all my big talk, I was never really able to sneak up on him as he did me. He could move as silently as a ghost, a trait I evidently never fully inherited. After awhile, I just gave up trying and accepted the constant ridicule he heaped upon me as a running joke. As I came near, and sat the small sack of food down alongside my assault rifle, he didn't speak so neither did I.

I sat on the opposite side of the fire. A small pile of wood had been placed nearby and I added a couple of logs to the flame. I removed two of the sandwiches from the bag and started to eat, the grumbling of my stomach reminding me it was long past time. I tossed the bag towards Steven. He remained motionless. After I finished eating, I took long swallows of the cool spring water I had brought in my canteen, then settled back to wait.

After a time, Steven absently reached for the bag and began eating without taking his eyes from the sunset which was blossoming into a thing of rare beauty. Shades of muted purple mixed with vivid orange and deep red against lengthening grays. Huge clouds of color were pasted against the brightness of the fading sunlight. The mountain pinnacles rolled towards the retreating radiance of the sun; chasing it like waves after a departing ship. The rising mist from the valleys mixed with the light, softening the lines and blending the tints like a soft pastel watercolor.

Steven finished his sandwiches and brought out his own canteen, turning it up to drink deeply from its contents. He replaced the top, and without even looking my way, tossed it over his shoulder in my general direction. I grabbed the canteen from the air and opened it, taking a sip of the strong bourbon. With Steven, I never bothered to ask what was in the canteen. The contents rarely deviated.

"This shit is really beginning to piss me off, Morgan." He kept his eyes on the setting sun. That was all he said.

"Yeah, I know what you mean." It was all I could think to say.

Silence settled between us again, heavy and dense. Dog ran up, sniffed at Steven, made a pass or two around the fire, then settled near my feet and promptly went to sleep. The sky slowly darkened, losing shades of red in favor of dark blues, heavier grays and much later the familiar purple and black of night. Still, we didn't speak. I added more logs to the fire as the temperature dropped with the sun. I hadn't brought a jacket and I used that as reasoning for taking another long swallow from Steven's canteen. You could rationalize anything if you thought about it long enough—something I was relearning from Ben.

"Heads up Steven." I tossed it back to him and watched as he took a swig and dropped it absently by his side. He stretched out on his back by the fire, staring at the roof of bright stars. The moon had risen even before the sun went down, and it was almost to fullness, maybe a day shy of a complete circle. I sat directly across the fire from Steven with my back against one of the fallen foundation rocks, the assault rifle close beside me. I noticed his shotgun was within easy reach. I closed my eyes and took cleansing breaths to clear my mind; practicing breathing techniques I had learned years before. The cool night air was fresh and clean, vastly different from the Charleston air I had breathed for the last year or two. There was no trace of salt air, exhaust fumes, or the normal city pollutants. It was crisp and clean and pure.

Steven finally spoke to me from his side of the fire, pulling me from my thoughts. "You know, I can remember the exact moment I changed the way I thought about my old man. You know what I mean; I always thought he was just my old man that he had no idea of what I thought about things. You remember when we were young and used to bitch about them not letting us do things on our own and shit like that? I never thought he had any idea what it was like to be young, you know?"

I remained silent. I felt like it was good for him to talk and I didn't want to risk saying anything to stop him. Of course, I don't think he really wanted an answer, anyway. He was just talking to heal himself.

"Well, after the old man had his heart attack, one day I was going riding on the parkway by myself. I was headin' towards Asheville and then thought I'd cut over into the Great Smokies towards Gattlinburg, you know? I think he must have wanted me to stay around and talk or somethin', being confined to the house was driving him crazy then."

"Anyway, we were sittin' on the front porch and I told him he didn't understand what it was like, that was all. I told him ridin' through and around these mountains was the nearest thing to heaven on earth for me. I tried to explain to him about the ridin'. Then he said something that really blew my mind; not right away, but later on when I had time to think about it. He said he understood, 'cause he used to get the same feeling hiking and climbing the high mountains. I'll never forget he said it was like "walking through the clouds". You know what he meant; when the fog is thick and you're really high up and the clouds are all around you, even below you in some places. I get those same feelings around Mitchell, or high up in the peaks around here. I mean when you really are passing through a cloud. That's a feeling I never thought any-one would ever really understand—unless they had been there, you know? But the old man really knew, he really did."

"I think that was when I started thinking about him as a person and not just my old man. It's hard to explain, but that's just what I been thinkin' about. I'm not even sure why, but I just can't get it out of my head. It's crazy." He was quiet for a minute or two. "Ain't this some shit, Morgan?" It was hard to see his face through the flames of the fire, but I could have sworn his eyes watered. He lit another cigarette and rose on his elbow to look at me across the fire. "It'll never be the same without em."

"I know."

He thought about it for a minute, "Yeah, I guess you do."

He retrieved the canteen and took another drink, then passed it to me and I did the same. "It sure as hell hurts right now Morgan, seeing them like that and all."

I said nothing.

"Tell me this is going to get easier to deal with, Morgan."

"I can't do that." And I really couldn't. I hadn't been forced to see my parents demise as he had, but I still had not come to grips with the loss. Even my father's death, the man I hated most of the years of my adult life, tormented my thoughts and dreams of late. I had a feeling, how-ever, that Steven was a lot stronger than I was, and in more ways than one.

"We'll get this asshole Steven. I promise." I couldn't believe I was making yet another promise I didn't believe myself.

"Will we Morgan?" His voice was quiet and I didn't know how to answer.

The fire died down and we added more wood.

Steven finally asked, "Alright Morgan, you got some kind of plan on what we do next?"

"Not really. I mean I don't think we're going to be able to hunt this killer down. I think the only thing we can do is lay a trap here and just wait on him, or her, to come to us. I've got a few ideas and maybe if we can buy a little luck; we might have a chance. I just hope we get the opportunity to do something before anyone else dies that's all. This thing is getting way out of hand."

"Yeah, I agree with that."

I hesitated, trying to make out his features in the firelight, "I'm sorry, Steven. I wish there was something more I could say."

"I know Morgan, but there's not. You know how it is with something like this. It's just going to take some time, that's all."

"Yeah, that's what I hear, anyway." If it took time to get over death, maybe enough had not passed with me. I decided to turn to something more tangible as a way to occupy both our minds. The train of thought we were on was a one-way track to despair, and I had been there before. Nothing about it appealed to me.

"Steven, I've been thinking about this a lot and maybe we might have a chance. The idea is a little risky, but I think this calls for some drastic measures. We've got to make sure, once and for all, that this killer does not leave this mountain alive."

"Okay, let's hear what you got in mind, cousin."

For the next quarter-hour I explained the idea I had formulated, then I let him think about it for awhile—let him realize the possibility of mortal danger to one or both of us. In the end, he agreed it was the only sure-fire way we had, and after some discussion, we decided it was the only possible plan that might work.

We let the fire die to embers, and then we made our way back to the cabin in the dark. The brightness of the moon supplied more than enough light, but it wouldn't have mattered anyway. We could have trod the trail with our eyes closed, day or night, made no difference. It was a beautiful night, as it could only be in the high Appalachians.

After we returned, we began our preparations for our defenses for the evening, just in case. We opened the wooden crates I had brought from Charleston, and removed the implements of destruction we needed. We worked long into the night, preparing the trap. As we worked, neither of us stopped listening to the sounds of the night. We listened for the sudden silence that would signal the approach of something unknown, something foreign to the forest. The nocturnal animals, birds, and insects, were natural alarm systems if you knew how to listen. When an unfamiliar silence arrived, there would be little time to react. Yet some warning was better than no warning.

When we finished, we took turns sleeping and watching until daylight. But it wasn't necessary. That night trouble never came knocking on our door…it came to the door of others.

CHAPTER THIRTY

When morning came, we put the finishing touches on our little "surprise package", with that finished, we had little left to do but wait. We each carried a small radio transmitter with a safety switch and an arming button. The small battery powered devices clipped to our belts and the plan called for us not to be without them. There was nothing else we could do but sit like cheese in a trap.

After I fed Dog, I went inside and watched while Steven tried his luck at preparing breakfast, failing miserably in the attempt. I thought it only fair that I point that out to him—trying to occupy his mind with familiar taunting, "Nice job with those eggs Steven. You always eat them black like that?"

"I didn't hear you offer to cook." It was good to hear him joke with me after the night he had spent. His tone was still abnormally subdued beneath the chiding exterior.

"No thanks. If you recall, I fixed supper last night."

"Oh yeah, sandwiches—big deal?"

"They were at least edible."

"So what. Who can mess up a sandwich?"

"I don't know. I used to think that same thing about eggs, and look what happened."

"Don't push me, Morgan." He pointed his spatula at me.

I sarcastically echoed his remark, "Don't push me." I smiled at him. "That supposed to scare me or something?"

"Just shut up and eat your eggs so we can go. I want to come back and take a nap."

We decided earlier that we would go down to the pay phone and make a couple of calls. I wanted to check in with Kathy and Ben, then call Marilyn to see what was happening in Charleston. After the breakfast we had, I thought we might even find a place down the mountain for a decent lunch. The gas supply for the generator was running a little low and we needed to top off the cans so we tossed those in the back of the truck. I had no idea how long we were going to be up on the mountain and didn't want to take any chances.

The morning was sort of overcast but nice as we made our way down. Dog rode in the back. At first Steven rode in silence, then finally he gradually began to talk more, joked around and even laughed a little. I considered it a good sign, but didn't know if he really felt better or if it was fatigue from another long night or the whole thing another facade of his. I didn't question it. I just went along like nothing had happened. He was a great guy, my cousin. But, or course, I couldn't ever tell him so—that would have been violating one of those unwritten rules between the two of us. We'd insult each other or tell one another to go to hell, but it came out meaning the same thing...to us anyway.

The black top road into town was deserted. Steven took our short shopping list and headed towards the store as I walked to the now familiar phone booth.

I closed the door, drew a slow, deep breath, and dialed a number from the past just as if I had called it the day before. It was a number I would never forget. Kathy answered on the third ring.

"Hello."

"Hi, Kath. What's up?"

"Lots." Her tone was subdued. Something was wrong. "How's Steven?"

"He's much better, I think. You know, sometimes it's hard to tell with Steven."

"Yeah—he's not the only one either."

"Ouch! Can't you lighten up on a frustrated man? Everything okay?"

"No Morgan, it's not. There were five murders last night that we know about on the reservation. One of them was a family with a small child, a ten-year-old boy."

"That's terrible." I remained silent for a moment as the news she had given me sank in. "I don't know what to say. What does your grandfather think?"

"I don't know. He was out most of the night and came home just long enough to eat and leave again. He was very upset Morgan. I think he feels somehow responsible for this—like he's failing his people when they need him the most. The phone has been ringing off the hook all morning and he's running himself to death. If this doesn't stop soon, I'm afraid he's going to hurt himself."

Her tone was heavy with concern, "When he told me about the boy he was near tears. I don't know what to do."

"There's nothing you can do, Kath. You just stay around the phone and keep a shotgun loaded by the door. I don't think you're in any danger. The killer doesn't seem to care about women or people outside our family tree, but I want you to take precautions just in case. I would come down but I think that would just be more dangerous for you. I know we're on the hit list and I don't want to draw any more attention to you or your grandfather than necessary." I paused, "I can't believe someone's killing children now too."

"I know, Morgan. I've tried not to think about it all morning but I can't get it out of my mind." Her voice reflected how much it bothered her; "The people here are nearly hysterical. They're afraid for their children now and that could bring on a full-scale panic before too long. The tribal police have already notified the authorities and I understand a Federal Task Force is on the way here now."

I didn't bother to ask how she had come about such information. With her political ties and connections she would know everything that was going on.

"Kathy, when they get there I want you to contact them."

"What? Why?"

"Well, ask for this Agent Smith we've been dealing with. He's a little stuffy but he's not a bad guy. I'll give him a call when I get off the phone. I think it wouldn't hurt if you two had some protection for tonight, at least. If he thinks you're a possible target, he'll put men on it."

"But I thought you just said you didn't think I would be a target." She took a stubborn tone; "I will not accept special treatment Morgan, not while our people are in such danger."

"I'm not asking you to Kathy, but if this killer is as smart as everyone seems to think, it won't take long for her to find out about your grandfather's efforts to thwart her plans." I caught myself again using the female term freely. "I don't want to take any chances. The killer may decide to come after Ben and I don't want anything to happen to you or him, okay?"

She hesitated before she replied. "Okay Morgan, I'll do what you ask for grandfather's sake, but he's not going to like it either you know."

"I'm counting on you to convince him of it, Kath. If anything happened and we didn't take this precaution, I would never forgive myself and neither would you."

She thought for a second, "Yeah, you're right. Anything you need? Anything I can do from here?"

"No, I don't think so. Just hang tight and I'll check in from time to time. We've sort of laid a trap up here and we've got to stay as the bait. The sooner the killer comes for us the sooner this whole mess will be over." I tried to put as much confidence as I could in my words, even though I actually wasn't so sure myself.

"Just be careful okay?" I could hear the concern in her voice and in a way it made me feel good.

"I will Kathy. You too. Don't forget to contact Smith when he gets there."

"I won't, but are you sure he'll come himself?"

"I'll make sure. Look, I need to go. You take care of your grandfather."

"I will...Morgan..."

"Yeah?"

"Don't take any chances you don't have to. I do want to see you when this whole thing is done, you know? I don't want anything to happen to you, with you thinking...I...you know..."

"Don't worry your pretty little head about me. I'm too mean to get hurt. That's what you've always told me anyway."

"I'm not trying to be funny here Morgan."

"Neither am I, Kathy." The silence rose between us. "I have to go now. Tell Ben I said to be careful."

"Goodbye Morgan." There was something in her voice I didn't quite recognize.

"Bye Kath." I hung up the phone.

I dug the number from my pocket and the same type deadpan voice answered; maybe not the same one but it sounded the same. "Hello."

"Agent Smith please."

"Who may I say is calling?"

"Morgan Roberts."

"Hold the line."

Several moments passed. Steven returned and put the supplies in the truck bed beside Dog. He came to the front of the truck and leaned on the grill; lit a cigarette and watched a couple of kids playing across the street.

"Smith here."

"Fred, how's it going?"

"Look Roberts, I don't have time to chat with you today. Where are you?"

"Around."

"Did you happen to be around your Aunt and Uncle's house yesterday after you left our meeting?"

"What makes you ask?"

"Don't play with me, Roberts; I don't have time for this right now."

I thought about it and then answered. "Yeah, we were there."

"I thought so. What happened? Never mind…just tell me where you are and I'll send a car for you. I have other things going on and I don't have time to argue with you."

I could hear the road noise from the car phone he was speaking on. "On your way to Cherokee are you?"

"What…how do you know that?"

"I heard about the killings."

"What do you mean, you heard? This whole thing is secret! No one's supposed to know. Only the local police know."

"There are no secrets on the reservation, Smith. You'll find that out soon enough."

"Did you hear that a child was killed this time?"

"Yes, I did." I paused, "Was it as bad as the others?"

"Well, I haven't visited the murder scene yet, but from what I understand, they may have been worse. The brutality and the mutilations have gotten more intense, if that's at all possible."

"I hope you get this guy, Smith."

"Yeah, so do I. So do I. Now, where are you, Roberts? I need to talk to you and soon. This time I don't want to hear your ideas on the best place for us to meet. You seem to be constantly involved with a Federal investigation and I think I've allowed you as much latitude as possible, much more than I ever should have."

"No dice. I'm not coming in Fred. I'll tell you what you need to know but make it quick."

"Look Mr. Roberts, when I get off this phone I am going to issue a federal warrant for your arrest. I want you where I can get to you when

I need to. You're coming in on your own or I'll come and get you, that's the deal."

"Okay, then no deal. Come and get me." I paused and added, "If you think you can that is."

I heard his exasperated sigh before he continued, "Okay Roberts, just tell me; was your cousin's parents killed by our guy?"

"Yes, no doubt about it."

"Was there anything different? Why was the house burnt down?"

"We did that."

"What?"

"Calm down, Fred. There was a reason for it. Steven didn't want your ghouls cutting up his parents and I can see his point."

"Mr. Roberts, I want you to understand that you have just admitted to a federal agent that you and your cousin committed a felony. I have no choice but to have you arrested."

"I understand that Fred. Take your best shot, but there was something unusual about the murders you need to know. You interested, or you want to wait until you have me arrested?" I snickered, "Of course, you'll have to find me to arrest me."

"Yes Mr. Roberts, I want to know. What was done that was so different?"

I told him about the writing on the wall in my uncle's house. I tried to quickly describe the scene and all I could remember about the bodies. I knew that if I stayed on the line much longer there was the possibility of a trace.

When I finished, Smith replied, "I wish you hadn't destroyed the crime scene Mr. Roberts. That may have been the first real hard evidence we have had, and now it will do us no good. Of course, you realize this makes your cousin's theory harder to believe?"

"How so?"

"Well, if I even remotely believed this myth nonsense, which I don't, how would a witch several hundred years old learn to write as she supposedly did?"

"Yeah, I've wondered that myself. Look, Smith, I can't stay on this line any longer. I can't take the chance of you tracing the call. I need you to do us both a favor."

I told him briefly about Kathy and Ben, where they lived and how to contact them. I told him Ben might be able to assist him in his investigation and that he may even be a possible victim. After a moment or two he agreed to help.

"Okay Smith, that's all I have to say. I'll be seeing you."

"Yes, you will Mr. Roberts. Of that, I'm certain. That is, if you don't get yourself killed first. This killer is coming for you and even if I can't find you, he may. I don't want to see your name next on a crime scene report."

"Woah, do I detect a note of concern on your part, Smith?"

"No, I just don't want anything to happen to you before I get a chance to arrest you, that's all."

"Of course, I should have known. Be seeing you Fred." I hung up, then dialed another number.

"Robert's Cycles. May I help you?" Her voice was coolly professional.

"Not from there you can't."

"Well…well…well, Mr. Roberts. How are you this morning? Got yourself in any more trouble since I saw you last?"

"Well Marilyn, let's see—nothing really interesting. I did just get a federal warrant issued for me though, that's something different I guess."

"Yeah, but considering it's you, I'm not really surprised. You stopped surprising me a long time ago."

"Really?"

"Really. Don't worry though, if the Feds get you, they'll let you go soon enough. They'll never be able to stand being around you for any extended period of time." She laughed at her little joke, "Seriously, what's up?"

I filled her in on what had happened since I talked with her last. She listened patiently as I told her of the most recent murders and the situation we were in. I told her about Steven's parents. She asked several questions to fill gaps that I had left from the story. She asked how Steven was holding up.

"He's doing alright, I guess—handling it much better than I could." I paused, realizing just how true that was. "I know you don't know him very well, but sometimes he's sort of hard to read."

"Oh, now there's a surprise! Is that a family trait or something? Where is he now?"

"He's about twenty feet from me, leaning on my truck and smoking what must be his tenth cigarette in ten minutes."

"Put him on the phone."

"You got to be kidding me."

"No, I'm not. Everything is fine here in case you're wondering. We're making you lots of money."

I hesitated for a second, "No, I'm through I guess, but listen, I don't know if this is the best time for..."

"Morgan, put him on the phone and take a chill pill, alright. And take care of yourself. I need to talk to you about a raise and I prefer to do it in person. I didn't know I was going to have to put up with all this kind of crap and I think I'm being grossly underpaid. Now put the phone down and get your good-looking cousin on the phone."

"I don't have a good looking cousin, only Steven."

"Don't be a smart ass, just do what I say."

"Don't I always?"

"Bye Morgan, and be careful okay?"

"Sure thing ma'am...yes ma'am...whatever you say, ma'am."

I let the phone dangle by the cord and motioned for Steven. He walked up with a look of bewilderment on his face.

"Telephone."

He looked confused. "Who..."

"Just answer the phone. Don't ask me what's going on." I shook my head, "Hell, I don't know myself."

I returned to the pick-up and watched as Steven talked to Marilyn. He removed the dangling cigarette from his lips and crushed it under his boot. He saw me watching and turned his back towards me with a smirk. After a minute or two, I saw him laugh as he turned back towards me, shaking his head and speaking into the receiver. I had to smile at the picture. Over three hundred miles away and Marilyn was still able to work her magic. She was amazing even from a distance.

Steven hung up the phone and returned to the truck with a half smile on his face. I looked at him as I started the truck and backed out of the parking space. I didn't say anything I just looked at him expectantly.

"What?" He asked with a silly grin, "What?"

I just shook my head and laughed. It felt good to laugh.

CHAPTER THIRTY-ONE

We did what man has done to catch his prey since the dawn of time. We laid a trap and baited it with what the killer wanted—us. It was not the first plan of attack; it was a last option. It carried a lot more risk than I would have liked.

A few years back, I used some contacts I developed while in the military to secure a small amount of plastic explosives. I was planning to blast a few stumps around the cabin and thought it would work better than dynamite. I had been well trained in how to handle it, courtesy of Uncle Sam, and I felt more comfortable with it than dynamite, which was much less stable. Possession of the plastic could have sent me to jail if Smith ever got wind of it, but I really didn't give a damn about Smith or his minions. Steven and I wired both the council house and the main cabin with explosives.

The plan was to lure the killer into one of the structures and set off the explosives without killing us in the process. With a little timing, we hoped to get the killer through the front door and into the cabin, then exit the back before the killing blast. There were a few possible hitches of course; it would be hard to exit the cabin fast enough via the back door and the old council house only had one door, which made that almost a suicidal choice. If luck had us closer to the council house when the killer struck, one of us would have to make a fast and mortal decision.

This, of course, was the last resort. I didn't want either one of us to die, but we had to have a back-up, sure fire plan if all else failed. Besides, it was the best one we could come up with. For further protection, we armed ourselves with powerful assault rifles, and carried large caliber handguns wherever we went. Steven still insisted on carrying his old shotgun slung over his shoulder. I couldn't imagine anything human standing up to such firepower, or anything inhuman for that matter. At the moment, even the impossible was beginning to seem plausible. The circumstances were making me question many things I once thought impossible.

Since the killer evidently preferred to kill late in the night, we would sit up and wait for her to call. It was that simple. I doubted she would visit us so soon, but I intended to leave nothing to chance. We were going to be ready each and every night until the situation altered. During the late evening hours, we would separate in the brush near the cabin, making sure the killer had to expose herself to one of us in order to attack the other. When she did, we would have her in crossfire. It was the same ambush made popular in similar mountain ranges in a country halfway around the world, Vietnam. The plan worked there and I hoped it would work for us. I didn't know what else we could try.

When Steven and I returned from the phone booth, it was just after midday. We took time to eat the burgers we purchased from the small grill in Bakersfield as we checked our work from the night before. We disassembled and cleaned every weapon and inspected the ammunition. After that, we had nothing else to do but wait.

To fight boredom as much as anything else, I dug out a couple of axes and a small chain saw and threw them in the back of the truck. Dog jumped in the rear and we worked our way down the road doing the maintenance we had talked about. We had to have something to do to occupy our minds and bodies until nightfall, and hard work soothed the mind. Or so my grandfather used to say. Every one to two hundred yards we stopped to cut a branch or small tree that sprouted too close to the road. For a time, Steven was able to ride in the back and use the power saw to cut overhanging limbs without getting out of the truck.

The day was becoming hot for the mountains, almost muggy. Before we were half way down, our shirts were plastered to our backs; our hands dirty from dark earth and pinesap. It felt good to be working that way, sweating out the worries, stress and grief I accumulated during the week of hell Steven and I had been through. The afternoon of manual labor reminded me of how much I enjoyed working with my hands and it filled out the afternoon hours nicely.

I pulled to the side of the road, noticing a medium-sized pine tree leaning dramatically towards the rocky road. Steven spoke to me from the truck bed through the sliding rear window, "What do you think, Cuz? Cut it or not?"

"I think we better cut it. The first ice storm hits, it's gone. If it breaks, I'll just have to clear it out of the way later. Might as well do it now. We've got plenty of time before dark."

I got out of the truck as Steven jumped off the back. Dog jogged into the nearby brush. She never stayed around when work was to be done. We grabbed an axe and the chain saw from the back. Steven cleared surrounding brush from the base of the pine and I retrieved the water bottle from the cab. After he finished, I sat down on the side of the bank and handed him the bottle. He drank deeply then handed it back to me as he lit a cigarette and sat on the bank. He squatted on his haunches, in the only way possible to balance yourself on a steep incline.

As he quietly smoked, I was reminded again of how much he resembled what the world perceived a true Indian to be. His long, black hair, still worn down with the single, telling braid, glistened in the faint sunlight escaping through the leaves. His profile was distinct and his skin color was extremely dark, with a cinnamon tint. His deep, brown eyes, the same as mine, seemed to stare at nothing in the nearby brush. Here, on the mountain of our forefathers, there was something different about him. He was not the same man I had seen just days before, in

Charleston or Florida. In the mountain forest, his "hood", he was in charge, and few would doubt his authority. There was an air of power and confidence about him that was almost tangible. He was a Cherokee warrior in every sense of the word. I was proud to be his kin.

"Tell me something, Steven, how can you possibly want a cigarette now? Those things are going to kill you one day."

"Well, I gotta' go one way or another. I think I'll go doing what I like and minding my own business. How about you?" He punctuated his words in his familiar way, pointing with the lit cigarette like a mountain preacher in a revival meeting.

"Oh, I wasn't giving you hell. I just truly can not understand how you could want a cigarette while you're working."

"Sure, sure. I know it's a bad habit, but it's my bad habit. I just don't want to quit that's all. I like it, so what? I didn't know I had to ask your permission or anything. You turned democrat or something?"

"Yeah, you mean it's a habit you can't quit." I smiled and taunted him, glad his sense of humor had returned; "Just like a few other things I know."

"Yeah, that too." He laughed.

I started the saw and made a forty-five degree wedge cut on the side of the tree in the direction I wanted it to fall. I pulled the saw and began a second cut an inch above the wedge on the opposite side of the tree. The saw buzzed through the tree until I felt it just begin to bind. I removed it, and after checking the path to insure Dog had not come back while I wasn't looking, gave the tree a big push with my hand and shoulder. The tree cracked and popped, loudly breaking it's final bonds with the earth. I moved back towards Steven as the heavy tree began it's decent. It rushed towards the earth with a distinctive sound, breaking limbs off the smaller trees around it as it fell. It hit with a thud I felt beneath my feet.

"Nice job there, cousin. I think you've done this before."

I laughed. "A time or two, yeah." In the households we grew up in, wood was the primary source of heat. In the cold mountain winters of the Appalachians, little things like warmth were taken very seriously. Both of us learned to work trees not long after we began to walk. I straddled the tree and began to "limb" it, cutting each limb carefully away from the trunk and trying not to cut my legs in the process.

After I finished, I cut the trunk into logs of a size Steven and I could manage and we moved the brush back along the bank to fight erosion. Even in death the tree returned something to the earth, not much different from human beings if you thought about it.

I looked at Steven with a bemused grin, "What did you and the Divine Miss M have to talk about, cousin?"

He dropped down on the bank near me; his huge hands intertwined beneath his head. He looked up at the Carolina blue of the sky, and it was a few minutes before he spoke, "I don't know that is any of your business. I don't want to get her fired or anything."

"I make it a habit to refrain from firing anyone I'm afraid of, and Lord knows I'm afraid of that one. Are you?"

He laughed without looking around, "Hell, yeah! She's female ain't she? That makes me afraid of her from the git go. But I sort of like her attitude."

"Well, she definitely has an attitude."

"She told me that I had to look out for you cause for all your uppity-ness, you need all the help you can get."

"Oh really? And what did you tell her?"

"I told her she didn't know the half of it."

"And what did she say?"

"She told me how sorry she was that I was up here with you, and how glad you weren't getting in her hair while she was trying to run your business."

"Ha! Don't quit your day job for comedy big guy."

"She said the next time she saw me; she'll owe me one. I told her that would be just great. That, I'd look forward to collecting. We talked about a few other things, but I ain't telling your nosey ass anything else."

"Thanks for the kind words on my behalf, by the way."

"Don't mention it, Cuz."

After that, we didn't speak for some time. We just listened to the woods. The sounds were again familiar and soothing. I think that is one of the many reasons why man has always searched for the mountaintop as his sanctuary, his place of spiritual enlightenment. On the mountain, there is peace and solitude like no other place on earth. I don't mean the mountains of the tourists, I mean the wilderness of the mountains, where no cars reach and few care to tread.

Dog came back from the woods; sniffed around where we had just cut the tree, searched around the piles of brush, then settled for a nap. She led such a tough life.

When I could think about it no longer, I looked at my cousin carefully and asked in a measured voice, emotionless as I could make it; "Steven, the other night, when we were on Jordan's balcony, were you scared?"

"Hell, yeah. Weren't you?" He looked back at me, puzzled by my question.

"Yeah, yeah...I mean really scared?"

"Were you?"

"Yeah, I was. I mean I have been scared before, I've been in life and death situations before, but this was different somehow, sort of weird."

"Of course it was different! How many times you think people saw what we did? That bitch would have scared the shit out of Rambo for God's sake!"

"I know, but this...I've never been that close to death before I guess. It made me think about dying, really dying. No matter how bad the fight before, I never really thought about it that way. This thing, this serial killer, seemed to breathe evil, to suck fear right out of me like fuel.

It's like it wanted me to be afraid." I spread my hands and looked to him, "Did you feel anything like that?"

He seemed sort of perplexed, began to answer, then just stopped and turned away.

After a minute or two, I continued, "You think about death, Steven?"

"Not much."

"I do."

"So?"

"So nothing. I'm just not ready to die. That's all. Sometimes I question being here in the first place, but I'm not ready to check out anytime soon."

"Who is?" He lit yet another cigarette.

"People do it every day…some by choice."

"Well, who gives a shit? All that matters is you and yours cousin. There's only room for one in that casket, bubba, and by then you won't care about company anyway. Way I look at it is; when my time comes, I'm ready. I ain't afraid of it so much anymore. Things went on just fine without me before I was here and I reckon they gonna' be fine when I'm gone. I plan to enjoy what I got, while I got it, and I'll fight tooth and nail to keep it when the time comes." He took a big draw of his cigarette and boasted, "Screw death! Bring it on. Hell, I'm ready, but I sure as shit ain't going without a fight." He held up a finger, "But I ain't worrying about it between now and then. When we go, we go."

I didn't comment.

He hesitated a moment, and became a little more serious; "I will tell you one thing Rising Wolf told me not long ago." At the mention of Ben's name, his manner became almost reverent." He seemed to think it was real important, so it must be. Rising Wolf said; there can be no courage, without fear."

"Sounds rather Zen like to me."

"Yeah, maybe so, but it makes a bunch more sense than most of that Zen and Taoist crap that I've heard you spout."

I thought about his comments but didn't say anything. I had spent a good portion of my life reading and studying everything I could get my hands on regarding philosophy and religion. Like so many, I was still looking for answers I had yet to find.

Finally Steven added; "There is one thing that bothers me though." He looked at me with a strange, half smirk on his face.

"And that is?"

"Who will take care of your skinny little ass when I ain't here?" He laughed and easily dodged the punch I half directed at his head. He got up and danced around a bit, using his arms to make the motion of a fisherman hauling in his catch. "Hook, line and sinker Morgan…hook, line and sinker!"

Dog woke, looked over at him like he was crazy, got up and moved a few feet further away, and went back to sleep.

It was late afternoon by the time we finished the upper half of the road. We decided to call it quits and finish the remainder later. The idea of a rest before we faced the long night ahead held some merit.

After a hot shower the front porch rocker felt soft as a recliner as I settled in, weapons within easy reach. Just because someone usually attacked in the night didn't mean they couldn't have a strategic change of heart. It had happened before, and I didn't intend to let history repeat itself at my expense.

Steven spoke, reminding me of plans we had agreed upon earlier, "Well, if I'm going to get back before dark, I better be leaving." Steven was going down to make our "check-in" calls at my suggestion. I think he wanted to go so he would have an excuse to talk to Marilyn again and I thought that might be the best thing for him under the circumstances.

"Alright, just don't wreck my truck if you know what's good for you, Stevey. Remember the gas is the long pedal on the right and the brake is the small pedal on the left."

"Morgan, one of these days I'm not going to say a word. You're gonna' call me that one time too many and I'm going to knock that smartass grin right off your face. You ain't even gonna' know what hit you until you wake up." He snatched the keys from my outstretched hand and Dog growled at him as he shuffled towards the truck with his shotgun in one hand and the automatic rifle in the other. He put the rifle behind the seat and the shotgun in the rack on the rear window, an item standard on all pick-ups in our part of the country.

"Watch your head Cuz, while I'm gone."

"You just watch my truck and let me worry about my own head, you redneck. And be sure and tell Kathy I said everything is fine and not to worry." I didn't get up from my chair.

He shot me the bird as he backed out of the drive and turned around to head down the mountain. I saw him wave from the drivers window, just before he disappeared around the turn. I waved back but I don't know if he saw it or not.

I tilted the rocker back and propped my feet on the rail, just as I did in my mother's kitchen chair when I was young. I remember my father severely beating my ass for it one night at our dinner table. He hadn't worked in weeks but had somehow managed to find the necessary funds to stay intoxicated every day. That afternoon, he was definitely feeling no pain. Without warning, he kicked the chair from under me and I ended up being tossed through the front storm door of the rental house before it was all said and done. The glass door was closed and locked at the time.

My drunken father made me clean up the glass before he allowed my mother to take me to the hospital to be stitched. I remembered the shards of glass at my feet as I moved to pick them up, turning them crimson red with my touch. The harsh kitchen light highlighted the splats of bright red blood as they dripped from the deep cuts on my arms onto the white linoleum of the floor. I could vividly recall his boots as he towered over me in his drunken rage. He forbid me to look up while I worked, but I will always remember the way those boots looked inches from my downcast eyes. Both toes were badly scuffed and in need of polish, with red mud caked on the heels.

My mother cried and pleaded at his side and I can still hear the first open-handed slap as he turned on her. When I finally got to the hospital, I passed out from loss of blood. I told them I had fallen through the door by accident. My mother cried while struggling her best to hide the half of her face blackened and swollen from the beating that she had taken to get me there.

I absently rubbed one of the scars on my left arm as I rose from the rocker and went inside the cabin to find something to do. Anything, to change the tracks of my thoughts. Dog followed behind. My eyes kept moving to the box that my grandfather's manuscript had been in, and something compelled me to place it on the table.

I went to fix myself a cup of coffee. As I prepared the pot by the sink, I looked out at the fading afternoon sun already darkening the fringes of the forest. There was still enough light struggling through the trees to shine brightly through the window. Small dust particles danced in front of me as I filled the pot from the cold water flowing out of the high, curved spigot. I turned the cool ceramic knob marked "cold" in fading black letters. The fixtures were at least thirty years older than me, and still functioning perfectly except for a small little drip every now and then, only noticeable when the cabin was at its most quiet.

I realized it was the first time I had been alone in the cabin in a long time. The first time I had any kind of chance to notice the quiet. In the past years, I had spent almost all my time at the mountain retreat alone, with only an occasional guest. I was glad for the brief time to myself. If nothing else, to help myself calm down and to get back as much "control" as I could before things got worse.

When the coffee was done, I poured myself a cup, added cream and sugar, and returned to the couch. I sat on the patchwork quilt which hid the deteriorating upholstery beneath, and propped my feet on the table.

I looked at the box beside my right shoe as I sipped. Finally, surrendering to curiosity, I pulled the box in front of me, opened it and peered inside.

The box held a number of items from my grandfather's past; things that were important to him, for his own reasons. It felt sort of strange to sort through someone else's memories. There were the normal things; birth certificates, death certificates, army discharge papers dated 1946, a Purple Heart and a Bronze Star from World War Two. There were two broken pocket watches; one with a fast moving train etched on the cover; the other with a faded worn inscription, no longer readable.

Two scratched, brass frames held small, wallet-sized photographs. The first was a dim picture of a beautiful young Indian girl, smiling brightly for the camera. Her dress was clearly of buckskin, hand-sewn with lots of beadwork, clean and neat. I removed it from the frame and didn't need to look at the writing on the back to know who it was. I had seen that picture on my grandfather's dresser many times when I was young. On the back, in faint black ink, were the words "Maggie Sylvia Roberts, 1924". My grandmother passed away after giving birth to my father. The other frame held a picture I had never seen before. It was of my grandfather, my father, and me. The date on the back was 1965. I was six years old at the time. For some reason I didn't understand I put both pictures into my wallet and returned the empty frames to the box. I removed an ancient medicine rattle like the one I had seen Ben carry. The red paint was so faded it was impossible for me to read anything etched upon it, even if I could have understood the language. I put it gently beside the box so, as not to damage it any further. I was careful that it didn't roll off the table.

I found a bone sided pocketknife with a worn blade so sharp I could have shaved with it. I placed the knife in my pants pocket. In a canvas drawstring pouch I found fifteen silver dollars, dates from the late 1800's up to 1902. There was a smooth twenty dollar gold piece, the date impossible to read. The coins went back in the pouch and into the cardboard container.

In the bottom of the box, wrapped in a tattered red bandanna, I found a leather-covered Bible. The pages were soft to the touch and smelling as only an old book could. The dim inscription on the inside cover read, "To my darling daughter on her birthday, Maggie Sylvia Powell, February 25, 1900, from your mother, Mamie Powell." There was a family tree filled out on one of the first pages. All the names of my ancestors were recorded in my grandmother's handwriting up until her death. The birth of my father had been recorded on the same date as my grandmother's death in the familiar handwriting of my grandfather. I imagined the great hurt those few words must have caused him. Later entries showed the names of my mother, myself, then Jordan. There was nothing after that. With Jordan's death, I became the only living person on that list. The last of my line.

It was strange reading those names. I carefully wrapped the worn volume, and placed it reverently back inside the box. I returned the papers and my grandfather's military decorations. I picked up the medicine rattle and hesitated with the smooth wooden handle in my hand. I leaned back and closed my eyes, trying to picture my grandfather; trying to remember him as I had seen him last. I could recall his worn face, his soft yet authoritative voice, rarely raised above a whisper, yet always heard. His contagious laughter and the stories he told me during long hours by a campfire, under the moonlight or the dense canopy of the mountain forest, would remain with me always. Such hours passed like minutes in the magic of his company.

Maybe Steven was right; maybe I didn't understand how truly great the man was I called Papaw. Maybe I took both him and all he believed for granted, but I loved him and I would never forget. Still, something had stirred inside me the last few days. The words of Rising Wolf, Steven, even Kathy, suggested to me that I only knew a fraction of what my grandfather was really about. I had forsaken the beliefs and the knowledge he held so dear, that he had devoted his whole life to preserving. I knew next to nothing about those things, yet I had whole-heartedly condemned them without proper consideration. Pushing them aside, always looking for something better. I chose to believe the things I had been taught by society over everything Screaming Eagle had believed and worked to preserve. I felt like I had dishonored my grandfather's memory. I placed the rattle that symbolized everything he stood for back in the box; I didn't deserve to hold it in my hand any longer, felt somehow foolish and more than a little disgusted with myself. I felt unworthy.

CHAPTER THIRTY-TWO

My coffee had gotten cold and darkness had crept up the mountain while I was lost to thoughts of my family's past. I warmed my coffee and walked to the porch wondering what was keeping Steven. The first stars of the night were beginning to sparkle in the evening sky. The sun had long since finalized its descent. I cut my eyes to the assault rifle leaning on the porch and whistled for Dog. After a moment or two, when she didn't come right away, I stepped off into the front yard, away from the cabin and called for her again. There was no answer. I thought she was probably chasing after some poor rabbit and decided to give her a break. She loved running through the woods around the mountain and she couldn't really get into any trouble she didn't start in the first place. There were no cars around to end her life, so again, I just let her run.

"Morgan." Steven's voice startled me from the darkness. I hated the way he could sneak up on me and he knew it. I think that's the main reason he found such delight in doing so. One second he wasn't there and the next second he was. It was sort of scary sometimes. He walked over to the porch and sat in one of the chairs. He didn't say anything, just propped his boots on the rail and sat quietly staring into the darkening forest.

"What's up Steven? Everything okay?" I already knew everything wasn't. Steven was working real hard at not telling me something. When he didn't answer, I asked him jokingly, "Where's the truck? I didn't hear it. You didn't run it into a tree did you?"

"No, it's broken." His voice was strangely monotone and subdued.

"Broken? What the hell do you mean it's broken?"

"It's at the bottom of the mountain road." His features were hidden in shadow and I couldn't see the expression on his face, but I knew there was something he wasn't telling me.

"And?"

"It just stopped running, that's all. I came up on foot as fast as I could. We can't fix it now. We'll have to wait until morning." His voice was angry; his responses clipped and short.

"Guess so." I said, becoming really confused by his attitude. I decided to do what normally worked best for Steven when he acted strange— stranger than normal; I kept my mouth shut and listened. If it was important he would get to it soon enough, but only when he felt like it. I thought I recognized the mood and just waited for him to tell me the rest. I moved into the chair beside him, retrieving my rifle and placing it closer to me. It was then I noticed Steven was unarmed. He didn't even have his pistol that I could see.

"Where's your guns Stevey?" I used my nickname for him, the one he hated, and waited for his normal retort.

"I left them in the truck." He made no mention of my name-calling.

The faint light of the forest filtered through the canopy of leaves and cast open shadows across his face. I still couldn't make out his expression. I propped my feet on the porch rail and decided to wait him out. If he wanted to drag things out, fine. I could wait. I had more time than money, or so I hoped anyway.

"Sorry about the truck." He finally mumbled several minutes later, his voice empty and emotionless, as if he didn't mean it. The tone of his voice worried me. I had never heard it before, not even when his parents were killed. Something was bad wrong and he was pissing me off by not telling me.

"Can we fix it? I mean, come on Stevey! What's going on here?" I asked impatiently, using the name again, purposely trying to provoke some kind of emotion on his part. "Give me some idea of what's happened! I mean, you walk in here from nowhere, no truck, no guns, no discussion, and you expect me to wait until you get around to telling me what happened. Just tell me what the hell is going on, Stevey." I used the nickname again and he let it pass again—for the third time.

"We can fix it, just not tonight. It's dark now. We need to wait until morning." He leaned his chair further into shadow and asked, "Morgan, were you afraid the other night at your brother's house?"

"You know I was. We talked about that earlier today. Where in the hell is your mind, Steven? Are you going to tell me what's wrong or do I have to wait for my credit cards to expire first?"

"Yeah, I'll tell you." He rose abruptly from his reclined position and was off the porch before I could react, walking quickly towards the rear of the cabin. "Come with me, Morgan."

"Okay, okay, just slow down a little," I called after his retreating figure. He was acting strange even for Steven, and was already around the corner of the cabin before I could get off the porch and retrieve the assault rifle from the rail. I hurried to catch up with him.

As I rounded the corner, I called, "Hey wait up…" That's when he appeared from hiding and knocked the gun from my hand, then grabbed me roughly by the throat. I struggled to escape, wondering what his game was. He wasn't playing or joking around, that was obvious. The pressure on my throat increased and I stopped moving and managed to croak, "What the hell are you doing?"

Steven's face, inches from my own, slowly took on a sadistic, unfamiliar grin. His breath was fetid and hot. "Are you afraid now, Morgan?" His hands were no longer pressing hard enough to hurt me, but escape was impossible without one of us getting hurt in the process.

I ceased my struggle and looked closer at him, concerned and frustrated. "I don't...I don't understand Steven. What the hell's the matter with you?"

He laughed. Turned his head upward and literally laughed at the night sky. The sound was strange in a way I couldn't put my finger on. I felt a chill run up my spine. "What's the matter? Why, nothing is the matter. Can't you see? Everything is just as it should be."

"Let me go, Steven. This isn't funny anymore." My tone became angry.

"Let you go?" The big Cherokee laughed again, this time his eyes never left mine. There was something different about his eyes, something I couldn't recognize. They glinted like glass in the faint moonlight, with no life in them. "I can't let you go Morgan." His voice became somehow different.

"And why not Steven?"

"Because you have to die, Morgan." He said it simply, as if he were commenting on the weather. He pulled me closer, our faces almost touching. "Can't you see that?" The foul smell of his breath was like rotting meat. Steven smiled that sinister smile again and began to tighten his hold on my throat.

I gave up conversation and began to struggle again. I was able to kick him pretty hard on his upper thigh. It didn't seem to faze him at all; he just smiled that much wider. I noticed then, it wasn't just his breath that smelled it was he. His whole body reeked and the smell was growing stronger. It was an odor I had smelled before. It was becoming more intense by the second. His eyes took on a wild appearance, seeming to change color as I watched, taking on a feverish red glow.

"Don't you see, Morgan? I killed all those people." He laughed again, but it was really more a strange giggle than a laugh, "I am your worst nightmare come to life, Morgan, and now it is your turn to die."

"What?" I managed to croak, totally and completely confused.

"I killed them for they had to be punished." His teeth clenched, his face filled with such abnormal anger I could barely recognize him. "Now it's time for you to be punished. Your worst fears are about to come true for you little cousin. Your world has reached its end."

"I..." The hand tightened around my throat, stopping my words before they could reach my lips.

I knew then what was happening. I didn't want to believe it, but it was becoming painfully obvious.

The face in front of mine startled me by abruptly changing. One moment I was looking into the face of my cousin as he effortlessly choked me and held me at arm's length, the next, the wrinkled face of my Aunt Mary appeared and I heard her voice. "Don't worry, Morgan, you will like it here with us, that is, after you pay the price." The face that had cooked me dinners and washed my hands since before I could walk broke into the same demented laugh that I heard from Steven...or what had pretended to be Steven.

I shut my eyes to the horror of what was happening; hoping against hope it was a sick dream that I would awaken from at any moment. I didn't wake up. The vise-like fingers at my throat increased their pressure even more and I felt my head begin to swim. When I managed to open my eyes, Uncle Frank was crushing my windpipe.

"You better listen now, boy. You know they ain't any use in fightin' it son. You gonna' give in just like the rest of us, it's just a matter of time I'm a tellin' you." As he smiled at me, I felt myself slipping away. The lack of blood and oxygen flow to my brain was causing me to move quickly towards unconsciousness. I gave one last ditch effort to get away from the killer as I was held, helpless, inches above the ground. I briefly pictured what it must look like, as a tiny, withered old man held a man twice his size overhead with no effort. I remember thinking it was a strange thing to be thinking at the time.

As I began to lose my last hold on consciousness, it was somehow fitting that I heard my brother's voice and felt his hands on me, "Why did you leave mom, Morgan? It's your entire fault she's dead. We all know it. Why don't you admit it?" His smirking grin was familiar, but his eyes, they were glazed with hatred and anger, beyond recognition. They appeared fire red, smoldering with evil, so intense I could feel the heat of them seeming to sear into my head.

As blackness overtook me, I heard yet another voice. It was harsh and brutal, an unknown, deadly voice, and it asked, "Are you afraid, Morgan?"

Then the voice added coldly, "You should be."

That was the last I remember before I passed out.

CHAPTER THIRTY-THREE

My first thought was how bad my head hurt. It pounded like it did when I forgot I couldn't drink champagne and tried anyway, only much, much worse. I struggled to open my eyes and when I finally managed, I could see hazy pinpoints that turned out to be stars. The amount of light suggested the moon had risen full, though not yet within my line of sight. For some reason, I couldn't move my head to look. I tried, but just couldn't seem to make my body respond. All I could see was the dark silhouette of the tree line against the night sky. My chest hurt like hell. There was an unusual, sharp, burning pain, just over my heart, like acid eating at my skin.

I started to rise from my prone position. Nothing happened. My limbs didn't respond. Despite my best efforts, I couldn't move a finger. A fleeting moment of panic seized me as I tried again to move and failed. I could sense every part of my body and knew nothing held me, yet I couldn't budge, couldn't even twitch. It was as if my limbs were made of stone. I seemed to be able to move my eyes but that was all. A sensation of fear crept over me and I quickly pushed it aside as best I could. I was helpless, totally vulnerable, and evidently there wasn't a damn thing I could do about it. Then I understood just how much trouble I was really in as I recalled what happened just before I blacked out.

I looked frantically side to side, but could detect nothing out of the ordinary from my position. Then, something else dimly registered through the haze I seemed to be viewing everything through. The terrible smell was still in the air, still intense and overpowering, and close. Once again, I felt the faint stirrings of fear in my gut, and couldn't keep myself from searching the darkness in a futile attempt to find the source. It seemed I was about forty or fifty feet from the cabin, on the back side nearest the woods. I recognized the corner of the generator shed just barely in view.

It was a weird feeling to be so exposed with no means of defending myself. I tried to calm myself, to find some way out of my dilemma. I needed something to occupy my mind, some thread of hope that I might cling to, something to ward off the steady approach of panic which threatened to overcome me as I lay there on the cold ground. I couldn't seem to think of anything. I tried to yell for help, hoping against hope someone might hear, even though I knew it was useless. I tried to scream, but no sound reached my lips. I lay helpless and afraid, unable even to speak.

Some time later, twenty feet or more away, near the shed; I heard a low, menacing snarl. The sound came from below me, and I struggled to see over my boots into the shadows. At first I could make out nothing, as the deep animal growl rose in intensity. Out of the darkness, Dog materialized, teeth barred, fur standing up on her back, bunched on her hind legs ready to attack at any second. I knew the look. She was no more than ten feet from me, as I lay helpless in her path.

My mind struggled to understand, but I could not accept what I was seeing. I knew Dog better than I knew myself, and knew she could never, ever attack me. Yet, there she was, so close to me I could see her sharp, exposed teeth, her ears folded back in anger. She had never appeared more ferocious. Something was wrong, and my mind couldn't quite latch on to what it was. My head was still fuzzy, or perhaps it was near panic, which kept my mind clouded. Still, a little bell was going off in my head, way in the back where I couldn't hear it too well. Why was she doing such a crazy thing?

Dog continued to growl, moving anxiously side to side then bunching her weight on her rear legs. The rancid smell of death hung in the air, heavy and vile. Suddenly, she bolted towards me and I shut my eyes for an instant against the imagined onslaught of her attack, but her attack never came.

I opened my eyes just as she jumped over my body. She leaped high into the darkness over my head and I heard the sound of another growl, and it wasn't Dog. Her attack came abruptly to an end. There was a brief yelp of pain, a heavy thud, then an empty, nauseating silence. The nocturnal sounds of the forest ceased in the wake of the brief encounter. Something had scared even the creatures of the night, something that was out of place and shouldn't have been there.

The killer had been with me all along. She must have waited quietly in the darkness, watching silently until I came fully awake, waiting until I became afraid and fully understood my predicament. The beast had to be just feet from me in the darkness. I was hesitant to raise my eyes. When I finally managed, I still could see nothing, only blackness. I waited, but heard nothing more of Dog. Her heroic attack had surely cost her life, and in a fraction of a second her time on earth was over, just like so many others who were closest to me. There was a hollow, emptiness in my chest, a brief touch of grief, which quickly gave way to an almost welcome anger. Rage, my great enemy for so long, was becoming my only ally against the fear.

"Are you afraid?"

The words came from the night, seemingly from all around me. It was as if they sucked all emotion from me like a vacuum. It was a harsh voice, vaguely human, like something from a bad horror picture. It was no longer a voice I recognized. The words were unhurried, simple, and almost childish. I could not sense anyone close to me, but obviously someone was. For long minutes I heard nothing else, only quiet. I lay there, straining to see into the forest, trying my best to hear even the breathing of my tormentor. I tried again to free myself from the invisible bonds, which held me rooted to the cold earth, to no avail. I could swallow, blink and move my eyes, but that was all. That was torture in itself.

"Come Morgan, you can tell me. Are you afraid?" A pause, then, "You should be. You will be. That is a promise."

My name! The unearthly voice knew my name and used it freely, and that familiarity really hit me deep. For some reason it bothered me more than anything else did up to that point did.

"What, you can't answer? Cat got your tongue?"

The voice was raspy yet possessed a faintly feminine quality. Evil seemed to ride along with each word. It reminded me of the voice of the girl from The Exorcist. Though calm and quiet, the voice was touched with a sinister quality, perhaps even insanity. I could do nothing to protect myself. I just lay and stared at the sky, awaiting the next move in the sick game, struggling to calm myself, to regain control of my racing emotions. There was little else I could do, and I think that was what scared me the most. I tried to find some thought to help me and could only remember what Steven had told me—what Ben had said, "There can be no courage without fear." I needed courage to survive, but the last thing I was feeling was courageous.

"Oh yes, I forgot. My little love bite keeps you from moving doesn't it? Can you move Morgan?" The words were even and calmer then, almost rational.

"You know damned well I can't!" I wanted to scream, but couldn't. "No courage without fear." I repeated it to myself in my head like a mantra.

"That is good, very good. I will talk, and you will listen, because I want you to fully understand what is going to happen to you. You will listen and soon you will come to know what pain waits. Your punishment will be harsh and vile." The disembodied voice grew louder—raspier, "After I tire of you, I will rip your beating heart from your body and eat it in front of you before you die. But before that, long before that, you will beg me for your worthless life. Beg me to take it, not to give it. When I am finished with you, you will thank me for the gift of your death. You will plead for the peace it should bring. But you will never find peace Morgan, for you will always be mine. Always. Even in death."

Ragged laughter spilled into the night and seemed to go on forever. I repeated Ben's words in my head, trying to focus on only them. "No courage without fear, no courage without fear..."

"You will suffer for an eternity here with me, just like all the others. Just like the rest of your kind." The voice rose violently, with no warning, "You will want to die as much as I want you to! You will beg me!"

The maniacal brain behind the words reached out, grabbing me, clutching at me like a live thing, pushing me closer to the boundaries of reason. I wondered if Steven was already dead, if she killed him like the others. I found myself hoping she hadn't with all my heart, all my hope. At that moment, I needed an emotional lifeline no matter how slim the chance of salvation.

"But before even that..." The words again became soft and smooth. "...long before the moment when I rip your life from you...I will make you pay for the sins of your fathers! Just like the others before you and the others yet to come!" The sound of my captor's words rose and fell like a devilish fire and brimstone sermon. The fetid odor covered me like an oily blanket and I fought for control as my pulse raced far ahead of my mind.

"You haven't told me about your fear, Morgan, but then you don't need to tell me. I know it's there. I can feel it. I can taste it on you like salt on the skin. You are afraid, very afraid and you should be. I can smell it on you just as you smell the stench of old death on me."

The voice was correct. The rotten foulness was almost unbearable; sickly sweet and suffocating. I was overpowered by the words, afraid in ways no sane person could imagine. My death would be slow and filled with torment, worse than the most terrible nightmare, but I sensed even that would not be enough. The demon wanted something more from me. It wanted my sanity. It wanted to rape my mind with my own intense fear.

"Oh, I know you very well. I know all about you Morgan and I will prove it to you. I know your thoughts, your past and I know your future." There was a giggle like a crazed little schoolgirl. The familiar use of my name taunted me and the killer seemed to understand that as well and repeated it on purpose.

"You see, when I punish one of you puny animals, I liberate more than your soul, I take your mind and make it part of me. Just after I eat your beating heart, I will eat your brain, Morgan." Again, the sadistic laughter echoed loudly, echoing from the trees around me. "Doesn't that scare you, Morgan? You will feel everything, my pet, every precious flick of agony, and each perfect taste of pain. You will be spared nothing. I will take it all from you and then make you mine forever. You will plead for an end to the fear and the pain."

The voice softened, taking on an almost sensuous, dark quality, "Give up Morgan; give yourself to me now. It is useless to fight me, as you will see. Even now, your great fear threatens your sanity, does it not? I can feel it as it seeps from your soul. It is fear like you have never known. Isn't it Morgan?" The words stopped as if waiting for an answer. I heard only heavy breathing, and then, "I know you are afraid because my little kiss upon your chest contained things to help free your weak human mind, a great magic that is far stronger than you Morgan. It will make you let go of your resolve and give yourself up to me. It will be as it should be my sweet."

That helped explain, or at least excuse, the flood of emotion that threatened me as I never felt before. My blood had been polluted with toxins to freeze my body and accelerate my fear. I had been afraid before, but this was different. My heart raced as fast as my mind, fighting the enticing, hypnotic effect of the voice. I struggled to breathe and, for a brief moment, thought I had lost control of that ability as well, but it was just the panic pushing me along its pathway, closer to the edge. An edge I didn't want to see over.

"Do you know I have killed so many of your people that I have lost count? Your kind have fed me for century upon century and I can recall each and every morsel of flesh and each sweet swallow of hot blood. I relished the painful cries and the taste of each beating heart, and I have kept all those pitiful souls inside me. When I sleep, I can still hear their screams and their senseless pleading for mercy. Just like the ones I shall soon hear from you. I have all their memories. I know everything they ever knew. I even learned your language from those I killed since my release." There was a pause, and then, "I even know all about you, Morgan."

For a time, there was quiet. Long minutes passed like hours before the sinister voice spoke again.

"I know about your pitiful drunkard of a father and your whore of a mother who would marry one such as he. They deserved to die just as they did. I am only sorry that I was not the one to suck their meaning- less lives from their worthless bodies." The voice dripped hostility like venom.

My heart felt as if it might erupt, the sound of its pulsation pounding loudly against my temples like ancient drums. The toxins were much too strong for me to fight, but I kept trying. The idea of giving up to the monster made me angry and I tried to use that emotion to fuel my resistance, to give me courage. For there to be courage, there must be fear. Hadn't Ben said so?

"And do you know how I know? Because as I sucked the life from the pitiful one you called an uncle, I took his knowledge of you. I devoured it along with his rotting flesh. What your aunt knew of you, I took that too. I know you. Do you understand me? I know how you abandoned your family, your tribe, and I know about your pitifully weak mind that has already deserted you once and will yet again." The words became as soft as a caress. "I know what makes you afraid and soon, very soon, you will know the true meaning of torment. You will beg and plead and it will not matter, for you are mine now Morgan Roberts."

It seemed as if I felt something lightly trail across my cheek.

"We will share such sweet pleasure you and I, such sweet pain."

The words were uttered in a faint hiss that carried the promise of something unpleasant and deadly. The killer seemed closer to me, just above me, somewhere in the dark and out of my line of sight. The tone changed so fast it was hard for me to follow. It was at one moment sedate, then frantic and angry, like a wild roller coaster ride through the demented emotions of a lunatic.

"Would you like to know about me Morgan? How I came to be here and why you are about to die?" There was a pause then, "As you wish. I will tell you all you need to know."

I tried not to listen to the jumble of words and curses, the stories of torture and rape, and death. I vaguely heard as she confirmed the story of the little village by the Hiawassee River and the forced imprisonment as well as her eventual escape after her tomb was inadvertently opened.

"Do you see what your people did?" The demon yelled at me, "Do you see? You see why you must be punished?"

She related detailed descriptions of my aunt and uncle's death and many others, too many others to count. I heard of the hideous tortures that she inflicted, the senseless killings, the long years of nightmares and death in the night. She told me of her pursuit of the tribal members and their deaths. She spoke of how she relished tormenting my aunt and uncle before she ended their lives.

Time stood still as the bloody narrative unfolded with maniacal clarity. The voice told of the atrocities with an obscene pride and pleasure that was sickening. The deranged mind raved on and on, slipping again into a soft feminine purr, as I struggled not to listen; tried not to hear of the mutilations inflicted upon others, and those soon to be my own.

It was not really the words that touched me so deeply, but the deadly sound of the voice. It held no trace of sanity or reason. It reached for me like a familiar lover in the afterglow of passion. I felt the touch of the words on my skin as real as any caress, invading me, violating me in an eerie fashion, which defied sane description. It made me feel dirty and soiled. The words burned into my soul, eating at me like a hungry rat at garbage. I hated the voice then, wanted to fight back with all my soul, but could do nothing. I was helpless and alone, and was about to die.

Delirious laughter came from the darkness. "Do you know the best part Morgan? Do you? I took each one of your family members and used them as I wished. I took them all inside me and forced them to please me."

I felt renewed revulsion at the thoughts of such an act. For an instant, I imagined the same happening to me. "No courage without fear, no courage without fear…"

"When I took them, they sparked a new life within me and that life will be born into your world very soon Morgan. That life will live on into the future, feeding off the helpless and the old, as we have done for centuries. Even my kind, do not live forever. We must reproduce and be reborn, and it is fitting your people will help give birth to one who will torture your children. That is the best punishment of all!"

A welcome silence returned for what seemed an impossibly long time. I knew that the killer was a master at the twisted game of fear and that periods of silence were added in measured doses, like spices to a stew pot. Still, knowing it didn't help much. The moon had risen almost to within eyesight, and yet, even in the growing light, I still couldn't separate shadows from darkness.

"Now, do you know what I think?" After the long period of quiet, the sound startled me. "I think it is time for you to see my face. My real face, one which will haunt you to the edge of your sanity and beyond. Would you like that Morgan? Would you like to see the face of your lover?" The question was as quiet as a church whisper.

No, I did not want to see, but I wanted to know. I wanted to know what kind of creature could speak so easily the horrible words. I wanted to know if it was human. If it was all real or just a nightmare of the worst kind. I worried for a moment that it might not be real, that I might have already crossed the invisible line to the dark side of insanity, finally losing the fight I had fought so valiantly for so long. No! I knew it was real! It had to be! I knew it was! But then again, maybe everything was all in my head. Maybe it was all a wicked dream and I was dreaming my way towards death. Either way, I was afraid of what waited there in the darkness.

"I could appear in many ways, as anything I wish, but I think now is the time for you to see your lover."

I felt the light touch of what I thought was a gentle breeze upon my cheek.

"I want to feel you inside me when I rip the flesh from your body. I want to suck the lifeblood from you and I want you to see my true face as I do. Then, only then, will you understand." The voice abruptly filled again with hostility; "You will understand why you must pay!"

I opened my eyes to look into the dark sky, refusing to face death with my eyes closed. I glimpsed a few weak stars and the edge of the upcoming moon. Then, without warning, everything changed; even the pale light was blocked. I felt a heavy weight settle upon my chest and a face appeared in front of mine, inches away. It was a reflection of the most horrible nightmare imaginable. There was no way I could adequately describe the ugliness.

It may have once been sickly white, but that whiteness was almost completely obscured by dirt, caked with gore and dried blood. Open, festering sores covered the face, neck and torso. Once white hair, matted with who knew what from year upon year of neglect, fell about the grotesque parody of a face. The hideous mouth opened to speak, revealing sharp, yellow-brown teeth. The acid breath reeked of something from the very depths of hell. Seeing the cracked parched lips form words called to mind some faint discord from my childhood but I couldn't quite remember what it was.

"Well, am I everything you thought I would be?"

Demented laughter returned and I felt the wetness of her vile spittle across my face. The figure rose slightly and I was startled to see huge, thick, rubbery wings unfold from the immense back. Flabby, sagging breasts drooped towards an obviously pregnant stomach and more of the large, open sores covered almost every inch of her exposed body. The killer of my people and family was indeed female. The laughter ceased.

"You see? You see what you have done? Years of rotting like a corpse in a grave brought this on, years without proper feeding! During those long decades in the cave, I was forced to feed upon my babies of the night. They came to me and offered their little, winged bodies to me when I awakened, needing to feed, to live. They gave themselves willingly so I could survive. As I devoured their loyal souls, I took on more and more of their traits; grew and changed to become more like them. Now, this is the form I am stuck with thanks to your fathers. I can shift, for a time, to another's body as my kind have always done, but this is what I must return to." She hissed between clenched, discolored teeth as the sickly sweet stench of her breath assaulted me in a great wave. "All because of you!"

I could not believe what I was seeing. It dispelled everything I had ever believed could be real. Everything about the legend had been true, for the monster in front of me was the farthest thing from human. The insane creature was something from a devil's dream and it was very much alive. The worst part was, I could do nothing. I couldn't run, nor fight, nor hide. All I could do was lay there and wait for the torture the unworldly monstrosity was about to inflict upon me. The Night Goer had come after all.

She raised her massive hands towards me. Her fingers were long, tapering into pointed nails several inches in length. The razor sharpness

of her touch trailed lightly down my left cheek and instantly, I could feel
blood pool, seeping from the shallow incisions.

"Do you not want me, Morgan?" Her voice was a soft parody of sen-
suality. Her deathly perfume gushed to overpower me. She lightly
touched her bloated stomach, ghastly white like the underbelly of a fish.

Bile rose in my throat and I struggled to stop it, knowing that it
would strangle me if it came, then briefly thought that might be best.
Death would be a welcome choice over what lay in store for me.

"Morgan, when next I bite, you will want me like you have never
wanted a human woman before. Your body will betray your mind
completely; it will rise to give me the pleasure I need before I take your
cowardly life."

My insides crawled as she described the humiliation. Her deformed
hands trailed down the sides of my chest, slicing the remains of my shirt
into bloody rags.

She whispered, "When you give yourself fully to me, I will feed upon
your body even as your lifeblood leaves it!" Her nails brushed my chest
with a faint caress, her grotesque face forming an inhuman parody of a
smile.

"What kind of man would do the things you have done, Morgan?
You are not like the others. You willingly abandoned all they fought and
died for, all your grandfather ever believed in."

She laughed, "What? Are you surprised I know of your grandfather?
The one you betrayed with your arrogance? Your grandfather may have
stood against one such as me, but in the end it would make no difference. None of your kind can stop me. They have tried before and they
have always failed. Just as you have failed. You are just fodder for me.
You will never be anything more." The Night Goer leaned closer, "I
think the time has come for you to feel pain Morgan, don't you? No?"

Her nailed hand once again raked the side of my face, moving so fast
I couldn't see it, but I felt the explosion of searing agony easily enough.
Her clawed hand dug deeply across the right side of my face but not

shallow like before. She slashed my face deep, from eye socket to chin. Her sharp nails scraped against the bone of my jaw before she drew her hand away. I could feel each cut as my face was laid open and my blood flowed freely to the cold earth beneath me. All I could do was lie there as liquid fire washed over my face like acid. Before my mind registered it completely, she struck me hard against the opposite side of my head, driving my bloody face into the dirt. I saw stars and fought for consciousness, for control. She struck me again, flinging my head upright so I was once more looking into her wicked face as she laughed maniacally.

My vision blurred and I struggled to hold on, fighting with all I had left, every ounce of hope, every scrap of determination I could muster. I focused on the four words; "no courage without fear."

Her laughter stopped and she shouted at me, her face inches above mine, "You see! You see what it is going to be like?" I could see her rotting teeth in the faint light of the moon. "It will be much, much worse before I am done!"

It was then that I finally realized what it was about her words that scared me so. When I was young, I remembered being terrified by movies of ventriloquist dummies or possessed dolls that somehow came to life. Their ability to speak was an obscenely evil parody of human speech—seeing the words coming from their wooden lips caused my skin to crawl. It was somehow, well, unholy. Seeing her speak brought back those same feelings. That monstrous mouth forming human words was disconcerting..

I closed my eyes so I would not see her face. My breathing was fast, my heart racing. The ache in my head caused by the powerful blows briefly masked the burning agony of my facial wounds. Try as I might to hold on, hope left me then. It abandoned me for what I knew was the last time. I had struggled as long as I could. At that moment, I just wanted it all to end. I didn't care how or why any longer. I wanted it to be over. She was right—had I been able, I would have begged for her to take my life then, pleaded for my own death.

I just gave up.
That's when the first bullets struck her.

CHAPTER THIRTY-FOUR

The first shot hit her high up on the shoulder and drove her forward across my body. Her great shape covered mine for a brief instant, and I felt the heavy weight of her before she pulled herself upright, just as the second magnum slug tore into her upper chest.

Steven's voice, the real Steven's voice, reached from the front of the cabin. "What do you think of that bitch? Why don't you come and pick on someone your own size, or are you a coward too? Either way, I'm going to blow your ass all over this mountain." I will remember the reassuring sound of his voice the rest of my life. I wanted to yell for him to shoot her again, to hurry before she hurt me more.

Incredibly, she laughed. She laughed loudly at the disappearing moon and then spoke to me so only I could hear, "You see Morgan, your kind can never hurt me." There was very little evidence of any damage to her body and there seemed no blood whatsoever. Where the exit wounds were, there was some damage but, incredibly, they seemed to be healing themselves as she spoke.

One moment she was sitting astride me, the next she seemed to shoot up into the darkness like a kite in a March wind. She just disappeared into the sky, only to come back down again almost immediately. There was a surprised cry just as she plummeted back to the ground. I heard what sounded like a twig snap followed by a grunt of pain and a sharp intake of air, then she was in the air again, vanishing quickly from sight.

Seconds later, I heard Steven's voice and loud gunfire, this time from the heavy assault rifle. A long burst from the automatic weapon erupted only to be abruptly cut short. Her laughter rang through the woods, and even though she was far from me, I heard every word as if she were still astride me.

"Are you afraid Steven?" It seemed her maniacal laugh echoed from everywhere; from the trees, from the leaves, from the very darkness, "You should be." She snarled and spat the words and I heard her every word as if she were inside my head. "You will be."

I heard Steven yell something from inside the cabin. A couple of seconds later, it blew. Fire mushroomed up in a brilliant flash of light as the C-4 exploded. The trees above me suddenly erupted into blinding whiteness. The intensity of the light burned my eyes as fire, logs, and rock flew high into the air. Debris rained down in great pellets of rubble and shrapnel. I kept my eyes closed and lay there as heavy logs dropped back to the ground after their airborne journey. Small rocks and splinters of wood landed on my chest seconds before something really heavy slammed into my legs bringing an excruciating burst of pain. I don't think it broke any bones but it hurt like a son-of-a-bitch. That's when the second explosion occurred and a new whoosh of flame jumped skyward, the normal quiet of the night again violated by a thunderous blast. I sucked in my breath and waited tensely as the last of the rubbish rained around me. I opened my eyes as a second wall of flame leapt skyward joining in the blaze as it greedily consumed what remained of my grandfather's cabin. The trees were painted with shimmering shadows of fire as it danced in the misty waves of great heat. I could feel the burning upon on my skin as it singed the hair. I waited and watched the tree line above, the fire blocking out the stars and the sky. The suffocating heat washed over me in waves, as I lay there helpless before its caress.

I waited for the sound of the white witch. I waited for the sound of my cousin's voice. I concentrated to hear anything over the loud roar of the fire, and heard nothing. Seconds passed with agonizing slowness. Long minutes later; still nothing. No Steven. No killer. Only the furious burning, the loud pops and crackles and tall waves of flame. Steven should have had plenty of time to get back to me...if he was alive. If everything had gone according to plan, he should have exited in time. If the plan had worked.

As the fire consumed itself, I was able to see black patches of sky through the gathering clouds and billowing smoke. I could make out the line of three stars together in a row, the ones whose name I could never remember, but always searched for. Nothing moved in the forest around me. As the fire died and the smoke drifted away, time allowed a gradual return of my senses. My head still swam from the harsh blows and it was extremely hard for me to concentrate. I fought to keep myself conscious as I waited for something, anything, but the only noises that reached me were the welcoming sounds of the forest as the world slowly returned to normal. The crickets and a lone, Brown Owl seemed to sound an "all clear" with their return. Nothing had changed in their world, just a brief interruption and everything before was forgotten.

I began to wonder if she could have survived the fire. I felt afraid again for just an instant, but knew she had to be dead. She had to be in thousands of tiny little pieces. Didn't she? Nothing could have made it through such an explosion.

I also had to consider the very real possibility that Steven might not have made it either. My cousin had to be dead, or he would have come for me. I closed my eyes and tried to think about something else.

After a time, I surprisingly began to relax, perhaps with the lessening of the drug's power over me or from sheer exhaustion I don't know which. Whatever the reason, my adrenaline flow slowed and my heart-beat eased. I felt myself dozing off, drifting as I watched the dancing, dying blaze from my limited vantage point. The night took on a faint, red glow. I know I fell asleep for a time because I remember closing my eyes, just for a minute I thought, and the firelight changed, faded much too fast. Eventually I opened my eyes to a return of darkness.

The stars were not as easy to see as approaching clouds obscured them from view. The air was still filled with smoke, but the smell of a coming rain crept through the mist and eased over me as I lay there on the forest floor. Dew formed on my outstretched arms and face. The blood flow from the wound on my cheek slowed, but it didn't lessen the hurt. My head ached and my body begged for movement. I remember looking up and trying to figure what time it was at one point, my best guess; three, maybe four, a.m. It must have been an hour or so later when I was able to move my left index finger.

I thought at first I only imagined it and tried over and over to move it again, and failed. Finally, I moved it, just a twitch, then once more. I kept working and the finger beside it jerked. I struggled harder to pull myself fully awake and started working on other parts of my body. A few minutes later, I shifted my right foot, just a little, and you would have thought I moved a mountain. After the feeling of lying helpless and immobile for so long, like lying dead in a coffin, it felt comforting to be able to move. There was wonder in my ability just to flex my foot. I tried again and to my surprise, the whole leg twitched. Finally, after tremendous effort, I was able to turn my head to the side, wincing as my wounded cheek came into contact with the wet, bloody ground.

By that time, the weak glow of the rising sun was just beginning to touch the mountain. I struggled to see my hand. It seemed a long, long way from me as I tried to focus on what lay beside me. There, within inches of my fingertips, Dog stared at me, her eyes glassy and empty. They were just visible in the pale light, already covered by the tarnished, hazy film of death.

I turned my face away. Swallowed. Closed my eyes, and tried not to think about anything but moving my legs. That's all that mattered then, just moving my legs. As the light grew and the rain clouds thickened, I was able to move both, then later, to roll over. It seemed hours before I was finally able to push myself from under the heavy log that pinned my legs, but in reality I suspect it was only a few minutes. I was able to roll away from where she lay and turned towards the nearest tree, a large pine, near the storage building. I crawled towards the tree, first using only my feet as my arms hung useless by my side.

I came upon one of Ben's arrows that he had planted near the corner of the cabin. It was broken in half and was covered with blood and gore. The arrow must have been what knocked the witch from the sky. Maybe Ben's magic worked after all.

I continued to crawl.

The tree appeared miles away as I made my way over the soggy ground. Each inch of the journey seemed a mile as I pulled myself through the wet leaves and fallen pine needles. I spent impossibly long minutes trying to move with limbs that refused to cooperate. Once, my injured cheek scraped against a rock and I scared myself when I cried out. I stopped dragging my body along and tried to clear my throat. My voice was faint and raspy and at first I didn't recognize it as my own.

I called weakly for Steven, waited for a reply, struggled to hear something, but only crickets and frogs answered me. I returned to my torturous journey across the litter-strewn forest floor. After a few minutes of exertion, my arms finally remembered what they were for and joined the battle. By the time I reached the tree, dawn had arrived on the mountain. As I grasped the smooth trunk and struggled to pull myself up, I yelled again for Steven and again got no response. I managed a "Damn it!" under my breath. The silence was really pissing me off. The not knowing was the worst part.

Using my stiff arms and legs to push and pull myself to an upright position, I leaned heavily on a low, dead branch and struggled to force my weight on it, trying to break it from the tree. The limb broke away and I crashed heavily to the earth along with it. All the air slammed out of my lungs when I hit the ground and the world got swimmy for a second or two. I managed to hold on to the three-foot limb and used it to help push me back up against the tree to a semi-standing position. On wobbly legs, I rested there for a few minutes, just breathing and trying to make the world stop spinning. Shaking the cobwebs from my brain, I could almost see around the edge of the generator shed, but was only able to make out one corner of what had been my grandfather's home. The home his father's father had built was only charred logs and smoldering ash.

I turned my head away, back to where I had crawled from, and looked again at the animal who had been the closest living being to me for what I thought were the worst years of my life. I could see where she had been struck down, well over ten yards from where her body lay. She had drug her mutilated body through the wet undergrowth in a final effort to reach me. She never had a chance; her wounds were far too extensive. I turned away and hoped for one bizarre moment that the witch wouldn't be dead.

I wanted more than anything to kill her myself.

I used the tree branch like a crutch and managed to hobble along, slowly at first, but improving with each clumsy, shuffling stride. My legs shook and it was all I could do not to fall down, but I got a little better with each step. Working to navigate around huge piles of debris, I felt as a child must feel; struggling with the supreme effort of putting one foot in front of the other, and just as proud of myself with each step. Granted it was a small victory, but at that point I was taking anything I could get. By the time I reached the clearing in front of the cabin, I was doing a hell of a lot better. My arms and legs had almost returned to normal, and I was finally able to toss my crude crutch aside.

The second explosion had been Steven's Harley. The heat must have ignited the gas tank and it was reduced to a smoking pile of melted rubber and steel. Small tendrils of smoke slowly waved their way skyward from the remains of the once beautiful machine. All that remained of the cabin were bits and pieces of the ancient rock foundation, blackened and smoking like everything else in sight. Small fires still smoldered, and smoke rose like morning fog on a lake, but the fire was over for the most part. It had destroyed all within its reach and burned itself out fairly quick. C-4 did that kind of thing, precise, controlled explosions with quick after burns. Perhaps the luckiest point was the fire had contented itself mostly with the cabin and hadn't made the jump to the surrounding trees. The whole mountain might have burned had it not.

Things could have been a lot worse, but all I could think of at the time was the box of my grandfather's things that I left inside on the table, lost forever…just like my past. Just like Steven. I was thankful Ben had taken my grandfather's manuscript with him. If not, it too would have been useless cinders. At least it had been saved. For some strange reason, that was very important to me. I'm not sure when it became so important, but it had. Maybe it was while I lay helpless under the stars and understood for the first time that anything could be real. Or maybe it was because Steven had died and the legacy of my birth lay smoldering at my feet. Then again, maybe it was important to me all along.

I heard a noise. I didn't recognize it at first but it came from the rear of the cabin. Limping slowly in the direction of the sound, calling Steven's name. I heard it again…just couldn't quite make it out. I tried to hurry my limbs along, but they were still stubborn and stiff. I stopped, swaying in place, wishing for a minute that I hadn't thrown my makeshift crutch away. I didn't know who was making the sound. It could as easily have been her and not Steven and I could be walking right back into danger. She could have survived—had survived before. After what I had seen, I was willing to believe anything was possible. She could be alive.

And if she were? I stopped and stood for long minutes, then called again but didn't hear a damn thing but wind in the trees. I cautiously moved closer. There was a badly charred oak tree not far from the remains of the cabin. The tree's upper limbs were burnt and barren but the lower part had been relatively untouched by the fire. The explosion had literally blown up the side of the tree and consumed all the leaves.

The giant oak looked barren and lifeless and out of place among the soft green all around it. From behind the twisted roots of the tree trunk, I could see Steven's right boot.

The tree had blocked most of the effects of the blaze. He had pulled himself behind the tree, using it as a shield from the fire. The path of his journey was marked with a faint trail of caked blood. I swallowed and tried to move a little faster. It was a miracle he was able to get even that far. As I reached my cousin, I could see the unbelievable damage he had suffered. Evidently, the splintering logs had become deadly shrapnel and were propelled through the air with great force. Steven had been much too close to the explosion and his body had been riddled with huge pieces of the oak logs from the cabin. As I bent down beside him, my legs literally giving way beneath me, I knew he was dead. I cradled my throbbing head in my hands, careful not to touch the wounds on my face. I thought I could feel my heart beat in the wound on my face—the pain pulsing in time to it's rapid pace.

Even Steven's massive body would never have withstood such incredible damage. He never had a chance. That's why when he spoke, it shocked me so much. I never considered for a second he could possibly have survived.

"Morg…" He coughed, startling me as I looked to his blackened face. I was surprised to see him returning my look, his eyes weak, but open and alive. His long black mane had been almost completely burned away; even his facial hair was singed and blackened. "Morg…I'm…"

Crazy as it may seem, I smiled.

I took his hand and I felt an ever so slight squeeze, as he sucked in his breath and closed his eyes. When he breathed out again seconds later, his grip on my hand relaxed as he struggled to speak. "Morgan, I got her, Morg…I waited to see her face. I had to Morgan…I wanted her to know."

He attempted to say something else just as his body was rocked by another wave of pain. I looked closer at his wounds while his eyes were closed. It was even worse than I thought. There was nothing I could do, nothing anyone could have done. That he made it through the long night was a miracle in itself. I realized the heroic effort, the immense will to live, which allowed him to stay alive as long as he had. Steven was going to die after battle, just as he always wanted to, right there on the side of my grandfather's mountain. He had defeated his enemy and he was giving his life for his people like a true Cherokee warrior. My cousin was dying a hero's death with no one but me as a witness. But then, he had been my hero all along.

"Morg…" his eyes looked to mine as I struggled to return his gaze. I had to look away. He knew what I was thinking. He managed a weak smile, "Yeah…yeah, I know, but it's alright Morgan. Don't get so damned upset. You're always gettin' carried away when there's no reason to…relax…be happy man."

I managed to fake a smile of my own, "Yeah, that's easy for you to say."

He swallowed, obviously in intense agony, then continued, "I wanted to wait for you…I had to tell you…" He squeezed my hand again, hard then relaxed. When he next spoke it seemed a bit easier, with maybe a little less hurt, "I'm sorry Morg. She pushed over a bunch of trees at the foot of the mountain. I knew something was wrong but I couldn't get the truck through. I had to run…I should have been here sooner."

"It's okay, Steven. You made it that's all that matters. You killed the bitch that's what we came here for, remember?" I tried to smile and failed miserably. "You saved my ass that's for sure."

He coughed wetly and I cringed at the pain it must have caused. "Again." He managed a smile.

"Yeah, again." I whispered.

"Yeah." He managed the word before he breathed in harshly and closed his eyes. He held his breath for an impossibly long time before he continued, sounding a bit stronger at least for the moment, "You don't look all that great yourself, Cuz." His valiant effort at a weak grin made me appreciate what it took for him to speak, and I squeezed his hand in response.

"I've been better, Stevey, that's for sure." I tried not to show what I felt, wanting to show him a strong front, to hide the anxiety and the sorrow I really felt. I would not dishonor him that way, especially not in the face of the supreme courage he was showing.

He coughed again, and a light trickle of blood leaked from the corner of his mouth. "Don't…call me Stevey…asshole."

I couldn't help but smile then, a genuine smile of relief at his welcome response. It was indeed my cousin dying beside me on that lonely mountain, and not some demon imposter from our past. The bitch really was dead. Too bad.

"Get me a cigarette will you?" he asked, and motioned towards his bloody shirt pocket.

I removed the pack, lit one for him, placed it in his mouth and returned the pack to what remained of his T-shirt pocket. He inhaled deeply and almost immediately began coughing in short agonizing spasms.

We didn't say anything for a minute or two. His cigarette dangled, momentarily forgotten, from the corner of his mouth. He turned his eyes skyward, "Looks like rain."

And it did. At any moment the clouds were going to break open and rain was going to fall, washing away the smoke and ash. Everything would go on in the world just like before, everywhere but on that mountain. There, it would never be the same again.

"Morgan, you have to do something for me." He blew a thick cloud of smoke in my direction, an act I normally would have bitched about, and I could tell by his mocking smile he knew as well. He almost seemed himself again, just a little subdued like he was about to fall asleep or something. His eyes seemed clearer too, or maybe it was the desire of my imagination.

"Anything Steven. What is it?" I leaned closer to hear him better.

"We both know I'm dying Morgan."

"Steven...." I began.

"No, don't give me any shit Morgan; I know and you know." He looked at me and inclined his head toward his waist where his 45 automatic was stuck in his belt. "I need my gun and I can't get it. Get it for me, Morgan." He was beginning to slur his words more and more, and a thin steady trickle of blood flowed slowly but constantly from the corner of his mouth and down onto his huge chest.

I realized what he was getting at and I started to argue, then stopped. I hobbled around painfully, cussing out loud and kicking at the blackened dirt. I stopped pacing and looked at him without saying anything.

He concentrated on smoking his cigarette, his eyes closed and his teeth clenched.

I had to accept the cards fate had dealt, horrible though they were.

I reached for the gun. I had little choice.

There was nothing that could be done for him and we both knew it. Also, we both understood he could die any minute or he might hang on for an hour, maybe two, but no longer. Either way I would never get help in time, even if I had two goods legs. Even if I did somehow manage to get down the mountain, to the nearest doctor, hours away, no doctor in the world could have helped Steven. The pain he was feeling had to be incredible and I knew he wanted to be spared the humiliation his final time would surely bring. I pulled back the slide, chambering a round in his old 45. I pushed off the safety for him. I didn't know what to do next. I waited in silence without looking at him. I just stared at the gun in my hand.

"Morgan...I can't do it myself. I can't. It's not the way of our people. I cannot die by my own hand. You know that." He paused to let what he was saying sink in. "Morgan, you gotta' help me."

I looked away, hating what he was asking, not wanting to believe it, not wanting to decide something of such great consequence. It was a long time before I could speak. "Steven, I can't. I can't do that, surely you know…"

"You have to do this for me Morgan…you have to. I want you to Morg." He coughed violently, much harder than before and fresh blood dripped down his chin and onto his chest. He tried to wipe it and couldn't. I tore one of the rags from what once had been my shirt and helped him, not meeting his eyes. "You have to do it Morg." His hand reached for mine and squeezed it hard. "I wouldn't ask if there was any other way." His voice rose a bit, "Damn it! I'll say please if I have to!"

"Please" was a word I rarely remember him use. My cousin never asked for anything. Steven was always the one who was there for others. He never needed anyone but himself. He was always the one asked, not the one asking. I will never forget that moment as long as I live. It was the hardest, most painful decision anyone could ever make, taking the life of another. Life had played some mean tricks on me over the years, but nothing compared to this. I loved my cousin and I would do any-thing I could for him, but I also knew what he was asking would mark me for life. I knew it would haunt my dreams and scar my soul forever. I didn't want my cousin to die, but more than that; I didn't want him to die by my hand no matter how right it was.

I stood up and stumbled around in a circle, my back and my face to Steven, mumbling to myself, the handgun dangling by my side. My legs were prickly, like they had fallen asleep.

I looked up at the dark rain clouds overhead and heard the morning birds singing without a care.

I couldn't do it!

Without turning to him I whispered, "I don't know if I can do it, Steven. I don't know if I can live with it."

When I looked at him, Steven smiled at me. A knowing smile I had seen a million times and one that I will carry to my grave.

"Being a little selfish aren't you cousin?"

And in an instant, I knew he was right. It was like satori, all at once I just knew. While I didn't understand it, I accepted it. It was his life after all, not mine. He had given everything to save me and he asked very little compared to his ultimate gift.

"It's the only way, Morgan." Steven spoke softly and calmly, "It hurts like hell, Morg."

"I know that damn it!"

"It's okay Cuz, I told you, I'm ready. I ain't afraid man…it's my time and you're doing what you have to. That's the deal Cuz and I love you for it, now pull the damn trigger already? It is the only choice I got, man. It's the only choice we got."

I knelt beside him and looked in his eyes; "I love you, Steven." My voice sounded strange and unfamiliar to me; saying those words I always had such a problem with…but then, I rarely meant them before. I meant them then.

He tried once more to reassure me with his own kind of encouragement. His joking smile returned and he tried to laugh like I had seen him do a million times since our childhood. "Yeah, me too. You keep it between the lines, okay?" His cigarette dangled from his mouth, just ash and filter. It had burned itself out.

"Yeah." I rose to stand above him.

"I'll be seeing you Cuz." And he closed his eyes for the final time.

"Yeah." It was the only word I could get out.

My chest pounded as if it might explode as I raised the gun. I looked up to the sky, damning any and everything that could have caused such a thing to happen. I pleaded for divine intervention and cursed the divine and myself when none came. Trees creaked and their leaves danced gently in the early morning breeze; deep dark clouds, pregnant with pending rain drifted slowly across the mountain sky as if they had all the time in the world.

I closed my eyes and pulled the trigger, flinching at the loud retort. I dropped the gun and I turned to begin the long walk down the mountain. I never looked back.

Big, wet drops of rain began to fall before I reached the first curve in the road and the tears started just after that.

EPILOGUE

There are no happy endings anymore. Maybe there never were. Yeah, I've read the books, seen the television shows and the movies. But what happens after the last page has been read; the screen fades to black; the theater empties? I'm not saying there's no happiness in life, I just don't think it's a permanent condition that's all. It never has been for me anyway.

In the almost two years since the dawn of Steven's death, a lot of things have changed for me. The greatest change has been the way I view life itself. I once had brief glimpses of the way things ought to be, but I, like so many others, never realized how things could have been. I've begun to understand the great wisdom in the simplistic attitude towards life Rising Wolf has adopted. Happiness, depression, prosperity, pain; all those things are just brief stops along a road everyone shares. No matter how we travel life's road, the origin and destination are the same for each of us. We are all born, and we all die; it's just that simple. What really counts is how we make the journey from start to finish, from womb to grave. When you get right down to it, in the end, the trip is all that matters.

I've given up trying to justify things; it's much easier for me to just accept things as they are. I've decided the best thing for me anyway, is to just let life come to me and take whatever it has to offer and accept that as real, and the hell with everything else. Questioning too much is never going to work for me. I think that's the way life was really meant to be;

free from all the encumbrances, rules, regulations and unnecessary justifications. Life doesn't need all that bullshit; it just happens, and we can do little to change it and nothing to stop it. There's no great or complicated answer. The only answer is—there is no answer. There never really was a need for one. I remember a cartoon I once saw where a "seeker of truth" finally climbed his proverbial mountain. At the top of the mountain, he discovered the wise man he had sought so hard and so long to find. He asked that wise man the meaning of life. Without hesitation the wise man asked, seemingly dumbfounded, "Life is a question?"

I've frustrated myself far too long by searching for all the solutions, all the reasons why, needing to justify everything, when it never really mattered in the first place. I realize now that I was losing sight of what was really important by chasing ghosts of reason, which wouldn't help, even if I caught up with them. All my life I have been taught the false hopes and empty promises of society; told that there was only one right way and any other was lunacy. I was forced to accept what was right and wrong as dictated by others.

People from the past, parents, politicians, teachers, advertising companies, preachers, priests and prophets—they all joined to shape my perceptions of life from the moment I first drew breath. I was robbed of my individuality, my freedom of choice. Life itself was stolen from me, and I'm really pissed off about it too. The sad thing is that I'm not the only victim. The good thing is that I believe I have found another way, and that way was within my reach all along. It was so close I never saw it. So easy to find I passed it by, time and time again. Now that I've found my own road to peace, I'm going to be damned careful I don't make any wrong turns from now on. It cost me much too dearly to get where I am, and I have no desire to relive my sins.

When I walked down the mountain that day, almost two long years ago, I had no idea what I was going to do, or how I was going to explain what had happened the night before. I was in shock from the emotional roller coaster ride and I was overcome by doubt and guilt at what happened—at what I had been forced to do. I found some solace in the thought that I was certain, had the situation been reversed, I would have asked Steven to do the same thing, and he would have answered as I had. I am sure in my heart I had no choice. I had to pull that trigger, but that knowledge never made the hurt any less. There was no way I could relate the events of that horrible night and morning, no way I could make people understand the pain and the uncertainty.

So, I made a mistake. One I won't make again under the same conditions; I told the truth. I should have known that was not the thing to do. I told them about their killer and, of course, they didn't believe me. I told them why I had to kill Steven and they thought I was crazy. Maybe I was. Maybe they were right. Maybe the whole thing was some insane nightmare. I could always pretend to believe such things, but I would only be kidding myself. Everything that happened on that mountain was painfully and sadly real. I may have been a little crazy then by the standards of some, and I may be a little crazy now, but that doesn't change a damn thing. I know...I was there.

As I sit here in front of this computer screen, I can look out the window and see the snowcapped mountains of home. I can look through the wire reinforced glass and the steel bars, and see the softness of the new snow as it once again blankets the ground, just as it has for the past three days. I have sat, day after day in this same room, alone but for the visits of the doctors and a few select visitors. I have sat here and relived my painful past, feeding empty lines into a lifeless computer with as little emotion as possible. I tried as best I could to detach myself and wrote freely of the hurt and the anguish and the great demons of doubt and fear. I kept my part of the bargain. The computer just took it. No emotion, no judgement, no discussion—just input that's all it was. But what I thought an exercise in futility, came to mean a lot more to me. I guess Dr. Fischer was right after all; it does help to write things down sometimes. God, I hate to admit a psychiatrist could be right about anything! It's a rather disturbing concept to accept. (Dr. Fischer, as you read this; don't take it personally.)

As soon as the prosecuting attorney dug into my past and discovered my previous "psychiatric problems" as he put it, my fate was sealed. My attorney suggested we jump at the chance for a reduced sentence, and at the time I just didn't give a damn anymore. Too much had happened as it was, and I wasn't about to give anyone the satisfaction of punishing me anymore than I was already punishing myself. Hell, I lived through the torment of that night and morning. I dream of it every time I close my eyes. I know damn well what I was guilty of and what I wasn't! No one needed to remind me! At the time of my arrest, I damned sure wasn't going to talk about what happened in front of a jury of my so-called peers.

I remember thinking, to hell with them all. And I tried to play it that way for a time. It didn't help any when both the local authorities and the FBI commented on what they termed my "uncooperative attitude". The judge agreed to a semi-voluntary commitment, with a minimum of one year in the State Mental Hospital in Morganton, and that's where I've been ever since. The judge decreed my doctor would have the ability to extend my stay if he saw fit to do so. Dr. Fischer did just that. (See Doc, I haven't forgotten. No hard feelings right?)

When I first arrived, I decided I would keep to myself for the year period, you know, do my time, get the hell out, and go home. It didn't work that way though. The first few months I gave everyone the silent treatment. I refused to talk unless I needed to, and would not participate in the program prescribed by the honorable psychiatrist, Dr. George M. Fischer. He called my bluff and extended my stay another six months, minimum. Needless to say, we reached a compromise.

Dr. Fischer excused me from the indignity of his earlier proposed projects and agreed to lay off me, if I agreed to write it all down for him; no holds barred, just as it happened, all I could remember. First I told him to piss off, (No offense Doc) but later warmed to the idea. He was holding all the cards after all—at least all the aces anyway.

This manuscript started as a penance of sorts, and I suppose it remained that all along. In any case, I caught myself using the manuscript as an outlet for many things, and an excuse for many others. Hell, all I had was time anyway. Days upon days spent in this small private cell I've been assigned, with its double-locked door and cheap motel furniture. Night upon night spent remembering and writing.

I asked for books and began to research the past of my people. I read everything I could find, or Rising Wolf and Kathy could find, on the history of the tribe. Through Rising Wolf's efforts and occasional visits, I learned the beauty of the Cherokee language, the pride of the Cherokee's past, and their frail hopes for the future. I found I needed to learn such things, truly needed them for my own reasons I have yet to fully understand. I used the excuse of the book at first, but that wore off as I came to realize more and more about myself.

Marilyn visited a few times. She already had a power of attorney before my incarceration, and has been able to run the shop pretty well without me. As a matter of fact, I have given her and her new husband to be, Mike, half of the business as a wedding gift. I still can't believe she's marrying the guy after all the time they spent fighting with each other. I guess in his case persistence paid off. They don't need me there, and I don't need the heartaches or worldly ties associated with a business anymore. Besides, I have other, perhaps more rewarding, plans for my future. That is, if and when I ever get the hell out of this God-forsaken place. (Once again, Dr. Fischer, no offense.) When I told Marilyn about Steven, she was deeply hurt. I think she felt sorry for me more than anything else. I've felt that way too for quite a long time. Still do, just not as often lately.

Kathy has been here every weekend since I was allowed visitors. She brings me books and I tell her what I have done in the time since our last visit. She has read the words I have written. I couldn't hold them all to myself. I wanted someone who really knew me, knew my life and how I had gotten to where I am today, to read the words. Perhaps I wanted someone to assure me that I might not be so mixed-up after all, that I didn't imagine the whole thing. That it really did happen. Most of all, that it was really over.

I don't think I could have written a word without her support and encouragement. Once again, she came around when I really needed her the most; helping me in ways I can never say and never repay. I suppose life has not been totally unkind to me. We have not spoken much of what will happen after I am released. We have just taken everything between us one visit at a time. I think I like it better that way for now. It's not like I have any other choices right at the moment anyway.

The visits I most look forward to are those of Rising Wolf. He has kept the promise he once made to my grandfather. The old shaman comes and we walk the manicured grounds surrounding the hospital, the snow-capped mountain peaks beckoning from the distance. He brings me writings in the old language, which I devour like a man starving for something, yet not exactly clear what it might be. I question him relentlessly, yet he remains patient and understanding with my ignorance. Rising Wolf has advised me and helped guide me along my path of mental salvation. I have now read the words of my grandfather as he wrote them, in the "old" language in which they were written. I have read the writings of those who went before him. It is true; there is great magic hidden within those words and stories. For me, the greatest magic has been the doors that have opened within me. I have learned much about myself among the faded scribbling, the myths, the legends, and the old formulas of the Cherokee.

I have found an inner peace of sorts within those ancient words and sentences, a guiding light in a stormy mental sea, alive with wave upon wave of confusion and doubt. I have come to understand the great value of those age-yellowed pages, both to the people of the Cherokee and to myself. I can never hope to understand everything within those ancient stories, but I have come to accept the wisdom contained in the writings, and to realize their worth. I now see the beauty within the peaceful philosophies of the Cherokee people of old. I understand there may indeed be a better way and I want to explore further along the path that Rising Wolf has chosen to follow; the path my grandfather followed and those who went before him. I want to know as much as I possibly can before I make any real decisions about my life. After all, every coin has two sides.

There is a great beauty among the ways of the Cherokee people, unfortunately a beauty very near extinction. I have discovered there is a lot to be learned among the writings and teachings of the "Real People". I also uncovered something within me. Something buried deeply. Something I haven't felt in years; desire. I have a desire to learn now, wholly for the sake of learning. It's the first time I've been driven, really driven, by something in far too long. I missed that feeling in my world. It was gone from my life for so long I had forgotten how fulfilling and how important it is to the human spirit.

Steven told me once that he felt there were few left to carry on the old ways. That no one wanted to study and to preserve the history of our people for future generations. He told me the reason he wanted to learn from Rising Wolf was, he thought, if not him, then who? After a great deal of anguish, I have reached a similar decision in my own life…if not me, then who? I honestly feel it is possible to carry the old traditions and beliefs into my life today and make them work. I want to try anyway. What have I got to lose?

Now, we get right down to it…those nagging questions that I'm suppose to be answering in this narrative. I feel I've answered quite a few already, but I know how shrinks think, so I'll finish up as best I can. (Don't want me to leave anything out right Doc?)

Did I feel guilt for what I did, for killing Steven? What do you think?

I have not spent an hour of my life since that morning when I didn't relive that horrible moment at least once or twice. I dream of it when I

finally manage to sleep at night. It is a sin I will live with everyday of my
life. But if I had it to do over, I would do the same thing again, painful as
it was. I loved my cousin and I did what I had to do, and that's all I'm
going to say about it. I don't give a damn what anyone else thinks.
(Including you Dr. Fischer.) It's my own battle and no one can fight it
but me.

Was I afraid? You're damned right I was afraid, still am. That creature
scared me more than I ever thought possible. I don't know if it was the
toxins or the whole insane nightmare, but I will never forget, never, ever.
Every time I look in a mirror and catch myself reaching to touch the
jagged scars on my face, I am reminded anew. Even now, I wake up at
night and think she's standing over me again, waiting; waiting on me to
be afraid, to feed her hunger. She frightened me with her faces of change
and her calculated invasion of my mind. Her presence scared me yes, but
her words scared me more.

I remember what she said that dark night on the mountain…that she
was not the only one of her kind—that there were more like her which
still had the power of shape shifting, and they would always be with us. I
can't help but wonder; what if she was right? If her words were true, I
may never sleep another full night in my life. To think monsters like her
could be living among us; hiding in the house next door or sitting next
to us on a bus—that's what really makes me afraid. It scares the hell out
of me, if you want to know the truth about it. I will never look at those
around me again without suspicion and doubt. Maybe none of us
should.

What will I do when (if?) I get out of here? First, I intend to ride my
motorcycle from the beginning of the Blue Ridge Parkway near the
Cherokee reservation, to its finish on Skyline Drive in upper Virginia.
When I get there, I'm going to turn right around and come back. I'm
going to ride until I'm exhausted then try to sleep without all the nightmares which now plague me whenever I close my eyes. I'm going to try to

find a cloud or two to ride through for Steven. I'm going to find that part of life he loved so much and live it one last time for him…and for me.

After that, I'm going to return to my grandfather's mountain, my mountain, and build a cabin on the summit, among the wild flowers and the butterflies of summer. I figure I can fix the broken-down foundation of the abandoned farmhouse and fashion a home just as my ancestors did. Maybe I'll ask Kathy to help me. I plan to stay on top of that mountain and continue my studies with Rising Wolf for as long as he will let me, and I want to write as much as I can. I want to rewrite my grandfather's book so the fading words get a new life, perhaps even a new generation of readers one day. Maybe in a few months I'll venture down to my grandfather's cabin and the old council house and rebuild, make a few repairs. But I won't be doing that anytime soon. I'm not ready yet.

Am I crazy? I don't know the answer to that. Only my doctors are supposedly qualified to make such a decision, at least officially anyway. I do know that if I am crazy, I want someone to tell me what guidelines they use to make the determination. I know there's a very fine line between sanity and insanity. I think that maybe I saw both terrifying faces that night on the mountain. I think sometimes it's hard to tell the difference between sane and not, and harder still to say who is really qualified to judge them apart. I'm as sane now as I have ever been— whatever the hell that might mean.

What did I learn? I learned many lessons there on the mountain and the long and many nights since. Some things I can relate and some things I can't. I learned there are always more reasons than the obvious ones, and sometimes they never become apparent until it's too damn late. I learned that whatever we might believe in, no matter how strongly we believe in it, believing will never make it right when it's not. I think all truths are different for all people and that we all must help each other if we have a snowball's chance in hell of getting through the fragile test of life. I now realize there are things about our world we will never know and I hope never to be foolish enough again to think I have all the answers. At this point in my life, I would be happy just to know the right questions.

And that's it. That's all I've got to say. I'm damned tired now. I'm tired of the writing. I'm tired of this place, and I'm tired of reliving my past. It's time now for the future...my future. It's time for me to live again and, hopefully, to learn to forgive myself.

Yeah, I've made a lot of mistakes. I know that better than anyone, but I now believe I have an idea of where I'm going, at least where I need to be. I think it's where I should have been all along. I can't recall the last time in my life I was overcome by desire and now I have something I truly believe in, and it drives me. It helps me focus on what can be rather than what was, and most of all; it helps me believe in me for a change. I've shaken off my lifelong partners of guilt and remorse, and even, the anger. I need to start anew. I need to start a whole new life and I can't do that in here. I need out. All I want now is the freedom to follow my heart for the first time in my life. Hopefully, it will lead me home. That's all I want, and I want it more than anything I have ever wanted before.

For now, I just want to go home.

POSTSCRIPT

...They found the evil ones entranced,
And cleansed the world
Of them and their possessions
With fire.
Standing all around the house
As the burning rafters fell,
As the smoke rose,
As the fire sank down to cinders and ash,
They stood, shivering with cold,
For they knew, as we all know,
That these who love life so much
That they would steal it
Are not evil strangers, but kinsman,
And every Raven Mocker
Is one of us,
One of us.

> The Raven Mockers
> Tales from the Cherokee Hills
> Jean Starr, 1988

Bibliography

Mooney, James. "Myths of the Cherokee."
    Washington, D.C.
    Bureau of American Ethnology, 1900

Mooney, James. "Sacred Formulas of the Cherokees."
    Washington, D.C.
    Bureau of American Ethnology, 1901

Starr, Jean. "Tales from the Cherokee Hills."
    Winston-Salem, North Carolina: John F. Blair Publishing, 1988

Underwood, Tom. "The Story of the Cherokee People"
    Cherokee, North Carolina: Cherokee Publications, 1961

0-595-20451-1